MW00784007

NOTHING BUT THE TRUTH

Books by Robyn Gigl

BY WAY OF SORROW

SURVIVOR'S GUILT

REMAIN SILENT

NOTHING BUT THE TRUTH

Published by Kensington Publishing Corp.

ROBYN GIGL

NOTHING BUT THE TRUTH

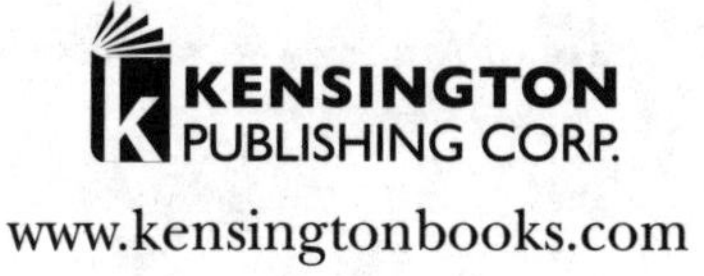

www.kensingtonbooks.com

KENSINGTON BOOKS are published by

Kensington Publishing Corp.
900 Third Avenue
New York, NY 10022

Library of Congress Card Catalogue Number: 2024932252

The K with book logo Reg. U.S. Pat. & TM Off.

ISBN: 978-1-4967-4179-0

First Kensington Hardcover Edition: July 2024

ISBN: 978-1-4967-4181-3 (ebook)

10 9 8 7 6 5 4 3 2 1

Printed in the United States of America

For Doreen, Virginia, and Tom

PROLOGUE

HE LAY COMATOSE, ENTANGLED IN A WEB OF TUBES AND WIRES. THE blue flexible hose ran from the ventilator and disappeared down his throat, the rhythmic pulse of the machine forcing air in and out. His hands and arms were secured to the bed rails, and periodically the cuffs strapped to his lower legs inflated, trying to prevent a clot from forming.

Monitors displayed his vitals with a glance—heart rate, respiratory rate, blood oxygen, temperature, and blood pressure. All were within normal limits now, but she knew all too well what the alarm meant when one or more fell into dangerous territory, having been in his room yesterday when his temperature spiked at 104.5.

IVs were attached to veins of all sorts, so she couldn't even hold his hand. All she could do was sit and talk to him, hoping that, somewhere in the darkness of his drug-induced coma, he knew she was there. She reached over the bed rail and gently placed her hand on his arm.

Later, she'd quietly castigate herself, but she found herself mumbling a prayer. She hadn't believed in God with a capital *G* since freshman year in high school when Brother Mathias had told her religion class that people like her were going to burn in the fires of hell for all eternity. But still, she found herself beseeching a deity she didn't believe in to spare his life. He had to live; he just had to. After all they'd been through together, she wasn't sure how she'd be able to go on without him.

She also remembered a promise she had made to him—a promise she knew she'd keep, but one she hoped upon hope wasn't necessary.

The alarm startled her. She quickly jumped out of the chair to get his nurse, but the nurse was in his room before she could even make it to the door. The nurse scurried over to the monitor, grabbed for the phone, hit a button, and yelled, "Code blue, ICU room ten. I repeat, code blue, ICU room ten." The nurse turned quickly toward her. "Go to the ICU waiting room. Someone will come and speak to you there."

She looked at the nurse, her eyes pleading. "Please save him—please!"

CHAPTER 1

Approximately one year earlier
October 19, 2009

RUSSELL MARSHALL MUTTERED UNDER HIS BREATH AS THE DOORbell chimed. He flipped on the front porch light, annoyed that his sources apparently felt they could meet with him anytime they wanted. *It's fucking Monday night, for God sakes. I have a life too.*

Except the truth was, for this story he'd give up his Monday night, and Tuesday through Sunday nights as well. If everything went right, this story was going to put him on the map as one of the premiere investigative reporters in the metropolitan area. This story would open up doors—the *Times*, the *Post*—there was no telling where it might take him. No, for this story there were no limits.

Marshall pulled open the door, the chill in the fall evening air catching him by surprise. Framed in the doorway was a tall, well-built man, his hands jammed into his coat pockets.

"Hey," Russell said. "Come on in," he offered, stepping back to allow the man to enter. "A little surprised to see you. What's up?"

"Yeah. Sorry to bother you, but I need to discuss something with you," the man responded, making his way into the foyer.

"Sure. Come on in," Russell said, nodding toward the kitchen. "I'm just cleaning up from dinner. Can I get you anything—coffee, soda, a beer?"

"Nah, I'm good."

They walked into the kitchen, and Russell closed the laptop sitting on the counter.

"So, what's on your mind?" he asked.

"This," the man replied, taking his right hand out of his coat pocket, a 9mm Glock in his gloved hand.

"What the hell are you doing?" Russell said, taking a step back, panic creeping into his voice at the sight of the gun pointed at his chest.

"Putting a stop to this nonsense."

"What are you talking about?"

"Your article."

"You've known about the article for months. You talked to me about it. Come on, man. Let's talk this out."

"Not much to talk about. I've watched this game play out long enough. Time to pull the plug."

"Sure. I can pull the article. Just don't do anything you'll regret."

The man's laugh had an ethereal quality. "Don't worry. I won't regret anything—not even a little. And, as for you pulling the article, you're a reporter. Even if you killed it, do you really think, given who I am, I can trust you to keep the fact that I'm pointing a gun at you under wraps? You and I both know that's not going to happen."

Russell tried to do some quick calculations. In the dish rack was a frying pan he had just washed. If he could grab that and throw it, maybe it would be enough of a distraction so he could tackle him. He wasn't sure he could overpower him; it was a bit of a mismatch—a forty-five-year-old, out-of-shape reporter versus a fit guy with a gun—but he didn't have too many other options. He inched back toward the sink. "Let's talk. Why . . . why are you doing this?" His question really a plea, trying to buy a little more time.

"Because," the man replied, and then he squeezed the trigger, the roar from the gun reverberating around the room.

The shot hit Russell squarely in the chest, knocking him backward against the sink.

"Unfortunately for you, you've gotten to the truth," the man said. "And the truth, the whole truth, and nothing but the truth isn't good for me."

"Please," Russell gasped, his eyes wide with fear as he grabbed the counter for support, trying to stay on his feet. "I don't . . ."

The second round struck Russell directly in his heart, causing him to stagger and collapse, his blood quickly starting to pool beneath him as he laid spread-eagle on the linoleum floor.

The man calmly walked around the L-shaped counter so he could have a clear view of Russell sprawled on the floor.

Shock was frozen on Russell's face; his eyes were wide open, staring at the ceiling. As the man stood there watching Russell's twitching body, he momentarily thought about doing a head shot to ensure the job was finished, but a bullet exploding the skull would likely leave a lot of back spatter. Safer to do one more into his heart.

Russell's body bounced when the third shot hit his inert body, and there was no further movement after that.

The house sat at the end of a cul-de-sac that backed up to the Dismal Swamp, so the man was confident the gunshots would go unnoticed. He made his way to the front door and, with his gloved hand, turned off the porch light. He checked the thermostat, turning it to "off," and opened the windows in the dining area and living room. Then he returned to the kitchen, careful to avoid stepping in the blood, spreading across the floor, and opened a window near the kitchen table. He collected two of the three bullet casings and placed them in his pocket. Finally, he disconnected the laptop and tucked it under his arm.

After scanning the scene to make sure he hadn't left any evidence, he made his way out the back door and across the backyard to the waiting woods.

CHAPTER 2

November 20, 2009

THE CANDLES ON THE ALTAR FLICKERED, THROWING STRANGE SHADOWS across the enormous stained-glass windows that rose up to the vaulted roof of the chapel. Erin McCabe stood among a group of people she had come to know over the last five years. Their journeys were all very different, but they were compatriots nonetheless, joined by a common thread. A thread that also knitted them to the names being solemnly read to the fifty or so people gathered in the pews near the front of the chapel.

"From the United States—Caprice Curry, age thirty-one; Jimmy McCollough, age thirty-four; Foxy Ivy, age twenty-five; Kelly Watson, no age; Eric 'Beyoncé' Lee, age twenty-one; Paulina Ibarra, age twenty-four; Mariah Qualis, age twenty-one; Carson Stevenson, age forty-seven; Jacqueline Ford, age sixty . . ."

As each name was read, it was displayed on a large screen. Each name a life lost, most of them young, most women of color, all of them killed in the last twelve months because they were transgender, nonbinary, or gender nonconforming. Tears rolled from the corners of Erin's eyes. This was her third year attending the International Transgender Day of Remembrance at the Princeton Chapel, and each year was harder than the previous one, as the list of names grew longer every year. Tonight, she and her companions took turns reading each of the 163 names of the people lost.

After the last name was read, they slowly returned to the pews and took their seats among the others in attendance. When they were seated, a Unitarian Universalist minister slowly climbed up to the pulpit and offered a moving prayer about love, compassion, and acceptance. When the minister finished, a singer sat down at the piano and, in a beautiful contralto, offered moving renditions of "Imagine" followed by "I Will Remember You." As the final chords faded, Erin remained anchored in place, allowing the solemnity of the moment to linger, taking a few more seconds to remember those who had lost their lives, especially those who were remembered simply as "Name Unknown," a final indignity to lives tragically cut short.

After several minutes, Erin turned to the woman on her right, Rachel Stern, a retired IRS Special Agent, and gave her a hug. "I hope you didn't mind that I added Jacqueline's name to the list," Erin whispered, referring to Rachel's friend Bradford Montgomery, who had also gone by the name Jacqueline Ford.

"No. It was nice," Rachel replied. "I know Brad spent his life in the closet, but he was one of us. Although, we both know Brad's murder was politically motivated, and not because he was trans."

"That doesn't make her loss any easier," Erin replied, purposely switching pronouns to reflect who Brad truly was.

"No. You're right," Rachel replied, and sighed. "I still miss her."

Once they slid out of the pew, Erin gave Logan Stevens a hug. Logan, a self-described biracial, pansexual, genderqueer attorney, had played a huge role in Erin's last case, and was now dating Rachel.

Gathering their belongings, they made their way out into the unseasonably warm evening. They stood outside the chapel in the well-lit area by the walkway to Nassau Street.

"A few of us are heading over to the Alchemist & Barrister to grab something to eat. You want to join us?" Logan asked.

"Sure," Erin replied.

"Excuse me," a man called out as he approached. "Would you be Erin McCabe?"

"I am," Erin replied, catching Rachel and Logan eyeing the man suspiciously.

"I don't mean to be rude, but are you the criminal defense lawyer?" he asked skeptically.

"Yes. I'm that Erin McCabe," she responded with a small grin. "And to answer your next question, as far as I know, I'm the only Erin McCabe who's a criminal defense attorney in New Jersey."

"I'm sorry," the man stammered. "I apologize. You . . . well . . . you just look . . ."

"Too young to be the infamous Erin McCabe, criminal defense lawyer," Logan suggested with a chuckle.

Erin tried not to blush, but at five foot five with a dusting of freckles across the bridge of her nose and a slim, athletic figure, she was still blessed with a youthful appearance that belied the fact that she was a seasoned attorney with a unique backstory.

"Is there something I can help you with?" Erin asked.

The man rubbed the back of his neck, appearing uncertain. "Um, is it possible for us to speak privately? I promise I won't keep you from your friends. I know what today is. I was inside for part of the ceremony. I only need a couple of minutes. It's about a potential case."

Sensing that Rachel was about to spring into special agent mode, Erin turned to her. "Why don't you go on ahead with the others and save seats for Logan and me?" she said, hoping that Logan's presence would reassure Rachel.

Rachel gave Erin a sidelong glance, but headed off to the restaurant.

Erin studied the man. He appeared to be in his early thirties, and was significantly taller than her, so her guess was that he was close to six foot. He was a good-looking guy, well-built. He was wearing a black suit, with a white shirt that was unbuttoned at the collar, exposing a gold crucifix hanging from a chain around his neck. And even though Erin didn't sense any danger, she felt better with Logan standing next to her.

"Is this about representing you?" Erin asked.

"No. Not me; I have a friend who needs help."

Erin pursed her lips. "Okay, but just so you know, if it's not about representing you, the attorney-client privilege doesn't apply."

"What's that mean?" he asked.

"Basically, it means that whatever you tell me isn't confidential," she said.

He sighed and looked down at the ground, seeming to weigh his options.

"Okay," he finally said. "I guess I don't have a choice. But can we speak alone?"

Now it was Erin's turn to consider her options. She had certainly pissed off enough rich and powerful people over the last four years to be wary of someone wanting to speak to her alone about representing someone else. Perhaps she was being paranoid, but as she was known to say, "It's not paranoia if they're really out to get you." Then there was also the issue of Logan, who Erin could sense was now in full protect mode. Erin finally landed on being cautious.

"Please don't take this the wrong way, but I prefer to have Logan here. Logan's also an attorney and we sometimes work together, so anything you want to discuss with me you should feel free to discuss with them here as well."

"Them?" the man repeated, looking around.

"Yes. Logan's genderqueer and uses they, them, theirs pronouns."

"Oh," he replied, unable to mask his confusion.

"I apologize. I don't know your name," Erin said.

"Oh, I'm sorry. I didn't introduce myself. I'm Gabriel, Gabriel DeAngelis. But please call me Gabe," he replied, offering his hand to Erin and Logan in turn.

"How can I help you, Gabe?" Erin asked.

DeAngelis seemed to glance around to see if anyone was within earshot. "Like I said, it's not for me. It's for my . . . my friend. He was arrested two days ago. He's charged with murder and he desperately needs an attorney and you come highly recommended."

"Nice to know someone highly recommends me," Erin said. "What's your friend's name and who's he charged with murdering?"

"My friend is Jon Mazer and he's charged with murdering—"

"Russell Marshall," Erin said, finishing the sentence.

DeAngelis took a deep breath. "I guess you saw it on the news."

"Gabe, unless I was living in a cave on Borneo, it would be pretty hard for me not to know about the case. A white state trooper shoots a Black newspaper reporter, in the reporter's home—a reporter who allegedly was working on an exposé of the state police. I mean, the governor, state attorney general, and the superintendent of the state police have all condemned your friend as a bad apple in an otherwise stellar law enforcement agency."

"They're all full of it!" Gabe shouted.

"I won't argue with you about that," Erin said. "But from what I've read, it still sounds like the state has a pretty solid case."

"That's exactly why Jon needs you. He didn't do it. He was the one working with Marshall to expose the corruption within the state police."

"Look, Gabe, let me be blunt. I presume you know that I'm a transgender woman, and generally speaking, law enforcement doesn't have a great reputation within the LGBTQ community. On top of that, my law partner, Duane Swisher, is a Black man. I'm sure I don't have to tell you how sick and tired Black people are of being killed by white law enforcement officers."

"Ms. McCabe . . ."

"Please call me Erin."

"Erin. I get it, but Jon's not just any trooper—he's gay. He's the only out gay male trooper we're aware of, and since he was outed, other troopers have put him through hell. They literally hate him." He bit down on his lip, closed his eyes, and exhaled. "Jon's a close friend. Trust me, he didn't do it. You have to help him."

Erin stared at him for several seconds. "Based on the fact that you're here, I'm assuming he's in custody."

"Yeah. Bail's been set at two million dollars. There's no way he can make that."

"The case is in Middlesex County, right?"

Gabe nodded.

"Not to be crass, but does he have money to pay for a lawyer?"

"We'll find a way."

Erin reached into her purse and took out a business card and handed it to DeAngelis. "Let me talk to my partner. Do you have a card?"

He reached into his pocket, took out a card, quickly jotted something on the back, and handed it to her.

She looked at the card, then at him. "That's interesting."

"Please don't call my work number," he said. "I wrote my cell number on the back."

"Can you call me around ten a.m. Monday?" she asked.

"Yeah. Ten will work."

"Okay. I'll talk to you then."

He turned and headed down the walkway toward Nassau Street. Once he was out of sight, they made their way down Witherspoon Street to join the others at the restaurant. "You going to take the case?" Logan asked.

Erin shrugged. "Don't know. At this point I don't even know if he can afford a lawyer. Not to mention, I'm not sure how Duane will feel about the racial overtones of the case. I guess we'll see."

"How about the fact that, based on what's been in the press, his friend is guilty as sin," Logan asked.

"Nah. That's not a consideration. If Duane and I only took on clients who were innocent, we would've been out of business years ago."

Logan laughed. "You think Gabe and Mazer are more than friends?"

"Don't know," Erin said. "But it would explain Gabe's desire for confidentiality."

"Why?" Logan asked.

Erin handed Gabe's card to Logan.

Logan looked down at the card, stopped in their tracks, and screamed, "What the fuck! Are you shitting me? Reverend Gabriel DeAngelis, Saint Raymond's Roman Catholic Church, Franklin, New Jersey."

"You can't make this stuff up," Erin said.

"Damn, woman," Logan said. "You sure do get some crazy-ass cases."

CHAPTER 3

November 21, 2009

ERIN AND HER MOTHER SAT OPPOSITE EACH OTHER IN THE BOOTH at their favorite diner. They had just come from Erin's final wedding dress fitting—a wedding a mere three weeks away.

"Your dress is beautiful," Peg offered.

It had been a wonderful morning, but Erin could tell that her mom was putting on a brave front for her. It'd only been a little over four months since Erin's dad, Patrick, had died suddenly, and just two weeks ago, it would've been his sixty-eighth birthday. Erin's parents had met in high school, and had been married for forty-five years, so her dad's death had rocked her mom's world.

Although she was now sixty-seven, with her almost wrinkle-free face, and her brown hair cut in a short bob, Peg McCabe could easily pass for someone in her midfifties. She still worked full-time as a guidance counselor at Cranford High School and stayed in shape mainly by doing yoga. But now, for the first time in her life, she was living alone.

"Thank you," Erin replied. "But I don't want to talk about my dress. I don't want to talk about my wedding. I want to talk about you."

Peg's eyes widened. "Me? Why do you want to talk about me?"

"Because I'm worried about you, that's why," Erin responded. "It's only been a year since you finished treatment for breast cancer. Then out of nowhere, Dad died, and you're still beating yourself up over the fact that you believe that you could have saved him," Erin fired back.

Her mother reached across the table and patted Erin's hand. "Thank you for your concern, my dear. I'll be fine."

"Are you seeing anyone?" Erin asked.

"Honey, it's only been four months since your father died. Too soon."

"Sorry," Erin said, barely suppressing a laugh. "A very poorly worded question. Are you seeing a therapist or a grief counselor? You've been through a lot."

Her mother smiled, apparently at her own misunderstanding of the question. "I talk with my friends," her mother said. "Some have been through similar things, so that helps."

"Mom, you're a guidance counselor; you should know better than most that talking to a professional can be really helpful."

"I don't disagree," Peg replied, "but for my generation, we just tend to muddle through. Besides, you've been through a lot, and I don't see you running off to see a therapist."

Erin smiled. "Actually, I've been seeing my therapist for almost seven years now."

"You have?" her mother said. "How come I didn't know that?"

"You knew I had a therapist. I started seeing her before I transitioned," Erin replied.

"Yes, but I didn't know you were still seeing her. Why are you still seeing a therapist? Is it my fault?" her mother asked.

"No, Mom," Erin said, shaking her head. "The reasons I see a therapist are not because of you. And you're doing what you always do—you're deflecting. This isn't about me, it's about you."

"But you've been through a lot too. I mean, after you came out, your marriage fell apart. Your father and brother stopped talking to you for two years. Someone tried to kill you, and you feel guilty over your last conversation with your father."

Erin's face twisted as if she had just sucked on a lemon. "You left out that I recently spent three weeks in jail, where I was beaten and groped. So now that we know why I see a therapist every week, let's talk about you."

"You see someone every week?"

"Mom!"

"What? I'm your mother. I'm allowed to worry about you."

"And I'm your daughter and I'm allowed to worry about you."

Peg let out a small laugh. "Seems to me we're doing far too much worrying here."

"Mom, I'm serious."

"Honey, I am too." Peg paused. "I appreciate the fact that you're worried about me. But right now, I have to find my own way through my grief. I will. But it'll take time. Your dad was part of my life for over fifty years. It's hard for me to imagine my life without him, and I'm not sure I'll ever be able to imagine it, but at some point, it'll happen. And honestly, sometimes that scares me more than the fact that I don't have him—moving on without him. I don't want that, but . . ." Peg chewed on her lower lip, and wiped a tear away with the back of her hand. "Sorry," she whispered.

"Don't be sorry, Mom," Erin said, fighting back her own tears. "Thank you for letting me in—even a little. I love you."

"I know you do, dear. I love you too. And trust me, there are times that the only thing that keeps me going is you, Sean, Liz, and the boys," she said, referring to Erin's brother, his wife, and their sons, Patrick and Brennan. "But I worry about you too because I know you struggle over the way things ended between you and your father."

All Erin could do was close her eyes and nod. Her last conversation with her father was one that, try as she might, she would never forget. What made things worse was that every time Erin walked into her parents' kitchen, the sights, the sounds, the smells brought the entire encounter back to her. It was a Sunday morning. She was going to have breakfast with her parents and then take them to her nephews' soccer game. But the night before she had gone to her twentieth high school reunion—a reunion made slightly uncomfortable by the fact that she had gone to an all-boys high school. When she got to her parents' that morning, her father had unloaded on her. After church a couple of his friends had let him know that his "daughter" had made quite the impression at the reunion. Why couldn't she have cut him some slack and just skipped the reunion? he had asked. He told her that he was tired of all the transgender stuff and that she embarrassed him. After a few other tense words, he had walked out of the kitchen, closing the door to the den behind him.

They'd never talk again. The long heart-to-heart she hoped to have with him—the tearful reconciliation, the warm embrace of forgiveness—none of it happened. He died. He was gone; end of story. True, her mother, brother, Liz, and Mark all told her that her father felt awful about what had happened and wanted to make it up to her, but destiny had other plans—for him, and for her.

Erin felt her mother's arms wrap around her before she had even realized that her mother had slid into the booth next to her.

"I wanted so much for him to be proud of me," Erin said, sobbing. "And all I'll ever have is the image of him closing the door on me in disgust."

"You can't keep doing this to yourself, Erin," her mother gently scolded. "Your dad loved you. Stop beating yourself up."

"I'm trying," Erin responded. "There's one more reason I see a therapist—guilt."

After a few minutes, her mother went back to her side of the booth and each of them sat silently, lost in their thoughts.

The waitress stopping at the booth to take their lunch order finally broke the solemnity of the moment.

"Can I change the subject?" Peg asked, after the waitress had headed to the kitchen with their order.

Erin gave her a weak smile. "Mom, one thing I've learned over the years is that even if I said no, you'll do it anyway."

Her mother shrugged. "I'd like to help pay for your wedding. After all, you are my daughter. The bride's parents are supposed to pay. And thanks to your father's life insurance, I have more than enough money."

"That's very generous of you, Mom, but no, you can't," Erin

replied. "First of all, this isn't my first marriage. Secondly, I've done okay over the last three years. I mean, I have a condo in Bradley Beach. We were able to put the money from the sale of Mark's house in Clark toward the house we just bought in Cranford." Erin paused. "And, last, but not least, the bride's parents paying is a sexist, misogynistic anachronism going back to the days when a woman's father had to pay a dowry to get his daughter married off."

Peg took a sip of her coffee. "Wow! Were you such a feminist before you transitioned?"

Erin grinned. "I wish I could say yes, but probably not. As they say, 'Perception is reality.'"

The waitress slid their plates down in front of them, asked if they needed anything else, and was gone.

"Can I ask a delicate question? Is anyone from Mark's family coming to the wedding?"

"Molly and Robin. Other than that, no," Erin replied, with a sigh.

Mark's sister Molly was a sweetheart. And, as she and her civil union partner, Robin Hansen, liked to joke, as soon as Erin came along, suddenly having a lesbian couple in the family wasn't so bad. In addition to Molly, Mark had two older brothers, Jack, the oldest, and Brian. After his brothers found out Erin was transgender, all hell had broken loose. Jack would constantly mock Mark about being gay. "Well, you are dating a guy," Jack would taunt, and he and Mark had almost come to blows over Jack's refusal to stop referring to Erin as "he." Brian was never as blatant, but his laughing at Jack's insults let everyone know where he stood. Things had gotten to the point where Mark's mother told Mark that Erin was no longer welcome in her home as long as they were dating. Of course, Mark took that to mean he wasn't welcome either. As a result, Mark had not seen his mother or brothers in over a year and Erin felt horrible. She couldn't help but feel that their marriage would make the rift permanent.

"Don't blame yourself for Mark's family," her mother cautioned.

"Too late," Erin replied. "Remember what I said? I do guilt really well."

"Unfortunately, you're right," her mother agreed. "It must be your Irish Catholic upbringing. But we've been through this several times before; you can't let close-minded people decide how you're going to live your life."

"Even if they're your in-laws?"

"Especially if they're your in-laws," Peg replied.

There was a long silence.

"Do you really like my wedding dress?" Erin asked.

CHAPTER 4

THE LAW OFFICES OF McCABE & SWISHER WERE LOCATED ON THE outskirts of the business district in Cranford, New Jersey, occupying the second floor of a former Victorian home that had been converted into an office building over twenty years ago. Erin had started her own firm almost seven years ago, after she left the Public Defender's Office. At the time, she knew Duane because his wife, Corrine, and Erin's then wife, Lauren, had been college roommates at Brown. Before they became partners, Duane had been an FBI agent, and probably still would be if he hadn't been forced to resign when he was set up to be the fall guy in a leak of classified materials involving the illegal surveillance of Muslim Americans after 9/11. When he left the Bureau, he had a lot of options, but to Erin's surprise, he had agreed to partner with her. Of course, at the time, Erin was still living as Ian McCabe. It was only a year after they became partners that Erin had come out as a transgender woman.

"Good morning," Erin said to Cheryl, the firm's receptionist, secretary, and paralegal all rolled into one, as Erin stopped to collect her messages. "Did you have a nice weekend?"

"I did. How about you?" Cheryl replied.

"A bit of a mixed bag," Erin said. "But the good news is that I really love my wedding dress."

"Oh, I can't wait to see it," Cheryl offered with a warm smile.

"I assume Swish is in," Erin asked, referring to her partner by his nickname, which, depending on where you knew him from, derived either from his last name, or, since he had been an All-Ivy basketball player at Brown, his prowess from three-point range on the basketball court.

Cheryl gave a knowing nod before Erin continued down the hallway toward Swish's office. It was always safe for Erin to assume that Swish was in before her because he and Cori had two children—Austin, who was now four, and their baby, Alysha, who was nine months old. Every morning Duane dropped Austin off at preschool and Alysha off at day care, then arrived at the office by 8:15 a.m.

Erin stood in the doorway to his office, which, unlike the clutter and chaos of Erin's, was always neat and orderly. "Hey, big guy," she said.

"Morning," he said with a warm smile, waving her in. Swish, who was six months older than Erin, kept himself in great shape playing in various adult basketball leagues. With his chiseled physique, dark brown skin, and a well-trimmed goatee, he had a commanding presence.

"You seem bright and chipper this morning," she said, taking a seat in front of his desk.

"For the first time since Alysha was born, both kids slept through the night. I never realized how wonderful a good night's sleep can be."

"Well, I'm glad you're feeling invigorated. Do you have time to talk about the case I called you about?"

He gave a small snort and nodded. "Sure. White state trooper kills Black man. Anything else we need to talk about?"

"His friend claims he didn't do it and that he's being set up."

"His friend the Catholic priest?" he replied, a hint of sarcasm creeping into his voice.

"You have something against Catholic priests?" she asked.

"Nope. It's got nothing to do with whom Mazer hangs out with. It's just . . . look, how can I ignore the racial overtones of this case?"

"I get the racial implications," she said.

"Do you?" he asked, his tone questioning.

She hesitated. "All right, let me admit that I don't understand it from a Black person's perspective. I don't have that lived experience. But suppose Mazer didn't do it. Then he's not racist at all, but he's being set up to take the fall by troopers who *are.* Shouldn't we at least hear what he has to say? I mean, Swish, you of all people know what it's like to be set up for something you didn't do—in your case it was because you were Black. In Mazer's case, it may well be because he's gay."

He stroked his goatee, seemingly lost in thought. "Would you defend someone accused of murdering a transgender person?" he finally asked.

She leaned back in her chair. *Good question,* she thought. "I honestly don't know. I guess it would depend on the circumstances. If they did it, I don't think I could. If they said they were innocent, I suppose I'd have to make a judgment call."

"Fair enough," Swish said. "You willing to let me make the judgment call?"

She smiled. "Absolutely. No case is worth our friendship. If you say no, we don't take the case, no questions asked."

"Deal," he replied.

The following afternoon, they sat at a small table in the attorney visiting room of the Middlesex County Adult Corrections Center, waiting to meet Jon Mazer. The sound of a key was followed by the clang of metal as the door was pulled open and two guards led in a shackled Jon Mazer.

Even though Erin had seen pictures of Mazer in the paper, she was still taken aback. Mazer looked like he was in his early thirties. He was every bit as tall as Swish, and looked just as solid, with close-cropped blond hair and blue eyes. It took all of Erin's willpower not to swoon. She was embarrassed that her own implicit bias had conjured up a far different image of what a gay man would look like.

The guards deposited Mazer in the chair opposite Erin and Duane.

"Use the phone behind you when you want out," one of the guards informed them, before turning and locking the door behind them.

"Hello, Trooper Mazer. I'm Erin McCabe and this is my law partner, Duane Swisher. I wish it was under better circumstances, but it's nice to meet you."

Mazer closed his eyes momentarily before responding. "Thanks for coming. And we can dispense with the Trooper Mazer, Jon works fine," he said in a voice that was a rich, deep baritone and as smooth as the silk of an expensive blouse.

This guy should be in Hollywood, not the New Jersey State Police, she thought.

"Jon," she began, "when we spoke to Gabe on the phone yesterday, we explained that in most cases we rarely ask a client if they've committed the crime they're charged with because, depending on their answer, it can limit our options in presenting a defense. But we have a little problem in your case."

"Yeah, Gabe explained the situation to me. I get it. I'm the exception to the rule."

Jon looked directly at Duane. "Look, Mr. Swisher, I know what it looks like—white cop, dead Black man. It happens all too often. And here I sit, the white cop, asking you, a Black lawyer, to represent me. I understand that not only am I putting you in an awkward situation, but many people will look at it as if I'm trying to game the system—hire a Black lawyer because I'm charged with killing a Black man." He hesitated and sighed. "The truth is that when I asked Gabe to reach out, it was to hire Ms. McCabe. From my perspective, being a gay man, I thought it might be helpful for me to have an attorney who's part of the LGBTQ community. I didn't even know that her partner was a Black man. Please don't hold it against me, but you were never even part of the equation." Jon looked down at the table before looking back up at Duane with a pained expression. "Sorry."

Duane gave a small chuckle. "Well, I'll give you points for honesty. How about we focus on the first part of my dilemma—white cop, dead Black man?"

"I swear to you that I did not kill Russell Marshall. I had no reason to kill him. I was helping him with a story he believed was the most important one of his career—mine as well."

"There's been speculation in the press, provided by the proverbial anonymous source who is 'someone close to the investigation' that Russell's article was going to 'out' you as gay, and you wanted to stop him," Erin suggested.

"That's bullshit," Jon responded. "Yes. The fact that I was gay was going to be in the article, but as part of the bigger picture to show how the Lords of Discipline were harassing women, minorities, and anyone who opposed them."

"Who are the Lords of Discipline?" Duane asked.

"Well, according to the task force the Attorney General's Office set up a few years back, they don't exist, but it's a badly kept secret that they're a group of rogue troopers, who operate clandestinely within the state police. They openly target and falsely arrest minorities. They're also hostile to minority troopers and go after any trooper who attempts to expose them. Do an internet search. You'll find them and the task force report."

"How many troopers we talking about?" Duane asked.

"Honestly, I'm not sure. My best guess is around thirty or forty. But in addition to the hardcore members, there's a number of troopers, including some of the superior officers, who look the other way. I don't have to tell you that there are all kinds of people who go into law enforcement. Most of them are decent people. But the Lords are a bunch of bigots who get their kicks using their power to abuse people and intimidating everyone else into keeping their mouth shut."

"Why'd they come after you?" Erin inquired.

"When they found out I was gay, they made my life a living hell. When I couldn't take their abuse anymore, I filed a formal Internal Affairs complaint. Since then, their goal has been to destroy me." He shook his head, and motioned with his shackled hands to his surroundings. "As you can see, so far it's working."

"Who's the 'they' you referred to?" Erin asked.

"The three guys I named in the complaint were Troopers David

Britton, Edward Stone, and Kiernan Lyons. There were others, but those guys were the ringleaders," he said.

Duane crossed his arms across his chest and leaned back in his chair. "What happened with the IA?"

"Dismissed as unsubstantiated. On top of that they found no evidence of the existence of the Lords of Discipline," Mazer replied.

"IAs are confidential; how'd they find out you were behind it?" Duane asked.

"I'm not sure," Mazer said. "The simplest answer is that someone in Internal Affairs leaked it. But then I remembered that when I was trying to figure out what to do, I contacted one of the lawyers the union pays for, a guy by the name of Spencer Drummond. As best I can tell, when he submitted his bills to the union, he either inadvertently—or not so inadvertently—included details about why I consulted with him, and then some of the higher ups in the union passed the information along to the guys connected to the Lords."

Duane nodded slowly. "Can you afford to retain us? We each bill at three hundred dollars an hour."

"You have a guesstimate on what it'll cost?" Jon asked.

"It's a pure guess at this point, but if the case goes to trial, a hundred thousand," Duane answered.

Jon's head snapped back. "Holy shit. I had no idea. I don't have that kind of money."

"Not to add insult to injury, but if we need to retain experts—forensics, fingerprints, things like that—their fees are on top of that," Erin interjected.

"I'm fucked," Jon mumbled. Then his face seemed to brighten. "Um—if I'm found not guilty, doesn't Middlesex County or the state have to pay my legal fees?"

"They do," Duane replied. "But if you're found guilty . . ."

It was as if Duane had just told him there was no Santa Claus; Jon physically seemed to deflate. "I get it," he said. "I'm sorry I wasted your time. I appreciate you coming."

Erin waited, but said nothing. Normally, this is where she'd jump in trying to find a way to give a client a break on their fees, but not today. She had promised Swish, this case was his call—no questions asked.

Finally, when she couldn't take the silence any longer, she said, "Listen, we wish you well. Hopefully, it will work out for you." She reached for the phone to summon the corrections officers to end the interview.

"How much can you afford?" Duane asked.

She turned back, surprised by Duane's question, and saw a look on his face that she couldn't place.

"I don't know. I can probably get you twenty-five up-front, and then another twenty-five as we go along," Jon replied.

"You know your bail is two million, which means, even if we get it cut in half, you'd need to come up with a hundred thousand just to secure a bail bond," Duane stated.

Jon choked back a laugh. "Yeah, well, that's not happening. Whatever money I can get, I'd rather put toward your fee. I know I've only been here a few days, but it hasn't been too bad. Every once in a while, I catch some shit from the COs about being gay, but because I'm a trooper, I'm in PC," he said, using the initials for protective custody, "so everybody pretty much leaves me alone."

"How soon before you'll know if you can raise the initial twenty-five?" Duane asked.

"Hopefully, by later today. I can have Gabe call you."

"By the way, what exactly is your relationship with Father DeAngelis?" Duane inquired.

"We're friends," he replied.

Erin raised an eyebrow, but decided not to dig further—at least for now. "One other thing," she said. "You don't talk to anyone about your case. Not the guy in the next cell, not a friendly CO, and not Gabe. Got it?" she asked.

"Gabe wouldn't say anything. Besides, aren't our conversations protected by the priest-penitent relationship?"

"No," Erin replied. "You may be friends, but I don't think the court would classify it as a priest-penitent relationship. Do yourself a favor, Jon, and don't talk about the case with anyone. And just so you know, any phone calls you make, other than to a lawyer, are recorded—including calls to Gabe."

After they had returned to Duane's car, Erin turned to Duane. "Do you mind telling me what just happened in there?"

"What do you mean?"

"I mean, I was ready to end our visit, and suddenly you're talking about taking the case. What changed?"

There suddenly seemed to be a fire burning behind Duane's eyes. "The Lords of Discipline," he responded. "They're there. They're real. We didn't know the name, but we wanted there to be a criminal investigation."

Erin was confused. "I'm not following."

Swish sighed. "One of the first investigations I worked on when I was with the FBI was the racial profiling of people by the New Jersey State Police. I guess they figured since I was one of the few Black agents, I'd be good for the job. They actually talked about using me undercover, riding up and down the Turnpike to see if I got stopped. Ultimately that didn't happen, but I was involved in interviewing the people who had been stopped, and some of the troopers, most of whom refused to cooperate with the investigation. For those of us working the investigation, there was no doubt in our minds that there was an organized group within the state police that helped create the overall culture where it was common practice to stop people for driving while Black. We just didn't know who it was—or have a name for it."

He stopped and inhaled, as if reliving a painful memory.

"We wanted the U.S. Attorney's Office to convene a grand jury to pursue charges under federal civil rights statutes and the hate crime laws based on the fact that so many people were racially profiled, falsely arrested on trumped-up charges, and a lot of them were assaulted as well." He paused, but only for a second. "It didn't happen. The U.S. Attorney's Office pursued a civil lawsuit, and the investigation of whether there was a group operating within the state police got put on hold and ultimately sent over to the New Jersey Attorney General's Office."

"The task force?" Erin asked.

Swish nodded and slammed his hand against the steering wheel. "We had been so fucking close to finding out who ran the group," he said, holding his fingers millimeters apart. "When we were in the initial stages, there had been a trooper who had agreed to talk to us."

"And?" Erin asked.

"And because it was a potential criminal case, his lawyer came in and made a proffer about the information the trooper had, which included being able to provide us with the name of the leaders of a rogue group of troopers. In return the trooper was looking for immunity." Swish rubbed his goatee. "While the immunity agreement was being negotiated, he took his own life."

"Do you believe he took his own life, or did someone take it for him?" Erin asked.

"Don't know. It was investigated by the Somerset County Prosecutor's Office. Wife claimed he was despondent. Single gunshot to his temple from his duty weapon." Swish turned and looked at her. "I always thought it was suspicious."

"You think it was the Lords that he was going to tell you about?" Erin asked.

"That's my guess," Swish replied. "What Mazer said rang true based on what we were looking at ten years ago."

"Are you concerned about the racial overtones in representing Mazer? I mean, you could face some tough questions," she said.

"Maybe," he said. "But I don't think Mazer did it and I'm not going to let some racist troopers hang him for it."

"Okay then," she said, her look of admiration for her partner slowly morphing into a smile. "Looks like we have our work cut out for us."

CHAPTER 5

IT WAS OVERCAST AND MISTY AS ERIN AND MARK DROVE THE TEN MINutes to her mother's house to help her get things ready for Thanksgiving dinner. It was one of those days where the moisture in the air made it seem far colder than the actual temperature—a day that just seemed to chill you to the bone.

Thanksgiving had always been Erin's favorite holiday. She enjoyed the focus on food and family, without the shopping, wrapping, and holiday parties that crowded the December calendar. But Erin's love of Thanksgiving had been put on hold after she transitioned. For the first two years after her transition, faced with a father and brother who refused to acknowledge her, she had spent Thanksgiving alone. Then, three years ago, as her brother's attitude toward her had softened as a result of the efforts of Liz, Patrick, and Brennan, her mother had convinced her to come for Thanksgiving dinner. Despite knowing that her father still wasn't ready to accept her, she had given in and gone to her parents, only to have her father refuse to deal with her as Erin. Leaving in tears, she had once again spent the day alone. It wasn't until a month later, the day before Christmas Eve, when she had been shot, that her father realized he needed to come to terms with Erin for who she was. But even then, their relationship had its ups and downs. The last down occurring the final time they spoke.

Erin stole a glance at Mark as he drove and not for the first time marveled at how her journey had brought her here. This wasn't her first marriage; she had been married once before, to Lauren. But when Erin came out as transgender, their marriage fell apart. Erin understood why. There was no rancor. Lauren simply wasn't a lesbian and didn't want to be married to another woman. Even Erin banking her sperm before she transitioned in hopes that the prospect of having children could save their marriage had been futile. But had anyone told her before she transitioned that someday she'd be marrying a man, she would have told them that they were insane. Yet here she was. She remembered being surprised when she realized she was attracted to Mark. True, he was handsome, with his jet-black hair that somehow was always stylishly messy, a sexy stubble, and green eyes, and a fit, six-foot frame, but it had still taken her a while to acknowledge that looking at a handsome man stirred something in her. It had taken her even longer to accept that she was bisexual.

Peg McCabe stood at the end of the dining room table, holding a glass of white wine. "I've never done this, so bear with me," she began. "Every year, as far back as I can remember, Pat would start our Thanksgiving dinner by giving a toast. But since this is the first year he's not with us, I decided I wanted to give the toast." She paused, looking around the table at each of them. "Pat and I have been blessed with an incredible family. Like any family, we've had a few bumps, but whether you called him Dad, Grandpa, or Pat, he loved each of you with all his heart. So, here's to Patrick Sean McCabe. Thank you for everything you've given to each of us over the years. We miss you and love you." She raised her glass, then took a sip.

"To Dad," Sean said, as he clinked his wineglass against Liz's glass. Everyone around the table took turns tapping everyone else's glass and wishing each other a happy Thanksgiving.

"By the way," Peg said, as the food was passed around the table, "since your father is no longer here, this is my last year hosting Thanksgiving dinner. One of you will have to take over now."

Sean smiled. "Mom, we know you too well. We'll be here next Thanksgiving."

"I agree with Sean," Erin said, holding up her glass. "Here's to the first annual last Thanksgiving dinner at Mom's. May there be many more."

"I'm thinking we'll still be here for the thirtieth annual last Thanksgiving dinner," Sean offered as he went over to their mom and gave her a hug.

"Oh sweet Lord, no," Peg replied. "That would make me ninety-seven!"

"Here's to ninety-seven," Erin said as they all managed to laugh and enjoy dinner and each other's company.

Later, as Erin lay in bed, that moment weighed on her. She never thought of her parents as mortals, but the absence of her father forced her to think of mortality—always a difficult concept. But she had grappled with mortality before—when her mom was diagnosed with cancer, when people had died during her cases—but the one wrestling match with death that always haunted her like the ghost of Christmas past was her own. Like so many transgender people, she had sometimes felt that the world would be a better place if she wasn't in it. The urge to spare the people she loved the indignity of being associated with a transgender person made death seem so attractive. They'd never know. She'd be gone and her secret would be gone with her. No one would know she had taken her own life, not if she staged a horrible car accident. She knew where, and she had narrowed down the when. Then Lauren opened the mail one day and found a new life insurance policy—a two-million-dollar life insurance policy. Lauren had saved her. Lauren had called the therapist Erin saw sporadically, who in turn had called Erin and threatened to have her involuntarily committed unless she got to her office immediately. The rest, as they say, was history.

The day after Thanksgiving, Erin and Mark made their way into Jersey City to have dinner with Molly and Robin, who lived in a two-bedroom condo on Third Street. With parking spaces in Jersey City sometimes harder to find than a unicorn, they took

Erin's Mazda Miata instead of Mark's Jeep—much easier to squeeze in between cars.

"It's nice of your sister to invite us for dinner," Erin said as she negotiated the narrow side streets.

"Yeah, I wonder what's up," Mark said. "I mean, yes, it'll be nice to see my sister, but I'm wondering what she wants to talk to me about."

"Do you think maybe she's trying to broker a truce between you and your brothers?" Erin asked, wondering if there was still a chance for a rapprochement before the wedding.

"I don't know. But there's something going on," he added.

"I guess we'll find out," she said, shooting him a smile.

Both Molly and Robin were foodies who, like Mark, loved to cook, and dinner was amazing. They cooked up a mini Italian feast, with an antipasto followed by tortellini and clams in a broth, then a main course of lamb osso buco accompanied by a Caesar salad. Over dinner they talked about Mark and Erin's upcoming wedding, and the discussion at the Simpson household on Thanksgiving. Erin could tell that Molly was sugarcoating things as best she could, but even covered in sugar, the bitterness of Mark's mother and brothers was unmistakable. Molly apologized several times, but Mark told her he and Erin wanted to know how they felt.

After they finished Robin's delicious tiramisu, and were having coffee, Molly put her finger to her lip. "I guess it's time we talk about why we asked you over," Molly began.

"Other than it's always great to see you," Robin added.

"Yes," Molly said, blushing at her faux pas. "Let me start with the easy part," Molly continued. She reached over and held Robin's hand. "Robin and I have decided we'd like to start a family," she said, her face beaming.

"That's wonderful," Erin said.

"How?" Mark asked.

Molly smiled at her brother's confusion. "We've been to a number of doctors to discuss artificial insemination, and we also consulted with two amazing lawyers. And as long as one of us is inseminated under the care of a doctor, the person who is the sperm donor is not legally the father and has no parental rights. And here's the best part—we can both be listed as the parents on our baby's birth certificate because we're in a civil union."

"Wow! That's fantastic," Erin said.

"Yeah. We're thrilled," Molly said.

"Sounds like you've really done your homework," Erin remarked. "Um, can I ask a sensitive question?"

"Sure," Molly replied.

"Have you done it already?" Erin asked, unable to hide her anticipation.

Molly glanced at Robin. "No. Not yet. And actually, that's why you're here," she responded, squeezing Robin's hand, before turning her attention to Mark. "We were wondering if you'd consider being our sperm donor."

Mark looked back and forth between his sister and Robin. "Wait. What? Sperm donor? What are you talking about? I don't understand."

Molly nodded. "Let me try and keep this very clinical. We're asking if you'd consider donating your sperm for a doctor to use to inseminate Robin. That way, Robin would be the biological mother of our baby, but the baby would also have my mitochondrial DNA because you and I have the same mother. It's the closest we can come to having the baby that will be both of ours genetically."

Erin leaned back in her chair, totally caught off guard. And when she glanced at Mark he looked like the proverbial deer in the headlights.

"I know you said I wouldn't legally be the father, but I'd still be the child's biological father. Don't you think that would be a little awkward?" he asked.

"Why?" Molly asked. "We know you and think you're amazing. Why wouldn't we want our child to be like you? I mean, our only alternative would be to get the sperm of a total stranger. Plus, like I said, by using your sperm, there'd be the added advantage of giving me a genetic connection to our baby."

Silence enveloped the room like a London fog. Finally, Mark turned to Erin. "You have any problem with this?"

Before Erin could even respond, Robin jumped in. "Erin, don't answer that. It's not fair to put either of you on the spot in front of us. We don't expect an answer from you tonight. We realize this is a big ask. Think about it, talk to each other, take your time, and let us know. Whatever you decide is good with us. We honestly hadn't even thought about it until we were talking with the physician's assistant, and she asked us if we knew anyone whom we'd like to be the sperm donor. Up until that point, we just assumed we had to use an anonymous donor. But when she told us we could use someone we knew, as long as everything was handled by the doctor, that's when we thought of you."

"What do you think?" Erin asked as she merged onto the NJ Turnpike.

"I think Molly and Robin will make great moms," he replied.

"And?"

"And . . . and, I guess I'm not sure what comes after 'and.' I can't say I ever contemplated that anyone would ask me to be a sperm donor." He shrugged. "Don't know how I feel about it."

"I suppose the question is how would you feel knowing that your niece or nephew was biologically part of you?" Erin suggested.

Her eyes were on the road, but she could feel him looking at her. "I think I'd be fine with that." He grew quiet for a long time before he continued. "I know I rarely talk to you about the situation with my family because it makes you feel guilty, as if, somehow, you're responsible for my family's ignorance. You're not. But my situation with them hurts. I miss my mom. She's not a bad person. Unfortunately, her view of you, and me, is totally influenced by my brothers. I wish I could repair things, but I'm not willing to betray the person I love—you—for them." He hesitated. "It was my decision, and I chose you. I never regret that we're together."

"Got it," Erin said, trying to plaster over her guilt.

"What I mean is that Molly's the only family I have right now. And, although she never says anything, I'm sure she catches a fair amount of shit because she stays in touch with us." He gave a small snort. "It's not like she's asking me to do a whole lot. I've never donated sperm before, but it sounds like the process might be something I'm familiar with, albeit in a different context."

Erin laughed. "If it makes your decision any easier, I'd be happy to lend a hand."

"Sounds like fun," Mark said with a chuckle. "But seriously, do you have any concerns?"

"No," she replied. "Like you, I think Molly and Robin will make terrific moms. And I certainly understand why they'd want sperm from someone they knew as opposed to a total stranger. So, you don't need my permission, but, if you're asking, I'm all for it."

Mark pulled his cell phone out of his pocket, searched his contacts, and hit send. "Hey, Mol," he said when his sister answered. "I just wanted to let you and Robin know that I'm in."

Erin could hear the squeal of delight coming from Mark's phone as he held it away from his ear.

"Yes, we're both a hundred percent certain. Just let me know what the next steps are."

There was a short pause, and then Mark said, "Hold on. Let me put my phone on speaker."

"Thank you, Mark and Erin," Robin and Molly were screaming.

"You're welcome!" Mark and Erin replied in unison.

"I'm happy for them," Erin said after the call ended.

"Me too," Mark responded. "Have you ever thought about being a mom?"

"Yeah, you know I have," Erin replied wistfully.

"Then there's no reason we can't look into similar procedures when the time is right."

Erin sheepishly stole a glance in his direction. "I guess, but it's a little more complicated because we not only need a woman to donate an ovum, we also need a gestational surrogate."

"What's a gestational surrogate?" he asked.

"A woman willing to carry and birth the baby."

“Right,” he replied. “Got it.”

The engine revved as she downshifted to go through the toll plaza. She tried not to think about how difficult the road to motherhood might be for her. It didn’t matter if they tried to adopt or pursue a gestational surrogate, there would be those who would scream she was unfit to be a parent—especially a mother. “How about we get married first?” she said, shifting gears and accelerating as she merged onto I-78. “We can discuss a family after that.”

“Sounds like a plan,” he replied.

CHAPTER 6

Friday, December 4, 2009

THERE WERE VERY FEW MEN WHO COULD PULL OFF A MAUVE SUIT, but Swish was one of them. And with his white shirt and black polka-dotted tie, he looked like he just stepped from the pages of *GQ* rather than court.

"How'd sentencing go?" she asked from behind her desk, motioning him into her office.

"Flat three," Swish responded, referring to a three-year custodial sentence without any minimum parole disqualifiers. "He'll be out in a year. If it hadn't been his third conviction, I probably could have gotten him six months in the county jail."

"I guess if your job description is bookmaker, jail time is the cost of doing business," Erin replied.

He nodded. "How'd Mazer's arraignment go?"

"Haven't lost one yet," she quipped.

"Seriously. Everything go okay?" he asked.

"I suspect this case is going to be a shit show," she replied.

"Why?"

"We've already seen what happened when Jon was arrested. The governor, AG, and the state police superintendent all blasted Jon as a bad apple. Today, the court was packed—lots of media and press, Marshall's family in the front row, a lot of people from the *Newark Journal*, folks from the Committee to Protect Journalists. Any day now, we're going to be dealing with all kinds of articles and reports convicting him in the media. We have our work cut out for us."

"How's Judge Bader?" Swish asked.

"She seems all right. Denied my oral motion to reduce bail and told me to file a written motion. By the way, can you handle that? I have a feeling I'm going to be busy until the end of next week," she said with a wide grin.

"No worries," Swish replied. "You're allowed a day off for your wedding."

"Thanks," she replied.

"You think Bader will be able to keep this from turning into a circus?" he asked.

"Hopefully," Erin said. "Struck me as a 'no-nonsense' type, which is good. Assistant Attorney General Ward Rivers and Deputy Attorney General Carol Roy gave me some of the discovery today and said they'd have most of the rest by next week. I told them that we'd be filing a notice of an alibi defense. Let's see, what else?" she said, looking down at the yellow legal pad with her notes from the arraignment. "The judge scheduled a status conference for January 22, 2010, at eleven a.m. She'd like to get a sense from us at that point if there are any motions that we think we'll be filing."

"You find out why the Division of Criminal Justice from the Attorney General's Office took over the case from the Middlesex County Prosecutor's Office?" Swish asked.

"Nothing official, but I got the sense that it was a bit of a turf war. Middlesex had the investigation initially, but when the AG's Office was advised the lead suspect was an on-duty trooper, they jumped on it. Sounds like we'll get a mixed bag of county detectives who started the investigation and AG investigators who finished it. Might allow us to have some fun," Erin replied.

"How's Jon doing?"

"Okay, I guess. Happy we agreed to represent him." She paused.

"Why do I feel there's a 'but' there?"

"I don't know, Swish. Like I said, the court was packed, but there was no one there for Jon. No family, no troopers, no friends—no one. I feel bad for the guy. I get the sense that other than DeAngelis, he's got no one."

"Unfortunately, that's par for the course for a lot of our clients," Swish offered.

"I know, but this guy's a trooper. I don't think I've ever defended someone in law enforcement who didn't have some kind of cheering section, no matter what they're accused of doing."

"I remember when I was at the FBI and word got around that the DOJ was investigating me, no one would talk to me. I felt like a pariah. And I never was even charged with anything," Swish recounted. "I suspect if it had been a white agent accused there may have been a different reaction."

"Yeah, and in Jon's case he was already on the shit list because he was gay and filed an IA," Erin added. "Listen," she continued, "next week is going to be crazy for me, so I had Cheryl make two copies of the discovery. If you have some time, how about we each review it and see what's there?"

"Sure," he responded. "Why don't we order a couple of salads from the Gourmet Deli and spread out in the conference room?"

"Sounds like a plan. But let's start by taking a look at the crime scene photos before lunch gets here."

He nodded. "Fine with me. But you may not have much of an appetite after you look at them."

"Probably better that way," she responded. "I have a wedding dress I have to get into next week. The less I eat the better." She gave a slight shrug. "I know," she continued before he could say anything, "I can be so stereotypical at times it scares me too."

Thirty minutes later, Erin nibbled on her Caesar salad. As crime scene photos went, these weren't god-awful. The photos showed Marshall sprawled on the kitchen floor, blood pooled beneath him. At least she was able to eat lunch. But bad or not, she hated any crime scene photos in a homicide case. Someone was dead. Their life unexpectedly over, and under violent circumstances. She always wondered what their last day was like. They had gotten out of bed that morning full of life, made plans, maybe went to work or a social engagement, and then wound up dead. What were they thinking right before the end came? She knew what had been going through her brain two years earlier when faced with a man who was hell-bent on assaulting and murdering her—*how the hell do I get out of this?* And ever since then, she assumed that was pretty much the last thought of every victim she looked at. *How the hell do I get out of this?* Somehow, she had made it out alive; they hadn't.

She took a forkful of salad and picked up the report of Detective Marco Cornish from the Middlesex County Prosecutor's Office Major Crimes Unit, who was the lead detective on the investigation. She recalled that there was a Detective Cornish who had served a subpoena on her to testify before the grand jury in the Michelle Costello case. If it was the same guy, he was moving up in the world, having gone from a glorified process server to the lead detective on a homicide case. "Lead" didn't mean he was in charge, but it did mean he had the responsibility of preparing the main report that provided the road map for the investigative team.

Cornish's twelve-page report started with the MCPO receiving a call from Edison PD at 1103 hours advising that a body had been discovered at 304 Saka Court. Edison PD had responded to the address after receiving a call from Douglas Rudnicki, an editor at the *Newark Journal,* requesting a wellness check on Russell Marshall, a reporter for the paper. Marshall had failed to show up for an eight thirty a.m. editorial meeting, and calls to his home phone and cell phone went unanswered. When a colleague had gone to his home, his car was in the driveway, but no one answered the door.

Upon gaining access to the house, Edison PD discovered Marshall's body in the kitchen, with what appeared to be two to three gunshot wounds to the chest. He was pronounced deceased via telemetry by Doctor Klab from Robert Wood Johnson University Hospital in New Brunswick.

There was no sign of forced entry, although three windows, one in the dining area, one in the kitchen, and another in the living room, had been opened, albeit from the inside. Forensics discovered numerous latent fingerprints in the kitchen, and fibers were collected from the carpet in the foyer and living room.

Erin quickly shuffled through the reports until she found the one from the state police lab. Most of the fingerprints in the kitchen were conclusively identified as belonging to the victim, however, six full or partial prints were all conclusively matched to Jon Mazer. Curious, she thought, double-checking the report. There were no fingerprints on any of the open windows.

After jotting down a note about the prints, she returned her attention to Cornish's report.

One bullet had perforated Marshall's body and was located in the kitchen, the other two were recovered during his autopsy. One bullet casing was recovered from the grate of a floor air-conditioning vent near the body. A cell phone was found in the kitchen, and a search warrant and communications data warrant for the phone had been applied for. It also appeared that, based on the type of power cords present in the kitchen, a MacBook had, at some point, been on the counter, however a search of the premises failed to locate any laptops.

She took a sip from her diet soda. "What are you looking at?" she asked Swish.

"First, I read the ME's report," he said, using the common abbreviation for the medical examiner. "It's a pretty quick read. I'll spare you the medical mumbo jumbo; three shots to the chest, two in the heart. Whoever shot him was standing nearby—probably within ten feet. First two rounds look like they were fired when Marshall was still standing. The third was a make-sure shot fired from above Marshall's body when he was already prone. All three were mortal wounds. Two bullets recovered from his body. The ME estimates the time of death to be between five p.m. and ten p.m. She states that exact time is difficult to pinpoint because there were several windows open, the overnight temperatures were in the midforties, the body was on a cold linoleum floor, and the heat was off in the house.

"Then I picked up the ballistics report. One spent hollow-point bullet was found in the kitchen in the linoleum directly underneath Marshall's body. The other two bullets the ME removed from the body, but all three were too deformed to match forensically. Unfortunately, there was one bullet casing found at the scene. Based on their testing and examination, the casing came from the 9mm seized from Mazer's home—a Glock 26—it's Mazer's registered off-duty weapon."

"Ouch," Erin said with a grimace. "That doesn't sound good."

"Agreed," he replied.

"How many bullets in the magazine when it was seized?" she asked.

"When fully loaded, the magazine holds ten rounds, plus one in the chamber; when it was seized, there were ten rounds in the magazine, plus one in the chamber." He gave her a knowing grin. "Look, whether it was Jon or someone else, it would be normal to reload. Besides, if I was going to pop someone with another person's gun, I'd swap magazines, and then put the original back in after the shooting. That way, if the owner looks, they're not wondering why they're missing three rounds. Even if I used their mag, I'd put three new rounds in just to be safe."

She thought for a moment. "If the shooter just put three new rounds in the magazine, there might be prints on the bullets," she suggested.

"Maybe, but that would be really careless."

"If there were no careless criminals, there'd be no cases solved," she said.

"Or maybe our guy did it," he said, raising an eyebrow. "You come across what gave them the PC to search Mazer's apartment?" he asked, referring to the probable cause needed for a search warrant.

"I haven't reviewed the warrant yet, but the state police lab had conclusive matches for Mazer's prints in Marshall's house and MCPO got a burner number off Marshall's cell. There were two calls to Marshall from that phone on the day he was murdered. It looks like when they got the call detail records they had enough to connect the burner to Mazer."

"Shit," Swish said, folding his arms across his chest.

"However, there is one interesting fun fact," she said. "Jon's prints are on the door and in the kitchen, but there are no prints on any of the open windows. Let's assume the windows were opened by the killer in an effort to make it harder to determine time of death. Why would Jon go in, carelessly leave his prints in the kitchen and on the door, but make sure they're not on the windows?"

"Unless he was there twice," Swish said, causing Erin to wince.

They spent the next two hours reviewing more of the reports. When they were done, they had learned that, according to the NJSP records, Mazer was working the six p.m. to six a.m. shift the night of the murder, and one of his assigned highways was I-287. Marshall's home in Edison was only a half mile from New Durham Road, which had both an exit and entrance connecting it to I-287. The records showed that around eleven thirty p.m., Mazer returned to the station to partner with a second trooper, Edward Stone, which was pursuant to the NJSP policy requiring two troopers per vehicle between midnight to six a.m.

In addition to the murder weapon, the search of Mazer's apartment turned up the burner phone that MCPO had gotten the call detail records on. A forensic extraction of the data confirmed two calls to Marshall's cell phone on the day he was murdered: a three-minute call at 2:51 p.m. and a twenty-five second call at 7:03:36 p.m. The cell tower data for the burner showed that the phone was turned on minutes before the last call was made and then turned off for the remainder of the night. When the phone was activated to make the second call, it connected to a cell tower near Somerville, within five miles of the state police barracks.

During the search of Mazer's apartment, fiber samples from his carpeting were taken and subsequent lab analysis showed that they matched fibers found in Marshall's home.

Cell tower data on Mazer's regular cell phone showed that his phone was turned off from 5:30 p.m. until 9:00 p.m., meaning there'd be no cell tower data to try and match the location of the regular cell phone with the burner when the 7:03:36 p.m. call was made. When his regular cell was turned on at 9:00 p.m., it connected to a cell tower near Bridgewater, about a twenty-minute drive from New Durham Road and I-287. The cell tower data showed that he was in the vicinity of New Durham Road around 9:45 p.m., and then again at 10:05 p.m. The rest of the data was consistent with some driving back and forth on major highways, with the cell pinging off different tower locations every few minutes, until the phone was turned off again around 11:30 p.m.

The records for Marshall's phone showed a number of calls on the day he was murdered, including the two calls from Mazer's burner. They also showed that two minutes after the 7:03 p.m. call from Mazer's burner, Marshall received a call from an unknown number that lasted fifty-eight seconds, and he made a call to an unknown number at 7:10 p.m. that lasted five minutes. Marshall received two other calls that night—8:25 p.m. and 9:45 p.m., both from a phone number listed to his sister that lasted only seconds, consistent with a quick voice mail message.

Finally, Cornish's report referenced several statements from troopers who told investigators that there were rumors Marshall was doing a story on the state police and that Mazer, who made a number of racist comments about Marshall, was paranoid that Marshall was going to "out" him.

"You know, no matter how we spin this, a good prosecutor will be able to spin it a hundred and eighty degrees around," she said laying down the investigation report.

"You're right," Swish said.

Erin hoisted herself out of her chair and stretched. "I'm sure there's a logical explanation for all of this," she said, walking over to the corner of the room and tossing her mostly uneaten salad in the garbage. "But we won't figure it out until we have a chance to go over this with Jon. Whadya say we blow this joint? I have plans for tonight."

A smile slowly stretched across Swish's face. "Sounds good," he said. "Besides, I have to get home because I'm babysitting tonight. My wife is going out with some friends to celebrate an upcoming wedding."

"Wasn't my idea!" Erin said.

Swish walked over to where she was standing and gave her a hug. "Have a good time. You deserve it. Besides, I get my revenge tomorrow when we take Mark out."

"Just don't get him in any trouble. Remember, he's a teacher," she said with a grin.

"No worries," Swish replied. "You in at all next week?"

"Yeah, I'm working through Wednesday and then I'll be back on Tuesday. We're just going into the City for our honeymoon."

"You know, you can take off as much time as you want."

She chuckled. "Mark's a teacher, remember?" She then looked at the reports spread out on the table and gestured with a wide sweep of her arm. "Besides, based on what we've read so far, we're going to be busy."

CHAPTER 7

ERIN HUDDLED NERVOUSLY IN A SMALL ROOM WAITING FOR THE guests to take their seats, while Liz and Corrine showed Peg pictures from the bachelorette party. Erin took one last look in the full-length mirror, and smiled. She had to agree with her mother, her dress was beautiful. It was a tea-length ivory sheath, with lace running from the bustline up to her neck, which then ran across her shoulders and finished as long sleeves. It clung to her, accentuating her figure. Her three-inch pumps matched her dress perfectly, and her hair was swept up, braided, coiled on her head, and held in place by an ivory headpiece. Completing her look were a pair of pearl drop earrings her mother had given her.

She and Mark had decided to have both the ceremony and reception at the Westwood, a popular venue in Garwood. Erin was initially reluctant because it had been the venue for so many of her high school sports banquets—somehow the thought of having her wedding in the same room as where she received "Boys" All-County Soccer honors her senior year was less than appealing. But with only four months between their engagement and wedding, there had been very few venues that could accommodate their schedule. It also helped that the Westwood had been substantially remodeled, and the available room looked spectacular. It only held a hundred people, but with just Molly and Robin from Mark's family attending, and most of Erin's father's side of the family not coming, there were very few relatives. Most of the guests were friends of Mark from school or his basketball league, and people that Erin knew either professionally or friends from the LGBTQ community.

There was a knock on the door and when Liz opened it, Judge Peter Fowler was standing there in his black judicial robe. Fowler was a New Jersey Superior Court judge who had recently been elevated to sit on the Appellate Division. Despite only being forty-five, Fowler had already been on the bench for ten years. His appointment had made headlines. Not because of his age or because he was a brilliant Rhodes scholar, but because he was the first openly gay man appointed as a judge in New Jersey. Erin had gotten to know him while trying cases, the last one memorable because in the midst of the trial her client disappeared, only to be discovered a day later, shot and stuffed in the trunk of a car. Erin would always remember the compassion Fowler showed her that day when, while sitting in his chambers with the assistant prosecutor, she learned her client was dead.

"Everybody ready?" Fowler asked Liz.

Liz looked over her shoulder at Erin, who did her best impression of a smile.

Standing in the hallway were Mark, Duane, and Sean in black tuxes with red vests. Also there, looking very uncomfortable in navy-blue suits, were Patrick and Brennan.

Erin tried not to dwell on what would have happened had her dad still been alive. She hadn't been raised and socialized as a woman, so she had never experienced what it was like to have been Daddy's little girl. She also never had the dream of her father walking her down the aisle. She was also certain he had *never* had that dream either. *Let it go,* she thought.

What she and Mark had decided was that Judge Fowler would walk out first and stand in front of the head table. Patrick and Brennan would walk Peg out and sit on either side of her. Then Sean and Liz, followed by Swish and Corrine, and then Mark and Erin would walk out together, arm in arm.

Standing there waiting, Mark clasped her hand, brought it up to his lips and kissed it. "You look stunning," he said.

"Thank you." She blushed. "You look pretty damn handsome yourself. You clean up nicely."

Since they were walking in together, Mark had asked Erin if he could pick the song that would play as they walked in. What she didn't know when she agreed was that he wasn't going to tell her what song it was.

Now, as she heard the opening words, joy swept across her face. It was Marvin Gaye and Tammi Terrell singing "You're All I Need to Get By." She squeezed his hand remembering the first night he had come back to her apartment for coffee and they wound up sitting on her couch kissing as Marvin Gaye played in the background.

They walked across the dance floor until they stood in front of Judge Fowler. Liz, who was her matron of honor, and Swish, who was Mark's best man, stood next to them.

"Good evening, Erin and Mark, and thank you for giving me the honor of officiating at your wedding," Fowler began. "We are here this evening to join Erin and Mark together as husband and wife. If there is anyone here that has reservations about this union, please speak now."

A wave of dread washed over Erin. She half expected one of Mark's brothers to come bursting into the room, screaming for them to stop. But there was nothing, just welcoming silence.

"Hearing no objection, Erin and Mark, please face each other, take each other's hands, and share the vows that you have written for each other," Fowler said.

Erin took Mark's hands and looked into his green eyes. "Mark, my love. I have heard it said that there are only two emotions—fear and love. In fear we find our anger, our prejudices, our self-doubt, and our rejection of others who are different from us. In love we find acceptance, compassion, and joy. A little over six months ago we stood on a beach and looked into each other's eyes, much like the way we're doing now. I told you then, and I now want to repeat in front of all these witnesses, that from the moment we became a couple you have opened my eyes to love—honestly, a love that I never felt I was worthy of. Up until I met you, I lived in fear. Fear that it was impossible for anyone to love me for who I was. But your love, and your acceptance of me, did something I didn't think was possible. You showed me that fear wasn't the answer; love was the answer. Your love saved me from my fears and self-doubt. Your love allowed me to open my heart. Your love allowed me to fill my heart with love for the most incredible man I've ever known—you. And for that, I will love you all the days of my life."

Mark gently touched Erin's cheek. "Erin, my love, I know there's a song in your favorite Broadway show about people being in our lives for a reason. Standing here with you now, I know that you are in my life for a reason. You've shown me what courage is about. What determination looks like. That there are no limits to forgiveness. And most of all, that with love, we can overcome anything. Because of you, I am a better man than I was before I met you. And for that, I will love you all the days of my life."

"And now for my part," Judge Fowler said. "Under the law, you both must declare your intent before all these wonderful people." Fowler turned to Mark. "We'll start with you. Mark, do you take Erin to be your lawfully wedded wife, to have and to hold, in sickness and in health, in good times and bad, for richer or poorer for as long as you both shall live? If so, answer 'I do.'"

"I do," Mark responded, his joy evident in his smile.

Fowler then turned to Erin. "Erin, do you take Mark to be your lawfully wedded husband, to have and to hold, in sickness and in health, in good times and bad, for richer or poorer for as long as you both shall live? If so, answer 'I do.'"

"I do," Erin said, beaming.

Fowler turned to Duane, who seemed momentarily confused, before reaching into the pocket of his tuxedo, removing a ring box, and handing it to Fowler.

Fowler took the first ring out of the box and handed it to Mark. "As you put this on Erin's finger, please repeat after me," Fowler said, as Erin held out her left hand. "Erin, please take this ring as a token of my love for you." Fowler paused, allowing Mark to repeat the words as he gently guided the ring onto Erin's finger.

"Please wear it as a reminder of my love for you today, tomorrow, and always."

Duane then handed Erin the ring for Mark, and Fowler repeated the same pledge as Erin slid the ring onto Mark's finger.

Fowler took a step back, folded his hands, and said, "By the power vested in me by the state of New Jersey, I now pronounce you wife and husband." His face broke into a broad smile. "Please don't take this as a court order, but if you would like to seal your marriage with a kiss, you have my permission."

Erin threw her arms around Mark's neck and they shared a soulful kiss.

When Erin and Mark finally broke their embrace, Fowler gestured with his arms outstretched. "I know that Erin is keeping her maiden name, so, family and friends, I present to you the married couple, Erin McCabe and Mark Simpson."

As the guests applauded, Erin and Mark shook Judge Fowler's hand and thanked him for a beautiful ceremony.

"Now the happy couple will share their first dance together as husband and wife," the DJ announced as the opening notes of Norah Jones's version of "The Nearness of You" started to float across the room.

Erin felt like she was floating as Mark took her by the hand and led her onto the dance floor, wrapping her in his arms as they slowly two-stepped to the song.

"This is the happiest day of my life. I love you," Erin whispered in his ear.

He leaned back slightly. "You're amazing," he said, before kissing her.

They were soon joined on the dance floor by Liz and Duane and Corrine and Sean, and halfway through the song, Liz and Corrine switched partners so they could dance with their husbands.

When the song was over, Erin walked up to Swish, grabbed his arm, and then signaled to the DJ. As the beginning strains of James Taylor, singing Carole King's "You've Got a Friend," wafted across the room, Erin took Swish by the hand and started dancing.

"Duane Abraham Swisher," she said as she looked up at him. "This song is for you. You have been my rock. Not too long ago, I was describing you to a woman who doesn't know you and when I was done, she said, 'Everybody needs a Swish.' And she was right, because I know I wouldn't be here tonight if it hadn't been for your friendship."

"Stop it. Don't get all mushy on me," he replied, his eyes smiling.

"It's my wedding. I'm allowed to get mushy."

"Well, it's mutual, you know. You offered me a spot when I left the FBI, and when they came around and investigated me a second time, you were there for me."

"Yeah, but I know some of your friends thought you had lost your mind for staying with me after I transitioned."

He shrugged. "Maybe one or two." He looked down on her. "But here we are. And I wouldn't trade our friendship for anything."

"Thank you," she said, leaning her head into his chest as they danced alone on the floor.

When the dance ended, they made their way to the head table. "By the way, how did the bail motion on Mazer go today?"

"Denied," he said, with his hands turned up in the universal "What do you want from me" gesture.

"I give you one simple motion to handle because I'm getting married, and you screw it up," she said with a laugh.

"That'll teach you to get married," he replied, as he veered off to avoid her playful punch.

After everyone was seated at the head table, the DJ introduced Sean for the toast.

"Good evening, everyone," Sean began. "Before the ceremony started there was a big argument over who was going to give the toast, so we drew straws—I lost," he said with a shrug, then he smiled. "Don't worry, E," he said. "I promised Mom I wouldn't turn this into a roast, so I will be serious now. Please raise your glasses."

Erin had grown up idolizing Sean, who, four years older, had always been the fair-haired son, literally and figuratively. He'd gone to Princeton undergraduate and the University of Pennsylvania Medical School, and was considered one of New Jersey's preeminent orthopedic surgeons. She had been devastated when he stopped talking to her after she transitioned. Thankfully, over the last few years, things between them had returned to normal.

"Erin and Mark, this is a wonderful day and I am so happy for both of you. It's a day for you to celebrate, a day to savor, a day to revel in your love for one another. Love is a gift, and yet, over time, we can lose sight of just how special a gift it is. Try not to forget. And when times get hard, when you've had a bad day, try to hold on to your love for each other and wrap yourselves in it just as you would wrap yourselves in a blanket on a cold day. Cherish the gift of love you've been given; nurture it; and hold on to that love every day of your lives together. Godspeed," Sean ended, raising his glass.

Erin looked up at her big brother and couldn't help being struck by how much he looked like their dad. She smiled. *Love is a gift,* she thought, echoing his words, and she silently gave thanks for all the gifts she'd been given.

She lowered her gaze from Sean to Mark, and gently tapped her glass against his. "I love you," she said.

"I love you too," he replied.

"Cheers," some of the guests said as everyone took a sip from their drinks.

Duane was having a blast. It had been a while since he and Corrine had enjoyed a night out together without the kids, but with her parents staying at their house to babysit, he was going to enjoy every moment and he'd spent most of the night out on the dance floor. He was also getting to see a side of his law partner he rarely saw—free and uninhibited, and as the night wore on, literally letting her hair down.

Resting between songs, he felt a tap on his shoulder. "Can I borrow you?" Logan asked.

"Sure. What's up?"

"There's a situation out in the main foyer—well, I think you should come with me."

A situation? What the hell does that mean?

"I'll be right back," Duane said to Corrine, and followed Logan into the lobby. Once there, Duane saw Jamal Johnson, JJ to his friends, standing rigid, like a member of the Queen's Guard at Buckingham Palace, with his arms folded across his chest, while a man standing in front of him screamed at him. Swish had been friends with JJ since high school, where they both starred on the basketball team. JJ would have been a lock to turn pro, but in his freshman year of college he suffered a career-ending injury. JJ and Erin had met through Swish, and he had been one of the first people Erin spoke to about coming out as trans, because JJ had been through a similar experience when he had come out as a gay man. Even as a gifted athlete, with his shaved head and multiple tattoos, JJ hadn't been immune from homophobic slurs questioning his masculinity.

"Who the fuck do you think you are?" the man screamed at JJ, his face red with anger. "One of the faggots getting married is my brother. I have every right to go in there."

"Dude, I don't care who you are, you're not going in," JJ responded in a measured tone.

Duane took a spot next to JJ's right shoulder. "It's Jack, right?" Duane asked.

The man's eyes narrowed as he stared Duane up and down. "You're his fucking partner. I've seen your picture in the paper. You're probably the one who introduced my brother to the queer fuck," he spit out, with a sneer, his fists clenching.

Duane's body tensed as it prepared for a physical confrontation, although he wasn't worried about who would prevail. Even though Jack seemed to be in decent shape, JJ was a second-level black belt in karate, and Duane had his own training from the FBI. But Duane was desperate to avoid a confrontation that would mar Erin and Mark's wedding.

"Jack, I think you should leave now, before you force us to call the police."

Jack glared at both of them. Suddenly he leaned to his left and then quickly turned right, trying to run around JJ. JJ's left arm shot out and he grabbed him by the jacket before he had taken three steps.

"Not a very good fake, Jack; besides, I'm pretty good with my left hand," JJ said with a smirk. "Now you either leave voluntarily, or we call the police. Your choice. But one way or the other, you're out of here."

"Motherfucking sons of a bitches," Jack spit out. "I'm leaving." He turned so he was looking at Duane. "But you tell that trannie partner of yours—"

JJ tightened his grip on Jack's jacket, bringing his fist up under Jack's chin. "Don't make a threat you'll regret, my friend. And if you try to do anything to Erin, you won't have to worry about the police. You'll have to worry about me finding you first," JJ said, pulling Jack toward the door.

When they got to the exit, JJ released his hold on Jack's coat to let him walk through the door, but he and Duane followed Jack outside, and stood watching as he got in his car and drove away.

"How'd that come about?" Duane asked.

"I was heading to the men's room, and Jackie boy was screaming at one of the waitstaff about the Simpson wedding. Being a trained social worker, I thought my intervention might be helpful," JJ replied innocently.

"Thanks," Duane said, exhaling. "What is it with some people? Why can't he just be happy for his brother?"

"You asking me?" JJ responded with a snort.

Duane shook his head. "Rhetorical," he replied, knowing that JJ had seen the same type of vitriol when he and his partner, Gary, had decided to have a civil union ceremony.

"What are you going to tell E?" JJ asked. "She and Mark need to be on the lookout for this guy."

Duane sighed. "Nothing tonight. It's her fucking wedding. They're heading into the City for the weekend, coming back on Monday. I'll talk to her when I see her on Tuesday." They headed back to the entrance. "Hopefully, your words of caution had the desired deterrent effect—at least for now."

CHAPTER 8

DUANE PORED OVER HIS HANDWRITTEN NOTES FROM HIS MEETING with Jon, periodically adding to the memo he had started on his computer, outlining his discussion with Jon, as well as including a list of things they'd need to follow up on.

Some of the things Jon had told him helped put some of the prosecution's evidence in a different light. Jon's admission that he had been at Marshall's home on multiple occasions, including on the day he was murdered, explained his fingerprints and the fibers from his apartment. Jon also claimed that when he went to the station that evening before going on duty, he had left his off-duty weapon and a burner phone he owned in a lockbox, locked in the trunk of his personal vehicle. Duane made a note to obtain the Computer-Aided Dispatch records, what the troopers referred to as the CAD records, which would give some indication of Jon's official activities on the night of the murder. Jon had told him that he remembered making a traffic stop in Bedminster, which was about ten minutes from Somerville, near the intersection of I-287 and I-78, for a suspected DWI. He said he had the driver do field sobriety tests, which he passed, so he accepted the driver's explanation that he was distracted by a cell phone call and let him go with a warning. Jon thought the stop was around 7:00 p.m. If he was right, his dashcam video could verify he wasn't on a cell phone at the time the call was made to Marshall at 7:03:36 p.m.

The one thing that troubled him was when he asked Jon why his personal cell phone was off between five thirty p.m. and nine p.m., Jon seemed a little taken aback, and finally said he couldn't remember why he had turned it off. Between his demeanor and how he responded, Duane felt like Jon was holding something back. And then, when Duane asked him why it was off after eleven thirty p.m., he easily volunteered that at that point he was partnered with Trooper Edward Stone, someone Jon had charged in his IA, so he would never talk on his cell in front of Stone.

Duane glanced down at his watch and realized Erin would be in shortly. He hadn't said anything to her at the wedding about Jack Simpson, and was torn as to what to tell her now. He had to tell her something, if for no other reason than for her personal safety. While he found it difficult to understand the anger and fear that, as a trans woman, Erin stoked in people, he could understand their confusion. When Erin had first come out to him, Duane remembered thinking, how the hell could his friend be trans, he was such a regular guy. He felt lied to, and was getting ready to start looking for another firm, but both Corrine and Lauren prevailed on him to give it a chance. And despite his doubts, as he watched his friend morph into this new version of themselves—confident and at peace with who they were—he found himself growing at ease with her, so much so that within weeks of her coming back to work as Erin, they had settled into a new normal.

"Good morning, Mr. Swisher," a familiar voice purred from his doorway.

"Well, well, well—nice to see you, Ms. McCabe. And how is married life treating you?" he said.

"I don't know, seems about the same as unmarried life," Erin replied with a laugh.

"You have a nice time in the City?"

"Yeah, we did," she replied. "We saw *Jersey Boys* and *In the Heights.* Both were amazing. How are things here?" she asked, taking a seat across from him.

"Moving along. I met with Jon yesterday, and he gave me some things to investigate and documents we have to get a hold of. He also explained why his prints and fibers were located in Marshall's house."

"I presume because he was there," Erin responded.

"Not only was he there, but there the same day Marshall was murdered. Still a long way to go, but it's a start."

"Yeah, but we only get that before the jury if he takes the stand. Too early to tell if that's a good idea," she said.

"True," he replied. "Ah, listen," he said before Erin could continue. "There's something else I need to talk to you about."

"What's that?" she asked.

"Your brother-in-law," he replied.

Erin looked puzzled. "Jack?"

"He showed up at the Westwood on Friday."

"What?" Erin said, her voice rising.

Duane proceeded to tell her what had occurred and the concerns that he and JJ had over Jack's behavior. "E, Jack sounds like a bit of a loose cannon, and if he was willing to mess with JJ, he's not going to be intimidated by you."

"I hear you," she nodded. "But after three and a half years of Krav Maga classes, I'm closing in on my blue belt. So even though I hope I never have to put it to the test, I think I can take care of myself."

"You carry the pepper spray I got you?" he asked.

She reached into her purse and produced a three-inch canister on a key chain. "Don't leave home without it," she replied with a weak grin. "Seriously, Swish, Jack is an annoying pain in the ass, and God knows what else he might do to make our lives miserable, but I don't think he's dangerous—at least, not physically dangerous."

"Let's hope not. Just be careful."

"Got it," she replied. "Let's get back to Jon," she continued before Duane could add anything further.

"What do you think about reaching out to Rich Rudolph?" he suggested, referring to a reporter for the *Newark Journal* that they both knew from when Rudolph worked the courthouse beat. "See what, if anything, he knows about the situation."

"Worth a shot," Erin replied.

Duane dialed Rudolph's cell phone number and left a message when it went to voice mail. Erin was about to leave when Cheryl buzzed to let them know Rudolph was on the line.

"Hi, Rich," Duane answered. "I have you on the speaker because I'm here with Erin."

"Hi," Rudolph replied, his tone as cool as the December air outside.

"Be careful," Erin whispered. "Make sure we're off the record."

Duane nodded. "Rich, can we speak to you off the record?"

There was a long silence. "Sure," Rudolph finally responded in the same frosty tone.

"Rich, we believe our client is innocent. It's our understanding that Mazer was helping Russell with the exposé he was working on. We think Russell was killed by someone else who didn't want the article to come out, and who framed our client."

Once again, silence filled the air.

"Rich, are you there?" Duane finally asked.

"I'm here," he replied. "Even if I believed you, and I don't, Russell was a friend. This is really personal for me."

"We understand, Rich," Duane said.

"No, you don't understand, Duane," he bellowed, his anger catching Duane off guard. "I get it. You're just doing your job. But Russell was just doing his job too—and doing his job really well—and as a result he's dead. I know the story he was working on. Because I've covered the courts and law enforcement for so long, I helped him with background. The bottom line is, I won't help you. Besides, anything I know is probably covered by the Shield law, so I couldn't say anything to you without talking to the paper's lawyers."

"Rich, can we at least ask you who Russell's editor was on the story?" Erin asked.

There was a slight pause. "Doug Rudnicki."

"Thanks," Erin said.

"Look, Russell was my best friend in the business. We started at the paper around the same time. I'm sorry if I sound pissed off, but honestly, I am. I've seen the discovery and from what I've seen, your guy is as guilty as sin. Now, you guys are good lawyers and maybe you'll get him off, but damn it, I hope you don't." He paused. "Anything else?"

"No, Rich. Nothing, other than we're sorry for your loss," Erin offered.

"Yeah, me too," Rudolph replied, his phone suddenly disconnecting.

"That went well," Erin said with a sigh.

"Kind of gives us a clue as to what we're up against. Seems like all the publicity has poisoned the well against our client," Duane said.

"Yeah," Erin agreed. "How often do we hammer the jury about the presumption of innocence? But outside the courtroom, and unfortunately, even sometimes in the courtroom, there's a presumption of guilt. That's what we're facing," she said, her frown matching her melancholy tone.

Duane turned to his computer and started an internet search. A few clicks later, he looked up at her. "I need to set up an appointment to see Mr. Rudnicki," he said.

She gave him a puzzled look. "Just you?"

"Yeah, I think so."

"Why?" she asked.

"We have a little history. He was my AAU basketball coach when I was in seventh and eighth grades. He was a good guy."

"You think he'll remember you?" Erin asked.

"Yeah. He came to see me and JJ play a few times in high school. Especially when JJ was a senior and I was a junior. We were ranked number two in the country that year." He paused; his gaze unfocused as he appeared to reflect on some memories from his past. "He'll remember me."

They sat cuddled on the couch, sharing a glass of Chardonnay. "I hate to break the mood, but there's something we need to talk about," Erin said.

"What's that?" Mark asked.

"Your brother, Jack," she replied.

Mark looked puzzled. "Jack?" he responded.

"Do you know what happened Friday night?" she asked.

"Yeah, he called Molly around one in the morning drunk as a skunk, screaming about all the queers in the family. But how do you know about that?" he asked.

"I didn't," she replied. "But I guess you didn't know he showed up at the Westwood on Friday."

"What!" Mark said, his voice rising.

After Erin repeated what Swish had told her, he closed his eyes, his face showing his anguish. "Shit," he said softly. "I'm sorry, E. I honestly don't know why my brother is like this."

"I only met him a couple of times, and you don't really talk about him. Besides hating me, what's he like?"

"Jack's the oldest. He started working construction right out of high school—no college. About ten years ago he started his own construction company. He flips houses—buys a fixer upper, remodels it, and flips it. He's been really successful. He and his wife have a huge house in Clark. Wouldn't surprise me if he nets seven figures a year. He's always been pretty conservative and he probably had the roughest time dealing with Molly when she came out, but over the last five years since my dad died, he's really bought into some crazy nonsense. And there's something about you—well, not exactly you specifically, more transgender people generally—that really sets him off. I wish I could tell you I knew what it was and that he'll come around, but I don't think he will."

"Swish and JJ think he's dangerous," she said.

Mark was quiet. "Not to you—at least not physically," he finally said.

"What about toward you?" she asked, concern rising in her voice.

"Nah. He might pick a fight with me if we were face to face, but other than being an asshole, I don't think he's dangerous. If it's any consolation, he did call Molly back on Saturday and apologize for waking her up."

"But not for his tirade?" she asked.

Mark's shrug said it all.

CHAPTER 9

"DUANE SWISHER," DOUG RUDNICKI SAID, STEPPING OUT FROM behind his desk, his arm outstretched.

"Hi, Coach," Duane said, taking the man's hand and shaking it. "Good to see you again."

"Coach? My God. You're dating both of us. I haven't coached in close to twenty-four years. How about you call me Doug?"

Duane grinned. "I don't know. Lots of good memories, and in all of them, you're Coach."

"Have a seat," Rudnicki said with a laugh, pointing to a worn, black, upholstered guest chair. As Duane sat, Rudnicki grabbed the matching guest chair and plopped down opposite him.

"You look good, Swish. Still playing?"

"Yeah. It's in my blood. I play in an adult league, one night a week, and sometimes, if my wife is sick of looking at me, I head to the gym for some pickup games. What about you?"

Rudnicki chuckled and looked down at his beer belly. "Come on. Do I look like I could get up and down the court? Nah, I stopped playing right around the time I stopped coaching. That's when I got the job as a reporter. So having any kind of regular schedule went out the window. I lived vicariously through you and JJ." Rudnicki hesitated. "You still see JJ? I kind of lost track of him after his injury. How's he doing?"

"He's good. We're still good friends. We play on the same team in the adult league and he was the best man at my wedding."

Rudnicki smiled. "Glad to hear that. I had heard through the grapevine that some of his friends turned on him after he came out."

"Yeah, some guys gave him a lot of grief. But I've known JJ since the seventh grade and whom he's attracted to doesn't change that he's one of the best people I know."

"He was also the best damn player I ever coached," Rudnicki said. "Next to you, of course," he quickly added.

Duane grinned. "No, you were right the first time. If JJ didn't get injured, he would have played in the NBA."

They reminisced for several minutes about life growing up in Elizabeth. Even though Rudnicki was twelve years older, they had grown up not too far from each other, Rudnicki in the Polish Bayway section of town, Duane in the nearby Peterstown section, the Burg to the folks who lived there. And while Duane and JJ had stayed local and gone to St. Cecilia's, a basketball powerhouse, Rudnicki's parents had sent him to Cardinal O'Hara, the high school Erin had attended.

"Look, Swish, as much fun as it is to catch up on the good old days, we both know that's not why you're here. Obviously, I know you and your partner are representing Mazer. And frankly, the only reason you got in my door is because of our history. Russell Marshall was a great reporter and an even better man, and I hope whoever murdered him spends the rest of their life in jail."

Swish noticed that, unlike Rudolph, Rudnicki hadn't voiced an opinion on Mazer's guilt.

"Coach, I do appreciate you meeting with me. And in the interest of full disclosure, we did reach out to Rich Rudolph, but he refused to talk to us and it wasn't just because of the Shield law."

"I know. He called to warn me you'd be reaching out," Rudnicki responded casually.

"Can I ask you some questions about Marshall and the story he was working on?"

Rudnicki laughed. "You still got it, Swish. You walk up the court dribbling slowly, then stutter step, suddenly accelerate, and blow by the defense."

Duane slowly shook his head. "Coach, if you throw me out right now, it was still worth the trip just to see you again and say hello.

There was a lot of shit going down in my neighborhood growing up. But you, my parents, and a few other folks made sure I stayed on the straight and narrow. And you taught me that basketball wasn't the end, it was a means to the end, and I'll always be grateful."

Rudnicki rubbed his fingers across his chin, and his weak grin slowly morphed into a smile. "Thanks, Swish. Nice to know I helped." He sucked in a deep breath. "I'm going to play it straight with you. I'm willing to tell you what I told the detectives from the Prosecutor's Office."

"Fair enough," Duane responded. "And honestly, that's my first question. We haven't received all of the discovery yet, but in what we do have, I haven't seen any motions to quash. Did the paper cooperate with the investigation?"

Rudnicki frowned. "On the advice of counsel, we cooperated. Understand, this was a unique situation. Everything pointed to the fact that Russell was murdered by one of the sources for the story he was working on."

Duane leaned forward in his chair. "His story was about the New Jersey State Police and the Lords of Discipline, right?"

"Correct."

"Where'd the story come from—I mean, who was the original source?" Duane asked.

"When he pitched the idea, Russell told us that shortly after the state police entered into a consent decree in 1999 with the U.S. Attorney's Office over allegations of racial and ethnic profiling involving traffic stops on the Turnpike, he had begun to hear rumors about a group within the state police ignoring the decree and also harassing some of their fellow troopers who were trying to do the right thing. Then about nine months ago, Russell met with a source, who told him about Mazer and an IA investigation. When Russell presented it to us, he had spoken to Mazer once, and was looking for permission to do a deep dive, which we gave him." Rudnicki stopped, studying Duane. "If your next question is, who gave Russell the information about Mazer, the honest answer is that to this day I don't know."

"Any reason he kept that a secret from you?" Duane asked.

Rudnicki snorted. "Yeah, probably to avoid me being forced to tell someone."

Duane gave Rudnicki a skeptical look. "You're his editor, Coach. Why is he keeping it from you?"

"Swish, I got the impression the information was given to him in the strictest of confidences. I suspect it was someone in the state police, but the bottom line for me was that it didn't matter who gave Russell the info about Mazer. What mattered was whether the information Russell got from Mazer about the Lords was accurate."

"I'm assuming he gave you updates as he went along?" Swish asked.

"He did," Rudnicki responded.

"Did he have sources other than Mazer?"

"He did, but again, if you ask me who they were, I don't know. I know most, if not all of them, were troopers."

"Have you checked his office computer to see if he left interview notes—things like that?" Swish probed.

Rudnicki closed his eyes as if he was in pain. "After he was murdered, our attorneys advised us not to go on his computer. They didn't want any allegations that we tampered with evidence. And then, when Mazer became the focus of the investigation, the Attorney General's Office came in with a search warrant and seized Marshall's computer and the contents of his desk."

"Wait!" Duane said, as he mentally went through the items seized during the investigation, sure that no computers were listed. "The AG has Marshall's office computer?"

Rudnicki nodded.

"Were you able to make a copy or download what was on it before they took it?"

"I told you, Swish, counsel advised us not to touch anything," Rudnicki responded, his tone indicating he wasn't happy about the situation.

"I saw in the police reports that the police speculated that whoever killed him might have taken a laptop," Swish said.

"Yeah. That's their theory. He definitely had a laptop and no one has been able to locate it."

"Marshall must have emailed you drafts of the article?" Swish suggested, his growing disappointment evident.

"I've seen drafts," he responded.

"When was the last draft he sent you?"

A shadow crossed Rudnicki's face. "Six o'clock the evening he was murdered. We had an editorial meeting the following morning, so he sent me what was supposed to be the penultimate draft."

Swish leaned back in his chair. "Can I get a copy?"

Rudnicki frowned. "No, Swish. That I can't give you." He allowed several seconds to pass before adding with a knowing grin, "Of course, since he was logged on to his work account when he sent it, there'd be a copy in his email on the computer the AG seized."

Okay, Swish thought, the article existed and one way or another, they'd be able to get the penultimate draft. "You never ran the story. Can I ask why?"

"First, since one of his main sources for the story is charged with murdering him, I didn't know if the information Russell relied on for the story was accurate or not. And . . ." He paused.

Swish waited. "And what?" he finally asked.

"The AG's Office asked us to kill the story," Rudnicki replied.

"Got it," Swish said with a nod. "Thanks, Coach. Great to see you," Swish said as they both stood and exchanged a man hug.

"They have his computer?" Erin asked incredulously, shocked that it hadn't been mentioned anywhere in the discovery.

"Yep. Confirmed it with Assistant AG Ward Rivers," Swish responded. "And get this, when I asked for a copy of the hard drive, his exact words were, 'Not a fucking chance. File a motion.' "

"Why?" Erin asked.

"Because it contains unrelated materials. He said they'd review it and give us anything they deemed relevant."

"That's bullshit," Erin fired back. "How did he explain that they didn't even disclose they had it?"

"A mere oversight," Swish replied in a voice clearly intended to mimic the tone in which Rivers had responded to him.

"What do you think—incompetence or intentional?" Erin posed.

"Always hard to tell when you're dealing with the AG's Office," Swish answered. "That said, it's kind of hard to forget you seized a desktop computer."

"Yeah," she agreed, "they do tend to take up space in the evidence vault."

She sorted through desk clutter until she found a thick red book—the *NJ Lawyers' Diary*. It listed every lawyer in New Jersey, along with virtually every other piece of information a lawyer needed for finding courts, judges, filing fees, or in this case, the schedule of motion days.

"Today's the 17th, so it looks like January 8th is the next motion day. If we get it filed by next Wednesday, the 23rd, they'll have to come up with their response over the holidays." She smiled. "I'm all in favor of making them work over the holidays."

"Count me in," he responded.

"I have something tomorrow. Would you have time to start on it?" she asked.

"Sure," he replied. "What do you have? You need help with anything?"

"No . . . well, um," she stumbled. "Actually, it's personal, and please don't say anything, especially to Mark, unless he says something to you."

"Sure. Is everything okay?" he asked.

"Yeah. Everything's fine. It's just that Mark and I are going tomorrow to meet with Molly and Robin and their lawyers about them having a baby." Erin chuckled when she saw the confusion on Swish's face. "Robin is going to be artificially inseminated, so they can have a baby."

"Okay?" he replied, seeming no less confused.

"Mark has agreed to donate his sperm as part of the process. That way the baby has Robin's DNA and Molly's, since he and Molly are siblings."

"So Mark is going to be the father?" he finally asked.

"No," Erin answered. "They're going to use his sperm, but the reason they're seeing the lawyers is so that legally Mark will *not* be the baby's father."

Swish shook his head and mumbled. "I don't know. Sounds to me like he's the father. You don't have a problem with this?"

"No. I think Robin and Molly will be great parents. And if they weren't using Mark's sperm, they'd have to use sperm from a total stranger."

"I guess," Swish said. He gave her a wide smile. "I gotta admit, I sure learn a lot of new shit hanging out with you."

CHAPTER 10

WITHIN FIVE MINUTES OF MEETING PHIL SONG, ERIN KNEW SHE loved him. He appeared to be about sixty years old. With his long gray hair hanging in a ponytail, a diamond stud in his right earlobe, and a neatly trimmed, full, gray beard, he looked like he could be on tour with a Grateful Dead tribute band rather than serving as one of the top lawyers in the country when it came to assisting members of the LGBTQ community in creating families. But it was the way he spoke that sealed the deal for Erin. His voice was rich and deep in timbre, and his tone conveyed his compassion and passion for everyone in the room. A gay man who had survived the ravages of the AIDS epidemic, he spoke from having litigated the issues he was explaining to them in courtrooms across the country.

Erin, who was seated at a large conference room table in the Newark offices of Song & Sutton, along with Mark, Molly, and Robin, listened as Song went over in detail every provision of the agreement he had prepared, which provided that Mark would donate sperm at the offices of Doctor David Weiss for use in inseminating Robin, and only Robin. As Song had previously explained to Robin and Molly, if done under medical supervision, New Jersey's artificial insemination statute automatically cut off Mark's parental rights and prevented Robin and Molly from claiming support from Mark.

"Who's going to be on the birth certificate?" Mark asked.

"As much as I hate the civil union statute, one benefit is that same sex couples are entitled to the same rights as married couples. Under the law, a husband is presumed to be the father of any child his wife gives birth to. Accordingly, unless someone objects, the husband is automatically listed on the birth certificate as a parent. In this case, since Molly is the civil union partner of Robin, she too will be presumed to be the parent of their child and will be listed on the birth certificate with Robin."

Song then explained that he would also file an action for Molly to become an adoptive parent of the child, as some states did not accept a birth certificate as proof of parentage. By going through an adoption proceeding, Molly would be legally protected as a parent. He also let them know that for purposes of the adoption proceeding, Molly would be treated as a stepparent, so there'd be no need for a home study, simply a criminal background check, child abuse clearance, and a hearing before a judge.

When he had finished, Robin had some questions about Doctor Weiss, which Song answered, and then Mark and Robin signed the agreement and passed it back to Song.

"Any other questions?" Song asked as he prepared to wrap up the meeting.

"Um . . ." Mark said, clearing his throat. "Molly and I were wondering if you have any experience with cases involving a gestational surrogate."

Erin's head tilted back as she tried to decipher why Mark was asking this. *Gestational surrogate*—she was shocked Mark had even remembered the term.

"All the time," Song replied. "What's going on?"

"Well, obviously it probably wouldn't be a good idea for Molly to be pregnant at the same time as Robin, or even while she and Robin had a toddler, so what Molly and I talked about was a situation where Molly had her eggs collected, inseminated, and then implanted into another woman who would agree to carry the baby to term."

"I'm confused," Song said. "Molly, you want to have a baby too?"

"I'm sorry," Mark said. "This isn't for Molly and Robin. It's for Erin and I."

Song smiled. "I'm still a little confused, but sure. The process is a little more complicated because there'd have to be a number of agreements in place with the gestational carrier—and even when there are, the woman who gives birth to the baby can still nullify the agreements within seventy-two hours of giving birth. But that's something I do on a regular basis, not just for LGBTQ couples, but for heterosexual couples who need alternative means of having children." Song paused and scratched the back of his neck before continuing. "Mark, I assume you realize you couldn't be the sperm donor in a situation where you were using Molly's ovum. Would you be using a sperm bank or do you have a donor in mind?"

"Actually, we have a donor in mind."

In the split second before Mark finished what he was about to say, everything fell into place for Erin. Her mind screamed *NO!* but before she could verbalize the thought, Mark continued.

"Before she transitioned, Erin banked her sperm. So, our thought was to use Molly's ovum and Erin's sperm, so that like Robin and Molly, we could have a child that contained Erin's DNA and my mitochondrial DNA through Molly."

Erin knew her mouth was probably agape, but before she could recover, Song said, "That's great. Sure, we can definitely talk about what would be involved if you want to retain us to help you navigate the process. The most important piece of advice I can give you is to think long and hard about who you'd want to be the gestational carrier. As I said, no matter what the signed agreements say, the carrier has the absolute legal right for seventy-two hours after the birth to void the agreements. When that happens, and I've seen it happen, it can be devastating."

"Thanks," Mark replied.

After leaving Song's office, Erin walked the entire way back to their car in silence.

"Why didn't you tell me about this before bringing it up in

front of everyone?" Erin snapped as soon as they reached the safety of Mark's Jeep in the parking garage.

He started the car, letting it warm up. "Because I suspected your reaction would be kind of what it is right now."

"What's that supposed to mean?" she demanded.

"That you'd be upset and wouldn't want me to ask." He faced her. "Have you ever heard the expression, 'It's better to beg forgiveness than ask permission'?"

"Yes," she said, her frustration barely subsiding. "But this is a deeply personal decision that you and I need to discuss."

"I agree," he said. "It is deeply personal, and we do need to discuss it. All I did was put it on the table. And it wasn't like I broadcast it to a wide audience. It was my sister and Robin, and the best attorney in the business. All I wanted to know was whether it was something he could do if, at some point, we were interested. And by the way, just for the record, I'm sorry. Forgive me," he added before she could say anything.

"But why not get an egg donor, and use your sperm?" she asked, her anger spent.

"Because like Robin and Molly, this is the only way we can have a child we both have a genetic link to."

Erin sighed. "When did you speak to your sister about your little plan?"

"A couple of days ago when she called to see if we could meet with Song today."

"And she's comfortable with using her ovum for us to have a baby?"

"Yeah. She was really excited about it. She thought we'd make great parents."

"But why didn't you . . ." She stopped. "I know; because I would have reacted just the way I am now."

"Yep," he said, trying to hide his grin.

She wanted to be mad, but she knew he was right. If he had broached the subject earlier, she would have told him not to raise it. And she had really come to admire Phil and the work he did, so it was good to know that if she and Mark ever did want to go down that road, Song could handle it. But as much as she wanted to be a parent, she was torn about this method. She had always just assumed that if they did decide to become parents, they'd adopt. But then the whole specter of the investigations by the adoption agencies and the inevitable questions about her transition made her feel like adoption might also be out of reach. As the conflicting thoughts danced through her head, she suddenly found herself on the verge of tears.

"What's wrong?" Mark asked.

"I don't know." The sobs escaped before she could stop them.

"Hey, hon, it's okay." He pulled her as close as he could, without either one being impaled on the gear shifter. "Talk to me. Honest, I'm sorry. I had no idea this would upset you so much."

She rested her head on his shoulder. "It's not that. It's just everything. How could I ever tell our child that I'm not their mother, I'm their father? Oh God, the shit they'd go through growing up. They'd be constantly bullied and humiliated. I've always wanted to have children—you know, that's why I banked my sperm in the first place—but how could I put a child through the hell that would follow from having me as a parent?"

"Erin, honey, I know why you banked your sperm. And I know this wasn't part of your plan at the time. But I have faith in the two of us to raise a child who will know they are loved beyond all measure and be strong enough to deal with whatever comes. Gay men, lesbians, and bi folks have been creating families together for years thanks, in part, to lawyers like Phil, and I'm sure lots of those kids have heard snide comments about having two dads or two moms. Lots of kids have to deal with issues over who their parents are. But that's not a reason to shy away. It's a reason to move forward. Because it's only when we refuse to be intimidated and we stand up to the bullies that we can move past the hatred and bias to a place of love."

Erin stared at him. "Ah, wow," she said. "That was beautiful."

He gave her a goofy grin, the one she had loved since the first moment she met him. "Thanks," he said.

"But, how will you feel knowing that you're not the biological dad to our child?"

His grin turned into a knowing smile. "One thing I've discovered in thinking through my situation with Robin and Molly is that being a parent, at least being a good parent, is a lot more than contributing genetic material. When they have their baby, Robin and Molly will be that child's parents—period, end of discussion. I will be the baby's uncle; that's it. And if you and I decide to have a baby, whether we adopt, or have a gestational carrier, I will be that baby's dad and you will be the baby's mom. And if we ever decide to use a surrogate, the fact you are the mom to a baby that came from your sperm will drive some people absolutely insane. But you know what, I couldn't give a shit. I gave up caring about what other people thought about you, or me, the day I realized I was in love with you. So, if at some point you want to take this journey called parenthood together, count me in."

Erin threw her arms around his neck and kissed him. "God, I love you, Mark Simpson."

The next morning, Erin sat across from her mom at their favorite diner, waiting for their brunch order to be served and anxious to talk to her about the possibility of having a baby.

"I think it's wonderful that Mark has agreed to let Robin and Molly use his sperm. They're such a beautiful couple. I'm really happy for them," Peg said, taking a sip from her coffee.

"Um, there's something else I'd like to discuss with you," Erin suggested tentatively.

"Is everything okay?" Peg asked.

"Yeah, everything's fine, just something else came up when we were with the lawyer that I'd like your advice on."

"Of course, dear," Peg said, reaching across the table and squeezing Erin's hand. "Talk to me."

Erin proceeded to tell her mom about Mark's idea for them having a baby and what it would entail, both medically and legally. During most of the explanation Erin found herself staring into her coffee cup, afraid of catching her mother's reaction. The hardest part was explaining that because Robin was going to be pregnant, Molly didn't want to be pregnant at the same time, so if they went ahead, they'd need to find a gestational surrogate. When she was finished, and finally looked up, her mother was beaming.

"I think that's a wonderful idea. You'll make a fantastic mom—and we already know that I am an amazing grandmother," she said.

Erin chuckled. "Thanks, Mom, but there are quite a few moving pieces. Not the least of which is finding someone willing to be pregnant for nine months only to give up the baby. It seems like it's too much to ask of anyone. I mean, what would I say? 'Hi, I'm Erin. I'm transgender. Would you allow yourself to be impregnated so I can have a baby?' " she said in a voice mimicking a late-night television infomercial. "It sounds so selfish."

"Erin, think about it. Isn't everyone's desire to have a baby inherently selfish? Mind you, I'm not talking about an unwanted pregnancy or someone who's raped, I'm talking about a mature couple that decides they want a baby. Why do we do that? Why do we think the world will be a better place if we create a child?"

"But maybe I should adopt," Erin countered.

"Maybe you should," Peg replied. "But doesn't that same argument apply to every other couple who decides to have a baby? You're doing what you always do—you make it sound like you have fewer rights than everyone else because you're transgender. You have just as much right to have a baby as any other couple. The fact that you're a transgender woman shouldn't make you feel like your desires are superficial, while everyone else's are legitimate."

Erin sat back against the padded booth. "Don't sugarcoat it, Mom. Tell me how you really feel."

"You know I'm right," Peg said, refusing to relent. "Stop looking at yourself as a second-class citizen. Any child would be blessed to have you and Mark as parents."

"Egg white omelet," the waitress interrupted, sliding the dish in front of Peg. "And blueberry pancakes for you," she said, plopping the plate down in front of Erin. "More coffee, ladies?"

"No thanks," they each replied.

They sat in silence for a while before Erin finally tried to broker a truce. "Even assuming you're right, there is still the minor detail of finding a gestational carrier. No small feat."

"Think about it. I'm sure there's someone you or Mark know that you could ask."

Erin gave a small laugh. "Okay, Mom. I'll think about it."

CHAPTER 11

"WHAT ARE YOU DOING HERE?" JON ASKED FROM BEHIND the glass partition, disoriented by Gabe's visit. Prisoners in protective custody were only allowed visitors once a week, on Friday mornings at ten. "I'll be the first to admit it's easy to lose track of time in here, especially in PC, but isn't today Wednesday the 23rd? How'd you get in to see me?"

Gabe smiled and motioned with his hands, sweeping down his chest to emphasize what he was wearing. Dressed in his black suit, with his clerical shirt and Roman collar, Gabe was in full clergy apparel.

"Visiting one of my incarcerated parishioners. Coming to wish them a merry Christmas," Gabe replied, seemingly proud of himself. "How you doing?" he asked.

Jon squeezed the back of his neck with his right hand as if he was working out a kink. *Yeah. Merry Christmas*, he thought. "I'm fine, I guess," he finally replied.

"You don't seem happy to see me," Gabe said.

"It's not that. I just don't need to get into any trouble. That's all."

"Why would my visit get you into any trouble?"

"Well, if anyone decided to check my intake records, for religion, I put down that I was an atheist."

"Lots of people find religion in prison, Jon," Gabe offered with a wry smile. "Don't worry, I won't get you into any trouble."

Jon wanted to add, *"other than what you've already gotten me into,"* but held his tongue.

"How are the lawyers?" Gabe asked.

"I only saw McCabe once, and Swisher twice. But they seem like they know what they're doing."

"They ask about us?"

"Yeah. But I said we're just friends."

"You're going to keep it that way, right?" Gabe asked, the hint of concern in his voice.

Jon hesitated.

"Jon, you promised. No one has to know. There's too much on the line."

"Gabe, we shouldn't be talking about this. They told me I shouldn't talk to anyone about the case—including you."

"Stop worrying, it's me. When did you stop trusting me? Besides, our conversations are covered by the priest-penitent relationship."

"It's not a question of trust. It's just . . ."

"It's just what, Jon?"

"It's just that I could go to jail for the rest of my life and the only reason I went there that day was because of you."

Gabe leaned back, as if he had been slapped. "Maybe I should leave?" he said softly.

Jon shook his head. "No. Wait. No. I'm sorry. I'm just scared. You know you're all I have. Please don't leave. I love you."

"Shh. Not so loud," Gabe said. He looked around the visiting area to make sure no one was close. "I love you too," he whispered.

Jon held him in his gaze for a long time. "Thanks," he finally said. "Oh, and by the way, the lawyers said our conversations aren't protected by the priest-penitent privilege."

"Of course they are, my son. Now say a good Act of Contrition and all your sins will be forgiven," Gabe said, holding out his arm and making the sign of the cross with his right hand.

If only it was that easy, Jon thought.

"Great brief," Erin offered, taking a seat in front of Swish's desk.

"You only say that to avoid writing our briefs," he replied.

"Guilty," she said.

"Cheryl told me we received another packet of discovery. You have a chance to see what they sent over?" she asked.

"Yeah, briefly. The grand jury transcripts are there. The NJSP CAD records for the two cars he was in that night were also there, but they've refused to turn over the IA that was conducted when Mazer filed his complaint."

"Why?" Erin asked.

"They claim that under the AG's Guidelines for Internal Affairs Investigations, the information is confidential."

"That's crazy," Erin replied. "This is a murder case, where our client says he was targeted because of that complaint."

"Don't worry," Swish said. "I did almost the exact same motion in the Donovan case. I'll just cut and paste, and get it filed along with the computer motion."

She smiled. "That's why I love you. You're always one step ahead of me."

He rolled his eyes. "You can stop sucking up now."

She shrugged. "Have you had a chance to go through the new stuff yet?"

"I took a quick look at the CAD records."

"And?"

"And, unfortunately the stop he made for the suspected DWI in Bedminster was at 19:14:03—sorry, 7:14:03 p.m. In other words, eleven minutes after the call to Marshall," he added, his disappointment obvious.

"Why do I feel like you've already checked GPS?" she asked.

"Because I have. The location of the stop is roughly nine minutes north of Somerville," he said. "In other words, he could still have made the call."

"Shit," Erin mumbled. "I guess that would have been too easy. But it still doesn't mean he made the call, just that he doesn't have an airtight alibi," she said, with more optimism than she felt.

They each took turns reading the two days of grand jury transcripts. When they were finished, they agreed that Swish would finish polishing the briefs for the motions, and Erin would start cataloging the discovery, analyzing what additional information they still needed, and working up what information they still needed from Mazer.

A little before five, Swish stuck his head in Erin's office. "Motions are all done and ready to file. Cheryl is sending them out for overnight delivery. I'm running into Westfield. I ordered Cori an engraved necklace for Christmas and I want to pick it up before the store closes. You good?"

"Yep. All good. Let Cheryl know that she can leave. I'll be out of here shortly."

He made a face like he had just gotten a whiff of a dirty diaper. "I don't like it when you or Cheryl are the last to leave—especially when it's dark. We've made more than our fair share of enemies in the last few years."

She gave him an appreciative grin. Feeling vulnerable was not something she'd experienced before she transitioned. Back then, she remembered going for a run in a strange city at ten o'clock at night and not thinking twice. Now, she was always aware of potential danger lurking in the shadows.

"Martial arts, pepper spray, and motion detector lighting on the parking lot—I'm good. Thanks," she replied.

His look betrayed both his skepticism and concern. "Call me if you need me."

"Go before the store closes," she said, shooing him out of the building.

Erin looked down at the papers scattered on her desk and picked up a heavily redacted report from the task force the AG's Office had set up a few years earlier to investigate whether the Lords of Discipline existed within the state police. As she read it, she grew increasingly frustrated by both the number of redactions and what appeared to be an investigation designed to come to a foregone conclusion—the Lords did not exist. Although the report highlighted the fact that troopers had been interviewed, the task force appeared to have no subpoena power or any other mechanism to compel the troopers to cooperate. Without that, many of the troopers simply refused to be interviewed. The report's conclusion hinged on the fact that the few troopers who did have the courage to come forward and admit that they were harassed or threatened couldn't prove the existence of an organized group. *Of course they couldn't*, Erin thought. *That's because they weren't part of the damn group.* Placing the burden on those troopers to prove the existence was not only unfair, it was downright impossible without the ability to compel testimony under oath.

She scanned the articles Swish had emailed her concerning the Lords, including several from the *New York Times*. When she finished those, she began doing her own internet research on her adversaries, Deputy Attorney General Carol Roy and Assistant Attorney General Ward Rivers.

Erin remembered Roy from the arraignment. She was an attractive woman, average height, with wide set brown eyes and high cheekbones. She was admitted in 1999, three years after Erin, meaning if she went straight through from high school to law school, she'd be about thirty-five. She had spent seven years as an assistant prosecutor in the Mercer County Prosecutor's Office before joining the AG's Office's Division of Criminal Justice, or DCJ as it was known, three years ago. Her years as an AP in Mercer had included two years trying homicide cases. So, unlike many DAGs, Roy had experience trying murder cases.

From what Erin could piece together, Rivers, who as an assistant attorney general was Roy's superior, had an unusual career path. After he graduated college, he spent thirteen years as a state trooper; five years on the road, before transferring to headquarters. While working a desk job, he managed to attend law school at night at Rutgers, Newark. After passing the bar, he resigned from the state police and set up a law practice specializing in representing law enforcement officers facing disciplinary or criminal charges. As Erin dug deeper, she found that Rivers had represented a number of troopers the task force investigating the Lords had sought to interview, all of whom declined to speak with investigators. Then, two years after the task force completed its work, Rivers was hired by the Attorney General's Office as an assistant AG and assigned to the section handling public corruption, police-involved shootings, and police misconduct.

Curious, Erin thought. Based on the date of his admission to the New Jersey Bar, he had only been practicing law for seven years. Almost all attorneys who went to work at the AG's Office started as a deputy AG. The title of assistant AG was usually reserved for attorneys who had risen through the ranks to a managerial position, or had substantial experience outside the office and were hired to fill a unique role.

Or, she pondered, *sometimes as a reward.*

Carol Roy reached into her desk drawer, pulled out a hair tie, and quickly swept her shoulder-length black hair into a ponytail, securing it with the tie, then checked her hair and makeup in the mirror she kept in the same drawer. Today being an office day as opposed to a court day, she kept her makeup to a minimum. But even without makeup, she received more than her share of uninvited attention from men, especially the men she had to deal with in law enforcement.

She looked up to see Ward Rivers strolling into her office with the bearing of a trooper approaching a vehicle they had just pulled over. *You could take the man out of the state police, but you couldn't take the state police out of the man,* she thought. Rivers was a good six or eight inches taller than her, with broad shoulders and a barrel chest. When he neared her, he casually flipped an envelope onto her desk.

"Mazer's attorneys are looking to get a copy of Marshall's hard drive and a copy of the IA Mazer filed. They're returnable on January 8. I need you to handle filing the opposition because I'll be off until January 4. I'm going hunting in Montana. Come see me after you've taken a look."

And as abruptly as he came, he was gone.

What an arrogant asshole, she thought, then reminded herself to be nice. Rumor had it Rivers had close ties to people who were friendly with the governor-elect. He was her boss now; soon, he might be lording over an entire division, like DCJ, the one she was in now. Either way, nothing good would come from pissing him off.

She turned her attention to the motions in front of her. They seemed pretty straightforward. While she knew her office always claimed IAs were confidential, Mazer was arguing it was relevant to his defense, and since he was the complainant in the IA, there was no way a judge would deny him access. Arguing against turning over a copy of the computer hard drive seemed equally as pointless. Under the court's discovery rules, a defendant in a criminal case was entitled to receive access to any tangible items in the possession, custody, or control of the prosecutor, including any electronically stored information, and the AG's Office had possession. Then she read Swisher's certification filed in support of the motion concerning his conversation with Rivers and cringed. *An oversight. Oh sweet Jesus.*

Thirty minutes later, Carol sat across the desk from Rivers.

"The motions are bullshit, right?" he said, his tone conveying the answer he expected.

"Not exactly," Carol replied.

"What do you mean, not exactly? Just tell 'em we'll give them what we think is important," he shot back.

"That's not what the court rules provide," she said.

"Fuck the court rules. Tell the judge that the victim is entitled to his privacy and defense counsel shouldn't be allowed unfettered access to his personal stuff."

"Unfortunately, Ward, we've had unfettered access—and it's his work computer, not his personal computer. Plus, they claim the IA is relevant to his defense."

"Look," he spat out, "I don't want to give them a copy of the hard drive or the fucking IA. End of discussion. Your job is to find a way to make that happen." His scowl left no room for debate. "Anything else?" he added dismissively, letting Carol know the meeting was over.

"Enjoy your trip," she said as she stood up. "What are you going hunting for?"

"Bear," he replied. "Black bear."

Walking back to her office she couldn't help but giggle as she recalled the title of an Ian Matthews album her dad used to listen to all the time when she was a kid. *Some Days You Eat the Bear . . . And Some Days the Bear Eats You.* She smiled. *Be nice,* she thought. *Be nice.*

CHAPTER 12

Erin propped herself up on one elbow and stared at her husband as he lay sleeping. Her husband—it still sounded strange. Yet, here she was, married to an incredibly handsome man, who knew her past and loved her regardless. Had someone told her six years ago when she transitioned that this is where she'd be, she would have thought they were crazy. And now, on top of everything, they were talking about having a baby.

She fell back onto the pillow thinking of all the times growing up that she had prayed for God to fix their mistake and make her a girl on the outside to match the girl on the inside. It had taken a while, but she was one of the fortunate ones—her prayers had been answered. Although in her case, God had come in the guise of two skilled surgeons, one who had done surgery on her face, the other who had performed gender-affirming surgery. She still vividly recalled the day about three weeks after her facial surgery when she had looked up while brushing her teeth and was stunned to see the woman she always knew she was, staring back at her. Tears of joy had slowly rolled down her still swollen cheeks and, in that moment, she realized how lucky she was. She had what so many trans people didn't have. She had resources, a mother who loved her, and a law partner who had stayed with her. She had the ability to live her life.

Still, as lucky as she was, there were still things that had changed—some forever, some she still hoped to repair.

She returned her gaze to her sleeping husband. As if sensing her stare, Mark rolled over and opened one eye.

"Hey, sleepy head. Merry Christmas," she said, planting a kiss on his forehead.

"Merry Christmas," he mumbled.

"What would you like first?" she asked. "Christmas sex or Christmas waffles?"

He opened his other eye. "Let's work up an appetite."

Later, after a postcoital breakfast of blueberry waffles, coffee, and juice, Erin and Mark opened their presents, then picked up Peg to head to Sean and Liz's so they could all enjoy Christmas Day together.

Liz's mother's family came from Poland, so she always served up some amazing Polish specialties, including red borscht, kielbasa, homemade pierogies, golabki, and a poppy-seed cake for dessert.

Liz, who was tall and thin, with long blond hair that framed a stunningly beautiful face, was the equal of Sean in every respect, and Erin had come to love her like a sister. It was Liz who had turned a blind eye to her sons' clandestine efforts to have Erin secretly attend their State Cup soccer games, which allowed Sean to see how comfortable his sons were with their "Aunt Erin," bringing an end to his estrangement from Erin.

After a wonderful dinner, the seven of them spread out in the living room to open presents. Based on Patrick's and Brennan's love of soccer, Erin had gotten them Arsenal replica jerseys: Robin van Persie for Patrick and Cesc Fàbregas for Brennan. And while they loved their jerseys, Erin could tell from the boys' reactions that Mark had scored the big hit of the day with his present of *FIFA 10* and *NBA Live 09* for the boys' PlayStation 3.

When all the presents were unwrapped and everyone had exchanged thanks and hugs, Patrick and Brennan approached Erin, who was sitting on the sofa leaning up against Mark.

"Aunt Erin," Patrick began, "there is one more gift that we'd like to give you. This is from all of us—Mom, Dad, Brennan, and me."

Brennan reached out with an envelope in his hand. "We hope you'll like it."

Erin immediately got the sense that everyone in the room but her knew what was in the envelope. With some trepidations, she took it. "Thanks, guys. I'm sure I'll love it."

Inside was a white card bearing a large bouquet of purple, yellow, pink, and white flowers. Above the flowers, in a gold print, were the words *With Love.* When she opened the card, written in what she immediately recognized as Liz's perfect penmanship, was a note. As she read, she could feel her hand begin to tremble.

Dearest Erin:

You have been such a wonderful aunt to the boys, we can't imagine anyone who would be a better mother. Your mom has explained your situation to us, and nothing would give me greater joy than for you to allow me to carry your baby. If you permit me the honor, I would love to be the gestational surrogate for your baby. Please know that this is not my decision alone. Sean is totally supportive, as are Patrick and Brennan. This is not just my gift to you; it is our gift to you and Mark.

With Love,

Liz, Sean, Patrick, & Brennan

Erin looked up, now the focus of everyone's attention. Brennan's hopeful eyes forced her to suppress her urge to scream "NO!"

"Wow. This is amazing," she said, hoping she had imitated enough enthusiasm to fool them. "I don't know what to say," she continued, this time with complete candor.

She stood up and quickly hugged Brennan, and then Patrick. "Thank you so much," she said to each of them.

"We can't wait to have a cousin," Brennan announced. "We're going to teach them all the cool soccer stuff, just like you taught us."

"Sounds very cool," Erin said, giving her nephew a high-five.

She then walked over to Liz and embraced her. "Thank you," Erin said.

Finally, she approached her brother. "Thank you," she said, giving him a hug.

When they separated, his look told her that he sensed something was wrong.

"Hey, guys," Sean said to his sons. "Why don't you go downstairs and try out the new games? I have a feeling Uncle Mark will be down shortly to challenge you on the NBA game."

After the boys had headed to the basement, Peg turned to Erin and asked softly, "What's wrong?"

Erin didn't know how to respond. At the moment her emotions were swirling like leaves caught in a strong autumn wind. "I," she mumbled. "I'm . . ." She shook her head, but no other words came out.

"Erin, I'm so sorry. I would never do anything to upset you. We thought this would make you happy," Liz offered, her voice soothing.

Erin turned to face her sister-in-law. "Oh my God, Liz. Please . . ." she stammered. "Please don't apologize. I don't know what to say. What you . . . what your whole family has offered me, us, is unbelievable. It's beyond kind and generous. It's overwhelming. But I could never ask you to do that for me. It's just too much to ask."

"Erin, you didn't ask me to do this. I want to do this, for you, for Mark, and for my family too."

"But, Liz, you don't understand."

"Honey, we talked about this," Peg interrupted. "Don't be so hard on yourself."

Erin gave her mom a weak smile. "Mom, I know I have lots of self-doubt, but this time my trepidations aren't about me; it's about Liz, Sean, and the boys. I could never put them through this."

"Erin, honest, we're all on board with this," Liz said. "Sean and I researched it and I'm the perfect candidate. I have children. I'm still young and healthy enough to go through another pregnancy, and the boys would be thrilled to have a cousin. I know Sean was a bit of a jerk when you first transitioned," she said, stealing a glance at her husband, "but this is something he really wants us to do for you and Mark."

"Liz is right, E," Sean stated. "You and Mark will be great parents, and we'd like to help."

Erin bit down on her lip, shook her head, and drew in a deep breath. "Oh God, it's not about me or Mark and me. It's . . . well, it's a lot more complicated than that." She stopped, collecting her thoughts. "I know having a baby seems like a very private and personal decision that shouldn't concern anyone else, but that won't be the case with me. Over the last three and a half years, I've received a lot of publicity, most of it unwanted, and much of it uncomplimentary. If Mark and I go through with this process, at some point we'd have to go to court for approval to have both of our names on the baby's birth certificate. While the court papers will be filed using initials, there are always people looking to cause me problems, so there are no guarantees that it will remain private. Which means it's possible that both of you and the boys could be thrown into the spotlight too. The stuff people write and say can be soul crushing. I love you all too much to put you through that meat grinder—especially the boys." Erin hesitated, a tear running down the side of her face. "Do you understand?" she asked, a catch in her voice.

Liz walked over to the sofa, sat down next to her, and drew Erin into an embrace. "Erin, I apologize." Liz lifted her head and glanced over at Sean. "We could have been more supportive with everything you've had to deal with since you transitioned."

"Please don't apologize," Erin replied, leaning back. "These are my issues. What I'm trying to avoid is making them your issues. You and the boys shouldn't have to deal with that crap because of me."

"Can I ask a question?" Peg interjected. "Are your concerns only about Liz, Sean, and the boys, or do you have your own reservations? Because, honey, if you have reservations, no one would ever want you to have a baby you don't want."

Erin looked down at her lap, trying to avoid her mother's probing eyes. "Yes, I have lots of reservations, the obvious ones anyone contemplating having a baby should have, like work-family balance." She looked at Mark and smiled. "But Mark has convinced me that we will arm our child with lots of love, and hope for the best—pretty much all that any parent can do to protect their child from the hatred that's out there in the world. So, to answer your question, there's nothing I would want more than to have a baby with Mark. But I can't in good conscience risk putting Liz, Sean, and the boys through that."

"But isn't that for Liz and her family to decide?" Peg asked.

Erin pursed her lips. "No," she said. "Having offered, even if they had second thoughts, they couldn't back out now. They'd feel awful. So, this makes it easy."

"Or we could feel awful that you didn't trust us enough to make our own decision," Liz suggested.

Erin winced. Even wrapped in velvet, Liz's words landed hard.

"Oh Liz, I trust you. I know you've always been there for me. I just don't want to see anyone get hurt because of me."

"Erin, don't you understand? How can Sean and I teach the boys that sometimes you have to do what's right, even if it's unpopular, unless we do what we believe in? It might not be popular, but offering you and Mark this opportunity is something that we truly believe is the right thing to do. Please let us do this for you."

Erin closed her eyes, torn. As much as she wanted this, there was another part of her that dreaded the thought of the people she loved suffering because of her. Then she looked up into Mark's eyes and her wedding vows came flooding back. *Up until I met you, I lived in fear. Fear that it was impossible for anyone to love me for who I was. But your love, and your acceptance of me, did something I didn't think was possible. You showed me that fear wasn't the answer; love was the answer. Your love saved me from my fears and self-doubt.* She knew—it was time to live up to her vow.

She turned to Liz. "Are you sure you want to go through another pregnancy?"

"I'm sure," Liz said.

"Oh God. I hope you don't regret this," Erin said.

"I won't," Liz responded with a wide smile.

Erin threw her arms around Liz and hugged her. "Thank you," she whispered.

Then Erin turned back to her mother. "By the way, for someone who's always lecturing me on making decisions for other people, seems to me you are a tad guilty of doing the same thing."

"I didn't have to ask you," Peg said without missing a beat. "I already knew."

Erin snorted and raised an eyebrow. "Really. And how did you know?"

"Mother's intuition," she replied with a faint grin. "You'll see," she said, giving her daughter a beatific grin.

With Peg staying at Sean and Liz's for the weekend, Mark and Erin had the car ride home to themselves.

"Are you upset?" Mark asked as soon as they were in the car.

She swiveled to face him. "No."

"You sure?" he asked.

"Yeah, I'm sure," she said.

"We don't have to do this, you know."

"Yeah, I know," she responded. "But if we want to have a family, there's always going to be someone saying I don't have the right. Whatever we do, there's always going to be someone against it. When all is said and done, I waste far too much of my life worrying about what other people think of me. It's time for me to forget what everyone else thinks and start living my life as best I can, and if that bothers people—well, as you told me a few weeks ago, that's their problem, not mine." She reached over and put her hand on his. "As long as I have you, I know we can do this. I'm ready if you are, Mr. Simpson."

He squeezed her hand. "Game on," he replied.

"By the way, speaking of game on, who won *NBA 09*?" she asked.

"They kicked my butt," he replied with a laugh.

"I knew they would," she replied, soaking in the joy that came from having a loving family.

CHAPTER 13

"HEY, MAZER, YOU GOT A VISITOR. YOU KNOW THE DRILL," THE voice called from outside his cell.

Jon got up from his bunk, went to the far wall of his cell, faced the wall, placing the palms of raised hands against the wall and spreading his legs. Two officers then entered his cell, and while one stood by the entrance, the other entered and patted Jon down.

"You like it when I pat you down, Mazer? You must miss all the boys running their hands down your legs," the officer said. He then told Jon to turn around, cuffed his hands in front of him, stepped behind Jon and smacked his hand on Jon's backside before letting out a derisive laugh.

"Knock it off, Carson," the officer at the door said. "Let's go."

A pat down and cuffs meant he was coming into contact with someone, and as they walked him through the corridor, he wondered if Gabe had parlayed his priestly garb into a contact visit. It was only when they turned onto J wing, where the attorney meeting rooms were located, that he realized he was about to see McCabe or Swisher.

"I didn't expect company the week between Christmas and New Year's," he said to Erin once the officers left. "What brings you here?" he asked.

She smiled politely. "I wanted to bring you up to date on what's going on."

"I don't want to make it sound like I don't appreciate the visit, but I'm sure you know that you could've arranged a phone call through my social worker."

"Sounds like you're not happy to see me," she replied.

"No. It's not that. It's just that I can't afford to pay you as it is, and . . . well, if I get convicted, there's no way I can pay you and I feel bad about that," Jon replied.

Erin squeezed her lower lip between her fingers. "Getting paid is great; it's what keeps us in business. But we understood the risk when we took the case. You're still entitled to the best legal defense we can provide."

"Thanks," Jon said softly.

"How you holding up?" she asked, changing the subject.

He looked up, and gave her a tight smile. "Not exactly the way I envisioned spending my holidays, but I'm hanging in there."

"Look, I know how hard ad seg can be," she said, referring to administrative segregation, which was just a nice term jails used for solitary confinement, which is what protective custody amounted to. "It can wear you down mentally really quickly."

Jon cocked his head to the side, his eyes narrowing as if to ask, "How would you know?"

"I spent almost ten days in solitary about six months ago when I was arrested on murder charges," she offered, answering his unasked question. "So, yeah, I know what it's like."

"I remember the stories about you being arrested, but I didn't know about the solitary part," Jon said.

"No reason you would know. It never made the press and it generally doesn't come up in casual conversation," she responded with a shrug. "But based on my experience, the best advice I can give you is to keep active mentally. Read as much as you can. They can't deny you materials from the law library, so ask for as much stuff as you can. It may not help your case, but it'll help keep you from going off the rails emotionally."

"Thanks," he replied.

"Have you been able to have visitors?" Erin asked.

"Yeah, Gabe's been here a couple of times," he said, deciding to leave out the pastoral visit.

"Anyone other than Gabe? Family? Friends?"

He shook his head. "No."

"Jon, let's talk about you. I need to get to know you better."

"Sure. What do you want to know?" he asked.

"Where'd you grow up?"

"Vineland—born and raised. Vineland High School class of '94. Starting quarterback my junior and senior years."

"I'm impressed," she said with a smile. "How about your family?"

"I'm the oldest of three kids. I have a sister two years younger and a brother who's five years younger."

"Are your parents still alive?" she asked.

"I presume so." Jon hesitated. "My family hasn't been in touch with me to let me know anything different." He took a deep breath and then exhaled slowly through his mouth. "I know that sounds cold, but my parents haven't spoken to me since my senior year in college. That's when I came out to them. They sent me to a therapist, who was a friend of my dad's. He was going to help make me straight. I saw the therapist once and afterward he told my parents it was a waste of time; I was gay and he knew I wasn't going to change. After that they told me I should pack up my stuff and leave. So, I did."

"I'm sorry," she said.

"Me too," he replied, trying his best not to touch the third rail where his emotions laid buried.

"How about your siblings—do you stay in touch with them?"

"No. Neither of them would risk my father's wrath."

"What's your dad do?"

"He's an emergency room doc."

"How about your mom? Did she reject you too?"

He could only nod.

"What's she do?" Erin asked.

"A matrimonial attorney. Which is ironic because she and my dad have such a shitty marriage," he replied.

He waited, but she didn't make the statement that so many others did about how surprised they were that well-educated people could reject their own children. Maybe she had the same experience as him—bias knew no class distinctions.

"Were you out when you went through the State Police Academy?" she asked.

"Good God, no! After coming out to my parents, I wasn't really publicly out to anyone. I guess you could say I learned my lesson. I basically had two lives—the private one where I dated guys, and the public version, Jon Mazer, state trooper."

"What year did you graduate the academy?" Erin asked, referring to the State Police Academy in Sea Girt, New Jersey.

"Class of '99," he replied.

"When we met the first time, you told us that the Lords of Discipline came after you when they found out you were gay. How'd they find out?"

He snorted. "You really don't know some of the assholes I worked with very well. Early on some of them started asking questions like, 'Hey, Mazer, how come we never see you with any women? What are you, a fag?' And I'd just try to laugh it off and tell them I'd never bring any woman I was dating around them. But they were suspicious. Then one night about three years ago, an Asbury cop who knew me spotted me coming out of Paradise in Asbury. It's no secret that Paradise is a gay club, so the next thing I know there's all kinds of nasty notes and gay porn being left by my locker or on the windshield of my car. And it went downhill from there."

She drew out in more detail the harassment he endured, and then filled him in on the motions they had filed to get a copy of Marshall's hard drive and the IA that was conducted as a result of his complaint.

"Jon, one piece of discovery that we did get were the CAD records. Unfortunately, the time of the stop you made was at 7:14, about eleven minutes after the call to Marshall was made from your burner. Meaning it doesn't eliminate you from making the call to Marshall on your burner."

"Shit," he mumbled.

"According to cell tower information, your regular cell phone was off from five thirty p.m. until nine p.m. When Duane asked you why, you said you couldn't remember. Jon, let me try again. Why was your phone off?"

He looked down, trying to avoid her gaze. He knew where this was going to go, and he didn't want to go there.

"Jon, the ME has estimated the time of death between five to ten p.m., which is basically the same time period that your phone is off. I'm not sure how we win this case if you don't take the stand and explain how, despite the fact that your off-duty weapon was used to murder Marshall, you're not the murderer. That means, unless you explain why your phone was off, you are going to get roasted on the stand. You have to help me help you."

Jon looked down at the table that separated them. "Gabe and I had an argument," he said without looking up. "It had gotten pretty heated, and I just didn't want to talk to him."

"What was the argument about?" she asked.

He looked up at her. His eyes pleading with her. Part of him holding on to his promise to Gabe.

"Jon, I need to know," Erin demanded.

"He wanted me to stop Marshall from doing the article. He was afraid . . . afraid the article might include him," he said, capitulating.

"Include what about him, Jon?"

Jon took his cuffed hands, placed them behind his head, and stared up at the ceiling.

"Jon, it's time you tell me the truth about Gabe. He's not just your friend; he's your lover, correct?"

Jon sighed and then nodded. "For obvious reasons, our relationship is something I've promised Gabe I'd never disclose."

"So how would Marshall even know about him?" Erin asked.

"The second time I met with Marshall, in Johnson Park in Piscataway, Gabe and I were together," he said haltingly. "I was delivering some documents, and I could tell Marshall was wondering who this guy with me was, and honestly, I wasn't really thinking, so I introduced Gabe by name as a friend. But for obvious reasons, Gabe is incredibly paranoid about being outed and wasn't happy I had just used his full name with a reporter."

"Is that why you went to Marshall's the day he was murdered, to try and convince him not to run the article?"

Jon rubbed his eyes, slowly bringing his hands together in front of his mouth as if he was praying. "Not exactly," he replied. "I asked him if he could delay the article because . . . well, not because, but to give me time to ease—well, I told Marshall they were my concerns, but really they were Gabe's."

"And?"

"And, he smiled and said there was nothing for me to worry about. He then took me over to his laptop on the kitchen counter and let me read the version of the article he was about to send to his editor. And it was fine—there was nothing about Gabe."

"So, if that's the case, why did you and Gabe argue?" Erin asked.

Jon let out a deep sigh. "Because even though I called Gabe and told him the article was fine, he begged me to go back and get Marshall to pull the article because he was afraid the article would generate further investigations, and he couldn't risk being exposed. When I told him I wouldn't do that, he started screaming at me, and accusing me of not caring." Jon stopped. "It's not that I didn't care; I do. It's just that exposing the Lords was—is—more important." Jon stared at the ceiling again as if he might find the answer there. "Gabe wasn't very happy with my response."

"Your phone was off until nine; did you call him after that?" she asked.

"I called him around ten, before I headed back to the barracks to double up."

"What happened?" Erin asked.

"He didn't pick up."

Erin looked down at her notes. "When I met Gabe for the first time, he gave me his phone number, but I've checked and it doesn't show up on your cell phone records or the calls on your burner phone. How is that possible?"

"Gabe had, maybe still has, a prepaid phone," he replied. "I only ever called that number."

"So, when you called him, you always called his prepaid cell?"

"Yeah."

"When you called him, did you use your regular cell or your prepaid cell?"

"I can't say I never called him from the prepaid, but usually from my regular cell," Mazer said.

"How about when you called Marshall?" she asked.

"For him, I always used my prepaid."

"I just want to make sure I have this straight. You used a prepaid to call Marshall, but your regular cell to call Gabe?" she asked.

"Yeah. I mean, Gabe was the one who was trying to keep us secret. I didn't care. It was just the opposite with Marshall. I didn't want anyone knowing I was talking to him."

"Got it," Erin said.

She flipped the page of her yellow legal pad and jotted a note at the top of the page. "Do you have a spare set of keys to your car?" she asked.

"Yeah, of course. Why?" he replied.

"Where were they the night Marshall was murdered?" she continued, ignoring his question.

"In my apartment," Jon replied, his tone quizzical.

"Does Gabe have a key to your apartment?"

Jon cocked his head to the side, realizing the implication inherent in her question. "What are you suggesting?"

"I'm not suggesting anything. I just want to know if he does."

"Gabe wouldn't hurt anyone," Jon fired back.

"I didn't say he would, or did. I just want to know if he had a key to your place," she persisted.

"Yeah, but he had five thirty mass that day, so it couldn't have been him."

Erin sighed. "Jon, Marshall was murdered on a Monday. It's been a long time since I've been to church, but I seriously doubt there was a five thirty p.m. weekday mass. But, even if there was, mass lasts about an hour, giving Gabe plenty of time to get to Marshall's after mass." Her eyes locked onto his. "Jon, I can't make you tell the truth, but if you're going to lie, it better be more believable than that one, otherwise they'll bury you."

There was nothing he could say. He felt like the kid caught with his hand in the candy jar.

"Jon, did you ever call Gabe at any number other than his prepaid phone?"

Jon shook his head. "No. Why?" he asked.

She ignored his question. "Did he have the prepaid phone when you met him, or did he buy it after you met?"

"Um, I don't . . . Actually, he had it before. I remember him giving me that number when we first met."

"Did he ever change his phone—burn it?" Erin asked.

"No. He used the same phone." Jon's eyes narrowed. "What's going on? Why are you asking these questions?"

"Jon, since you called Gabe's prepaid on a regular basis, and since he apparently didn't change phones after you were arrested, they could easily track Gabe's prepaid phone location, and eventually by following the phone, find out who was using it. In other words, by now I'm sure the AG knows about Gabe. Has he said anything about being contacted by the AG's Office?"

"No. Nothing," Jon said, shifting uncomfortably in his chair. "He would have told me if anybody contacted him."

"When's the last time you saw him?"

"Right before Christmas."

Erin nodded. "Okay. I'll touch base with him just so he knows he doesn't have to speak with anyone if he doesn't want to."

"Thanks," Mazer replied.

Erin paused. "And, Jon, I know how important Gabe is to you, but please remember what I told you the first time we met: don't talk to him about the case."

He nodded halfheartedly, wondering if Gabe would continue to press him to talk to him about things.

"Do you know who else besides you talked to Marshall for the article?" she asked.

"Honestly, I don't. He never told me who else he was talking to."

"But you must've given him names of some troopers you felt might be cooperative."

"Yeah. I did."

"Who are they?" she asked.

"If I tell you, you'll have someone speak to them, won't you?"

"Yes," she replied.

"Then I can't tell you," he said.

After he was back in his cell, he stretched out on his bunk, trying to figure out how in God's name he had wound up where he was. Thirty-three years old, and looking at spending the rest of his life behind bars.

How different his life was from what he had envisioned. He remembered his "Glory Days," as Bruce Springsteen would call them. The star quarterback, the guy everyone envied, the guy who dated the prettiest girl in the senior class, the guy who was the "king" of the senior prom, the guy voted most likely to be a movie star. The guy who carried a secret he had known since age twelve—the guy who was gay.

McCabe was right about one thing; the isolation of protective custody had worn him down pretty quickly. Too much time to think; too much time to explore "what ifs"; too much time to be swallowed by the pain of rejection, a pain he thought he had buried twelve years ago when his parents told him to leave and not come back. Why did it matter who he was attracted to? How could you disown your own child simply because he liked men instead of women? He didn't know why he was gay. It wasn't like he decided one day to be gay; he just was. But other than that, he was still the same person. But that didn't matter—not to his parents, and definitely not to his fellow state troopers.

He liked to think that he had become a trooper for all the right reasons—to help people. And there were times when he did, like when he pulled a young mother and baby from a burning car. He knew a lot of other troopers who were like him too, ones who really did want to help people. But somewhere along the way *protect and serve* seemed to become almost antithetical to the reality of the job—people hated the cops and the cops hated the people. So often it seemed like it was "us against them." And then he had become the "other." He was no longer part of the "us." Apparently, there was no room in the thin blue line for a gay trooper.

What a fucking mess. His life had revolved around going from one closet to the next—hiding he was gay from his friends on the job, and hiding he was a trooper from his gay friends. And then a year ago he met Gabe. Someone whose closets were even deeper than his. Only he would fall in love with a Catholic priest. But that wasn't true. He didn't know Gabe was a priest until they had been dating for two months. Gabe was so damn handsome, but he also carried so much baggage. And now, after McCabe's questions, the ultimate quandary—could Gabe be trusted? He wanted to believe in Gabe, but . . .

Swish, Corrine, and the kids were spending the week between Christmas and New Years at her parents in Virginia. Nevertheless, Erin had barely pulled out of the jail's parking lot when Swish called in response to her text about meeting with Mazer.

"Why are you calling me so quickly? You're supposed to be on vacation."

"I am," Swish responded. "Corrine is out with her parents, and both kids are napping. So, you have my undivided attention—at least until someone wakes up."

She went over her conversation with Jon in detail.

"Sounds like you think Father DeAngelis knows more than he's telling us," Swish said.

"I don't know if he does or not, but I suddenly have a lot more questions that we need answers to, and . . ." She hesitated. "And, Swish, the way Jon described it, DeAngelis was desperate to stop the article from being published. He also had access to the spare key to Jon's apartment, where there was a second set of keys to Jon's car. As I was talking to Jon, I suddenly began wondering if DeAngelis may have been in on setting Jon up, or worse."

"Wait. You think DeAngelis might be involved in Marshall's murder?"

Erin sucked in a deep breath. "I don't know," she finally said.

"But he was the one who contacted you to represent Jon."

"Yes, but remember, I wasn't Gabe's pick. I was recommended to Jon. Gabe reached out to me because Jon asked him to."

"Do me a favor," Swish said. "Wait until I'm back. I think we should speak to DeAngelis together."

"I agree. Let me know if this works. The argument on the discovery motions is right after you get back. Assuming we win those, we can set up a meeting with Gabe after we take a look at the new discovery. There may be things there we want to ask Gabe about."

"Perfect," Swish said. Then quickly added, "Gotta run, Alysha's screaming."

"Enjoy," she said as Swish hung up, leaving her to contemplate the joys and challenges that awaited if she were to join the ranks of being a working parent.

CHAPTER 14

JUDGE LILLIAN BADER MOVED HER READING GLASSES DOWN TO THE tip of her nose and peered over the top of the rims. "Ms. Roy, I don't think you've answered my question. I understand that you don't want to make Mr. Marshall's computer available to the defense. My question was, and is, under the discovery rules, specifically Rule 3:13-3(b)(1)(E), aren't you obligated to provide the defense with any 'electronically stored information' that's in your possession, custody, or control? And wouldn't that include Mr. Marshall's computer that your office has possession of?"

Erin leaned back in her chair and looked over at Roy. If Erin was reading Roy's body language correctly, she was trying hard to make the best out of an argument she really didn't believe in. Erin could certainly sympathize. Every lawyer who had ever entered the well of a courtroom had experienced those days when you knew from the opening bell that it was going to be an uphill battle—so far, it had been one of those days for Roy.

"Well, Your Honor . . ."

"Ms. Roy, excuse my interruption, but that seemed to be a yes or no answer." Bader folded her hands. "Let me see if I can break it down for you. The Attorney General's Office has in its possession Mr. Marshall's computer. Correct?"

Carol Roy nodded. "Yes, Your Honor," she said, glancing down at Rivers, who was seated next to her at counsel table doodling on a legal pad.

"Good. Now, on that computer there is electronically stored information, correct?"

"Yes, Judge."

"We're making progress," Judge Bader said with a hint of a grin. "See how easy this is, Ms. Roy, when you answer my questions? Would I also be correct that your office has reviewed the information on Mr. Marshall's computer?"

"You are correct, Your Honor."

"So, is there something specific that you can point to on the computer and say, 'Judge, we don't think the defense should see this because it's personal, confidential, or potentially embarrassing for the victim'?"

Rivers rose from his seat. "Your Honor, if I may."

"By all means, Mr. Rivers. Please enlighten me," Bader said with a tinge of sarcasm, which in Erin's estimation, was totally lost on him.

"Judge, we'll be happy to review Mr. Marshall's computer and provide defense counsel with any relevant information. But there's simply no need for them to have unfettered access."

Bader took off her glasses and laid them down in front of her, her look of irritation growing. "Mr. Rivers, while I'm sure Mr. Swisher and Ms. McCabe are deeply appreciative of your generous offer, I suspect they would prefer to decide for themselves what is relevant to their client's defense, and not rely on your determination. They may have a slightly different perspective from you and Ms. Roy. Now if you'd be so kind as to answer my last question, is there anything on Mr. Marshall's computer that is personal, confidential, or potentially embarrassing for the victim?"

"His emails, Your Honor," Rivers replied.

"Are these his personal emails or work emails?" Bader asked.

"A mix of both," Rivers asserted, his confidence seeming to grow.

"Are they all sent from or received on his work email address?" Bader inquired.

"I . . . I'm not certain, Judge."

"Ms. Roy, can you help us out? Do you know?"

Roy rose from her seat, her body language suggesting to Erin that she was not happy about being dragged back into the fray. "They're all on his work email account," she replied, drawing a disdainful glance from Rivers.

"Is there anything on his computer that is arguably not work related?" Bader asked.

Rivers turned to Roy, deferring once again.

"Ah, Judge, I haven't reviewed every single document in his documents file, so I can't say with certainty," Roy replied.

"Are there any other programs that might contain anything that's personal, confidential, or potentially embarrassing?" Bader asked.

"He has his iTunes library on there, Judge," Rivers replied.

"Anything else?" Bader inquired.

"No, Judge. Not that I can think of at the moment."

"Thank you, Mr. Rivers and Ms. Roy. Mr. Swisher, let me ask you this. Is there any reason you need Mr. Marshall's iTunes library?"

Erin watched as Duane rose to his feet and buttoned his suit jacket. "Actually, there is, Your Honor. If a user is utilizing iTunes as their default audio application, there may be interviews that Mr. Marshall conducted that he stored in iTunes."

"Mr. Swisher, I will confess that I am not the most tech-savvy person. Can you put that in English for me?"

"Sure, Judge. Let's say Mr. Marshall interviewed person A and when he did the interview, he recorded it. Now he wants to play that interview on his computer. If he uploads the audio of the interview to his computer, and iTunes is the program that he uses to listen to audio files, a copy of that interview may well be stored in the iTunes library. Now, because we haven't had access to Mr. Marshall's computer, I can't tell you if he did save interviews in that fashion, but if he did, we should be able to listen to them." Duane paused. "And if he didn't save interviews in iTunes, the worst thing that will happen is that we will find out what kind of music Mr. Marshall enjoyed."

"Thank you, Counsel. Let's turn to the Internal Affairs investigation. Ms. Roy, I've read your brief. Do you, or Mr. Rivers, have anything to add?"

Rivers slowly stood. "Your Honor. As you are well aware, the attorney general's guidelines on IA investigations makes them confidential. Accordingly, we believe the court should deny the defendant's request."

"Let me ask you this, Mr. Rivers. The defendant, Mr. Mazer, has proffered through his counsel that he believes he was targeted by other members of the state police, in part, because he filed an Internal Affairs complaint, which he asserts will be part of his defense. Since he was the complainant in the IA, and it's possible that some of the same people who were interviewed as part of the investigation of that complaint may be witnesses against him in this case, why shouldn't he have access to their prior sworn statements?"

"Because, Your Honor, the people who provided statements did so relying on the fact that those statements were going to be kept confidential."

"You're not suggesting that their statements to Internal Affairs would have been different if they knew the statements wouldn't be confidential, are you?"

"No. Of course not, Judge. To the extent the witnesses are sworn law enforcement officers, they're obligated to tell the truth. No, what I'm saying is they told the truth in the IA and they will tell the truth in the courtroom, so there's no reason to disclose the IA."

"Mr. Rivers, I suspect if I asked Mr. Swisher or Ms. McCabe if they've ever seen a witness, including sworn law enforcement officers, change their testimony, they'd tell me it happens with some regularity. I have certainly seen it enough times from my lofty perch on the bench. Accordingly, I'm not swayed by your argument. Thank you. You can have a seat."

Bader picked up a legal pad that she had been jotting notes on. "Here's what I'm going to do. I'm ordering that the state turn over a complete copy of Mr. Marshall's hard drive. I'm also ordering that a complete copy of the Internal Affairs investigation be turned over to the defendant. To ensure that nothing confidential or embarrassing about Mr. Marshall is inappropriately released, I'm going to enter a protective order. If and when we get to trial, we can address how we'll handle admissibility of these materials at that point in time. Anything further, Counsel?" Bader asked.

Duane quickly stood. "No, Your Honor. Thank you."

"No, Judge," Rivers added, halfway between standing and sitting.

Erin leaned over to her right and said softly to Jon, "Not a bad day. As soon as we get a look at the computer and IA, we'll come visit you to discuss what's there."

"Thanks," Jon said, allowing the sheriff's officers to help him out of his seat and escort him as he shuffled out of the courtroom.

"I think I like Judge Bader," Duane said with a chuckle.

"You should. She made you look brilliant," Erin said with a laugh. "Although, I do have to admit your iTunes argument was spot-on."

"Thanks. Let's go pick up some coffees for the ride back."

"I wonder how they'll split things up if it goes to trial," Erin said on the drive back to the office.

"What do you mean?" Duane asked.

She took a sip from her coffee. "Roy has a decent amount of trial experience, including doing murder cases. My gut tells me she'll be good in front of a jury. Rivers, on the other hand, if he's anything like he was today, may come across to the jury as a bit arrogant. Based on that, my hope is that the jury sees and hears more from Rivers. If he's annoying in small doses, just imagine how grating he'll become over the course of a lengthy trial."

"We're gonna need a computer expert to scour Marshall's computer. Got any ideas?"

Erin smiled. "Yeah, I do. Remember when we were defending Ann Parsons, there was the young computer guy who found the rootkit on her father's computer. His name is Aaron Tinsley and he works for Locksmith Computer Services, which is in the Williamsburg section of Brooklyn—so fairly local."

"Sounds like you looked him up," Duane said, stealing a glance in her direction.

"I did better than that. I spoke to him and his boss, Peter Geiger."

"And?"

"And, I think they'd be perfect for what we need. Both are former hackers, but only Aaron ever got caught—hacking into the NRA's computer system." She held up a hand before Duane could interrupt. "No criminal record. He was eighteen, so they admitted him into a Pretrial Intervention Program, which he successfully completed, and all charges were dismissed. They'd work on the case together, and if we needed someone to testify, it would probably be Geiger, because he's the owner and has a little more experience—plus he's never been caught hacking," she added with a lopsided grin.

"How much?"

"Retainer of seventy-five hundred, but if they go through the hard drive and don't find anything out of the ordinary, they'd be willing to refund twenty-five hundred of it. Of course, if they find anything helpful, and we want them to do an expert's report and testify, it would be another three grand for the report and five grand to testify."

"Whew!" he said. "You realize this is all coming out of our pocket, right?"

Erin cocked her head to the side. "Excuse me, but do me a favor, when you see my righteously indignant partner who decided to take this case, ask him to give me a call."

His face contorted in an apparent effort to suppress a smile. "Not fair shoving my own words back in my face."

"I'll try and remember that for future reference."

Each of them sipped their coffee as they rode in silence.

"Um, can we change the subject for a minute?" Erin asked.

"Happy to, since I'm getting my ass kicked on this one. What's up?"

"I haven't said anything to you, because there were some tests that needed to be run, but . . ." She stopped and took a deep breath, unsure as to what his reaction might be. "Ah, Mark and I may have a baby."

He stole another glance in her direction. "Wow! Didn't see that coming," he said, his look of surprise slowly transforming into one of joy. "That's great. Good for you. Are you adopting?"

"Not exactly," she said softly. "Maybe I should wait until we get back to the office. I don't want to cause an accident."

"You can talk to me. It can't be any more awkward than when you told me you were transitioning."

Her memory flashed back to when she had told him she was transgender. For that conversation, Erin had laid the groundwork by having Lauren tell Corrine, and telling Swish's best friend, JJ, herself, so JJ would be prepared to answer Swish's questions. For this conversation she'd have no backup—it was just her and Swish.

She inhaled. "I'm not sure if you'll remember, but at some point, I had told you that I had banked my sperm before I started female hormones."

"Yeah. I think I vaguely recall that."

"Well, Mark's sister Molly is going to donate some of her eggs, and we're planning to go to a doctor, who is going to use my sperm to fertilize Molly's egg."

"Wait, I'm confused. I thought Mark was donating his sperm to Molly and her partner so they could have a baby."

"He is," Erin replied.

"Huh? What's that got to do with you and Molly?"

"Nothing. We are creating a separate embryo from my sperm and Molly's ovum so Mark and I can have a baby."

"But you can't become pregnant—can you?"

"No. My sister-in-law Liz has agreed to have the embryo implanted in her uterus and carry the baby. We just went through a week of testing to make sure my sperm were viable and Liz was healthy enough to carry the baby. Next, we have to see the lawyers to make it all legal."

An unnerving quiet enveloped them. "Mark is okay with this?" Swish asked. "I mean, it's not his baby."

"It was his idea," she replied.

"Oh," he said in a tone that did nothing to hide his surprise.

"And he will be the baby's dad. We're going to get a court order, and once the baby is born and Liz waives her parental rights, Mark will be listed on the baby's birth certificate as the father, and I'll be listed as the mother."

She couldn't help but notice Swish wince.

"Yeah, but . . ." He stopped midsentence.

"Yeah, but?" she repeated.

Swish shook his head, as if clearing his mind. "Yeah, but nothing," he said. "I'm sorry. I don't know why I slip sometimes and think of you differently from any other woman I know."

"Maybe it's because there are things that I have to consider that other women don't—like will my child be safe because of who their mom is?"

"Maybe. But most parents worry if their kids will be safe. I worry all the time if my Black babies will be safe in this crazy country. All you can do is love them and try your best to protect them." He turned to look at her, a smile spreading across his face. "You'll make a great mom, and Mark will be a terrific father. I'm happy for you."

"Thanks. I appreciate that," Erin said. She wasn't sure if he meant it or just was being sensitive to not hurt her feelings. Regardless, it was what she needed to hear to quell the demons of self-doubt that had once again escaped and were running amok in her psyche.

Rivers stared at the screen of his burner phone and let out a disgruntled moan.

"I really wish you wouldn't call me," he said, his annoyance on full display. "Although I will give you credit for having the good sense to call this phone. So why the fuck are you calling?"

"Carol Roy just called me," a nervous voice responded. "She said the judge ruled that Mazer's lawyers are entitled to his IA complaint file, and that I have to send her a copy." He hesitated. "Ward, are his lawyers really entitled to get that information?"

"Jesus, man, stop whining," Rivers replied. "There's nothing there. What are you worried about?"

"I supervised the investigation. I signed off on the final report."

"Yeah, so what?"

"I don't want people asking me questions about the investigation, or . . . or about the task force."

"Stop being such a fucking pussy."

"I'm concerned. You know what I did. There are things I hid—"

"Yeah, there's a lot of things you hid," Rivers interrupted. "Especially from your wife and family."

"Please, Ward. I've done everything you asked."

"Keep it that way, and your secret will be safe."

"But—"

"There's no fucking buts. Send Roy what she wants and keep your mouth shut."

"What will they use it for?"

"How the fuck would I know? I'm not a fucking mind reader. Just do what you're told and then crawl back in your hole. *Capisci*?"

Rivers put the burner down on the table.

"That sounded interesting," David Britton said.

Rivers looked at Britton and shook his head. Britton was only about five nine, but built like a fireplug. Based on the size of his pecs and arms, Rivers figured him for a steroid user. To each his own, he thought. Britton had been one of the troopers Rivers represented during the task force investigation, and he had helped to make sure other troopers kept their mouth shut.

"Where were we?" Rivers asked.

"You were telling me about Mazer's lawyers," Britton said.

"Right," Rivers replied, refocusing on what needed to be done.

CHAPTER 15

IT HAD TAKEN TWO WEEKS TO RECEIVE THE DISCOVERY FROM THE AG'S Office. As soon as they had received the mirror image of the hard drive, they sent it to their experts to analyze. Now, she and Swish were trying to digest Mazer's IA investigation.

Swish looked up from the documents and sighed. "You get the sense that the outcome of the IA was a foregone conclusion?"

"Yeah," Erin replied. "There are more references in the IA's conclusions to the task force report from a few years ago, which found no credible evidence of the existence of the Lords, than there are to any real findings on Mazer's complaint. It reads almost like a rehash of the task force report."

She turned to the last page. "The investigation was primarily done by Sergeant Thomas Banks and DAG Albert Holmes, and reviewed and signed off on by Lieutenant Matthew Cole. I don't know the others, but I remember Holmes's name. He was part of the AG's task force investigation a few years ago. What do you think the chances are of any of them talking to us?"

"Slim and none," he responded.

"Really?" she replied.

"Why? What do you think the chances are?" he asked, seemingly surprised by her response.

"None," she said without any hesitation. "I thought your 'slim' was being overly optimistic."

He rolled his eyes. "Listen, I know I've been the one squawking about expenses, but if there's any chance that one of these people will talk, I think we're going to have to hire an investigator. None of them will talk to us, but maybe they'll talk to someone who's a former cop."

"You're right. Plus, we need to sit down and speak with Gabe and I want an investigator there for that. You want to use Rick and Alex?" she asked, referring to two retired NYC Narcotics detectives they had used in other cases.

"I spoke to them, and they felt that two Black private investigators might not be what's needed if the troopers involved are truly racist."

"You have someone else in mind?" she asked.

"Yeah. They gave me a guy by the name of Dylan Roberts. Worked ten years as a trooper and then went to the Monmouth County Prosecutor's Office. Retired four years ago as a lieutenant. According to them he's an honest guy, well respected, and knows what he's doing. Plus, he has the added benefit of having worked in the belly of the beast."

"Sounds good to me," Erin offered.

"There is one good thing in here," Swish said, tapping the report. "Mazer is consistent in the IA with who he told me he believes are the ringleaders of the Lords—Troopers David Britton, Edward Stone, and Kiernan Lyons."

"I'm glad Mazer's consistent about something," she said, still dismayed by his efforts to cover for Gabe.

Their conversation was interrupted by Cheryl buzzing them to let them know that there was a voice mail message from Rich Rudolph. He was calling to let them know that the U.S. Attorney's Office was holding a news conference involving the New Jersey State Police, and rumor was that it was to announce new charges against Mazer for violating Marshall's civil rights. He had left a number and suggested that they call him if they had any comment.

Erin looked over at Swish, whose expression mirrored her confusion. "That's weird," she said. "You don't think it's possible that the DOJ is indicting Jon, do you?"

"Absolutely not. Why would they charge our guy without even

talking to us? That makes no sense. Trust me, it's just not how the feds operate. They'd use that to try and get a plea."

The intercom buzzed again. "Erin. It's Peter Geiger and Aaron Tinsley."

"Busy day. Put it through, Cheryl." She hit the speaker button and waited for a beat. "Hi, guys. It's Erin and I'm here with my partner, Duane Swisher. You have any news for us?"

"Actually, we do," Geiger said. "And there's good news, bad news, and 'we don't know yet what it means' news."

"Okay," she replied with a small chuckle. "You pick the order."

"To be fair, I'm not sure if this falls under bad news or good news, but there are approximately twelve hundred emails, sent and received, during the date range you gave us. We've put those on a separate flash drive so that you can go through them. Also, just so you know, based on our analytics, it also appears that he deleted about two hundred emails in that time frame."

"Got it," Erin replied, also not sure if it was good news or bad news either. "Will you be able to recover the deleted emails?"

"Not sure yet. Hopefully, we'll be able to recover some of them," Geiger replied.

"What else?" she asked.

"The good news, at least based on what you told us the judge's concern might be, is that it really does look like Marshall used this computer solely for work-related stuff. In other words, nothing personal saved on his desktop, nothing embarrassing. It appears he did a lot of research on the Lords of Discipline and prior lawsuits, both individual troopers suing and lawsuits by the DOJ."

"That is good news," Duane said.

"In the category of 'we don't know what it means,' we've reviewed the documents saved on Marshall's computer. Drafts and final versions of his stories; research for various stories, including the one on the Lords; drafts of letters relating to his stories, things like that. The curious thing is that with the story on the Lords, including the penultimate draft he sent to his editor the day he was murdered, all of his sources are referenced as Source A, Source B, et cetera."

"That's not surprising," Erin interjected. "There's no way he'd reveal his sources like that in the actual story. It could put them in harm's way."

"We understand that. But we expected to find something that identified who each source was, simply so he'd have it documented if ever challenged. But we couldn't find it anywhere. And here's what's curious. We found steganography software on his computer."

"You found what?" Erin and Duane said almost in unison.

"Steganography software. It allows you to hide a message or information in something that's visible to everyone. So, for example, with this software, you can hide a secret message in a photo of your cat. Then, using the software again, you can decode it. We believe he used it to bury the information concerning who each of his sources were."

"Sounds like you haven't found yet where it's hidden—assuming he did," Erin said.

"Correct," Geiger replied. "We're guessing Marshall had a personal computer of some kind. Do you have access to that, because that would be the logical place to hide it?" Geiger asked.

"From what we're told, he did have a personal laptop, but no, we don't have access. In fact, no one has access. According to the police reports, they believe whoever murdered Mr. Marshall took his laptop."

"Shit," Geiger mumbled.

"You indicated that it could be embedded in a photo. Did Marshall have saved photos on the computer?" Duane asked.

"He did, but they've all been deleted."

"But even if you delete something, an expert can retrieve it. Is that wrong?" Erin asked.

"No, it's mostly accurate," Geiger replied. "That's why we may be able to retrieve some of the deleted emails, but remember, with this we're trying to find fragments that are embedded in something else. Basically, when we recreate a deleted file, there are often pieces missing. If we're missing fragments of the code, we're probably not going to be able to find what we're looking for."

"Does that mean it's lost forever?" she asked, with more than a hint of trepidation.

"Not necessarily," Tinsley replied. "It means that it's either buried somewhere on this computer and we just haven't found it yet, or we have to build a subset of emails that he sent from his work email to his personal email and search all the attachments and hope that he didn't go back and delete his sent emails."

"Are you sure you need the names of his sources?" Geiger asked.

Erin quickly glanced up at Duane, who with a nod confirmed her gut reaction. "Yeah, we do," she responded.

"All right. Give us about a week, and we'll let you know if we find anything."

"Sounds good. In the meantime, email us a copy of his last draft of the story on the Lords. And once we get the flash drive from you, we'll start looking through the emails and let you know if we find anything there that may help you."

After they ended the call, they sat in silence for a few minutes, both lost in thought.

"Have you thought about what we do if they do find Marshall's sources?" Duane asked.

"What do you mean?" Erin asked.

"Play it out," Duane responded. "We find out Trooper A and Trooper B were giving information to Marshall and we want to call them as witnesses. Aren't we then obligated to turn that information over to Rivers and Roy? And what do they do with it? Most likely, sit down with folks in the state police and let them know. Then what happens to Trooper A and B? Are they in trouble for giving information to a reporter? Have we put them in physical danger? What do we do?"

Suddenly, Jon's refusal to give her the names of the troopers he had given to Marshall made perfect sense. If they didn't disclose the names, they couldn't use them as witnesses, no matter how helpful their testimony. But as Swish had just articulated, disclosing them would bring a different set of risks. She put her head back and stared at the ceiling and then she allowed a smile to slowly stretch across her face.

"What?" Swish asked. "I've seen that smile before."

"We wait and see who's on the state's witness list and hope the names are there. If they're not, we list the names of every trooper in the barracks and say they all have knowledge of Mazer, his complaints, and information on the Lords. Then either the state interviews everyone, or no one, but we hide who we want to call," Erin said.

Swish returned her smile. "I like the way you think, woman."

Two hours later, Erin walked into Swish's office. "Rudolph's on line one."

Swish hit hands free and then line one.

"Hi, Rich. It's Duane and Erin."

"I figured I owed you a follow-up to my voice mail to let you know the news conference had nothing to do with Mazer."

"Mind if we ask what it was about?" Swish asked.

"DOJ is suing the state police claiming it's using racial profiling in determining when to stop a vehicle," Rudolph responded.

Swish's laugh was hollow. "Really. Nice to know that the DOJ finally figured out that the state police have been enforcing driving while Black for years."

"Was that on the record, Duane?" Rudolph asked.

Erin could see the anger in Swish bubbling up. She shook her head trying to discourage him from engaging.

"No," Swish said, his voice clipped, hiding the raging storm she could see brewing in his eyes.

"Rich, we appreciate the follow-up. We'll talk soon," Erin said, clicking off the call.

"I guess you didn't trust me to keep my mouth shut," Swish said, in a tone that hinted at some resentment.

"Swish, I don't know what it's like for you to hold your breath every time you pass a cop to see if they're going to pull you over because of the color of your skin. I'm sure it sucks. But before you went on the record with a reporter about the state police racially profiling motorists, I thought we should discuss it, because what you say could impact the case."

She watched his body tense, ready to fire back at her. But instead, he closed his eyes and waited, and as his anger seemed to recede, the muscles in his shoulders and upper body slowly relaxed.

"You're right," he said. "You don't know what it's like every time you pass a cop car, wondering if they're going to pull you over just because you're Black."

"No. I don't," Erin replied. "But maybe I had a taste of what it's like when I was transitioning and my license still was in my dead name. I was a nervous wreck every time I got behind the wheel. That said, I only experienced it for a few months; you've had to deal with it your entire adult life. But if half of what Mazer has told us about the Lords is true, we may get to expose some of that racial bias in the courtroom. That's why I didn't want you to go off now. Let's save it for when we have twelve people in the jury box."

"I hate being lectured to," he said, his scowl gradually fading. "However, for you, my friend, I'll make an exception—but only when you're right."

"Thanks," Erin replied. "Honestly, if the roles were reversed and you were asking me to hold my tongue over the way trans people are treated, I'd be biting your head off, telling you all the things you never experienced."

Swish laughed. "Um, you have—several times."

Erin tilted her head, knowing she was guilty as charged.

"Where were we?" she finally asked.

"How's Marshall's article?" Swish asked.

"Pretty explosive," she replied. "He lays out a pretty convincing case that the attorney general's task force report on the Lords was a whitewash."

"Pun intended?" he interrupted.

"No," she said, shaking her head. "No pun intended."

"Sorry," he replied, his smirk suggesting he wasn't.

She ran her hands through her hair. "Here's the opening of the article—*On the morning of October 1, 2005, the lifeless body of New Jersey State Trooper Steven Cook was discovered in the parking lot of Community Medical Center in Toms River, dead of a single gunshot wound to his temple, his off-duty weapon on the floor of his car. Six months earlier,*

Cook had filed a lawsuit against the New Jersey State Police and several fellow troopers. In his lawsuit Cook alleged the trooper defendants were part of an organized group that had targeted him for testifying that stops made by the troopers were part of a racial profiling campaign." Erin stopped reading and looked up at Swish. "It says Cook left behind a wife and two young daughters."

"Pretty damn similar to what I told you happened when I was with the FBI."

She sighed. "Yeah," she whispered. "It then goes through, in detail, the history of racial profiling allegations against the state police, and the consent decrees the state entered into with the feds to allow a federal monitor to oversee their data on traffic stops and arrests. He covers a number of civil lawsuits that have been brought by former troopers for racial and gender harassment and he quotes frequently from their attorney, Barry Goodman, about what his clients encountered. He then goes into Mazer's story, the harassment he endured for being gay and the IA complaint he filed. Of course, despite requesting a copy of the IA investigation through an open public records request, Marshall's request was refused under grounds of not being substantiated. But here's what doesn't make sense, Swish. Despite the article saying he didn't get the IA, he seemed to have information on the IA investigation that he couldn't have gotten from Mazer."

"What do you mean?" Swish asked.

"He compared what happened in the Mazer IA to the task force report. But how could he do that if he didn't have the IA?"

"You think someone leaked the IA to Marshall?" Swish asked.

"That's what it looks like," she replied.

"Wow. Be nice if we could find whoever that is," he said.

She nodded. "This case seems to hold lots of surprises. I can't wait to see what we find out when we talk to Gabe tomorrow."

"Ah, the good Father DeAngelis—Gabriel of the angels," Swish added with a sour look.

"You seem to have taken an instant dislike to DeAngelis; any particular reason?"

"Dislike is a strong word—just a healthy dose of skepticism," Swish offered.

She cocked her head to the side. "I hear you. I'm definitely in the skeptical camp."

The following morning, Erin walked out into the reception area where Father Gabriel DeAngelis was already waiting to meet with her and Duane. As he was the first time they met, he'd dressed casually—nothing that gave away his vocation. They had asked Dylan Roberts to sit in, because whenever they interviewed a potential witness, an investigator could testify as to what the witness had said during the interview, if they suddenly told a different story at trial.

After exchanging pleasantries with Gabe, Erin escorted him into the conference room.

Duane and Dylan stood when Erin brought DeAngelis into the room.

"Gabe, I know you and Duane have spoken on the phone, but here he is in the flesh. And this is Dylan Roberts. He's an investigator who is helping us out on Jon's case," Erin said.

"Nice to meet you both," Gabe said, shaking their hands.

"Likewise," Dylan replied.

"Please, sit," Erin said. "Gabe, let me start by saying we don't represent you. Which means nothing you tell us is confidential. If you feel you want or need legal representation before you speak with us, we can reschedule."

His eyes narrowed. "Why would I need a lawyer?" he asked.

"Because, like anyone connected to the case, you're a potential witness," Erin replied. "In fact, one of the reasons why we wanted to talk to you was because we're trying to figure out if you can help Jon's case if we call you as a witness. We—"

"Wait. Stop!" His voice was suddenly leery. "You can't call me as a witness."

"Can I ask why?" Duane asked.

"Because I have no connection to the case. I know Jon, and I know that he didn't kill Marshall. But that's all I know," he responded.

"Well, actually just knowing Jon connects you to the case. And that's really the main reason we wanted to meet with you, because we know Jon called your prepaid cell a lot, so it's likely that investigators from the AG's Office will want to talk to you," Erin said.

DeAngelis rubbed the fingers of his right hand with his left hand, avoiding eye contact. "Um, well, actually they've already contacted me."

Out of the corner of her eye, Erin saw her usually inscrutable partner raise an eyebrow.

"Did you talk to them?" Erin asked.

"Well, yeah. I mean, I thought it would've looked suspicious if I refused."

"When did you speak with them?" Duane asked.

"A few weeks ago," DeAngelis offered.

"Before the holidays?" she asked.

"Yeah. It was," he replied.

That's strange, Erin thought. She had seen Mazer after Christmas and he didn't know that DeAngelis had seen anyone from the AG's Office. "Do you remember who you met with?" Erin asked.

"Ah, there were three of them; two were investigators and the other one was a lawyer," he replied. "I don't remember their names, but I have their business cards at home. I can call you with their names."

"The attorney, was it a man or a woman?" Erin asked.

"Man," he replied.

"Was his name Rivers?" Erin suggested.

"Yeah. That sounds right."

"Did they tell you why they wanted to talk to you?"

"Well, like you just said, they saw that Jon and I spoke a lot, so they wanted to know what my connection was with Jon."

"What did you tell them?" Erin asked.

DeAngelis shrugged. "That we were friends."

"Friends?" Duane said, leaning forward. "That's all?"

"Yeah. That's it."

"Gabe, it's generally none of my business what a person's sexual orientation is, but they obviously know Jon is gay. Did they ask if you had an intimate relationship with him?" Erin probed.

"They asked, but I said we were just friends," he replied.

"Gabe, are you aware that it's a crime to lie to a law enforcement officer who's involved in an investigation?" Erin asked.

"Ah . . . what do you mean?" he asked, growing defensive.

"I mean, that if hypothetically you and Jon are more than just friends, say you're lovers, you could be charged with the crime of providing false information as part of a criminal investigation," Erin replied.

"So, then just don't call me as a witness," DeAngelis said flippantly.

"You realize that it's not just us; the state could also call you as a witness," Erin said.

"They told me that they're not going to call me as a witness," he replied.

"Really. That's interesting," Erin said. "My guess is they lied to you," she said calmly.

DeAngelis's brow furrowed. "What do you mean? They said they weren't going to ask me to testify."

"Sorry, Gabe. I wouldn't believe them if I were you."

"They can't," he said, concern gathering.

"I'm afraid they can," Erin said, allowing the confidence in her voice to grow.

"But they promised me," he said, as if trying to convince himself.

"In return for what?" she inquired.

"All they wanted was the truth," he said.

Erin allowed herself a sneaky grin as she studied DeAngelis. The line every lawyer took pains to tell their witnesses when asked, "What did they tell you to say?"—"Tell the truth."

"Did you tell them the truth, Gabe?" Erin asked.

He looked at her, his panic now on full display. "I . . . I need to get a lawyer."

"There's no way we can call him as a witness," Duane said after DeAngelis left. "He'll lie, or tell the truth, whichever one allows him to save himself." He paused. "And, in the process, he'll bury Mazer."

"I know," Erin replied. "That's why I tried to put the fear of God into him."

"Sorry, my friend," Duane replied. "I think that ship sailed a long time ago."

CHAPTER 16

JON WALKED INTO THE VISITING AREA AND TOOK HIS SEAT OPPOSITE DeAngelis, who once again was in full priest mode.

"I know what you're thinking, but I can explain," DeAngelis whispered as soon as the officer walked far enough away.

"Please do," Jon said. "McCabe told me you spoke to the folks from the AG's Office and now feel like you need a lawyer. Why didn't you tell me?"

"Jon, I know you. I didn't want you worried about the fact that the investigators had come to see me. Don't worry, I didn't tell them anything. They just wanted to know why you called me so much, and I told them we were friends. They asked me if you ever said anything about Marshall's murder and I told them no. That was it. It lasted all of about half an hour."

"So, why do you need a lawyer?"

"Because your lawyer scared the hell out of me. Within five minutes, she was cross-examining me and telling me I could be charged with a crime. I almost got the impression that she thinks I'm somehow involved in Marshall's death."

"All she's trying to do is protect me," Jon finally said. "That's her job."

Gabe looked around to make sure no one was close by. "Don't worry, babe. I'll protect you. I'll never let anything happen to you."

Jon smiled. It was the smile of a man who desperately wanted to believe, but didn't. It was the smile of a man who had been betrayed at every turn in his life, from his family to the people he worked with every day. It was the smile of a man who just once wanted to trust in someone other than himself. It was the smile of a man who had no other options.

Erin took a sip from her coffee as she waited for her mother. There were times when her pursuit of parenthood felt like an out of body experience. It was as if she was watching herself in a play, the actors around her strutting across the stage, all of them involved in a carefully choreographed scene, and she was the only one who didn't know their lines or where they were supposed to be on the stage. She felt lost—making it up as she went, trying to make sense of it all. Whatever it was, her becoming a parent seemed to have taken on a life of its own—*pun intended*, she thought.

Her mind slowly replayed yesterday's journey into the milieu of reproductive rights. First, she, Mark, Molly, and Robin had gathered once again to see the lawyer, Phil Song, this time joined by Liz and Sean. Song had reviewed the legal procedures involved, including the agreements that would be necessary for her and Mark to have with Liz and Sean, and separately with Molly. He explained that Sean and Liz should consult with separate counsel, but if they all went ahead using him as their attorney, they'd have to sign a waiver of any conflicts. Then Song walked them through the court proceedings that would be necessary to allow Erin and Mark to be listed on the baby's birth certificate. Based on his experience, Song was confident all would go well. Erin didn't verbalize her doubts, but she was less sanguine, especially since she would be Song's first trans client who had used their own sperm while seeking to be listed as the mother.

The six of them had left Song's office, gone to lunch, and then headed to their meeting with Doctor Marsha Grimes, who would be handling the medical aspects of their journey.

Like Song, as soon as Erin met Grimes, she felt not only seen, but embraced. Grimes appeared to be in her forties, but her gray hair left Erin unsure if she had gone prematurely gray, or just appeared younger than her years. She told them how wonderful it was to see families coming together to support one another, and reassured Erin and Mark that if the process was successful, it would be one of the most positive, life-changing experiences of their lives.

Grimes had started by explaining the psychological evaluations all of them would need to undergo to ensure they were mentally and emotionally prepared for how things would evolve. Erin had sensed that Liz and Sean had been a little surprised by the emphasis that Grimes had placed on Liz's evaluation, but Grimes had repeated several times that it was only normal for the gestational surrogate to build a deep emotional attachment with the baby she was carrying.

Grimes then went through the medical aspects, explaining that, although it seemed counterintuitive, Liz would need to stay on her birth control pills to assist the clinic in understanding her menstrual cycle. Grimes also let Liz know that she'd have to start on another drug, Lupron, which would be used in tandem with the birth control pills to make sure they had a good handle on her cycle.

Erin smiled as she recalled that Grimes had caught Erin's surprised reaction to the use of Lupron, a drug used to delay puberty in trans children. Seeming to immediately understand Erin's reaction, Grimes had explained that Lupron was used for many medical issues including endometriosis, precocious puberty, certain forms of cancer, and as with Liz, to regulate a woman's menstrual cycle.

After the clinic had a good understanding of Liz's cycle, she would then need to take estrogen for a period of time and finally, before they implanted the embryo, a shot of progesterone, to help prepare her uterine lining for the implantation of the embryo.

Grimes had then explained to Molly the tests she would need, and assuming all went well, they would start her on fertility medication to encourage her body to develop more eggs. Those eggs would then be retrieved and some would be fertilized with Erin's sperm, which had already been tested. Once those embryos were formed, one would be implanted in Liz's uterus and the remainder frozen in the event they were needed in the future.

Erin placed her hands on her coffee mug and closed her eyes, momentarily overwhelmed by how fortunate she was. There weren't many women, let alone trans women, who not only had the financial wherewithal to afford the process they were about to embark on, but who also had two other women willing to help, one willing to donate her eggs, the other to actually carry her baby. She was indeed blessed.

"Hi, dear. Sorry, I'm late," her mother said, sliding into the opposite booth.

Erin looked at her watch and smiled. "You're actually right on time. I was ten minutes early."

"On time is late," her mother responded with a wink. "How are you? No, wait. Before you answer that, I owe you an apology."

"For what?"

"I feel like I may have rushed you on the whole baby thing, by asking Liz without talking to you first," Peg said.

Erin pursed her lips in an attempt to suppress a laugh. "Ah, maybe just a tad."

"I'm sorry," her mother responded, her expression drooping.

"Honest, Mom, it's all good." Erin released a small snort. "Let's just say you gave me a gentle nudge in the right direction."

"Can I ask you a question?" Peg asked.

"Of course."

"Without what you call my 'gentle nudge,' would you have asked Liz to carry the baby?"

Erin inhaled and sighed. "Probably not."

"Why?"

Erin shrugged. "I don't know. I guess because I think it's too much to ask anyone to carry my baby."

"Why? Because of who you are?" Peg asked.

"Yes and no," Erin replied. "It's more than that. It's asking someone to go through nine difficult months so Mark and I can have a child. There's part of me that feels very selfish."

"But you know Liz doesn't feel like you're being selfish. She was thrilled to help."

"Yeah, we'll see if she's still thrilled when she's eight months pregnant."

They sat quietly, neither knowing what to say next.

"Can I get you coffee, hon?" the waitress said to Peg, breaking the silent impasse.

"Yes," Peg said, looking up at the waitress. "Thank you."

After the waitress had poured her mother's coffee and moved on, Erin twirled a strand of her red hair around her finger. "You know how much I've always wanted to have a child. And honestly, without your gentle nudge, I'm not sure I would have had the courage to move forward. That's what makes you a great mom—you give me the strength to live my life as I should, not as laid out by someone else." She paused, then added, "Thank you."

Her mother raised an eyebrow. "I think what you meant to say was that I'm a meddling know-it-all."

"No," Erin said, shaking her head. "Maybe there's a fine line between meddling and a gentle nudge, but you never crossed the line." Erin reached across the table and took her mother's hand. "I appreciate the nudge."

"You're welcome," her mother replied. "Am I allowed to ask how things are going?"

"Sure, but we better order first—it's been a bit of a journey."

After they placed their order, Erin shared with her mom what they had done so far.

When Erin finished, her mother stared at her. "I had no idea that it was so complicated."

"The good news is that both Song and Grimes seem to know what they're doing and they've certainly done it enough times before—unfortunately, just not with a trans woman as the parent whose sperm was used."

"Are you sure you're okay with everything? A baby is definitely going to change your life," Peg asked.

"Were you and Dad ready when you had Sean?"

"Are you kidding? No. We didn't have a clue as to what we were doing. But we muddled through somehow," Peg responded. "And you will too. Just remember one thing; you can never give your child too much love."

"Thanks," Erin replied.

"'Morning," Erin said from Swish's doorway. "Cheryl said you wanted to see me when I got in. What's up?"

Swish motioned for her to grab a seat.

"You ever listen to WTRA?" he asked.

"Not intentionally," Erin replied. "Some of the things their on-air personalities say can be really difficult to listen to. Why? Do you?"

"Keep your friends close and your enemies closer," he replied. "WTRA is one of the stations I've made a point of listening to from time to time in order to find out what conservative white folks are thinking. And I've listened enough over the last few years to suspect that there was a good chance that Drew Smith, the morning shock jock, would go off this morning about the DOJ's decision to sue the state police."

Duane laid his new iPhone that Cori had gotten him for Christmas on his desk, opened the VoiceMemo app, and hit play.

"Good morning, everyone, and thanks for tuning in. It's 7:57 and this is Drew Smith on WTRA, 108.2 FM, Somerville, New Jersey. Let the liberals listen to NPR. If you want to hear the real truth, listen to the voice of the real America. Coming up in a minute, we'll have traffic and weather and then at the top of the hour, I am going to go off on one of my rants against the Nazis working for the Department of Justice and their continuing attempts to paint the hardworking members of the New Jersey State Police as racist. Now here's Rachel with a look at the roadways and your local forecast."

Duane hit fast forward and skipped through the weather.

"Thanks, Rachel," Smith said, his rich baritone providing a seamless segue back to his portion of the show. *"Sounds like it's going to be a cold one out there, so bundle up, folks. Speaking of cold days, it looks like it will be a cold day in hell before the feds give our dedicated men and women in the New Jersey State Police the credit they deserve for*

keeping all of us safe. Yesterday, the Department of Justice, or as I like to call it, the Department of Injustice, filed a civil rights lawsuit against the state of New Jersey and the New Jersey State Police alleging that troopers improperly used racial profiling in making motor vehicle stops on the Parkway and Turnpike. Folks, let's call this for what it is—this is a blatant attack on white troopers just for doing their jobs. It's certainly not the troopers' fault that a large percentage of people engaging in criminal conduct or violating the motor vehicle statutes are African Americans and Hispanics. Those are just the facts of life.

"As some of you know, a couple of years ago I wrote a novel in which a few of the characters were state troopers. In doing my research, I had the opportunity to talk with a number of these brave troopers to discuss the dangers they face every day, and I must tell you, every one of them is a decent, honorable person. They are out on the front lines protecting all of us from the criminal element overrunning our state, and to do that they need to use all the tools at their disposal. Now, just as it's done in the past, DOJ is accusing these brave public servants of being racist. Well, I say, enough already! This nonsense has to stop and stop now!"

Smith's diatribe lasted for another ten minutes. When it was over, Duane turned off the app. "What do you think?"

"Wow! I can't believe you can listen to that guy," Erin offered. "I can only imagine what his novel is about."

"Here you go," Duane said, swinging his monitor around so she could see his screen. "This is what I found with a quick internet search."

"*The Guardians of Discipline*," she said, reading. "That's the name of Smith's book?"

"Yep. But it gets better," Swish said, turning the screen back around so he could read from it. "Here's the description of the book. *Vito Mancini is a hard-nosed state trooper, trying to stop an inner-city drug lord. However, the newly elected DA, a former community organizer, is out to ruin Vito's career—a move certain to let the drug lord spread his tentacles and expand his growing empire from the hood to the suburbs, destroying the lives of countless innocent suburban kids in the process.*"

"Is it self-published?" Erin asked.

"No. Published by Righteous Books, LLC."

"We need to get our hands on a copy. You think it's really as racist as the dog whistles in the description make it sound?"

"You said you never listened to Drew Smith's show?"

"No. I have zero desire to. I know who he is. I've heard some of his comments repeated by others, but honestly, all it would do is make me upset."

"Well then, the answer to your question is that it could be as racist as it sounds. But just as you shouldn't judge a book by its cover, you also shouldn't judge it based on a blurb on a website," Swish replied. "I called the bookstore and they have it in stock. I'll pick up an extra copy, just in case you want to read it too."

"Thanks. I love crime thrillers, but I have a feeling this one may leave me cold."

"Keep an open mind," Swish said with a small laugh. "Who knows, maybe we'll be surprised."

The following morning, they once again gathered in Swish's office.

"You get through it all?" Swish asked.

"Yeah, unfortunately, I skimmed through it. Vito Mancini makes Dirty Harry look like an Eagle Scout. He and the guys he works with violate every constitutional right a defendant has and the book glorifies vigilante justice. Not to mention, it's more racist than even I thought it would be. I can only imagine what your reaction is," Erin said.

Swish was sporting what could only be described as a shit-eating grin. "Did you read the acknowledgments at the end of the book?"

"No. Why?" Erin responded.

"Because you missed the best part," he replied smugly. Swish picked up his copy of the book and turned to the back. *"I am also extremely grateful to David Britton, who is the inspiration for this book, and who provided me with invaluable insights into what it's like to be on the front lines in law enforcement's current efforts to combat crime."*

"Wait," Erin said. "Britton's referenced in Mazer's IA. He's one of the people Mazer alleged was part of the Lords. Right?"

"Yep," Swish said, picking a piece of paper up off his glass desk. "But there's more—the state's initial witness list," he said. "Trooper David Britton, New Jersey State Police, Somerset Barracks."

"It's got to be the same guy," Erin said.

"One way to confirm—interview Smith."

"He'll never talk to us," Erin replied somewhat dismissively.

Swish laughed. "You're right. Not if we call him up. But maybe he'd be interested in doing an interview about his book—you know, see if he can boost his sales."

"You have something in mind?" Erin asked.

"I don't. But that's why we have an investigator. Maybe Dylan can use his law enforcement background as a hook to help him get access."

"Worth a shot," Erin replied.

One week later.

Britton slowly swirled the tumbler containing his bourbon on the rocks, the ice clanging on the side of the glass. He stopped, stared into his drink, took a healthy swig, and placed his glass on the bar in his finished basement that he had turned into a stereotypical man cave, complete with a large screen television and pool table. He uncorked the bottle and poured another three fingers into his glass, nodding silently as his compatriots, troopers Ed Stone and Kiernan Lyons, waited.

"What's eating you?" Stone asked.

Britton pointed his finger to the upstairs portion of the house. "David, why are your friends coming over again?" he said in a mock falsetto, in a weak imitation of his wife's voice. "We never do anything together anymore?" he said in the same voice. "I'm not sure when she went from a hot fuck to a fucking nag—probably the day I said 'I do,' but the only reason we're still together is I can't afford to get rid of her."

"Sorry, dude," Lyons said.

"Yeah, me too," Britton said. "All right, let's forget about Michelle," he said, taking another sip of his drink. "This is what we've learned about the investigator Mazer's lawyers have hired. His name is Dylan Roberts. He spent ten years with the outfit," he said, using the term troopers had for the state police. "He left to go to the Monmouth County Prosecutor's Office. Retired from there as a lieutenant and set up his own shop," he said, picking up his bourbon and taking a healthy draw.

Britton jiggled his glass, mixing the water from the melting ice with the bourbon. "My source tells me Roberts left the outfit because he was one of the guys who cooperated with DOJ when they brought their first racial-profiling case against us."

"Motherfucker," Stone said.

"What did Smith have to say about his conversation with Roberts?" Lyons asked.

"According to Smith, he got a call from Roberts at the radio station," Stone said. "Roberts told him he had been in law enforcement for over twenty-five years, including ten with the state police, and really liked his book. He asked if Smith had worked with any troopers in doing his research, and Smith said he had. Then Roberts repeated he had been a trooper and wondered if he spoke to anyone Roberts knew. Smith claims he started to get a little suspicious and refused to name any names. After that, they talked about the book for a few more minutes, and then Smith said Roberts said he'd like to meet with him to discuss what Smith had learned about the Lords of Discipline. At that point, Smith told him he had no interest in talking to him, and ended the call."

"Jesus, Dave," Lyons said. "We told you that talking to Smith for his book was a mistake. Now some investigator is snooping around—I don't fucking like it."

"You don't have to fucking like it," Britton fired back. "No one is asking you for your fucking opinion. Remember when our good friends at the Division of Criminal Justice had their task force investigating the Lords, almost everyone turned tail. But I was the guy that kept the core group together. Rivers and I made sure people got lawyers and kept their mouths shut. Now people are coming back. Last count we were close to a hundred. And a lot came back because of Smith's book. So don't give me any of your shit about whether it was a good idea or not."

Britton rested his arms on the bar and leaned forward. "Let's get down to the main reason why we're here. As I told you last week, Swisher was part of the FBI team that was investigating the outfit ten years ago. Fortunately, their main witness met an untimely death before he could spill his guts. But there's a concern about Swisher's involvement in the Mazer case based on his prior role with the FBI—that, and the fact he's Black. Our folks want to be able to exploit white cop shoots Black man—so we need him out of the picture."

"You worried that as a former agent he's untouchable?" Stone asked.

"Nah, they checked around. He left under a cloud. We'll be fine," Britton responded.

"What about the other lawyer, the woman? Are we going to deal with her too?" Lyons asked.

Britton laughed. "Nah, she's not a woman. She's a trannie. They'll be able to handle her. Swisher's the key. What did you find out?"

"We confirmed he plays in a basketball league on Wednesday nights in Metuchen," Stone said. "We tailed him after this week's game. He drove through Edison. I don't know how you feel about Edison, but I think it would be perfect for us. We know a number of people in the department."

"Edison's perfect," Britton said. "That department's a shit show on a good day. The only thing to be careful of is that there's so much infighting you don't want the cops in one clique trying to jam up the cops in another. From what I've seen it's like the cop version of the Crips and the Bloods over there."

"No worries," Stone said. "The guys I'm talking to all hang together. Trust me, these guys do some crazy-ass shit. They're a minor league version of the Lords. They wouldn't sell each other out. This will just be another day in the office for them. They'll know how to handle it so it goes down in a way that protects everyone."

"All right," Britton said. "I checked and as a former FBI he has a carry permit."

"Fine," Stone said. "But there's no reason for him to carry at a basketball game."

"No worries. We're going to give him a reason," Britton said, polishing off what was left of his drink and slamming his glass on the bar.

Two nights later, Britton called Stone. "How do we look for Wednesday night?"

"According to the folks in Edison, we're all set," Stone replied.

"Good. I don't want any fuckups."

"Understood."

"We all set with Swisher for tonight?" Britton asked.

"Yeah," Stone replied.

"Good," Britton said.

CHAPTER 17

DUANE WASN'T SURE WHICH HE HEARD FIRST, THE SPLINTERING sound of something shattering or the wail of the security system. Layered on top of each other, they put his own internal alarm system into overdrive. He caught a glimpse of the digital clock on his night table as he bolted out of bed—2:11 a.m. He headed straight to his chifforobe, reached into the top drawer, unlocked the gun box, and took out his Smith & Wesson 9mm. Corrine, who was now sitting upright in bed, seemed momentarily dazed.

"What's happening?" she asked.

"Go check on the kids," Swish said. "I'm going to check downstairs."

When he got to the top of the steps, he flicked on the light switch in the hallway that illuminated the foyer on the first floor just inside the front door—nothing.

He felt Corrine brush by him on her way to Austin's room, just as Alysha's screams joined the cacophony of the blaring alarm system.

He chambered a round, held the gun at his side, and slowly descended one step at a time. About halfway down, he was greeted by a rush of cold January air, causing him to once again eye the front door. *Secure,* he thought, looking at the door, which was clearly closed. But about three steps from the bottom, he noticed glass scattered on the living room floor. That, plus the flood of frigid air, could only mean that the window in the living room had been shattered. He leaned up against the wall of the stairwell, took two more steps down, and peered around the corner. Despite only dim light from the foyer, he could tell that the front bay window had been completely shattered. Realizing he couldn't walk into the room in bare feet, he dashed back up the stairs and threw on a pair of sneakers and grabbed his cell phone out of the charger.

"Is everything okay?" Corrine asked, emerging from Alysha's room with her cradled in one arm and Austin, barely awake, clinging to her leg.

"No. But I don't think we're in any danger."

As he quickly headed back down the stairs, his cell phone rang.

"Swisher residence," he answered.

"Mr. Swisher, this is Andy from Protect Systems. Your home security system has been activated. Do you need assistance?"

"Yes, please get the police here asap."

"Is anyone injured? Do you need an ambulance?"

"No, Andy. No injuries. Just get the police here."

When he got to the bottom of the stairs, he cautiously stepped into the room, the glass crunching under his shoes. *Shit!* The window was shards now, the drapes snapping like flags on a flagpole as the cold January winds swirled into the room. He found the switch and flipped the lights on, revealing the full extent of the damage. On the floor, about ten feet from the shattered window, was a brick. It had something wrapped around it, but he knew better than to mess with a crime scene.

In the distance he heard the blare of police sirens.

"Duane!" Corrine screamed.

He ran to the bottom of the stairs, his heart pounding.

"Duane, open the door and get up here," she hollered.

"What's wrong, the police are almost here?"

"Duane, you're what's wrong! You're a Black man holding a gun in a house where someone has just called nine-one-one. They'll shoot you and ask questions later. Get up here."

Damn, she's right.

He unlocked the front door and opened it about a quarter of

the way, punched in the code to turn off the alarm system, then scampered back up the stairs, quickly throwing his gun back into his drawer. He turned on the light in the upstairs hallway and picked up Austin, resting him on his shoulder.

The flashing lights from the police cars bounced around inside the house like some mad scene from a disco.

"Anyone in there?" came a voice from the doorway.

"We're up here, Officer," Duane hollered down the stairs.

The door slowly creaked open and a hand with a gun appeared, followed by the arm and then the torso of a large, white police officer.

"We're up here, at the top of the steps," Duane called down.

The officer entered the foyer and looked up at Duane and Corrine, each holding a child, and he appeared to relax.

"Is there anyone else in the house?" the officer asked.

"No one that belongs here," Duane responded.

Two other officers entered and headed in different directions. A few minutes later a sergeant came through the front door and glanced up the stairs.

"Swish, you okay?" he asked.

"Yeah, we're good," Duane replied, then turned to Corrine. "Everything will be fine now. I know Bernie. Why don't you see if you can get the kids back to sleep?" He placed Austin back on the ground. "It's okay, buddy. Mommy's going to put you back to bed."

He quickly stole a glance at Corrine. "Thanks," he said, taking a deep breath and exhaling. "I wasn't thinking."

He made his way down the steps and shook hands with Sergeant Bernie Downs of the Scotch Plains Police Department.

"Thanks for coming," Duane said.

"No problem. When I heard the street address, I remembered you lived on Chiplou Lane, so I headed over." Downs gave Duane a knowing smirk. "I didn't want any problems."

"Thanks," Duane replied again.

They looked around the living room, the only damage being from the brick thrown through the window.

"Looks like there's a note tied around it," Duane pointed out.

"Excuse me, Sarge," an officer who had just come through the front door said.

"Yeah, what's up?"

"Looks like the Honda SUV in the driveway has been vandalized."

"Shit," Duane mumbled.

Downs looked at Duane standing there in his boxers and T-shirt. "Maybe you want to throw on some clothes before you head out. It's pretty fucking cold."

Ten minutes later Duane, Downs, and the other officer stood in the driveway inspecting Duane and Corrine's white Honda SUV, which had the word *traitor* spray painted in black on both side doors and four flat tires.

"Any ideas what the hell *traitor* means?" Downs asked.

"Honestly, not a clue," Duane said.

"I know this is overkill, but I'd like to get the county's bomb-sniffing dog out here. I'm sure the car is safe, but I'd hate for you to start it and blow the fuck up."

"Yeah," Duane said. "That would definitely ruin my day."

"You also need to get some plywood up on that window."

Duane glanced at his watch. "Thanks, but where am I going to get plywood at three in the morning?"

"If you ask nicely, I can reach out to whoever is on call from the DPW tonight and get someone here in an hour or so."

"Thanks," Duane replied.

"Seriously, you have any idea as to who or why you were targeted?"

"Other than the fact that I'm Black?" Duane responded.

"Yeah, I don't think it's that. You and I both know that the racists in this town aren't real public about their racism. Plus, you've lived in town for what, six years?"

"Seven, but who's counting," Duane responded.

"And I suspect if it was about race, a different word would have been scrawled on your car."

Duane looked at Downs and knew he was right. "Then it's got to be the case that Erin and I . . . Oh shit, Erin."

* * *

It was almost eleven a.m. when Erin picked Duane up at the auto body shop.

"You sure you're okay?" Erin asked as they headed to the office.

"Yeah," was all he said, even though she could sense there was a lot more churning inside. "How about you?"

"I'm fine. Nobody threw any bricks through my window," she replied.

"Sorry I woke you," he offered.

She gave him a look like he was crazy. "Seriously, Swish, you're apologizing? For all you knew the wolves were at my door. I appreciated the call." She gave him a quick glance. "I'm just a little tired—and probably cranky," she offered with a grin. "I get that way if I don't get my eight hours of beauty sleep."

"Damn, you're going to be tough to deal with when the baby arrives."

In light of everything that had happened in the last eight hours, she appreciated his attempt at humor.

"Read me the note again?" she asked.

He looked down at the paper in his hand. *"Drop the white cop, you fucking Uncle Tom, or the next time the brick is a bomb, and there'll be lots of burned bodies."*

"What do you think?" she asked.

"I don't think it's from my side of the aisle. I think it's a message from the Lords, not some upset Black activist. A brick through the window—that's a scare tactic. If it was really some Black folks upset with me, they'd be protesting outside our law office. And, by the way, if I'm right, you're not immune. If it's the Lords, you and Mark could be next."

"I suppose," she said. "But does it matter? Whether it's someone angry that you're defending a white cop, or the Lords of Discipline, that brick was real. Whoever it was, they've gotten my attention."

"Mine as well," he said. "It's one thing to come after me, but when you threaten my family, you just upped the ante."

"So, what's the plan?" Erin asked.

Her question was met by a snort. "You're assuming I have a plan?"

She glanced in his direction. "Come on. You're a former FBI Special Agent. Aren't you always prepared?"

"That's the Boy Scouts."

"I don't suppose you were a Boy Scout?"

"Nope. Sorry."

"Shit. Just when I need a Boy Scout, I'm stuck with you." She gave him a weak grin. "Okay, seriously, any thoughts on how we keep you and your family safe?"

"Since I have a carry permit, I'm going back to carrying my gun. And Cori is a licensed owner, and probably a better shot than I am."

"Um, I hate to be a Debbie Downer, but guns aren't going to protect you if they do use some kind of bomb or Molotov cocktail."

"I hear you, but my security company is putting in some security cameras and Scotch Plains PD is going to make sure they keep my place on a regular patrol route, especially at night. Maybe Cranford PD will do the same for you."

"Sure," she replied, suspecting that because Swish was a former FBI agent, he might get a favor or two from the locals that she wouldn't get as a civilian.

"Short of moving or sending Cori and the kids out of town, not sure what else I can do," he added.

She felt his stare. "What about you and Mark? I've been after you for years to learn how to use a gun. No offense, but martial arts and pepper spray aren't going to help you in a gunfight."

She slowed to a stop at a red light, giving her the opportunity to turn and look at him. "You know, this is a very depressing conversation." She brushed the hair back from her face. "Swish, Mark and I are adults and we can decide what risks we're willing to take. But you have a family to think about. And no case is worth risking your family. If you want us to pull out, I'd understand perfectly."

The light turned green and she turned her focus back to the road, the roar of the engine as she shifted through the gears the only sound.

"Thanks," he finally said.

Erin found herself confused both by Swish's response and the silence that followed. Was he accepting her offer to be relieved as counsel?

It was probably only thirty seconds or so, but it seemed like an eternity before he spoke again. "It's kind of ironic. Before Cori and I married we talked about the personal risks of me being an FBI agent. I never imagined the greater risks would come after I left the FBI."

Again, he stopped, whatever he was thinking punctuated with silence.

"If anything ever happened to my family, I'd never forgive myself. So probably the smart thing to do is walk away. You're right, no case is worth my family. But I can't walk away, E. I know this is probably a strange comparison for a Black man to make, but I feel like Gary Cooper in *High Noon*. Someone is trying to scare us off and I don't know why. But I've never run scared in my life and I'm not going to start now. I guess there's always going to be part of me that thinks I'm still a special agent. If you're in, I'm in."

She nodded. "I'm in."

"Just do me one favor," he said.

"What's that?"

"I know that our partnership agreement has a buyout provision in the case of death or disability. If anything were to happen to me, please make sure Cori and the kids are taken care of."

"Nothing's going to happen to you," she said forcefully. But when she glanced in his direction all she saw was the steel-eyed resolve worthy of a soldier about to go into combat.

"Promise," he insisted.

"I promise," she replied, as a chill caused her to shiver.

CHAPTER 18

TWO DAYS LATER, ERIN AND DUANE TOOK THE RICKETY ELEVATOR TO the fourth floor and made their way into the offices of Locksmith Computer. Shortly after giving their names to the receptionist, they were greeted by Aaron Tinsley.

"Thanks for coming by," Tinsley said.

"No worries," Erin offered. "You guys sounded excited, so we're anxious to learn what you found."

"We are excited," he replied. "We managed to unlock what was hidden by Marshall's use of the steganography software, and we thought it was important for you to see it firsthand, especially if you're going to need an expert report and for us to testify."

Aaron led them back through a cramped work space that had eight cubicles, with cables and computer equipment scattered throughout, to a work area that had computers of various makes and models on two worktables. As they walked in, Peter Geiger slid his chair back from the computer he was working on and introduced himself.

After the introductions, Geiger guided them over to a section of the worktable that had a large monitor. "When we went through Marshall's emails," he began, "we noticed that he sometimes sent emails from his work email to his personal email account and then, for whatever reason, likely because he forgot, didn't delete his sent emails. On one of his emails that he sent to himself there was an attachment with a photo of a stream running through the countryside in a PNG format." Geiger paused and brought up a photo on the screen. "The photo intrigued us because it was during the period of time when he was working on the Lords of Discipline story, but it didn't seem to be related to anything else Marshall was doing. Using the steganography software that Marshall had on his computer, we discovered that every hundredth pixel in the photo concealed a letter of the alphabet. The change was so subtle that without the software you would never see the change."

"Wow," Erin said, watching as Geiger ran the software. "This is all pretty amazing, and above and beyond anything I've ever heard a reporter do to prevent people from learning his sources."

"We thought so too, but apparently Marshall was really sensitive about protecting his sources."

"Sensitive is an understatement," Duane said.

"As we decoded the letters, this is what we came up with—either Mo Donovan or M. Odonovan, A. Silvia, A. Urjinski, D. Britton—"

"Wait! Are you sure it said D. Britton?" Erin questioned.

"Yeah," Geiger replied. "That one's easy," he said, pointing to the picture.

Erin turned toward Duane. "D. Britton? There has to be more than one. Mazer named Britton in his IA as one of the ringleaders of the Lords."

"I hear you, but remember, all this is implying is that Britton was a source—a source of what remains unclear," Duane suggested.

"All right, but just the fact that Marshall was in touch with Britton is a little surprising," Erin added.

"Is it? Maybe it's just a sign of being a good reporter and taking nothing for granted," Duane posed.

"I guess," she replied.

"Or maybe Britton was a double agent," Duane offered.

"What do you mean?"

"Pretending to help Marshall, while at the same time trying to lead him astray with disinformation."

"Yeah, but Marshall had to know Mazer considered Britton to be one of the leaders of the Lords. Why would Marshall trust him?"

"Maybe he didn't. But, if he thought he could talk with someone allegedly well-placed in the Lords, why wouldn't he?"

Erin rubbed her forehead. "I guess you're right."

"There's also a fifth name," Geiger chimed in. "We're a little unsure of this one because the spelling of the last name makes no sense—'D. Agholmes.' But, like I said, we're having trouble figuring that one out. Do these make sense to you?" Geiger asked.

"You sure you have that spelling right?" Duane asked. "Could it be DeAngelis?"

Geiger looked at the screen. "I don't think so. But I guess it's possible he intentionally misspelled it."

"I guess," Duane said. "Was there anything else?" he asked Geiger.

"There was one other letter we uncovered," Geiger replied. "It was just the letter *W.* We couldn't find any other letters that went with it. So, we have no idea what that means."

"Where is it on the picture?" Duane asked.

"Down here," Geiger said, moving the cursor to where the letter was in the lower right-hand portion of the picture. "Right in the middle of the stream. Any ideas?" he asked.

"Beats me," Erin said.

"Me too," Duane agreed.

"Can you print us out several copies of your screen so we can share it with our client?" Erin asked.

"Sure. No problem," Geiger said, hitting a few keys and waiting a few seconds before high-resolution color photos slowly inched out of the printer.

"Can I ask an unrelated question?" Erin inquired.

"Sure," Geiger replied.

"Your website says that the company has twenty well-trained computer experts. Umm, do you have another location, because there's not enough room here for twenty people?"

Geiger smiled. "No. No other location. But most of our employees are out in the field at clients' offices or homes, working on their systems, trying to find viruses or install software." He gave her a knowing look. "Don't worry. We didn't fudge our credentials. I've testified enough to know that if I get up on the witness stand, everything about me and the company is fair game."

"Thanks," Erin replied, relieved Geiger was playing by the rules.

Later, sitting in the attorney visiting room at the Middlesex County Adult Corrections Center, they placed the picture on the table and laid out for Jon what they had learned.

"That's got to be a mistake," Jon reacted when he heard Britton's name. "There's no way Marshall would have spoken with Britton. I told him he was definitely one of the people heading up the Lords."

"We had the same initial reaction," Duane said. "But remember, Marshall was a reporter, so he probably would have spoken to the devil himself if he offered information. We also can't be certain yet what it means. For all we know, there was one conversation where Britton denied everything."

Jon appeared to consider what Duane suggested. "I guess it makes sense. When you're doing an investigation, you talk to anyone who's willing and evaluate it later," he finally replied.

"What about the other names? Do you know who they are?" Erin asked.

"Yeah, 'Mo Donovan' is Trooper Maureen Donovan; 'A. Silvia' is Trooper Anthony Silvia; and 'A. Urjinski' is Trooper Alec Urjinski."

"Those are the names that you wouldn't give me?" Erin asked.

Jon nodded slowly. "Yeah," he sighed. "I was trying not to expose them, but those were the troopers I thought might speak off the record about the Lords." Jon covered his mouth with his hand. "What happens now? I mean, will the prosecutors get their names?"

"We haven't decided what we're going to do yet, but it's certainly a possibility," Erin replied. "But remember, we're assuming at this point that the prosecution doesn't have these names. For all we know, they've gotten their own expert to look at Marshall's computer and they've already figured it out."

"If they have, and it gets back to Britton, it will be hell for these three," Jon said, slumped in defeat.

"Obviously, the information is there, so there's nothing we can do to prevent the prosecutors from finding it on their own, but remember, we're going to provide the name of every trooper at the barracks as a potential witness. We won't single these people out," Erin offered, in an attempt to ease Jon's concerns.

"Thanks," he responded without conviction.

"Did any of them ever say anything to you about speaking with Marshall?" Duane inquired.

"No. Remember, I was a pariah after the IA. No one wanted to risk being seen associating with me—they would have suffered the same fate."

"Of this group, who do you think would be most likely to speak with our investigator?" Erin asked.

"Urjinski," Mazer responded without hesitation. "He hated them as much as I did because they always made fun of his accent. I'm not sure where he was from—Poland, Ukraine, Russia, somewhere in that region—but he has an accent."

"What about 'D. Agholmes'? Do you know who that is?" Erin asked.

"No. Not a clue. That one didn't come from me," Jon replied.

As they drove back to the office, while Swish returned the call of another client, Erin studied the screenshot. *D. Agholmes*, she repeated several times to herself, trying to make sense of the fifth name. Then something clicked. *No. It couldn't be.* She quickly reached down into her purse, which doubled as her briefcase, and leafed through the file folders and took out a copy of what she was looking for. She hastily turned to the page she wanted. "Damn," she mumbled to herself.

Swish, who had just ended his call, glanced over. "You know you're talking to yourself," he said.

"I know who D. Agholmes is," she declared confidently.

"Father DeAngelis?" he said with a snarky grin.

"Deputy Attorney General Albert Holmes," she said.

"What?" Swish snapped incredulously.

"DAG Holmes. D-a-g-h-o-l-m-e-s," she repeated, this time spelling out the letters. "DAG Holmes who signed off on the IA report that resulted from Mazer's complaint," she said, waiving the report in front of her for emphasis.

"Shit," Swish said. "A trooper our client says is one of the mainstays of the Lords and the deputy attorney general who signed off on Mazer's IA were both talking to Marshall?"

"It's a potential explanation as to how Marshall's article had information from the IA. Perhaps Holmes shared a copy."

"But Marshall wouldn't know who from the AG's Office signed off on the IA," Swish replied.

"Maybe Holmes reached out to him," Erin offered.

"Damn," Swish replied. "The more we learn, the fewer answers we have." He glanced in Erin's direction. "We need to reach out to Roberts to see if he can get Holmes or any of the troopers to speak to him."

"Yeah, good luck with that," she replied.

She closed her eyes and rubbed her brow, wondering what all of this meant. After several minutes, she turned toward Swish. "Have Roberts contact the troopers. I'm going to reach out directly to Holmes."

"What? Why would you do that?" Swish asked.

"Look, whenever we interview a potential witness, we always have an investigator present. But if I'm alone, hopefully he'll be smart enough to realize that I can't testify as to anything he says. Maybe that way, I can convince him that I just want to know what he knows and he won't be exposed for talking to Marshall."

"Assuming he spoke with Marshall," Duane added.

Erin smiled. "If he didn't, I assume he'll tell me to bugger off."

"Bugger off?" Swish repeated.

"Sorry. Been watching too many *Doctor Who* episodes on PBS," she said with a small laugh. "But not tonight. Tonight, I'm coming to see you guys play hoops."

"Guess I better make sure Mark gets in the game," he said.

"That's weird, because Mark always tells me everyone is getting so old and slow, he plays almost the entire game."

"He said what?" Duane said, his voice rising as he turned toward her, only to be met with her gloating smile. "You—"

"Be nice," she said, unable to wipe the smile from her face.

CHAPTER 19

AS SHE WATCHED THE BACK AND FORTH BETWEEN THE BEARS AND the Knights, Erin had to admit that she was impressed by Mark's skills on the court. She had watched him messing around with her nephews on the hoop set up in her brother's driveway, but this was different. This was serious basketball and Mark was holding his own with some good players.

She already knew how talented Swish was because she had seen him play a couple of times in college when she had gone to visit her then girlfriend, Lauren. The intervening years may have robbed him of a step or two, but he could still bring his A game when he needed it. Then there was JJ. At six foot four, his natural position had been small forward, but now he used his bulk to play power forward. Despite the injury that kept him from becoming a pro, tonight he still was the best player on the court. Mark had a good outside shot, but his role on the Bears was to concentrate on defense.

But the players on the other team were no slouches either. From the chatter she picked up on while sitting in the stands, several of their players had recently played at Rutgers, FDU, and Seton Hall, so they were not only good, but about fifteen years younger than Mark's teammates. So, it wasn't a surprise that with a minute left to go, the Bears only led by three points and the Knights had the ball.

As the Knights quickly moved the ball around the perimeter

looking for an open shot, Erin watched nervously as the clock wound down. Suddenly, Mark cut in front of the player he was defending, perfectly anticipating the pass, and picked it off. Gaining control of the ball, Mark looked up, saw Swish making a dash up the side of the court, and made a perfect snap pass to him. As Swish crossed half-court, two guys from the Knights hustled back to cut him off from heading to the basket, but as they did, Swish lofted a perfect looping pass to JJ, who caught the ball in midair, slammed it into the net, and was fouled in the process. JJ calmly drained the free throw, giving the Bears a six-point lead and putting the game safely out of reach.

When the final whistle blew, the Bears embraced and high-fived each other, then went over and shook hands with all the players on the Knights.

"I'm impressed," she said, giving Mark a hug when he finally got his sweats on and made his way off the court.

"Thanks," he said with a huge smile. "You picked a good game to come to."

"You guys are pretty damn good for a bunch of old-timers," she said to Swish and JJ when they came over to say hello.

"Thanks, I think," JJ replied with a grin. "Your husband here saved the day," he said, throwing his arm around Mark's shoulder. "I think you're going to need to come to all our games, because he plays really well with you in the crowd."

"Nice to know I bring out the best in him," Erin said, giving Mark a playful squeeze.

"Anyone want to grab something to eat?" Swish asked.

"Thanks, but I have a busy day tomorrow and need to get some work done," JJ replied.

Erin looked to Mark, who nodded. "Sure," she replied. "Where'd you have in mind?" she asked.

"There's an Italian place up on Inman Avenue in Edison called Ferraro's. Want to stop there?"

"Sounds good. We'll follow you," Mark replied.

Duane popped open his trunk and threw his gym bag inside. Then he unlocked the case where he had stored his Smith & Wesson 9mm during the game. Hopping into the driver's seat, he started the car, turned the heater up full blast, opened the center console, and placed his gun inside. Normally, he didn't feel safe carrying his weapon because, just as Corrine had warned him Sunday night, it didn't matter where a Black man with a gun was—his home or his car—some cops would shoot first and ask questions later. But with the brick through his window still fresh in his mind, tonight it was worth the risk.

He pulled out and made sure Mark and Erin were following and headed up Plainfield Road, which became New Dover Road once he crossed Oaktree Road. He didn't think twice when he turned onto Tingley Lane and saw the Edison Police's black-and-white sitting in the parking lot of Bishop Ahr High School. Knowing that Mark and Erin were following him, he was keeping it safely within the speed limit.

About a quarter of a mile down the road, he saw Mark pulled to the side, and flashing lights suddenly appeared in his rearview mirror. As the police car flew past Mark's car, Duane pulled to the side of the road, hoping it would speed by him as well. Instead, the car pulled in behind him. That's when he saw the second car, with its lights swirling, pass him, then come to a stop in front of his car, blocking him in between the two cars.

Ah, fuck. What the hell is this about?

He took his iPhone out of his jacket pocket, opened up the VoiceMemo app, hit record, and slid it back in his left-hand coat pocket. He then lowered his window and waited, his hands on his steering wheel so everyone could see them. The fact that his Smith & Wesson was stowed in the center console, and not in the glove compartment where his registration and insurance card were located, at least gave him some comfort that he wouldn't be shot when they asked for his credentials.

Two white officers exited from the vehicle in front of him. One approached his side, the other, the passenger's side—both drew their weapons as they approached.

"Good evening, Officer," he said to the one who leaned into his window.

"Not for you, it's not, asshole," was the icy response. "I need your hands where I can see them."

"I have them on the steering wheel," Duane replied, stating the obvious.

"Fuck you, smart-ass," the cop shot back. "You match the description of someone who just robbed a gas station on Route 27 at gunpoint. I need you to get out of the car, keeping your hands so I can see them at all times. The second I don't see your fucking Black hands, that's your last."

"Officer, I'm not the person you're looking for," Duane said, choosing his words carefully knowing he was recording this. "I'm coming from a basketball game in Metuchen and about twenty people can verify that."

"Look, nigger, you and your vehicle match the descriptions exactly, and either you get out now, or I'll drag your motherfucking Black ass out," the cop said.

Swish swallowed hard. Every fiber of his being wanted to shove those words down the cop's throat until he choked on them. But he silently gave himself the talk, the talk that his father had given him many years ago—sometimes you had to let it go and accept that "yes, sir" and "no, sir" were the only acceptable responses.

"I don't want any trouble," Swish said. "I'm a former FBI Special Agent. Reach in and lower the window on the passenger side so your partner can open my glove compartment and take out my credentials."

"You may not want any trouble, but it's found you, boy," the cop said, sounding more like a stereotypical southern sheriff than an Edison police officer. "And former FBI don't mean shit. Probably some fucking affirmative action hire who couldn't hack it," he added.

Swish drew in a breath. The cop was clearly trying to push his buttons. He needed to stay calm. Corrine, Austin, and Alysha needed him. He bit his tongue.

"Let's go, asshole. I don't have all fucking night," the cop demanded, raising his weapon so it was pointed at the side of Duane's head.

Duane swiftly weighed his options. He feared they were going to use the gun in his center console as a pretext, not to arrest him, but to shoot him. Assuming he was right, his options were limited: get out and let them find it, or let them know that as a retired law enforcement officer in good standing, he not only had a permit to carry a gun, but he had a gun in the car. Either way, he wasn't sure the outcome would change, but since he was recording everything, if somehow the recording survived, maybe it would help convict them.

"Officer, as I told you, I'm retired FBI. As a result, I have a permit to carry a gun. My permit's with my credentials in the glove compartment. If you'd . . ."

Suddenly, Duane heard a commotion. Someone was yelling and screaming. The officer leaning in his window straightened up and turned toward the police car behind Duane's. In the rearview mirror, Duane saw a cop get out of the driver's side of the car behind him and continue yelling at someone. Duane then turned his head so he was looking outside his driver's side window. There, on the other side of the road, was Erin.

Erin? What the fuck is she doing?

"Hey! What are you doing?" the cop screamed. "You! I'm talking to you."

As soon as Erin saw the cops pull Swish over, she knew something was off. She and Mark had been following Swish. He hadn't been speeding. The two cars had boxed him in. And, as she watched the tableau unfold, her mind began to scream.

It's a setup.

She had grabbed her iPhone out of her purse, and despite Mark's protestations, had told him to drive past where Swish was pulled over, once he was out of sight, park, and call nine-one-one. "Give them your name and location and then tell them you are concerned that several officers are threatening a Black motorist. Give them your location, and then hang up," she told Mark. Then, before he could stop her, she jumped out of the car, sprinted across the street, and ran until she was directly across the street from where they had Swish pulled over. Now, she stood with her phone recording what was happening.

"Lady, get the hell out of here!" the cop yelled.

"I'm a lawyer and I'm filming the harassment of my law partner as evidence when we sue you," she hollered back.

"Get the fuck out of here or I'll arrest you for interfering with an arrest and obstruction."

"You can't. Under the law, it's not interference if I film from at least thirty feet away. Since the road is thirty-five feet wide, and I'm standing on the shoulder, I'm within my rights."

The cop gave her a quizzical look, but didn't seem deterred. "Look, bitch, if I have to come across the street and arrest you, it won't be pretty."

"Go ahead and try. Before I started filming, I hooked up with News12, so what I'm filming is being sent directly to them. You assault me and not only will you be on the news, you'll be arrested by dawn tomorrow."

The cop who had been at Duane's passenger window started walking back toward the one who was yelling at Erin, an air of uncertainty appearing to develop. A second cop got out of the passenger side of the car behind Duane and the three of them conferred for about thirty seconds. The cop who had been dealing with Duane watched from the side of Duane's car as the other three started across the road.

"Yes, they're approaching me now," she said as loud as she could, as if she was talking to someone.

Oh shit. This is about to get ugly, she thought.

Swish watched with dread as the cops started across the road toward Erin. If he got out of the car to try and protect Erin, they'd likely shoot him; if he did nothing, it looked like Erin would get arrested, and probably roughed up in the process. As he watched her, she slowly backed up as they approached, all the time yelling as if she was a broadcaster on the Weather Channel in the middle of a hurricane.

Suddenly, the flashing lights of a third police car appeared, coming toward them from the opposite direction. The third car stopped near where Erin was standing, her cell phone still in hand, her narration continuing.

A portly cop struggled out of the vehicle and lumbered toward the three officers who had been heading toward Erin. Swish couldn't hear what he was saying, but the four of them wandered back toward the car behind him.

This can't be good, Swish thought.

As they approached, the new arrival turned to the officer who was still standing by the side of his car. "Come here," he said.

"Everything's under control," the cop hollered back. But after another bark from the new arrival, he reluctantly headed over to where the others were huddled behind Swish's car.

Just when Swish thought the party couldn't get any larger, a fourth car pulled up, and another officer got out, and although it was hard to tell because it was dark and he had on a winter jacket, he looked like he could have been a superior officer. He walked over to the scrum of officers and immediately took over the conversation.

For the first time since he was pulled over, Swish began to have hope that he might get out of this in one piece. He tried to follow what was happening in his rearview mirror and strained to hear the muffled chatter going on behind his car. Finally, the portly late arrival ambled over to his window.

"License, registration, and insurance card, please," he said in a tone that indicated he had said it hundreds of times before.

Swish reached into his glove compartment, took out his registration and insurance card, then took his wallet out of his jacket, removed his license, and handed it to the officer.

The officer pulled a flashlight off his belt, shined it on the documents, and handed them back to Swish.

"Sorry for the mistaken identity, Mr. Swisher. You're free to go."

When the four of them arrived at Swish's house, Cori was waiting at the front door. As soon as Swish got in the door, she threw her arms around him and hugged him. "Are you okay?" she finally asked, taking a step back.

"Yeah," he said. "A little shaken up, but thanks to my partner, alive to tell the tale."

Swish walked over to Erin, who was standing just inside the door with Mark, and gave her a massive hug. "Thank you," he said. "I have no clue what possessed you to do what you did, but you may have just saved my life."

"Come on into the kitchen and tell me what happened," Cori said. "All I got from Duane when he called to say you were coming was that he had a close encounter with the Edison PD. Knowing my husband, it must have been bad for him to call me. Sit," she said, pointing to the chairs around the kitchen table. "You want something? Coffee, tea—a drink?"

They agreed on beers, and after Swish passed them around, he described for Cori what had taken place. Then he put his phone on the table and played his recording of his interactions with the cop. "Give a listen."

"Shit, that was messed up," Swish said when the recording was over.

"It sounds like they were looking for a reason to shoot you," Erin said.

Swish took a long swig from his beer. "Seemed that way to me too," he said, placing the bottle on the table. "Clearly this was not a routine traffic stop."

"Agreed. But why?" Erin asked.

"It's got to be about Mazer."

"But the Edison PD has nothing to do with the Marshall investigation. It doesn't make sense," Erin said. "You think it's related to the incident the other night?"

"My gut is telling me yes," Swish said. "I just don't know how or why."

They sat around the table in silence, shaken by what had taken place.

"Were you really recording?" Swish asked Erin.

"Yeah, I was," she replied, opening up the photo app and playing the video.

"I didn't know you could legally film from thirty feet away," Swish said.

"I don't know if you can either," she replied. "I made it up. I was just trying to slow things down, and put them on their back feet."

"What about News12? How did you connect with them?" Mark asked.

Erin raised an eyebrow. "I wasn't connected to News12. I made that up too. I just needed something so they would think that they could still get jammed up even if they destroyed me and my phone."

Cori reached out with her beer bottle and tapped Erin's. "You go, girl. Thank you."

Erin looked across the table at Swish. "Based on what's on your recording, there's a case to be made for violating your civil rights, and maybe, if we can get an investigation going, we can find out who's behind this. I say we make an appointment to go see someone at the U.S. Attorney's Office as soon as we can. I don't want state or local enforcement involved."

"Agreed," he replied.

"Goddamn it!" Britton screamed. "How the hell did they screw this up?"

"Looks like Lyons was right—we should've taken care of the bitch too. Based on what I was told, she was the one who threw a wrench into their plan," Stone replied.

"Assuming she filmed it, they'll be able to identify the cops involved. How solid are they?" Britton asked.

"I told you, they're solid. If someone investigates, it will show that Edison PD received an anonymous nine-one-one call of an alleged robbery with the perp fitting Swisher's physical description and describing a similar vehicle to his. Of course, the call turned out to be a hoax, but no one will be able to show that officers on the scene knew it was bogus at the time of the stop. There won't be any problems," Stone said emphatically.

"In case you didn't notice, there already are problems," Britton replied, allowing his annoyance to seep through.

Stone didn't take the bait. "What's plan B?" he asked.

"There is no plan B. I was told we needed to stand down.

There's a concern that someone might make a connection between what's happened to Swisher over the last few nights and the Mazer case. Right now, all they have are two unrelated incidents. Anything else happens and someone might start connecting dots," Rivers said. "Besides, there's apparently another issue that has to be dealt with."

"What's that?" Stone asked.

"I'm told that, based on the draft of Marshall's article, it looks like he saw a copy of Mazer's IA report."

"How the fuck is that possible?" Stone asked.

"It's not—unless someone leaked it to him."

"Who the fuck would do that?"

Britton mulled Stone's question. "I'm told there's a person of interest. Even so, keep your eyes and ears open, just in case it's someone in the outfit. Whoever it is, the leak needs to be fixed. . . ."

He let his voice trail off. No reason to say anything else.

CHAPTER 20

When Erin and Duane reached the lobby of the Peter Rodino Federal Building, they put on their coats and bundled up against the frigid February weather.

"Mind if we walk down to Ward's Coffee?" Erin asked. "I'd really like something stronger, but coffee's gonna have to do for now."

"Sure," Swish said, pulling the collar of his overcoat up around his neck and holding the door open for her.

"Aren't you freezing?" he asked as they waited to pay for their coffee.

"Nah," she said, shaking her head. "You didn't know that pantyhose magically traps in all of a person's body heat so that women wearing skirts in the middle of winter are always super warm?"

He tilted his head to the side. "Funny," he replied.

"I don't know what's colder, me or the reception we just got from Assistant U.S. Attorney Schmidt. I got the sense that the only reason he even saw us was because of our involvement in the Townsend case," she said.

"Yeah. He certainly didn't seem all that excited by what we had to offer."

"Maybe the cold shoulder has something to do with us representing Mazer," she speculated.

"How so?"

"Well, Marshall was doing an exposé on the state police and the DOJ just announced its lawsuit against them. Maybe Marshall was talking with the DOJ on background and . . ." She stopped. "I don't know. I'm just spitballing here because our reception wasn't what I expected."

"Agreed. But as long as we're spitballing, it's just as likely that given my history with the feds, they'd rather let the locals handle it."

Later, as they drove back to the office, Erin made a suggestion. "I thought Vanessa Talon, the Middlesex County prosecutor, was a straight shooter when we dealt with her last year in the Costello case. Why don't we see if she'll meet with us?"

"Yeah, she was good," Swish said, a reticence in his voice. "But I don't have to remind you that there were others in that office that tried to lock you up on contempt charges."

"Nope," Erin replied. Her battle with the Prosecutor's Office over her refusal to disclose the location of her client was still very fresh in her memory. "No need to remind me. That's why I suggested meeting with Talon and not anyone else."

"I guess it's worth a shot. But my experience is that county prosecutors never want to go after cops in their jurisdiction because they catch too much flak from other cops. It can be an incestuous relationship."

"Well, we can't do worse than we just did with Schmidt."

"That's true," Swish replied. "But I feel like we're going down the rabbit hole here."

"What do you mean?" Erin asked.

"I mean we're distracted from what's important—gathering what we need to convince a jury that Jon didn't kill Marshall," Swish said.

Erin gave him a sidelong look. "Okay, but in our defense, people have thrown a brick through your window, vandalized your car, and had cops trying to kill you. In my book those things all tend to be distracting. What are you suggesting—we ignore what's going on?"

"Basically, yes," Swish responded. "Look, let's see if Talon will see us. If she does, we give her what we got, let them handle it, and we move on. And even if they don't want to deal with it, we move on. We have to focus on Jon. If we're right, and what's happening to us is related to our involvement in his case, we need to keep going."

"So, it's basically the Winston Churchill philosophy," she said.

He gave her a funny look. "What's that?"

"If you're going through hell, keep going."

Swish smiled, then his expression hardened. "Yeah. Through is the only way to safety."

"If we don't get killed in the process," she added, her tone more ironic than fearful.

Swish turned toward her; his eyes narrowed. "Love your optimism."

Erin shrugged. "Well, if we're gonna go through hell, guess it's time we called Deputy Attorney General Albert Holmes and rattle some cages."

Duane's office phone was set up so that he could record calls digitally directly onto his computer. He moved his phone across his desk so it was in front of Erin, who was sitting opposite him, and pressed record. Then she dialed the number she had written on a piece of paper. On the second ring he answered.

"DAG Holmes," he said.

"Deputy Attorney General Holmes, my name is Erin McCabe. I'm an attorney and I'd like to speak to you about a case I'm involved in."

"Umm, I'm sorry, Ms. McCabe, but . . . ah, I don't believe that . . . ah, that I have any cases with you. Umm . . . I think you must . . . ah . . . have me confused with someone else in the office," he stuttered.

"Oh, I'm sorry, DAG Holmes. I apologize for the confusion. We don't have a case together. No, the reason I'm calling is because you're a potential witness in a case I'm handling. I represent Jon Mazer, who's charged in the murder of Russell Marshall—the newspaper reporter. The one who was doing a story on the Lords of Discipline, a group within the New Jersey State Police."

"Ah . . . a . . . again, I . . . I believe you must be mistaken. I . . . I don't have any in . . . involvement in the Mazer case."

His voice was quivering and Erin could sense his nervousness through the phone line.

"Actually, you are involved because you signed off on the IA that resulted from Mazer's Internal Affairs complaint, and"—Erin paused to punctuate what was coming next—"and we know that you communicated with Mr. Marshall when he was doing his story."

"I . . . I have nothing to say to you. I never spoke with . . . I work for the A . . . AG's Office. I can't speak with you. I don't want to lose my job."

Erin tried to dissect his response. "I understand your dilemma, DAG Holmes. Honest, I'm not looking to cause you any problems. I'm really not. And I understand you're in your office right now. So, I'm more than willing to meet you—just me, no investigator—anywhere you'd like to discuss these issues off the record."

She stopped, waiting to see if he'd respond. When he didn't, she continued. "Obviously, I can't force you to talk to me, but if you don't, when the case goes to trial—and there will be a trial because my client is innocent—I will subpoena you as a witness. I'd prefer not to do that, especially if you're going to perjure yourself. I'd much rather we speak confidentially and off the record. That way, you can tell me what you know, and then I won't have to put you on the stand. Let me give you the number of a phone you can reach me at. It's a burner, so you don't have to worry about my number showing up on your bill. Call me and let's meet."

Erin then provided him with the number for her burner phone and waited.

"You . . . you . . . I never . . . Marshall . . ." he fumbled.

At that moment, Erin decided to bluff. *Leave it vague,* she thought. "DAG Holmes, let's meet so I can discuss with you the fact that Marshall had a copy of Mazer's IA and how I know who provided it to him."

There it was. She had accused him, without accusing him.

The silence that followed enveloped them like a shroud. When Erin couldn't take the dead air any longer, she added, "We have a copy of Marshall's hard drive. We know his sources."

She couldn't be sure, but it sounded like a gasp on the other end of the line.

"I can't talk now. I . . . I have to . . . think what to do. I'll call you," he sputtered.

"That's fine. Wherever and whenever you want to meet; just let me know and we'll meet, just the two of us, and I promise, off the record."

The line clicked off and she looked up at Swish.

"What do you think?" she asked.

"Hard to know, but you certainly put him between a rock and a hard place," Swish responded. "I guess we'll find out."

The last few days had taken their toll, which meant neither of them felt like cooking, so they decided just to grab dinner at the Cranford Hotel. They each ordered a beer, Corona for Erin, a Brooklyn Ale for Mark.

"I heard from my sister today," Mark said.

"And?" Erin replied expectantly.

"And Robin is pregnant."

"Oh my God," Erin said. "That's amazing."

"Yeah. Needless to say, they're thrilled. But Robin's only two months pregnant, so Molly asked that we not tell anyone."

Erin smiled. "Understood. How's Robin feeling?"

"According to Molly, she has a little bit of morning sickness, but otherwise she's doing great."

"I hope her morning sickness passes quickly," Erin said. She did some quick mental math. "So, if she's two months pregnant, she'll be due in September."

"Sounds right," Mark responded.

"Does your mom know that Molly and Robin are trying to have a baby?" Erin asked.

"From what Molly has told me, yeah, she's aware—just not about my involvement."

"Gotcha," Erin nodded.

"How's Liz doing?" Mark asked.

"I spoke to her on the way home from the office. She's been cleared mentally and physically. Now they start tracking her cycle to make sure they know the optimum time to try and implant the fertilized egg."

The Mazer case was scheduled to go to trial on September 7, 2010, and would last two to three weeks. Based on that, if everything went right, and Liz became pregnant around the beginning of April, there'd be plenty of time for the trial because the baby wouldn't be due until January.

"You okay?" she asked.

"Yeah, I'm fine," he replied with a warm smile. "I guess I was just wondering if you were having any second thoughts."

"Second thoughts?" she said, a small chuckle interspersed with her words. "I passed second thoughts a while ago. I've already gone through third and fourth."

Mark frowned. "We don't have to do this."

She reached across the table and took his hand. "I'm sure I want to have a baby," she said, her tone strong. "And I'm sure I want us to have a family. But being sure doesn't mean I won't second, third, or fourth guess myself. Maybe it's the lawyer in me. Or maybe, it's just part of who I am." She squeezed his hand. "Don't worry. This is what I want. What about you?" she asked, looking into his green eyes.

"It was my idea, remember?"

"I remember. It's one thing for our family and friends to know, but aren't you worried what it will be like if the world knows?"

He gave her a wry grin. "I can't worry about things that might not happen. Or, as Mark Twain once said, 'Worrying is like paying a debt you don't owe.' All I can deal with is what is, not what might be." He sighed. "E, I can understand that you don't want the people you love to be tarred with the same brush that you've been. But if the people who love you don't stand up to people who hate you just for being who you are—the haters win. And I love you too much to let them win. We can do this. As long as I have you, I can deal with anything," he said. "And for our baby, I'll endure whatever I have to in order to make sure they're safe."

"Thanks," she offered, feeling renewed by his confidence.

"Whatever happens, we'll get through it together," he said.

She smiled, allowing herself to believe he was right.

CHAPTER 21

HOLMES PACED NERVOUSLY BACK AND FORTH ACROSS HIS OFFICE. How did McCabe know he had provided Marshall a copy of the IA? No, she hadn't said he gave it to Marshall, just that she knew who had. But if she knew who had, then she knew it was him. But how? Marshall had assured him that he'd never disclose it. But Marshall was dead and McCabe and others were crawling all over Marshall's computer. What if they discovered he had been the one to go to Marshall and tell him about the Lords—that he was the one who had unleashed Marshall on the Lords? *Shit, shit, shit!*

If she knew about the IA, then Rivers knew. No, not yet. One thing he could be sure of was that if Rivers knew, he'd be dead by now—maybe not literally, but figuratively. Rivers would let word leak out about his arrest five years ago, the arrest that led to Rivers owning him lock, stock, and barrel.

He stopped pacing, walked to his chair, sat down, and buried his head in his hands. *Oh sweet Jesus, what have I done?* His wife, his young kids, his parents, his in-laws, what would they think if they found out? The nausea washed over him like an unexpected swell. He quickly grabbed the trash can under his desk and vomited.

When his stomach was empty, he wiped his mouth with his handkerchief and took several deep breaths trying to calm himself, his thoughts ping-ponging between hope and despair. Rivers wasn't much for detail, so maybe he would never discover what

McCabe had uncovered. But even if Rivers never found it, if he didn't speak with her, McCabe said she'd subpoena him. Either way he was screwed.

His thoughts were a jumbled mess, like charger cords thrown haphazardly in a box, all intertwined, hard to separate. What could he do? Go to Rivers and confess. Maybe he could offer to testify and lie that Marshall had been afraid of Mazer and that Mazer had threatened him. After all, only he and Marshall knew what really happened, and Marshall was dead. Even if the testimony was inadmissible hearsay, perhaps just the offer would inoculate him against Rivers ruining him.

No, he thought. He could never lie and potentially put someone in prison for the rest of their life. Besides, Rivers was a psychopath. Rivers would destroy him either for the sport of watching him suffer or to eliminate him as a credible witness—or both.

Maybe he could speak with Carol Roy—she was rational. No, it would never work. Rivers was her boss. Roy was a good lawyer. She'd never be able to keep the information from Rivers.

His only alternative was to speak with McCabe. She promised she'd keep everything they discussed confidential and she wouldn't call him as a witness. Could he trust her?

He stared at the phone number he had scribbled on a yellow Post-it Note. Rivers, Roy, or her—talk about a Hobson's choice. *Shit!*

He dialed the number. "Hello, Ms. McCabe. We need to meet."

"I don't like it," Swish said as they drove back from their meeting with Prosecutor Talon. "I should go with you."

"We've been through this," Erin replied. "We need information—information it seems Holmes might have. We don't need him as a witness. All we want is for him to open up and not worry about what he tells me coming back to haunt him. Besides, he's a DAG, not a member of the Lords. And based on his demeanor in our two conversations, he's scared shitless."

"Call me paranoid, but with all that's gone on, I don't like you meeting with him alone. It could be a trap. Why not just speak to him on the phone?"

Erin laughed. “He said he had some documents to give me. Besides, we’re meeting in a freaking diner in East Brunswick for crying out loud. What could be safer?”

“You’re meeting at eleven p.m. There’ll be no one there.”

She shrugged. “It’s close to a multiplex. Maybe there’ll be a late night, after-movie crowd. But if it’s empty, so what? He’s not going to attack me.”

Swish stared at her. “I want Roberts there.” He quickly held up his hand before she could respond. “Hear me out. He can just have a late-night breakfast and keep an eye on you when you meet with Holmes.”

Erin shook her head no. “Won’t work. Remember, Dylan’s already been in touch with potential witnesses, plus he’s a former trooper and was in the Monmouth Prosecutor’s Office for a long time. Holmes could’ve worked with Dylan and may recognize him.”

“Then let me reach out to Rick Adams and Alex Fredericks,” Swish said, referring to two retired NYPD Narcotics detectives they had worked with on other cases. “It would make me feel better.”

She smiled. “Okay. Anything to make you feel better. By the way,” Erin said, “I thought the meeting with Talon went well. I like her more now than when she dismissed the charges in the Costello case. I think she might actually go after the Edison cops.”

Swish glanced at her. “Yeah, but like I said before, let’s stay focused on Jon’s case. And right now, that means your meeting with Holmes.”

“Got it,” she said.

Rivers sat in the passenger’s seat of Britton’s trooper vehicle idling in the parking lot of the Best Buy on Route 1 in Woodbridge.

“I know who gave Marshall the IA,” Rivers said coldly.

“Who?” Britton asked.

“Holmes. Deputy AG Albert Holmes,” Rivers replied.

“Holmes? That little faggot,” Britton spat. “Really? How do you know?”

“Because he’s stupid. Apparently, he forgot that all emails sent from the AG’s Office are stored on an automatic backup system.

All I had to do was give IT the names of all the people I wanted searched, along with some search terms, and bingo. IT found an email from Marshall reaching out to Holmes saying he needed to talk—again."

"Again?" Britton said.

"Yeah, but Holmes didn't respond. Instead, he sent a copy to his personal email address. Ten minutes later, he emailed a copy of the IA to his personal email address. I then had someone check Marshall's emails on the hard drive we have, and it looks like Holmes emailed Marshall and Marshall replied, but the emails were deleted and they couldn't reconstruct the substance of the emails. But the fact they were communicating is enough for me."

"How do you want to handle it?" Britton asked.

"I just sent Holmes a text from my burner letting him know I'm aware he leaked the IA. I also told him that he's not the only one who knows reporters. I told him that in seventy-two hours his wife, father, father-in-law, and a friendly reporter would be getting a copy of the police report from his arrest."

"Why'd you give him seventy-two hours?"

"Because he's a licensed gun owner. Hopefully, he'll do the right thing in order to avoid the information becoming public," Rivers said, unable to contain his smirk. "Apparently, he forgot that I own him. All I've done is remind him."

"Aren't you worried he could cause more problems?"

"Of course, I'm concerned! A cornered animal sometimes attacks a more formidable prey," he said, sneering. "In fact, before I texted him, he set up a meeting with McCabe for eleven p.m. tonight."

"How do you know they spoke and when and where they're meeting?" Britton asked.

"Have you ever heard of StingRay?" Rivers asked.

"The car? What the hell are you talking about?"

Rivers shook his head dismissively. "No. Not the fucking car. StingRay is a device that allows you to remotely pick up cell phone conversations. I had a van parked down the block from

McCabe's office for the last week, monitoring their cell phone calls, and we got lucky. Holmes called her burner yesterday to set up the meeting."

"Are you just going to let that happen?"

"Of course not. Why do you think I wanted to meet with you?"

Erin's booth was on the far side of the diner giving her a panoramic view of the seating area and the front door. There were two people sitting at the counter, and about twelve people scattered among various tables and booths, one of them Rick Adams. She peeked at her watch—eleven thirty p.m. She texted Swish.

How much longer do I wait?

She took a sip of her coffee and picked up her phone when it vibrated.

Give it another thirty minutes.

Thirty minutes later, she stood, left a ten-dollar bill on the table to cover her coffee and tip, nodded to Adams, and stepped outside into the crisp, dark February morning. She headed to her car, which was parked close to the entrance, but despite the cold, she took her time, giving Adams time to follow her out. She climbed into her car, and then watched as Adams, who was close to six feet tall and well over two hundred pounds, struggled to fold himself into the passenger seat of her Miata.

"Sorry to drag you out on such a cold night for nothing."

"No worries," Adams responded. "What do you think happened—cold feet? No pun intended," he quickly added, as the steam from their breath fogged the windshield.

"Don't know," Erin responded. "I hope that's all it is." But she couldn't shake the sense of foreboding.

She texted Swish.

No show. Rick & I are leaving. Talk in the morning.

She turned to Adams. "Where's your car?"

"Back side of the building," he replied.

As she drove around the side of the diner, she noticed a white panel van, with heavily tinted windows. She couldn't be sure, but she thought she remembered seeing a similar van near the office.

"See that van?" Erin asked. "I drove around the building when I got here. It wasn't here then."

"Yeah," Adams responded. "Wasn't there when I got here either, but it's on my radar now."

"This early in the morning it should be easy enough to see if we're followed when we leave," she suggested.

"That's not a tail van," Adams replied. "Electronic surveillance."

She gave him a puzzled look.

"If they're close enough, they can use a device to monitor cell phone conversations," he said. "NYPD does it all the time."

She drew in a deep breath. "Shit." If she was right about seeing a similar van near the office, whoever it was could have eavesdropped on her call with Holmes setting up the meeting. She thought she was being careful when she gave him her burner cell phone number to call. Instead, she may have inadvertently walked him right into a trap.

"Everything is resolved," Britton reported.

"Good. I'm glad to hear that," Rivers replied.

"He had an envelope with him. In it was his sworn affidavit. It talks about his arrest, and attaches the complaint and police report. He describes his role in the task force and IA and the fact that you were using his arrest to blackmail him to make sure that he found that the Lords didn't exist. He also relates a conversation he had with Marshall. It's not good for me, or for you. You want it shredded?"

There was pause. "No," Rivers finally said. "I want to see it, just in case there are any other copies."

"No problem. I'll get it over to you."

"And just so you know," Rivers said, his voice measured, "I will be leaking the police reports of his arrest, the complaint, and his plea as a lesson to anyone who tries to fuck with us. Even in death you can't hide from us."

CHAPTER 22

ERIN STARED BLANKLY AT HER DINNER. NEWS REPORTS THAT AN UNnamed deputy attorney general had been shot and killed had broken at lunchtime. According to the reports, the shooting had taken place in the parking lot of the Old Bridge Medical Center on Route 18, only five miles from the East Brunswick Diner. Swish had done a quick internet search, which showed that Holmes had lived in East Freehold, placing the location ominously along the route Holmes likely would have taken to get to the meeting with Erin. She and Swish had followed the developing story on News12 throughout the afternoon, hoping against hope it wasn't Holmes. Just before they left the office, the AG's Office released the identity of the deceased—Albert Holmes, age forty-two, married, father of two.

"You should try and eat something," Mark suggested.

"I screwed up. It's my fault he's dead," she said, explaining her belief that her cell phone calls had been monitored.

"You can't blame yourself. Based on the way that they've described things, it sounds like he may have taken his own life," Mark said.

"Yeah, maybe. But even if he did, I exposed him." She hesitated. "Someone knew exactly when and where we were meeting—the van was at the diner. That's not a coincidence."

"Did you get the license plate?" Mark asked.

"Yeah, but when Rick had it run, it came back as untraceable—meaning it was an undercover police vehicle."

"I don't get it," Mark said. "Why would the police be surveilling a meeting between you and Holmes?"

"It's only a guess, but if the cops were troopers involved in the Lords, maybe they didn't want Holmes sharing with us what he knew." She chewed on her lower lip, hoping the pain would keep her tears at bay. "He has a wife and two kids, and he'd still be alive if I hadn't called him."

"Stop! You don't know what happened," Mark replied. "Maybe it had nothing to do with you."

Before she could respond, her cell phone rang. It was Swish.

"Hey. What's up?" she said.

"You have the news on?" he asked.

"No. Why?" she responded, getting out of her chair, grabbing the remote, and turning the television on, the sound arriving a split second before the picture.

". . . of the New Jersey State Police confirming that all evidence at this time indicates that the deputy attorney general took his own life. And as you just heard, Captain Jorgenson has verified the accuracy of Newark Municipal Court records that have recently surfaced, detailing an arrest of the victim five years ago for soliciting an undercover male police officer for sex in Branch Brook Park. Those charges were ultimately downgraded to a municipal offense for loitering. Captain Jorgenson refused to comment on whether anyone in the Attorney General's Office was aware of the charges prior to today."

She dropped onto her couch, the remote in one hand, her cell phone in the other. "Shit," she mumbled into the phone. "They had him by the balls."

"Yeah. It appears that way," Swish replied.

"And when they found out we were meeting, they squeezed him," she observed, her tone despondent.

"You okay?" Swish asked.

"No," was all she could muster. "Let's talk tomorrow. I just can't now."

Mark came over and sat next to her on the couch. He put his

arm around her shoulders and pulled her into an embrace. "I'm sorry," he said.

She buried her head in his chest. Her guess was that five years ago Holmes had gotten caught up in an undercover sting operation. A feeling born from a recent spate of news reports about gay men being targeted by various police departments sending young, handsome undercover police officers into parks in sting operations trying to entice gay men into offering to hookup, only to arrest them for soliciting. The tactic had apparently gone on for a number of years, but the sheer scope of the operations hadn't emerged until the shooting death of one of the targeted men by an undercover officer four months ago. The officer involved in the shooting had claimed the man had lunged at him when the officer displayed his badge and attempted to arrest him. Of course, since there was no one to contradict the officer's version, the shooting had been deemed justified, proving once again the adage that dead men tell no tales.

But even for the targeted men who had escaped with their lives, it was often a life left in tatters. For some, the resulting publicity ruined their careers or destroyed their family. Others ended their lives rather than deal with the fallout. Maybe that list now included Albert Holmes—maybe not. One list Erin knew for sure Albert belonged on was the list of people whose lives had ended mysteriously while trying to expose the Lords.

"I didn't know that they had anything on him," Erin said, her voice muffled by Mark's chest. "I didn't know."

Mark stroked her hair, then kissed the top of her head. "There was no way for you to know," he said, trying to console her.

She lifted her head so she could look at him. "I understand, but it doesn't make it easier. A husband, a father, a son—is dead. The lives of the people who loved him have been changed forever, and I played a role in it. And even though my role was unintentional, it doesn't bring him back. He's gone—gone forever, and there's nothing I can do to make amends."

"No. You're right. Nothing you do will bring him back. But if you're right, and the Lords did play a role in his death, maybe . . ." He stopped.

"Maybe what?" she asked.

He shook his head. "I was just going to say, maybe whoever they are, and the evil they stand for, will be exposed in Mazer's trial. But I stopped because I know that's not what the trial's about. You don't have to prove anything. Your job's to prevent the prosecutor from proving Mazer guilty." He gave her a sad, crooked smile. "Sorry, I got carried away."

She looked into his soft, green eyes, thankful she had him by her side. She knew she could never undo what she had done. That pain would linger. But maybe Mark was right. If they could help expose the culture that existed in the state police, Holmes's death would not have been in vain. "Who knows?" she said, returning her head to his chest. "Sometimes the best defense is a good offense," she whispered.

"Morning," Erin said as she walked into Swish's office the next day. "Tinsley and Geiger are on the phone."

He looked at his partner, her anguish from the night before concealed by her "all business" attitude, but he knew from painful firsthand experience the self-recrimination she was putting herself through. He then glanced down at the blinking light on his phone, hit the hands-free button and then the flashing light.

"Hey, guys," Swish said. "I have you on speaker. Erin's here. What's up?"

"We came across something on Marshall's computer that we think may be important."

"Let me plug in the hard drive that has the mirror image of his computer." A few minutes later Swish had opened what he needed. "I'm there. What am I looking for?" he asked.

"Go to iTunes," Geiger said.

Swish looked up at Erin, who shrugged.

"Okay, I'm there."

"Open up various artists and look for 'The Britton Invasion.' "

"You mean the British Invasion?" Swish asked.

"No. The next one down—the Britton Invasion. It's about forty minutes long," Geiger said. "Listen to it and call us back when you're done."

"Okay," Swish replied, still puzzled.

When the recording ended forty minutes later, Swish pushed his chair back from his desk with such force it slammed into his credenza. He stood and started pacing his office. "Do you believe that motherfucker is a state trooper and my tax dollars help pay his fucking salary?" He looked in Erin's direction. "That fucking racist bigot. We'll destroy him with this. We'll—"

"Swish, slow down," she said, stopping his tirade. "I understand why you're furious, and I understand how helpful this recording might be. But first things first. We need to focus on how we get this before a jury, and exactly what it does and doesn't do. There's nothing on the recording that exonerates Jon. There's also a lot of language that could inflame a jury. In other words, if we don't play this right, the judge keeps it out because any relevancy is far outweighed by the prejudice to the state."

He looked at his partner and felt like his head was going to explode. But as he allowed what Erin had just said to slowly pierce through his raging anger, he realized she was right. This could be a clutch three pointer or an air ball. *Listen to her,* his internal voice said, while at the same time hoping that someday he'd come face to face with Trooper David Britton so he could show Britton exactly how he felt, even if he wound up locked up for assault.

When he finally calmed down, they called Geiger and Tinsley back.

"Where did that come from?' Swish asked.

"It was an MP3 attachment to an email," Geiger responded.

"Do you know who it's from?" Erin jumped in.

"Yeah, actually we do," Geiger said, his satisfaction apparent. "The source is a guy by the name of Scott Lewis, who sent it from his Yahoo account. And to answer your next question, no we don't have the email. We were able to extract that information from the MP3 download."

When they ended their call with Geiger and Tinsley, Swish looked up to see Erin grinning at him. "What?" he asked.

"I was just remembering your iTunes argument to Judge Bader. Pretty prophetic," she said.

"Dumb luck," he replied. "Now let's see if we can find Mr. Lewis."

"It's not exactly a unique name," Erin said.

"Worth a try," Swish said, turning back to his computer and beginning to search the internet. He scrolled through the results, stopped. "I think I found him," he proclaimed.

Erin walked around his desk so she was hovering over his shoulder. He was on the website for the radio station WTRA, 108.2 FM—the radio station where Drew Smith had his show. Under a drop-down menu for the station's on-air personalities and behind-the-scenes staff was Scott Lewis, sound engineer.

"We need Dylan to talk to him," Swish said.

"Yeah, but with Marshall getting killed, Lewis may be spooked and reluctant to talk," Erin replied. "This is going to require some finesse, because not only do we need to find out what Lewis knows, we may need him as a witness to authenticate the recording as accurate so we can get it into evidence."

"Given what's on that recording, I think we can get him to cooperate," Swish said.

"You're right. He did give the recording to Marshall, that's a plus." She paused. "Can you handle speaking with Dylan?" Erin asked.

"Sure. Why? What are you up to?"

"I need to go to the jail to talk with Mazer. At four o'clock this morning I thought of a rather routine question we forgot to ask him."

"What?"

"His keys—were his car keys in his locker or were they with him?"

Swish nodded, grasping the implications of what it could mean if Mazer had the keys with him.

"More importantly, I want to see if he knows Holmes and if he knows anything about Marshall and Holmes having been in contact," Erin added.

Swish studied his partner's face. Unlike when they had spoken last night, today she wore her poker face—her emotions no longer on full display. "We haven't talked about Holmes," Swish said. "I know you well enough to know you're blaming yourself. You can't do that, E."

"So I've been told," she replied.

"But you are," he said.

She gave him a tight smile. "Detective Vince Florio and Lenore Fredericks," she said, referencing two people who had been murdered after speaking with Swish when he and Erin had represented Sharise Barnes. "That was three years ago. Have you forgiven yourself yet?" she asked.

He exhaled before he responded. "No," was all he said.

"Some wounds heal completely; some leave scars," Erin said. "Holmes will leave a scar."

CHAPTER 23

"JON, WHERE WERE YOUR CAR KEYS THE NIGHT MARSHALL WAS murdered?" Erin asked, after they had exchanged some small talk.

"What do you mean, where were they?"

"I mean were they in your locker at the barracks or did you have them with you on patrol?"

"Are you trying to blame Gabe again?" Mazer fired back, confrontationally.

"Actually, right now I'm not blaming anyone," she said, her voice growing softer as she spoke. "I'm just trying to figure out what the possibilities are."

"What do you mean?" Mazer said.

"Jon, it's a simple question. Where were your car keys that night—in your locker or with you in the car?"

"In my pants pocket inside my locker," he said.

She gave him a "that wasn't so hard" look. Armed with the knowledge his keys were in his locker, she questioned him about the security, or what turned out to be the lack of security, at the barracks. By the time they were done, she had been shocked by some of his answers.

"Do you know a Deputy Attorney General Albert Holmes?" she asked, changing gears.

Mazer looked perplexed. "He was one of the people on the task force who investigated whether the Lords actually existed in the state police, and he was involved in the IA, but I don't know who he is. I don't remember if he was there when I was interviewed or not—maybe he was—nothing stands out."

"Did Marshall ever mention him?"

"No. Never. Why? What's Holmes got to do with anything?" he asked.

"He's dead," Erin replied. "He either took his own life, or was murdered on his way to meet with me."

Mazer flinched like he had just absorbed a punch in his gut.

Erin was surprised by his reaction, but it had been unmistakable.

"Let me ask again. Did you know DAG Holmes?" she asked.

"Yes," he whispered.

"How?" she asked.

Mazer took a deep breath. "After the IA was finished, he called me on my cell. We met at a restaurant in Perth Amboy."

"How did he have your cell?"

"I had provided it as part of the task force investigation."

"What was your meeting about?"

"He told me he knew the Lords existed and that he believed I was being singled out because I was gay. He suggested I talk to Marshall, who he knew was doing an investigative piece."

"Did he tell you why, if he knew the Lords existed, the task force report and the IA found to the contrary?"

"All he said was they had dirt on him, and if he didn't do what they wanted, they'd destroy him."

"Did he tell you what it was they had on him?"

"No. I didn't ask and he didn't volunteer."

Erin proceeded to tell Mazer about what had been revealed shortly after Holmes's death was announced and the role, she believed, her phone call had played in his death.

"I assume that if I asked you why you lied to me and said you didn't know him, you'd tell me that you were protecting him. Am I correct?"

He nodded. "Yeah," he said.

"Look, Jon. I've had a lot of clients lie to me over the years, and

I understand that in many cases, from a client's perspective, a lie works better than the truth. But just keep in mind, your best option may be to testify in your own defense. If you do, and you lie about something that the prosecution can prove is a lie, they will rip you a new asshole, and once a jury decides you've lied about one thing, there's nothing to prevent them from finding you lied about everything. 'False in one, false in all,' it's called, and it applies to any witness. So, even if I can't stop you from lying, I can warn you of the consequences."

Jon gave her a knowing look. "Erin, I appreciate that you're trying to protect me as best you can. From your perspective that means me telling you nothing but the truth. Unfortunately, I've seen what these guys can do, and it ain't pretty. Look what the truth did for Holmes. Trust me, I don't want to spend the rest of my life in jail. But I also don't want to be the cause of anyone else going through what I'm going through, or worse, ending up like Holmes."

His words stung. She knew he wasn't blaming her for Holmes's death, but he was right—confronting Holmes with the truth had ripples she had never intended. One thing was clear, the truth had not set him free.

When she got back to her car, she called Swish to fill him in on her visit, and he in turn updated her on his call with Dylan.

"A few other things," Swish said. "Dylan got hold of Trooper Urjinski. Urjinski's not anxious to get involved, but will if he has to. He said Britton, Stone, and others are brutal. He also gave Dylan a copy of a Facebook post Britton sent to a bunch of troopers after Smith's book was published."

"Sounds encouraging," Erin said.

"That's not the best part. There's more. I'll fill you in when I see you."

"Now you've piqued my curiosity."

"I prefer to tell you the other part in person," Swish said.

"Fair enough. Anything else?" she asked.

"What are you doing tomorrow morning?" Swish asked.

"I've got nothing on. Why, what's up?"

"I got a call from Prosecutor Talon's administrative assistant; the prosecutor would like to have a follow-up meeting with us at eight thirty."

"Meet at the office at seven thirty?" Erin asked.

"See you then," he replied.

Prosecutor Talon was already sitting in her conference room when Erin and Duane were shown in at eight twenty by Talon's admin. She stood when they entered and greeted each of them warmly by their first names. After they exchanged some pleasantries, she offered them coffee, which they politely declined.

"Thanks for coming in on such short notice," Talon began. "I realize it's only been a week since you provided me with the information on what took place in Edison, but I wanted you to hear this directly from me." She paused, her demeanor, which up until now had been cordial, suddenly shifting. "The Office of the Attorney General has notified me that they are superseding my office and they will be taking over the investigation."

Duane's face twisted with a mix of anger and confusion.

"I'm sorry," he said. "How does the AG's Office even know about what happened in Edison?"

"I don't know," Talon responded. "I had asked my people who are with the Professional Responsibility Unit to get the records of the stop, CAD records, any videos, etcetera. They did that the day after we spoke. Yesterday afternoon I received a call from the first assistant attorney general advising me they were taking over."

"Are you at liberty to tell us why?" Erin asked.

"I hope you'll believe me when I tell you—I don't know. I asked, and I was told that it was to avoid impinging on other ongoing investigations." She turned her hands palms up to express her uncertainty.

"Edison PD certainly has had more than its fair share of bad headlines; is the AG investigating them?" Duane asked.

Talon shifted in her chair. "Let me put it this way," she said. "If they are, I'm unaware of it." She pursed her lips. "And while there's no guarantee that I would be aware . . . I'm pretty sure I'd know."

Silence filled the room.

Duane pushed his chair back and stood. "Thank you," he said, extending his hand. "I really do appreciate your efforts."

Talon stood and shook Duane's hand. "I'm sorry. Having had the opportunity to listen to your recording and watch what Erin captured on video, I want to apologize to you for what happened and what was said to you by the officer." She paused for a beat. "And totally off the record, this is bullshit."

He gave her a weak smile. "Thanks," he said.

Later, they sat in the coffee shop across from the Prosecutor's Office. "I have an idea," Erin said.

"If it involves the CIA, Interpol, or the NSA, I don't think they'll be interested," Swish said, his frustration still on full display.

"Much simpler than that," she said.

"What? Go to the press with everything?" he asked.

She grinned. "Well, actually a little more devious than that."

He raised an eyebrow. "You have my attention. What are you thinking?"

"We provide copies of your recording and my video to Roy and Rivers as part of our ongoing discovery obligations."

Swish sat back in his chair, looking like he had a gas pain. "I don't get it. How's that help?"

"What's the first thing they're going to do after they look and listen to what we turn over?"

"Say 'what the fuck is this'? It has no relevance to the case."

"Exactly," Erin said. "Then they'll try to figure out what the hell is going on, and when they can't, they'll raise it with the judge."

"Yeah, but the judge is probably going to agree it's not relevant—and we've wasted everyone's time," Swish said.

"Probably. But first the judge has to watch and listen to what happened, which will educate her as to what happened to you, and hopefully set us up for the main event—the Britton Invasion. That's the recording we absolutely need to get in."

"So basically, you're suggesting we fake left, and go right," Swish said.

"Something like that."

"Okay. But to sell a fake you have to make it look real. How we going to do that when Edison PD played no role in this case?"

"Au contraire," Erin said, her smile widening. "Who were the first people at the scene of Marshall's murder? Who had control of the crime scene until the Middlesex County Prosecutor's Office showed up? If you take police departments for five hundred dollars, the answer is, 'Who is the Edison Police Department?' "

Swish let out a laugh. "Are you serious? We have no evidence anything improper happened at the crime scene."

"Let them think we do," Erin responded. "Besides, as I recently said to someone, sometimes the best defense is a good offense. It's time we started to push back. What's the worst that happens? We get a whole lot of publicity around the Edison PD calling you the *N* word. Think about it. If we can get the Britton interview in, we've hit gold."

Swish sat there, a shit-eating grin spreading across his face. "Damn, woman. I like the way you think. That is one bad-ass plan. How long did it take you to come up with that?"

She shrugged. "It just came to me," she said.

CHAPTER 24

Two months later
April 15, 2010

ERIN SAT ON A HARD, PLASTIC CHAIR NEXT TO LIZ IN DOCTOR GRIMES'S waiting room pretending to read a magazine. The nurse had just taken both a blood and urine sample from Liz. Two weeks earlier, they had been here for Grimes to implant the fertilized egg into Liz via a long catheter. Now they were back to determine if Liz was pregnant. The more conclusive blood test would take a few days to come back, but they'd have the results of the urine test momentarily.

After talking it over with Sean and Mark, they had decided that just Erin and Liz would come. This way, if it turned out that Liz wasn't pregnant, the two of them could commiserate together and talk to the doctor about when they would try again. And, if it turned out to be good news, there'd be time for all of them to celebrate together.

"You nervous?" Liz asked.

Erin put the magazine down and pursed her lips. "Nervous, no—scared out of my mind, definitely," she said with a weak grin. "What about you?"

"No. Not really. I suppose I should be. But I've been pregnant before, so I kind of know what to expect. Although," she added quickly, "it has been thirteen years since I had Brennan. I hope I remember how to do this." Liz stole a quick look at Erin. "Don't worry. I'm not having second thoughts."

Erin looked down sheepishly. "Guilty as charged."

"Will you ever be able to accept that I'm very happy to be able to do this for you and Mark?"

Erin frowned. "I'm trying—honest."

Their conversation was interrupted by the nurse standing in the doorway that led to the examining rooms. "Liz and Erin?"

They followed the nurse down the hallway to room 3. "The doctor will be with you shortly," she said before closing the door.

They each took a seat on the chairs. As they waited, Liz reached out and squeezed Erin's hand. "Don't worry. Everything's going to be great," she said, her smile warm and genuine.

There was a gentle rap on the door, and when it swung open, Doctor Grimes walked in holding a medical chart on a clipboard. "Nice to see both of you," she said pleasantly.

"Hi, Doctor," they said simultaneously.

A smile slowly inched across Grimes's face. "Well, I have some news. We won't have the results of the blood test for a couple of days, but, Liz, based on the urine test, you're pregnant. Congratulations!"

Erin turned toward Liz and her tears came without warning. She and Liz hugged each other and were laughing and crying at the same time. When they broke their embrace, Erin looked up at Doctor Grimes.

"Thank you," she said, her voice cracking.

"I don't want to pour cold water on your celebration—this is a wonderful first step. But let's remember, it's only a first step. We still need the blood test to confirm and then in four weeks, Liz, we'll schedule you for an ultrasound to see if we can detect a fetal heartbeat. Again, I'm not trying to be a Debbie Downer here, but, like every pregnancy, things can go wrong. And, as we discussed in our first meeting, there is a slightly increased risk of miscarriage with IVF. As I would caution any pregnant woman, and in this case, you as well, Erin, you may want to hold off telling most people the good news until after the first three months. Generally, that is when, if there's going to be any issues, they would occur." Grimes paused and smiled. "But this is a great first step."

After they had made the next appointment for Liz to have the ultrasound, they went out into the lobby. Erin looked at her watch—2:45 p.m.

"I'm going to give Mark a call because I know he's waiting for news, but he also has a meeting after school with the school newspaper staff today," Erin said. "But my mom said she'd be home by three and wanted to know the results. Rather than call, I thought I'd head over to her house. Why don't you come with me?"

Liz checked her own watch. "No. You go give your mom the news," she said, the warmth of her smile radiating joy. "I have to get back. The boys have soccer practice at four p.m., and if I leave now, I'll be home to get them to practice on time."

Erin embraced her sister-in-law. "I don't know how I'll ever be able to repay you."

"Be happy," Liz replied. "That will be repayment enough," she said, giving Erin a kiss on the cheek.

Peg's car was in the driveway, so Erin knew her mom was home. She used her key to let herself in the front door. "Mom, I'm here," Erin called out so as not to startle her.

"I'm just changing!" her mother yelled from upstairs. "I'll be right down."

Erin paused at the bottom of the stairs leading to the second floor. "You want a cup of tea?" she hollered.

"Sure!" came her mom's reply.

Erin continued into the kitchen, took the blue teakettle off the stove, filled it with water from the pitcher in the refrigerator, turned on the burner, and placed the kettle on the flame. She went into the pantry and retrieved two tea bags, grabbed two mugs from the cabinet, and placed the tea bags inside.

As she stood at the stove, she looked over at the kitchen table. Her father's half-empty beer was there. His motionless body lay sprawled on the kitchen floor. He was dead. It had been nine months. Nine months since her father had died, but those last images were seared into the photographic plates of her memory, just as fresh and vivid as if she was flipping through a group of photos.

And now as she stood there with the news that, if all went well, she'd be a mom—meaning he'd have been a grandfather again—she found herself wondering how he would have reacted. Would he have been thrilled, like he was when Sean and Liz had the boys, or disgusted by the prospect of her being a mom? She'd never know. He was gone. And despite the reassurance from her mom, Liz, and Sean that he had been anxious to mend fences with her, the pain of not knowing ate at her.

Her mother's sudden appearance in the kitchen startled her, and she quickly brushed away a tear that had leaked out of the corner of her eye.

"Is everything all right?" Peg asked, her concern evident.

"Yeah," Erin said, trying to quickly corral the conflicting emotions swirling inside. This was supposed to be a joyful moment, and yet she found to her dismay that even joy could trigger the guilt and self-doubt that still lingered just beneath the surface.

The whistle of the teakettle saved her from the awkward silence. It also allowed her time to realize that, given the pained look on her face, her mom would be expecting disappointing news.

Erin reached over and took the teakettle off the burner and then stepped toward her mom. "Don't get too excited," Erin said, "because it still has to be confirmed by a blood test, and there's still a long way to go, but according to the urine test, Liz is pregnant."

Her mother's look of concern morphed into one of sheer joy. "Oh my God! Erin . . ." Peg threw her arms around Erin and enveloped her in a hug.

When they finally broke their embrace, Peg hurriedly poured the hot water into the mugs, handed one to Erin and took her daughter by the hand, leading her to the kitchen table.

"Talk to me," Peg said. "What did the doctor say?"

Erin proceeded to explain everything to her mom, especially

trying to emphasize how early in the process they were and all the things that could go wrong. "Please don't say anything to anyone. It's way too early," Erin implored.

"Who would I tell?" Peg responded.

Erin giggled. "Ah, who would you tell? Given your enthusiasm for becoming a grandmother again, your sisters, sisters-in-law, my cousins, your coworkers, the butcher, the baker, the candlestick maker. . . ."

Peg gave Erin a sympathetic smile. "Don't worry," Peg said. "I know what it's like to be pregnant and I also know what it's like to have a miscarriage. I won't tell anyone until you give me the go-ahead."

Erin reacted as if she had touched a live wire—her mood shifting from playful to shock in a heartbeat. "Wait! What? You had a miscarriage? When?"

Her mother's face revealed a sense of melancholy Erin had never seen before.

"It was my first pregnancy—before Sean. We found out in October that I was a month pregnant. Your father and I heeded my ob-gyn's advice and we told no one—get through the first trimester, he told us. We planned to tell everyone on Christmas. We bought little baby carriage Christmas ornaments that we wrapped up and were going to give to my parents and your father's parents on Christmas Day. But two weeks before Christmas, I had a miscarriage." She paused, her look now far away. "We never told anyone. I was still feeling the effects of the D and C on Christmas Day, but we just let people assume I was having my period."

Erin got up and walked around the table, leaned over, and hugged her mom. "I'm so sorry, Mom. I never knew."

Peg patted Erin's hand. "No reason to apologize, dear. Other than your father and my doctor, you're the only person I've ever told."

Erin straightened up. "No one! Not even your mom, or your sisters?"

"Nope. No one," she replied.

"Why?" Erin asked.

"I don't know. It was a different time, I guess. People didn't share the intimate details of their lives. It was something your father and I knew—that was enough. And I don't mean this to sound cruel, but I don't think he felt the loss, the grief, the same way I did. To him the baby was still an abstraction. To me, it was our child growing inside me. But six months later, I got pregnant with Sean, and life went on."

"Thank you for sharing this with me," Erin said, once again leaning over and hugging her mom. "I wish I had known."

Peg gave Erin a sad smile. "You're welcome." She hesitated. "I guess this was the first time where it just seemed right to share and to let you know that, as thrilled as I am, I know to be cautious," she added. "But enough about me, how are you? Are you excited?"

"I am," Erin replied, retaking her seat. "But trying to keep my excitement in check. This is so early in the process; I don't want to get my hopes up too much."

They sipped their tea and discussed what would happen from here.

"Can I ask you a question?" Erin said.

"Of course."

"Did you breast-feed?" Erin asked.

Her mother's smile was quizzical. "I tried with Sean, but my milk just wouldn't come in, and I was getting so upset and frustrated, our pediatrician had me switch to formula. You—you were an entirely different story. Maybe I was just more relaxed, I don't know, but you breast-fed for the first six months without any problems. Why do you ask? Are you worried about not being able to breast-feed?"

Erin shrugged. "Well, actually, after speaking with my endocrinologist, there is a possibility that I may be able to breast-feed."

"But . . ." her mother said, her expression conveying her bewilderment. "How?"

Erin could only smile at her mother's confusion. "I won't bore you with the gory details, but with the right combinations of medications at the right time, there's a chance that I can lactate. It's the same thing they do for cisgender women who use a surrogate. But I certainly understand that breast-feeding can be challenging for women under the best of circumstances—you being exhibit A—but it's nice to know it's at least a possibility."

Peg raised an eyebrow. "You, my dear, never cease to amaze me."

Later she and Mark sat curled up on the couch having a glass of wine.

"This is it for me," Erin said, holding up her glass.

"What do you mean?" Mark asked.

"I mean, if I was the one who was pregnant, I wouldn't even be drinking this glass of wine."

"But you're not—pregnant, I mean."

"Don't worry, despite what some people might think, I'm not delusional. Maybe it's a meaningless gesture, but I just want to be able to share, even in a small way, a little bit of the experience with Liz. I understand this is nothing in comparison to what she'll have to go through, but I want to feel connected."

"You sound like you're excited," he said.

"Yeah," she replied. "I am, but I'm also trying to keep things in perspective—way too early yet. Lots can still happen," she said, deciding not to share her mother's miscarriage.

"What about you?" she asked.

"I guess like you, trying to keep things in perspective." He gave her a squeeze. "But I have to admit, I am pretty stoked."

She leaned into him. "That's good," she said. "I have a good feeling about this."

CHAPTER 25

THE WALLS OF JUDGE LILLIAN BADER'S CHAMBERS WERE NOT A DEfense lawyer's dream. On full display were numerous framed articles of the cases she had handled when she was an assistant prosecutor, most of them homicide cases. Not surprisingly, all involved convictions. Smattered among the newspaper mementos were framed photographs of her with governors, senators, and one with then President Clinton from her short stint in private practice before she was appointed as a superior court judge in 2000.

From what Erin had managed to glean from newspaper reports and old bios that she had been able to find online, Bader was sixty years old, a graduate of Columbia Law School, a Democrat, and married to U.S. Federal District Court Judge Harold Bader, who had been appointed to the federal bench by President George H.W. Bush, meaning he was a Republican—a mixed marriage, Erin had joked to Swish.

Erin's own experience with Bader had been limited to the few appearances in Mazer's case, but through the network of criminal defense attorneys that she and Swish knew, Bader had received high marks for her intellect and ability to conduct a fair trial. The one repeated warning was that she didn't suffer fools easily. That normally wouldn't have fazed Erin, but today she knew she might have to dance a little, and wondered how the judge might react.

As soon as Erin and Deputy Attorney General Roy came in,

Bader had greeted them warmly, then pointed to the two chairs in front of her desk. She wore a white silk blouse with a black pinstripe suit, which, because she owned the same suit, Erin recognized as Jones New York. Her brown hair had liberal blond highlights, and she looked younger than her sixty years.

Normally, Erin would have been at a distinct disadvantage if she was up against a local county prosecutor. But because Roy was from the Attorney General's Office in Trenton, she didn't have the home court advantage—instead both of them were on neutral turf, so to speak.

Bader flipped through a few papers on her desk until she found the most recent scheduling order. "Where are we on this, folks? According to the scheduling order, the state was to make its best plea offer by last Friday." She looked up at Roy. "Has that been done?"

"Yes, Your Honor," Roy replied. "The state has offered the defendant a plea to first-degree murder, with a thirty-year sentence, and an eighty-five-percent parole disqualifier. We think, given the overwhelming evidence of guilt and the cold-blooded nature of the murder, any offer that provides the defendant with the opportunity for parole is extremely generous."

Bader turned her focus to Erin, seeming a bit hopeful for a plea.

"Judge, there will be no plea in this case. My client is innocent and intends to go to trial."

If Bader was disappointed, it wasn't reflected in her response. "Well, that makes it easy," she said.

"How about discovery? Anything outstanding?" She put on her reading glasses and glanced down at her notes. "Ms. McCabe, have you received the victim's hard drive and a copy of the IA as I previously ordered?"

"I have, Your Honor. Additionally, we've previously provided notice of our alibi defense and reciprocal discovery. And at this point, I'm unaware of any outstanding discovery issues."

"Judge, if I may," Roy interjected.

"Yes, Ms. Roy?"

"Judge, about six weeks ago, we received from the counsel an audio recording and a video recording purporting to be of a traffic stop of Ms. McCabe's partner, Duane Swisher, by the Edison Police Department. According to the accompanying letter, Ms. McCabe indicated that these items were being produced pursuant to defense counsel's reciprocal discovery obligations. Judge, we strenuously object to these unauthenticated recordings as they have absolutely no relevance to any issues in this case and would ask that Your Honor prevent counsel from polluting this case with extraneous issues that have no bearing on the guilt or innocence of their client."

Bader turned her attention back to Erin. "Ms. McCabe?"

"Judge, obviously we are under no obligation to provide our defense strategy to the state. Suffice it to say that the initial officers on the scene of Mr. Marshall's murder were from the Edison Police Department. They controlled the murder scene until detectives from the Middlesex County Prosecutor's Office arrived. We therefore think that Mr. Swisher's subsequent interaction with the Edison PD and their clear racial animus and bias may well prove relevant. Most respectfully, Judge, to force me to reveal now, how we will use that in defense of our client, and when, without even the benefit of a formal motion and an opportunity for Your Honor to review the recordings, would be unduly prejudicial to the defense."

Bader took off her glasses, laid them on the desk, and gave Erin a look like she was about to call bullshit on her response. But the look passed and she instead turned to Roy.

"I will admit that what you describe sounds a bit out of the ordinary," she said. "But I am reluctant to bar it without the benefit of a formal motion to allow counsel to respond and without listening to the recording in question. As to what relevance the recording may have at the time of trial, I do agree with counsel that, at least at this point, it's not my role to dictate trial strategy. My suggestion, Ms. Roy, is for you to make a formal motion and let's go from there."

"Yes, Your Honor," Roy responded, unable to hide her disappointment.

"How much time will you need to file the motion?" Bader asked.

"Judge, normally I'd ask for thirty days, but I'm supposed to start a gang murder case in Mercer County next week that I anticipate will take three weeks to try, maybe a month. Could I have sixty days?"

"Any objection, Ms. McCabe?"

"No, Your Honor. If Ms. Roy needs more time, I have no problem with that."

"Good. Ms. McCabe, I'll give you two weeks to respond and I'll set it down for a hearing in July. Ms. Roy, what's your guesstimate on the length of the state's case?"

"Two—two and a half weeks, Judge," Roy replied.

"Ms. McCabe, I know you're under no obligation to present any evidence, and understanding things may change, but for scheduling purposes only, do you anticipate that there will be a defense case?"

"I do, Your Honor."

"Again, I'm sensitive that things may change, but if you had to guess, do you have an estimate?"

"Best guess, approximately a week," Erin replied.

"Okay, let's leave the trial on for September 7th and revisit it after I hear the motion in July. Anything else, Counsel?"

"No, Judge," they both replied.

When they were in the hallway outside the courtroom, Roy stopped Erin. "Ms. McCabe, do you have a couple of minutes to talk?"

"Please call me Erin," she replied. "And sure," Erin said, curious as to what this could be about.

They found an alcove with several places to sit. There was no one else there, so they sat opposite each other.

"Ms. . . . sorry, Erin. I wanted you to know, and please let Mr. Swisher know, that I watched and listened to the recordings of his encounter with the Edison PD. They are, to say the least, disturbing, and no one should be referred to or treated the way he was. I apologize for the way he was treated. However, as distasteful as what happened, the conduct of the officers has no relevance to this case."

Erin assumed that Roy's pause was designed for her to respond, so she did. "Thank you . . . ah, may I call you Carol?"

"Of course," Roy responded.

"Carol, there's no reason for you to apologize. We certainly don't hold you responsible for the conduct of the police officers. As to whether or not we get it into evidence, I guess we'll just have to wait and see."

Roy's eyes narrowed. "You're just using the recordings to try and poison the well. It won't work," she said emphatically.

"Unfortunately, the well is already poisoned," Erin replied. "We're just trying to make it drinkable again."

"You can't really believe that the stop of Mr. Swisher by the Edison Police Department is related in any way to this case."

Erin nodded. "I can and I do. Maybe you should check with whoever in your office is now investigating the stop and see what they think."

"My office? What are you talking about? Why would my office be investigating the stop of Mr. Swisher?"

"I don't know," Erin said as she stood. "Perhaps you should find out."

Erin reached Swish from the car. "It went down just the way we hoped," she said. "Bader's making Roy file the motion to bar. I don't think Bader's very impressed with our position, but we got what we wanted. The judge is going to have to listen to the recording and watch the video."

"Good," Swish said. "Unfortunately, we have a different problem."

"What's that?" she asked.

"Dylan met with Scott Lewis and Lewis really doesn't want to testify. He told Dylan that nobody knows he sent the recording to Marshall, and if Smith finds out, Lewis would probably lose his job. Sounds like he'll be a reluctant witness at best and we'll need to subpoena him."

"Damn. That means we'd have to put him on our witness list

and Rivers and Roy will know something's up," Erin said, mulling the problem as she drove. "Maybe there's a way to get the recording in without Lewis," she said. "It's a little risky, but even if it doesn't work, I think it'll provide us with enough cover that if we do need to subpoena him at the last minute, I don't think Bader will bar his testimony even if he's not on our witness list, if he's only coming in to authenticate the recording."

"I'm listening," Swish said.

"If we can establish through the state's witnesses that what's on Marshall's computer hasn't been changed since his murder on October 19, and then we can get Smith to admit that it's his voice and Britton's voice on the recording." She waited.

"It might work," Swish said.

"As much as we can, we need to ambush them with this," she said. "Honestly, it's really not even an ambush. It's really just our hackers are better than their computer experts."

Swish seemed to mull over her suggestion. "I'm on board," he finally said.

When Carol got back to the Justice Complex, she went straight to Rivers's office. She needed to follow up on the voice mail she had left him on what had happened at the conference, but, more importantly, based on what McCabe had told her, she wanted to find out who was involved in looking into the Edison PD. As second-in-command of the section, he'd know.

He looked up when she knocked on his glass door and motioned for her to enter. She hadn't even gotten two feet into the office when he barked, "Who the fuck does she think she is?"

Carol was momentarily confused and unsure who the "she" was that he was referring to—it soon became clear it was Bader.

"Those fucking recordings have nothing to do with Marshall's murder. Why the fuck is she allowing them to be part of this case? Fucking McCabe and Swisher—how the hell are they getting away with this shit?"

Carol waited until he stopped. "Ward, I'm sorry if my message wasn't clear, but Judge Bader hasn't decided whether she's going to allow them to use the recordings. My sense is that she's very skeptical of their position. All she did today was require us to file a formal motion. Which, if you think about it, is not necessarily bad for us."

"What's that supposed to mean?" he fired back.

"It means, if she's going to bar them from using the recordings, it's better to have a complete record, so that assuming Mazer is convicted and someone is filing an appeal on his behalf, there's a record of why she prohibited the use of them at trial."

Rivers's look conveyed that he hadn't considered that possibility.

"I met with McCabe afterward and told her that her position was bullshit and she was wasting everyone's time," Carol said.

"And?" he demanded.

"McCabe said that based on Edison's initial role in the investigation, she believed they were relevant. And," Carol continued before Rivers could deliver another torrent of obscenities, "she told me that our office was investigating what had occurred between Swisher and Edison PD. Is that true?"

"It's none of her fucking business what we're investigating," Rivers said.

"Ward, she didn't ask me if we were investigating, she told me we were."

"Well, I don't know where she got her fucking information, but she's wrong. There was a BOLO," he said, referring to a "be on the lookout for" in police jargon, "for a person and vehicle matching Swisher's description. All the cops were doing when they stopped him was their job. The matter was looked at, closed, and sent back to Edison for them to consider if any internal action was appropriate."

She wanted to believe him, but she was indignant over his total lack of concern regarding the officers' behavior. "Ward, I've listened to the recordings. Their language was totally inappropriate, and, if I had been Swisher, I would have been pretty damn certain it wasn't going to end well," Carol responded, her tone conveying her pique.

Rivers glared at her. "Whose side are you on?" he demanded.

"The side we're both supposed to be on. The side of justice," she said, knowing it wasn't the response he wanted to hear.

"Is there anything else?" he asked, the disdain in his voice clearly visible.

In for a penny, in for a pound, she thought. "Yes," she said. "Who from our office handled the investigation?"

His eyes gave her the response even before he opened his mouth. "I did. Anything else, Ms. Roy?"

Carol rose from her chair. "Because of my trial schedule, Judge Bader gave me until June 14th to file our motion to bar. I'll make sure you have a draft to review at least a week before that," she responded. "I think you told me everything else I need to know," she added, before turning and leaving his office.

CHAPTER 26

Three months later
July 12, 2010

ERIN LEANED CLOSE TO THE BARS OF THE HOLDING CELL AND SPOKE softly to avoid being overheard. Bader had just granted the state's motion to bar the recordings involving the stop of Swish, and Erin was surprised by how unnerved Jon appeared by her decision. "Don't worry. Remember this is what I told you we were expecting to happen. Our goal is to try and get into evidence the recording of Britton and Smith. This was just setting the stage for that."

"Okay," Jon said, sounding unconvinced.

She was worried about him. Over the last few months, he had lost a lot of weight and his skin had a milky pallor, the result of not being outside for eight months.

"We're in the home stretch, Jon. Less than two months to trial," she said in an effort to offer him some hope. "Hang in there," she said, knowing full well that for him the trial held the possibility of either redemption or damnation. "Have faith things are going to work out."

His eyes betrayed a sadness that seemed to transcend his current situation. "I lost my faith a long time ago," Jon replied.

She sensed his response was metaphoric, but it provided a segue into something she needed to ask. "You told me that Gabe spoke to a lawyer. Assuming you testify, have you given any more thought to how you will respond if you're asked about your relationship with him?"

"Nothing's changed," Jon offered with a rueful grin. "He's promised he won't hurt me." He held up his hand and shook his head before she could say anything. "I know," he said. "You've warned me. I get caught in a lie . . ." He didn't finish the sentence. "I understand, Erin. I understand. But I have to trust him."

As she walked back into the courtroom, she found herself drawn back to the memories of her own incarceration and the impotence of knowing that, in large part, your fate rested in the hands of others. The one difference, she thought, was that Jon did have some control over his own fate—he just needed to tell the truth—despite that she was pretty sure he wouldn't.

"Kind of what we figured," Erin said to Swish when she returned from the argument on the motion. "Bader made easy work of our relevancy argument. But we got what we set out to do; Bader's seen and heard the recordings."

"Good," Swish said.

"Let's hope," she replied. "Um, I need to talk to you about something else."

"Sure, what's up?" Swish asked.

"Remember I told you back in January that Mark and I were talking about having a baby?"

"How could I forget?" he replied, with a wink.

"Well, since then, we went ahead with the process and . . . and Liz is three and a half months pregnant. Mark and I are going to have a baby!" she said, her excitement tempered by her trepidations about how Swish would react.

Slowly the corners of Swish's mouth started to curl, and the smile that started there didn't stop until it lit up his face. He stood, walked around her desk, and guided her to her feet. Then he enveloped her in a bear hug. "I am so happy for you, E. You are going to be a wonderful mom, and Mark is going to be an amazing dad."

Erin leaned into his chest; thankful that she had Swish. When they finally broke their embrace, she drew in a deep breath. "As with most things about my life, us having a baby is a little more complicated than for the average couple."

"Why aren't I surprised?" Swish responded, retaking his seat. "*Qué pasa?*"

"Our lawyer, Phil Song, is going to file an application in the Family Part of the Superior Court to have Mark and I listed on the baby's birth certificate as the baby's mom and dad." She paused, giving time for what she just said to percolate.

Swish folded his arms across his chest, his brow furrowing. "I'm no family lawyer, but isn't Molly technically the bio mom?"

"Yes, but not legally. Just like we did when Mark donated his sperm, we all entered into an ovum donation agreement where Molly agreed to donate her ova to us with the intent that we'd use the ova to create embryos to build our own family. And it also provides that Molly doesn't have any right or responsibility of parentage. Of course, the wrinkle is that we used my sperm, so the question is, will the court be willing to allow me to be listed as mom on the birth certificate?"

Swish stroked his goatee. "Sounds complicated."

She shrugged. "All I can tell you is that Song is confident he's going to make it happen."

"Hey, good for you," Swish replied. "I hope it goes as smoothly as Song predicts."

Despite her best effort, Erin winced.

"What?" Swish said as soon as he saw her reaction.

"I didn't say he predicted it would go smoothly," she said before hesitating, "just that he's confident it will happen."

Swish closed his eyes and shook his head. He held his arms out and motioned with his hands for her to continue.

"Song is filing everything using initials, and he's filing the exhibits, under seal, but it has to be served on the Attorney General's Office . . . and . . . and they have the opportunity to object. Given the somewhat unique nature of the case, he's concerned that they may oppose the application."

"Not to mention, we don't have the best of relationships with the AG's Office," Swish added.

"Yeah, but this will go to the Division of Law, not the DCJ—it's civil, not criminal. No reason the folks who get notice of the application will even know that I'm involved in the Mazer case," she said with a confidence that tried to paper over her doubts.

"Your lips to God's ears," he replied.

Four weeks later, Erin and Mark sat in Song's conference room. He had called Erin that morning, asking if they could come in.

"Thanks for coming in on such short notice," Song said, shaking hands with each of them. He placed a file folder on the table as he dropped down into a chair. "I apologize for dragging you in here, but I knew this was something that we needed to discuss asap."

Erin's stomach started to tumble. *Oh shit. This can't be good news,* she reasoned.

"The AG's Office has filed opposition to you and Mark being listed on the baby's birth certificate as the baby's mom and dad. I can't say I'm shocked, because the AG's Office has opposed other applications in the past, but what is shocking is the stridency of their objection. And"—he paused to inhale, then exhale—"the fact that despite my request that the exhibits be treated as confidential and under seal, their objections to our requested relief were not filed under seal, and refer to both of you, as well as Liz and Sean, by name."

Over the years, Erin had had the unpleasant task of watching as a jury returned with a verdict finding her client guilty. It was the nature of her work—if you tried cases, you were bound to lose some of them. As a result, she had learned to mask her response. The anger, the disappointment, the second-guessing—all of it could wait. She'd needed to stay in the moment for her client's sake. Now she needed to stay in the moment for her sake and Mark's.

"Is there a way to stop the AG's filing from becoming public?" Erin asked.

"Unfortunately, it's already public," Song said. "They issued a press release announcing that they were opposing having you listed on the birth certificate as the mother, when in fact you're the father."

Song's words hit her like a blow to the solar plexus. Even in her worst nightmare, she hadn't seen this coming.

She steadied herself. "What did they say about Liz and Sean?"

"Just that Liz was the gestational carrier and was married to your brother, who was a well-respected orthopedic surgeon."

"They say anything about Molly?" she asked.

"No. In fact, they don't even reference her in their papers."

She glanced at Mark, trying to gauge his reaction. He in turn appeared to be solely focused on her.

"I need to get hold of Liz and Sean and let them know—especially so they can talk to the boys," she said to no one in particular. "Is it okay if I give them a quick call?"

"Of course," Song replied.

Erin quickly called Liz, and as Erin was explaining the situation to her, Erin's iPhone buzzed with a call from Swish. She ignored it. As soon as she hung up, her phone vibrated again with another incoming call from Swish.

"Hey," she said. "What's going on?"

"Just wanted you to know that Cheryl's already fielded about a dozen calls from various media outlets looking for you. What the hell is going on?"

Erin proceeded to explain what she had just learned and her guess the calls were about the AG's press release.

When she hung up, she let Mark and Song know about the calls that were coming into the office.

"I'm sorry," Song offered. "But candidly, I'm shocked. Not that they filed opposition, but that they appear to have gone out of their way to expose you." Song paused for a moment. "Any thoughts on how you want to handle this?"

Mark looked from Song to Erin. "Look, I'm a schoolteacher. I'm not used to dealing with the press. Whatever the two of you think is best, I'm good with."

Erin was of two minds. There was the part of her that wanted to go into full attack mode and excoriate the AG's Office. But her lawyer's instincts were telling her to play the long game. When Song filed the application, he had been pleased that the case had been assigned to Judge Lisa Jacobs. He had described Jacobs as fair, thoughtful, and intelligent.

"My feeling is we do nothing."

Song gave her a knowing look, but Mark seemed perplexed.

"I guess I just thought you'd be more upset," Mark said.

"Upset? I'm furious!" she replied. "I want to scream. But there's nothing to gain by fighting this in the press. Phil told us that Jacobs is a good judge. At the end of the day, she's the one who's going to rule on the application, not some newspaper. I want her to get our position directly from us."

Erin stopped and, for the first time, had to fight back her emotions. "Mark, this isn't about me . . . or us. This is about our child," she said. "They can say whatever they want about me, as long as ultimately the judge rules in our favor." Erin turned her gaze to Song. "Do you disagree, Phil?"

"No. I agree with you a hundred percent. You never know what a judge is truly thinking until they issue their ruling. But having been in front of Jacobs before, I don't think she's going to be very happy with what the AG did."

They spent the next thirty minutes reviewing the opposition filed by the AG and strategizing.

"Anything else?" Song asked.

"Yeah," Mark responded sheepishly. "There's one other thing that I just thought of that you should be aware of."

"What's that?" Song asked.

"The AG might not be alone in objecting," Mark said, closing his eyes.

Erin turned to look at her husband. "Who?"

"My family," he said, with a sigh.

Mark sat alone at the kitchen table waiting for Erin to get home from work. As he feared, his family was trying to insert themselves into the proceedings. Song's office had just emailed copies of the motion papers filed by Solomon Musto, a lawyer from the American Liberty Defense Alliance, a stridently anti-LGBTQ+ conservative legal advocacy organization, on behalf of his mother, Vivian Simpson, and his brother Jack, to intervene. As Mark read through the legal papers, including the certifications signed by his mother and brother, his anger mixed with his concern for how Erin would react to the vitriol contained in the papers. Musto's argument was summarized in the opening section of the brief, titled the *Preliminary Statement.*

> *It strains credulity for Plaintiff, Erin McCabe, who is a biological male, and who provided the sperm necessary for the creation of the embryo, to ask this court to declare him to be the mother of the child. This court should not even recognize the sham marriage between McCabe and Plaintiff, Mark Simpson. McCabe and Simpson are both males, engaged in a homosexual relationship, and at best their relationship can be characterized as a same sex, civil union. It certainly is not a legal marriage, an institution reserved solely for the union of one man and one woman. Since neither of the Plaintiffs are women, they are not legally married.*
>
> *It is respectfully submitted that based on the fraudulent nature of Plaintiffs' relationship, and in the case of McCabe, based on his deviant transgender lifestyle, McCabe should not only be disqualified from being listed as the mother on the child's birth certificate, but he should be barred from having any parental relationship with the child, including any subsequent attempt to adopt the child.*
>
> *Accordingly, prospective intervenors, Vivian Simpson and Jack Simpson, not only request that Plaintiffs' application to be listed on the birth certificate as the child's parents be denied, but that the court commence a separate proceeding to terminate any parental rights they may have.*

Mark heard the front door close and looked up to see Erin heading toward the kitchen. "Hey," he said, walking over to her and giving her a hug. "You're home early. Where you coming from?" he asked, trying to gauge if she had seen the motion or not.

"I was at the jail prepping Mazer. Why?"

Now he knew. She hadn't seen Musto's motion yet. He sighed as he tried to figure out how to tell his wife that she'd just been misgendered repeatedly in a court filing and that his family had argued that she was unfit to be a parent.

"It's my family," he said. "It's what I feared. They moved to intervene so they can oppose the application Song filed." He rubbed his forehead. "I'm sorry," he said, motioning her to his open laptop.

When she was finished reading what had been filed, she looked up at him, her face twisted into a frown. "I don't think I'll ever understand why your family hates me so much," she said.

"Please don't blame yourself," Mark said. "It's not you, it's them. I'm the one who owes you an apology."

She gave him a weak smile. "How about we agree that neither of us is to blame for your family. At this point, we need to focus on giving Phil what he needs to respond to what they've filed. Honestly, my feeling is that Musto has overplayed his hand. His argument is demeaning and annoying, but I don't think it's going to work. My gut tells me it's only going to make the judge more upset."

Mark stood behind her and kneaded her shoulders. "You're in the middle of preparing for trial. How about I give Song a call tomorrow and provide him with whatever I can."

"Thanks," she said. "I have so much work to do for the trial, if you can deal with Phil that would be a huge help."

"Happy to," he said, giving her a kiss on the top of her head. "How about I make us some dinner, while you work on whatever you need to do?"

"That sounds great," she said, her half smile showing her appreciation.

Erin rubbed her eyes and looked at the time on her laptop—one a.m. She was exhausted and the trial didn't even begin for another two weeks.

A reasonable doubt—that's all they needed—for the jury to have a reasonable doubt as to Jon's guilt. In theory, they didn't have to prove anything. But this case was different. Jon's gun was the murder weapon, so while in most cases the decision as to whether a client was going to take the stand was based on how the case was going, they didn't have that luxury here. Jon had to face the jury and explain his innocence—always a dangerous gambit. If he didn't take the stand there was no way to explain how Marshall was shot with his gun. Even if his testimony went perfectly, there were still risks, chief among them was whether they would be able to get the jury to believe who they claimed went into Jon's locker to get his car keys and took his off-duty weapon and burner. To acquit Jon the jury still needed to make a leap of faith . . . and if the leap fell short, Jon Mazer would spend a long time behind bars.

She powered down her computer, washed up, and made her way to bed.

She believed Jon was innocent, and the burden of representing an innocent man was weighing on her. And now there was the added pressure surrounding the birth certificate hearing that had to be dealt with. She'd let Mark deal with Phil, but she knew she needed to call Liz to alert her as to what was going on. No doubt the motion file by Mark's mother and brother would generate some renewed publicity, and she wanted to make sure Liz and Sean were prepared.

Shit, she thought. As tired as she was, she knew her sleep would be fitful—just too much going on.

CHAPTER 27

Tuesday, September 7, 2010

THERE WAS A LIGHT RAIN FALLING AS ERIN AND DUANE MADE THEIR way into the Middlesex County Courthouse for the start of the trial. They passed through security and went up to the fifth floor where Judge Bader's courtroom was located. Unlike some county courthouses, there was nothing fancy or ornate about the courtrooms in Middlesex County. The building itself was fairly modern looking for a structure originally built in 1959, but the courtrooms were about as basic as you could get. A judge's bench, a witness box on one side, and a box for the court clerk on the other, with room for the court reporter in the middle, a jury box, two basic wood counsel tables, and a spectators' gallery consisting of five rows of benches, separated by a center aisle.

Shortly before nine a.m., Mazer was led in by three sheriff's officers. He was dressed in a navy-blue suit, with a white shirt and a red tie. Gone, at least for the trial, was the orange standard-issue jail jumpsuit. Even though he was in custody, he was allowed to wear "street" clothes so the jury wouldn't know he was incarcerated.

Precisely at nine a.m. Bader took the bench. After a few preliminary matters, she had her clerk call down to the jury assembly room to request a pool of potential jurors. Approximately fifteen minutes later, a group of fifty people filed into Bader's courtroom and filled the seats of her gallery. From that group, and others if needed, they would begin the process of sitting fourteen jurors. Twelve of these people would ultimately decide Mazer's fate; the remaining two would become alternates. The dilemma for Erin and Duane was they wouldn't know *who* the alternates were until right before the jury retired to deliberate. The alternates could be the two jurors Erin and Duane liked the most, the least, or somewhere in between—it was a crapshoot that could impact the outcome of the case.

One by one the clerk called the names of fourteen potential jurors, each in turn taking their seats in the jury box. The judge then proceeded to ask each juror a series of questions that Roy, Rivers, Erin, Duane, and the judge had all agreed to in advance, questions designed to obtain background information, as well as to elicit evidence that a particular juror might hold certain biases or prejudices that would disqualify them. Because Mazer's sexual orientation played a role, not only in the prosecution's attempt to show his motive, but also as part of the defense's claim that he was targeted by the Lords because he was gay, Erin had been successful in getting the judge to ask questions concerning the prospective jurors' attitudes toward LGBTQ individuals. This would not only provide them with information to show if any potential jurors were biased against Mazer, but could also show if they were biased against Erin because she was trans.

Of the first fourteen potential jurors, eight requested to be relieved because they either didn't think they could be impartial or because they had job or personal issues that made serving a month a hardship. Once those eight were replaced, four of the new jurors asked to be let go. And on it went until they finally had fourteen people willing to serve.

Now, Erin thought, *the fun begins.*

Bader asked the attorneys to approach for a sidebar conference, which was a discussion between the attorneys and judge that took place on the side of the judge's bench furthest from the potential jurors to prevent them from hearing what was being said.

"Anyone have any challenges for cause?" she asked, which struck Erin as a very optimistic way of asking this required question—there were always challenges for cause and today was no exception. First the prosecution and then the defense asked that certain jurors be removed because one side or the other felt they could not be fair and unbiased, with the judge ruling on each request.

The process played out slowly, but by the lunch break, they had fourteen prospective jurors in the box that neither side challenged for cause.

"You notice anything about their challenges?" Swish asked as they grabbed some lunch.

"No. What?" Erin asked.

"They were all white," Swish replied.

Erin thought for a moment. "Yeah, you're right. Let's see if they continue to do that once we get to the peremptory challenges," she said, referring to the right to strike a potential juror without giving any reason.

Because Mazer was charged with murder, she and Swish had twenty peremptory challenges and the prosecution had twelve. The reasons for using a peremptory varied from an attorney's gut instinct, to the more nuanced analysis of the way a juror had responded to the judge's voir dire questions. The only exception to the rule was that the state couldn't use its peremptory challenges to strike jurors based on their race, gender, or ethnicity, and in this case, sexual orientation.

"Looks like we might have a reverse Batson," Swish said, referring to the Supreme Court case that prohibited the prosecution from using its peremptory challenges to strike all the potential Black jurors from the jury.

Erin chuckled. "That's good. Means that they don't know about the Smith recording yet."

When they returned for the afternoon, Rivers continued to use the state's peremptory challenges to remove white jurors. Erin, on the other hand, was more circumspect, using her challenges based more on whether she felt a particular juror would be able to accept that the Lords of Discipline existed and that Mazer had been set up.

When they finished for the day, Rivers had just used the state's tenth peremptory challenge. With Erin and Duane having used seventeen of their peremptories, it was clear they'd have a jury the following morning.

"What do you think?" Erin asked as they headed back to the office.

"I'm worried about juror eight," Swish said.

Erin glanced at her notes. *Juror eight—Karen Cosby, Old Bridge, NJ, white woman, age fifty-eight, divorced, paralegal in the bond department at the law firm of Smith Cranston in NYC, watches Fox News, Bader denied removal for cause.*

"Yeah, I'd like to strike her, but we keep getting people who are even worse. Depending on who goes in the box tomorrow, we should use a peremptory to remove her," Erin offered.

"Have you noticed the way she looks at you?" Swish asked.

"No," Erin said. "What do you mean?"

"She keeps staring at you. I know you're going to think I'm reading too much into it, but I think she knows you're trans, and isn't necessarily an ally."

"Great. Just what we need," Erin replied.

Jury selection continued the next morning. Shortly before eleven o'clock Erin surveyed the current fourteen jurors in the box—six were Black, three men and three women; three were South Asian-Americans, two men and a woman; one was Hispanic, a male; and four were white, two men and two women. To Erin's dismay, they were down to their last peremptory challenge and Karen Cosby was still on the jury. Even more troubling was that, in addition to Cosby, one of the white men, juror twelve, Robert Samuel, belonged to a mega church that was virulently homophobic. Despite Erin's pleas that Bader strike Samuel for cause, the judge had refused based on Samuel's repeated assertions that he could be fair and impartial.

After conferring with Duane and Mazer, they reluctantly decided that Samuel was more of a risk than Cosby.

Erin rose to her feet. "Your Honor, the defense thanks juror number twelve for his service, but requests the court excuse him."

As Mr. Samuel made his way out of the jury box, Erin held her breath as the clerk called out, "Juror number 704."

Juror 704 was young, twenty-two it turned out, white, a graduate of Vassar, and an associate literary agent at Linda Gittens Literary Agency. Both Erin and Duane heaved a sigh of relief as Jason Washburn answered Bader's questions. By all appearances, he was a far better juror than Samuel.

Now Erin waited. Rivers and Roy had one last peremptory challenge. Would they strike Washburn? Erin stole a glance as Rivers conferred quietly with Roy.

Rivers stood. "Your Honor, the jury is acceptable to the state."

Erin rose from her chair. "Your Honor, the jury is acceptable to the defendant."

Before the lunch break, the jury was sworn in and the judge gave them their preliminary instructions including the admonition not to read or listen to any news stories about the case. The instructions also forbade the jury from doing any research on any participants in the trial, such as the parties, the witnesses, or the lawyers. During this, Erin studied juror eight, Ms. Cosby, but either Swish had misread her or she was a very good poker player, because she gave no indication that she had violated the judge's instructions.

When Bader finished, they broke for lunch, allowing Erin and Duane to find a quiet place to go over his opening statement.

When they returned, Bader called on the state to give their opening statement.

Rivers rose to his feet, buttoned his suit jacket, gave a small nod to Russell Marshall's family, who were sitting in the first row right behind the railing, and made his way to a spot in front of the jurors. Given Roy's extensive trial experience, Erin had anticipated she would deliver the opening. But as Erin listened, she had to admit that Rivers was doing a good job. The arrogance so apparent pretrial was muted, and he laid out the state's case effectively and efficiently.

Mazer's cell phone records showed he had called Marshall twice the day he was murdered. Mazer's fingerprints were in the house. He had a motive—the article Marshall was writing was going to expose him as a gay man. And the most compelling evidence of all? Mazer's off-duty gun was the weapon used to shoot and kill Marshall.

"Ladies and gentlemen of the jury," Rivers said, his voice rising in righteous indignation as he reached the conclusion, "that man," he said, pointing at Mazer, "that man, a sworn member of the New Jersey State Police, planned the premeditated murder of a respected journalist in the prime of his career. And after planning it, he went and intentionally and purposely executed Russell Marshall. And I don't use the word *executed* lightly. Make no mistake, ladies and gentlemen, this was an execution. The testimony from the medical examiner will show you that after shooting Mr. Marshall twice, the defendant stood over Mr. Marshall and fired a third shot directly into Mr. Marshall's heart at almost point-blank range. The evidence will show you, beyond any reasonable doubt, that the man who fired those shots, the man who killed Russell Marshall in cold blood, was the defendant, Jon Mazer." Rivers drew in a deep breath, inflating his chest. "Thank you," he said, retaking his seat next to Roy.

"Counsel, does the defense wish to provide an opening statement?" Bader asked after Rivers had finished.

"Yes, Your Honor," Duane said, rising.

Normally, when they tried cases together, Erin took the lead, giving the opening and closing statements, as well as handling the cross-examination of most witnesses. But because of the racial overtones of the case, they had decided that Duane needed to play a bigger role in front of the jury, and no better place to start than to give the opening statement. After many long, hard discussions, she and Duane had agreed that it was better for him to do a generic "presumption of innocence, reasonable doubt, blah, blah, blah" opening, instead of giving Rivers and Roy a roadmap of what they really hoped to do.

Keeping in mind the admonition of their colleague, Logan Stevens, that there might be jurors who did not identify as a lady or a gentleman, Duane began with, "Members of the jury," instead of the usual gendered terms. "I suspect I know what I'd be asking myself if I were sitting in your position. If it was Jon Mazer's off-duty weapon that killed Russell Marshall, as Assistant Attorney General Rivers just told you he was going to prove, how is the defense going to prove Jon Mazer didn't do it?"

He strode the length of the jury box looking at each juror in turn.

"A good question?" he asked when he reached the end. "Or is it?" He paused. "No, I submit to you, it's not a good question. It's not a good question at all because Jon Mazer is under no obligation to prove anything to you. Not a thing. It's the state's burden to prove to you beyond a reasonable doubt that, not only was it Jon's gun that was used in the horrible murder of Russell Marshall, but, most importantly, they must show you that Jon pulled the trigger. And that's where the state's case falls apart. We don't dispute that Jon's gun was the murder weapon. What we vigorously dispute is that Jon had anything whatsoever to do with this senseless murder of Russell Marshall, a brave and respected journalist."

He walked back to counsel table and stood behind Jon so the jury would look at their client. He put his hands on Jon's shoulders. "Folks, take a look at Jon Mazer. Along with my partner Erin McCabe, it is our honor to represent Jon. He's had a distinguished career in the New Jersey State Police for over a decade. He's received numerous commendations. Most importantly, he did not kill Russell Marshall. Let me repeat that—despite what Assistant Attorney General Rivers has told you, the evidence will show that Jon Mazer did not kill Russell Marshall or have anything whatsoever to do with Mr. Marshall's tragic death."

Duane walked out from where he was standing behind Jon and stood facing the jury. "Please remember, it is never Jon's obligation to prove his innocence. As you look at Jon, he is an innocent man. He is presumed innocent throughout this trial. When you walk into the jury room to deliberate at the end of the case, he is still presumed innocent. It is the state who must prove to you that Jon is guilty beyond a reasonable doubt. We hear that expression all the time—the defendant is presumed innocent. And yet, if we're honest, sometimes that flies in the face of our everyday experience. A crime was committed. The authorities arrest a person they say committed the crime, and we all breathe a sigh of relief. The bad guy has been caught. But, as we know all too well, the authorities don't always get it right; sometimes they get it horribly wrong."

"Objection," Rivers said, slowly rising out of his chair.

"I'll see counsel at sidebar," Bader said.

Erin suppressed a smile as she joined Duane on the side of the judge's bench. It was rare for an attorney to object during an opening, but Duane had suggested that, at least some of the Black members of the jury might be skeptical of how police exercise their authority, and if he could get Rivers to object, it would help remind the jurors of their distrust.

Once they were in place, Bader turned to Rivers. "What's the basis of the objection, Mr. Rivers?"

"Your Honor, counsel is making an argument. This is an opening statement. Counsel is supposed to be laying out the facts for the jury—not argue."

Bader looked at Duane.

"Judge, I represent the defendant," he said. "I don't have to prove anything. All I'm doing is reminding the jury of what the presumption of innocence is, something defense counsel routinely do during an opening."

"I'm going to overrule the objection. Mr. Swisher is correct that he is permitted to remind the jury that his client is innocent until proven guilty. If I hear Mr. Swisher veering off into making an argument, I will cut him off. But for now, I find what he's saying is permissible." She paused. "Although, you are close to the line, Mr. Swisher," she said, seemingly as an afterthought that Erin took as Bader's attempt to stake out her neutrality.

Duane nodded. "Thank you, Your Honor."

Bader waited for counsel to return to their respective tables. "Ladies and gentlemen, from time to time you'll see me confer with counsel at the side of my bench. That's called a sidebar conference. It's just so we can discuss an issue out of your presence without forcing you to leave the room. It's perfectly normal and I'm sure it will happen from time to time during the course of the trial. The objection is overruled. Mr. Swisher, you may continue."

"Thank you, Judge. Folks, as I was saying, just because Jon has been arrested, just because Mr. Rivers has told you that Jon is guilty, that doesn't mean he is. Sometimes the state, with all its power, gets things wrong. You will hear a far different story when we get the opportunity to cross-examine the state's witnesses and, if necessary, present our witnesses. All we ask, all Jon asks, is that you keep an open mind.

"Please remember, Jon has no obligation to prove who did murder Mr. Marshall. The burden of proof always remains on the state. A burden that the state will not be able to meet, because the evidence will show that Jon Mazer did not murder Russell Marshall. Thank you."

Duane nodded to the jurors and made his way back to counsel table.

"Counsel, is the state ready to call its first witness?" Judge Bader asked in a pro forma tone signaling they had better be ready.

Roy rose to her feet. "Yes, Your Honor, the state calls Edison Police Officer Lawrence Andrews."

Interesting choice, Erin thought, not sure she would have led off with Andrews. But since Roy hadn't done the state's opening, this would be the first time for the jury to see her on her feet, and Andrews offered a safe witness. He was the first officer on the scene, responding to a request for a wellness check at Marshall's home. Erin had no reason to even cross-examine him. For now, she could afford to take a low-key approach. If all went according to plan, the fireworks would come later.

CHAPTER 28

THE FOLLOWING MORNING, ERIN POSITIONED HERSELF NEAR THE JURY box to begin her cross-examination of Dr. Christine O'Hara, the medical examiner who had performed Marshall's autopsy. Knowing that today would be the first time the jury saw her in action, and being superstitious, Erin had worn her lucky outfit—a navy-blue business suit over a white silk blouse and beige high heels.

"Good morning, Dr. O'Hara," Erin began.

"Good morning, Counsel," O'Hara replied graciously.

"Dr. O'Hara, you did not go to the crime scene, correct?"

"Yes, that's correct."

"And in making the findings you testified to on direct, you relied upon the examination of Mr. Marshall's body that was performed by a member of your staff at the scene. Is that accurate?"

"It is," O'Hara replied.

"And that examination occurred at approximately noon on October 20, is that correct?"

"Yes."

"You testified on direct that you and your team had some difficulty determining Mr. Marshall's time of death because windows in the house were open and it had been a very cool night, which likely resulted in Mr. Marshall's body cooling more rapidly than normal, do I have that right?"

"You do."

"And to help you make your determination, you utilized the

fact that rigor mortis had fully set in, which indicated to you that Mr. Marshall had been dead for approximately fourteen to twenty hours, correct?"

"Yes, it is," O'Hara replied, her tone relaxed and confident.

"As I understand your testimony, to help you further refine your estimate of the time of Mr. Marshall's death, you utilized his body temperature taken at the scene by your assistant, the ambient temperature of the room when the body was discovered, and your estimate of what the ambient temperature had been in the room overnight. Is that fair?"

"That's fair," she responded.

"Based on all of these things, your best estimate of Mr. Marshall's time of death was between five p.m. and ten p.m. on October 19, correct?"

"Yes, Counsel. That is correct."

"Do you ever utilize external factors? In other words, suppose hypothetically, a victim was in a meeting with five other people at seven in the evening, could you rely on that fact in determining that the time of death was after seven p.m.?"

For the first time, O'Hara paused before responding. "Well, in the situation presented by your hypothetical, yes, I could rely on information like that. Assuming of course that the information was reliable and accurate."

"Were you aware that Mr. Marshall sent an email at 6:01 p.m. on October 19?" Erin asked.

"Objection," Roy said, jumping to her feet.

"Reframe the question, Counsel," Bader said.

"Yes, Your Honor," Erin replied, knowing she had just planted two seeds for the jury. One was that the state didn't want them to know about Marshall's email, the second was establishing his time of death was after six p.m.

"Hypothetically, Dr. O'Hara, if it was established that Mr. Marshall sent an email at 6:01 p.m. on the day he was murdered, would that fact have an impact on your calculation of his time of death?"

O'Hara gave Erin a quizzical look. "Of course, if someone could establish it was Mr. Marshall who sent an email at 6:01 p.m., that would mean he was murdered sometime after that."

"And would you likewise agree, Dr. O'Hara, that if hypothetically it was established that Mr. Marshall spoke on his phone at 7:03 p.m., 7:05 p.m., and again at 7:10 p.m., that too would have an impact on your calculation of his time of death?"

"Again, Counsel, if it was established that it was Mr. Marshall on the phone at those times, then of course it would impact my estimate of his time of death."

"In the course of preparing your report, or for your testimony here today, were you shown any documents or emails that indicated that Mr. Marshall sent an email at 6:01 p.m. on October 19?"

"No."

"How about, were you shown any documents or phone records that indicated that Mr. Marshall was on his phone at 7:03 p.m., 7:05 p.m., or 7:10 p.m. on October 19?"

"No."

"Thank you, Doctor. No further questions."

"Any redirect?" Bader asked Roy.

"No, Your Honor."

"Next witness, please," Bader said mechanically.

"The state calls Detective Marco Cornish as its next witness," Rivers announced.

The courtroom deputy went through the double set of hallway doors and called Cornish's name. As was the standard procedure, the witnesses were sequestered outside the courtroom to prevent them from hearing what the other witnesses testified to, which might cause them to change their testimony.

As they waited for Cornish to make his entry, Jon leaned over and whispered to Erin. "Why is the time of death so important?"

"We need to establish it happened while you were on duty," she said sotto voce.

"Why?" Jon asked.

"Because otherwise your off-duty weapon and burner are with you, and not locked in the trunk of your car," Erin replied.

"Oh, right," he said, nodding.

When Detective Cornish walked by, Erin gave a knowing glance at Swish. She and Detective Cornish had a little history together as he had served a grand jury subpoena on her about a year ago in the Michelle Costello case. That meant that somewhere in between then and now, Cornish had been transferred to Major Crimes.

Rivers quickly took Cornish through what he had observed when he got to the scene on October 20—the location and condition of the body, the windows being open, and no signs of forced entry. He then testified concerning his recovery of one of the bullets that had killed Marshall, a power cord for a laptop, a cell phone, and a bullet casing stuck in the air-conditioning grate located on the floor in the kitchen. Finally, he laid the groundwork for the forensic witnesses who would follow.

When Rivers was finished, he confidently looked first to the judge and then the jury and announced that he had no further questions.

Erin stood and gave Cornish an impish grin, confident that he'd also remember their history. Sometimes, she thought, when you know the answer to a question can't hurt you, you just have to take a flyer.

"Good morning, Detective. You mentioned that you were the lead detective on the case. Was this the first homicide case in which you were assigned to be the lead detective?" she asked.

"Um, well, yes, ma'am, it was," he stammered, seemingly caught off guard.

"And in fact, you were subsequently replaced as the lead detective prior to Mr. Mazer's arrest, correct?"

"Objection," Rivers boomed, rising to his feet, his tone indignant.

"What's the objection, Mr. Rivers?" Bader asked when counsel arrived at sidebar.

"Judge, defense counsel is implying that Detective Cornish was replaced for incompetence," Rivers offered.

"Was he replaced?" Bader asked.

"Yes, Judge," Rivers began, "but . . ."

"Mr. Rivers," Bader interrupted, "if Detective Cornish was replaced, it's a perfectly legitimate question. If you believe Ms. McCabe's question has left the jury with a tainted view of the facts, you will have the opportunity on redirect to rehabilitate any incorrect impressions you feel cross-examination has created. I'm going to overrule the objection."

When the judge had returned to her seat, she turned to the jury. "Ladi . . . members of the jury," she said, her gaze shifting to Duane and Erin, "I've overruled the objection. Detective Cornish, you may answer the question."

"I'm not sure 'replaced' is the right word," Cornish replied defensively.

"Okay," Erin replied. "Let me ask it this way. Prior to the arrest of Mr. Mazer, someone else took over as lead detective in the case. Isn't that correct?" she asked.

"Well, yes. The Attorney General's Office took over the handling of the entire case."

"So then, you were replaced?" Erin said, returning to her original question and catching juror number one smiling.

"Yes, along with everyone else from the Middlesex County Prosecutor's Office."

Erin loved it when witnesses sparred with her and wound up digging an even deeper hole. If, as Rivers worried, the jury had been misled into believing Cornish had been replaced because of incompetence, now they'd think the entire Prosecutor's Office had been incompetent.

"How long had you been in Major Crimes before you were assigned to be the lead detective?" she asked.

"I went to Major Crimes on September 1, 2009," he replied.

"So approximately seven weeks?"

"Yes," he replied, a bit of belligerence creeping into his voice.

"And where were you assigned before Major Crimes?"

"Grand jury," he said, glaring at Erin.

"And while you were assigned to the grand jury, you were responsible for serving witnesses with subpoenas to compel them to testify, correct?" she said, standing with her back to the jury so they couldn't see her grin.

"Yes. Among other things," he replied.

"But those other things didn't involve being the lead detective in a homicide investigation, correct?"

"Correct," he replied.

"Move on, Ms. McCabe," Bader said. "You already established this was his first time as lead on a homicide case."

Thank you, Judge, for repeating it one more time for the jury, Erin thought as she sneaked a peek at the jury just to make sure they were still with her.

"Detective, you stated on direct that after Mr. Marshall's body was removed, you began a diligent search of the kitchen area looking for any evidence, do I have that correct?"

"You do."

"And it was during that process you found one bullet and a casing?"

"Correct."

"Where was the bullet located?"

"It was in the linoleum floor, directly underneath Mr. Marshall's body," Cornish replied.

"The bullet casing was located in the slats of an air-conditioning vent grate on the kitchen floor, is that accurate?" Erin asked.

"Yes."

"And if I understand the layout of the kitchen, the countertop runs along the wall where the sink is and then turns to form an L. Is that correct?"

"Yes. That's correct."

"And on the far side of the L were two stools, so someone could sit at the counter. Correct?"

"Yes, ma'am."

"And based on the physical evidence, it appears Mr. Marshall was standing near the sink when he was initially shot, correct?"

"Correct."

"And the bullet casing you found was located on the other side of the counter from the body. In other words, near where the stools were located."

"That's correct."

"Tell me how you found the bullet casing," she asked, knowing that whatever his testimony was to this open-ended question, it couldn't hurt.

"I got down on the floor, and I observed an air-conditioning grate, located on the floor under the counter, near where the stools were. I saw something in between the slats. I retrieved a pair of tweezers the office uses for picking up small objects, and using the tweezers I gently removed the object from the grate. When I examined the object, I recognized it as a bullet casing. I then placed it in a plastic evidence bag and labeled it with the date and my initials."

"So, if I understand you correctly, Detective, you never touched the casing with your finger, correct?"

"That is correct," Cornish replied.

"Detective, did you, or others working the crime scene that day, question the neighbors about whether they had seen or heard anything unusual that day?"

"We did, and no one reported seeing anything out of the ordinary," Cornish replied.

"Did anyone report seeing a state police vehicle there the afternoon, evening, or night of the shooting?"

"No, ma'am," Cornish said.

"Did any of the homes in the area have security cameras?"

"Three, I believe," Cornish replied.

"Did any of them show a view of Mr. Marshall's front porch?"

"No, ma'am."

"How about the street outside his home?" she asked.

"Yes, ma'am. One of them did."

"I presume you reviewed that video for October 19."

"I did."

"At any time did you see a state police vehicle on the video?"

"I did not," he replied.

"Nothing further," Erin said.

Rivers was out of his seat before Erin had even gotten back to counsel table.

"Why were you replaced as lead detective?" he asked the witness.

Erin spun around. "Objection—foundation and hearsay."

"Sustained. Lay a proper foundation, Mr. Rivers," Bader said.

Based on Rivers's facial expression and body language, he was stumped. And in that moment, Erin realized that Rivers's lack of trial experience was on full display—between them, Roy, not Rivers, was the experienced trial attorney. But for whatever reason, he was her boss.

Erin, on the other hand, had paid her dues with five years in the public defender's office. She had started with juvenile cases, which were tried before a judge without a jury, and then she had moved over to trying adult cases alongside a more experienced partner before being allowed to fly solo. She hoped that her inexperience in those early years had never caused any of her clients to be wrongfully convicted, because she knew she had made more than her fair share of mistakes.

One thing she had learned well—trying a case was much more than the mechanics; it all came down to the gentle art of persuasion. Getting the twelve jurors to see the case through the prism you had created. It required being likable, knowledgeable, forceful, confrontational, and humble all at the same time.

Watching him, Erin wondered if Rivers would have the humility to get help from Roy. Her intuition said his ego wouldn't allow it. She knew his type, and she smiled inwardly, knowing at some point, when it really mattered, she could exploit it.

"Were you told why you were replaced?" Rivers asked.

"Objection. Hearsay, Your Honor."

"Sustained," Bader said. "Counsel, please approach."

When they assembled at sidebar, Bader sighed. "Mr. Rivers,

here are the issues. First, you haven't laid the foundation for the question. Does the witness even know why he was replaced? But assuming he does, the source of his knowledge is almost certainly based on what someone else told him, thereby creating a hearsay issue."

"Judge, earlier when I objected to the questions defense counsel asked, you ruled I'd have the chance on redirect to correct any false impressions. Now, you're preventing me from doing exactly what you said I'd be allowed to do."

Bader rubbed the bridge of her nose. "Mr. Rivers, first I remind you that all Ms. McCabe did was ask if Detective Cornish had been replaced—he had. She never suggested or asked if it was for incompetence. The detective then volunteered that his entire office had been replaced. I'm sure someone told the detective why, but, as I said, what someone else said to him is inadmissible. My suggestion is that we take a break. Perhaps you and Ms. Roy can discuss the issue together and/or with Ms. McCabe and Mr. Swisher to see if you can reach a stipulation. Let's take our morning break and see where we are in fifteen minutes."

"Well, that was fun," Erin said when she, Swish, and Jon had gathered in the holding cell.

"I don't understand," Jon said. "Why are you attacking Cornish?"

"I hope it's not coming across that way to the jury," Erin responded, glancing at Swish.

"No worries," Swish said. "I've been watching them. Except for juror eight, you're good."

Erin then explained to Jon the situation where Cornish had served her with a grand jury subpoena and why she had decided to have some fun with it.

"At the end of the day, we have to make sure that when they go back to deliberate, the jurors have a reasonable doubt about your guilt. Sometimes there's a gaping hole in the state's case, but sometimes it's just a lot of little things that cause the jurors to have that doubt. Our job is to sow doubt wherever we can, and harvest it when we give our summation. If the jurors are left wondering why the AG's Office took over the case, we're fine with that because maybe it makes them wonder if Middlesex screwed up. Anything that causes doubt helps," Erin said.

Despite her explanation, Erin knew that the case would almost certainly rise and fall on Jon's testimony, but she decided not to say anything. He didn't need the added pressure of her emphasizing that his freedom depended on his credibility.

CHAPTER 29

AFTER THE MORNING BREAK, THE ATTORNEYS ADVISED BADER THAT they had reached an agreement that the jury could be told that the Office of the Attorney General had made an administrative decision to take over the investigation from the Middlesex County Prosecutor's Office based on investigative leads that had been developed by MCPO. From the state's perspective, it essentially removed the inference that MCPO had messed up, and from the defense perspective, it left open the inference that the AG didn't trust the MCPO to finish the investigation.

Roy had spent the rest of the morning and part of the afternoon calling two Edison police officers and two other MCPO detectives who had been on the scene during the initial crime scene investigation in what appeared to be an effort to negate any inference that Cornish was incompetent. Knowing that less is often more, Erin didn't cross-examine any of the witnesses.

Roy then called Detective Michael O'Malley from the MCPO and qualified him as a fingerprint expert. He described lifting latent prints from Marshall's home and subsequently having the prints screened through a fingerprint database. He testified that the vast majority belonged to Marshall, but there were six latent prints that, in his expert opinion, belonged to Jon Mazer.

"The fingerprints that you've identified as belonging to the defendant, where were they located?" Roy asked.

O'Malley walked over to two blown-up photos Roy had set up on easels. Using a laser pointer, O'Malley first indicated a photo of Marshall's kitchen. "There were three on the kitchen counter," he said, using the pointer to show where he had lifted the prints. "They were the index, middle, and ring fingers of the defendant's right hand," he said. "There were also two on a stool at the kitchen counter." Again, he used the pointer. "These were fingerprints from the thumb and index fingers of the defendant's left hand. And there was one on the inside of the front doorknob; the defendant's right thumb," O'Malley stated, pointing to the second picture, which was of Marshall's front door.

"Detective, did you check exhibit S-1, a 9mm, Glock 26 handgun, for fingerprints?" Roy asked.

"Yes, ma'am. The defendant's fingerprints were on the handle of S-1."

"Were there any other fingerprints, other than defendant's, on S-1?"

"No, ma'am. His were the only prints on the weapon."

"Thank you, Detective. Nothing further," Roy stated confidently, returning to her seat.

Duane rose slowly and approached the witness box. "Detective, fingerprints can tell you that someone touched a surface, but they can't tell you when the person touched the surface, isn't that right?"

"Yes, sir. You are correct," O'Malley responded.

"So, you have no way of knowing if Mr. Mazer touched the counter, the stool, and the doorknob on October 19, or a day before, or a week before, correct?"

"That's correct," he replied.

"Detective, did you dust for fingerprints on the windows that were open in the living room and dining room?"

"I did. There were no prints on any of the open windows."

"No prints at all," Duane repeated.

"Correct," O'Malley replied.

"Detective, there's been testimony that a bullet casing was found at the scene; are you aware of that fact?"

"Yes, sir," O'Malley responded.

"Did you attempt to determine if there were any prints on the casing, Detective?"

"I did, however, there were no identifiable prints because they were so badly smudged," O'Malley said.

"Do you have an opinion as to what caused the prints to be so badly smudged?"

"Not specifically in this case, sir. Although generally, the heat that a casing experiences when fired would destroy any fingerprints."

"Could it also be because someone wiped the casing to try and remove any prints?" Duane suggested.

"That's certainly a possibility, but I'm afraid I'd have no way of knowing if that's what happened or if some other equally plausible scenario occurred."

"You testified you found Mr. Mazer's prints on the handle of the gun—did you check for prints on the trigger of the weapon?"

"I did, sir, and there were no prints on the trigger."

"Did you check for prints on the magazine?"

"No, sir."

"Did you check for prints on the bullets in the magazine of the weapon?"

"Why . . ." O'Malley stopped. "No, sir. I did not."

"Thank you, Detective," Duane said, turning so he could make eye contact with each of the jurors as he headed back to counsel table.

"Not a bad day," Erin said to Swish as they drove back to the office.

Swish gave her a sidelong glance as he navigated the late afternoon rush hour traffic on Route 1. "Really?" he replied. "All they did was establish that a bullet casing from our client's gun was in the house and our client's fingerprints were on the gun and in the victim's house. Sounds like they did pretty good to me," he observed.

"When did you become such a 'glass half empty' kind of guy?" Erin responded good-naturedly. "Need I remind you that it's going to get a lot worse for us before we even get our chance? For now, all we can do is tread water and try not to drown." She let out a long, slow sigh. "My mentor at the PD's Office used to say, you chip away at the state's case every chance you get, because you never know what a jury will latch on to for reasonable doubt." She turned her head so she was looking at him. "I have to think that after your cross of O'Malley, at least one of the jurors has to be wondering why our client's prints weren't on the windows or the trigger, and why they didn't dust the magazine or the other bullets in the magazine."

"Maybe, but I thought Roy's redirect in establishing that three weeks had passed between the murder and the seizure of Jon's off-duty weapon was effective in explaining why they didn't check the magazine."

Erin laughed. "You know, there's still times when you think too much like a cop."

"Fair enough," Swish replied. "I think they made one other tactical mistake."

"What's that?" Erin asked.

"If I were them, I would have led with Doug Rudnicki as my first witness," Swish said. "They started the story with Russell already dead. The jury has no sense of who he was. To them, he's the dead guy. If they had started with Doug, he would have painted a picture of Russell as a living, vibrant journalist on the trail of the biggest story of his career. They could have humanized him."

Erin nodded. "Yeah, I hear you, but they'll get their chance tomorrow when Rudnicki testifies."

"For my money, it's still not the same," Swish replied. "It's like reading the chapters of a book out of order. You know the ending—he's dead. But they missed the buildup."

Erin mulled over Swish's point. At the end of the day, they wanted the jury to empathize with Marshall. They needed the jury to believe he was murdered for the groundbreaking story he was doing—just not by the guy who was charged with doing it.

"You still want me to handle the cross of Rudnicki tomorrow?" she asked.

"Yeah. I know we're not going to go after him—at least I hope there's no reason for us to go after him—but he means too much to me personally," Swish replied.

"No worries. I planned on it. Just wanted to make sure. Looks like based on what Roy told the judge, it's going to be a busy day."

"Although, not much for us to do," Swish said.

"True," she replied. "Still a few witnesses to go before the proverbial hits the fan."

When she got home, Mark was working on his laptop doing his lesson plans. She made her way over and gave him a kiss.

"How'd it go today?" he asked.

She thought for a moment. "Sorry, I was trying to come up with a good basketball analogy, but couldn't come up with one," she said with a shrug. "It went okay. All we can do is sit back and try to chip away when we can. How was your day?"

"Song called. The judge is going to have oral argument on my mother and brother's motion to intervene on Monday and then she's going to schedule the hearing on our application once your trial is over. He also said that the judge knows you're on trial so there's no need for us, or me, to be present at the argument. Song viewed the scheduling as a good sign."

"I agree," Erin said. "I think if she was leaning toward allowing them to intervene, she'd schedule it when we could be there," she said, hoping she was reading the tea leaves correctly.

"Let's talk about happy things," Erin said, changing subjects. "Did you speak with your sister today?"

"I did," Mark replied.

"How's Robin doing? She's only two weeks from her due date," Erin said.

Mark smiled. "According to Molly, Robin's good—a little tired and nervous, but otherwise feeling great."

"Um, how do you feel about things? Any"—Erin paused, searching for the right word—"qualms," she ultimately landed on, "about your connection to their baby?"

Mark shook his head. "No. Molly sounds so happy. No. No second thoughts or qualms at all," he said.

"Good," Erin said with a broad smile.

CHAPTER 30

DOUGLAS RUDNICKI LOOKED THE PART OF A NEWSPAPER EDITOR. He wore a black and white herringbone jacket, with gray slacks, a white shirt, and a silver tie. He was on the portly side, with thinning brown hair that was gray around the temples. At first Erin was confused because it appeared that Roy was treading very carefully with Rudnicki, but then it dawned on Erin that Rudnicki was a bit of a mixed bag for the prosecution. Based on what he had told Swish, he hadn't been happy with the way his paper had turned Marshall's computer over without maintaining a copy, and he seemed far from convinced that Mazer was the murderer. Erin could now see that Roy was trying to walk a fine line of being wary of what Rudnicki might say, while at the same time making the jury think everything was going exactly as planned. What Roy did get right was allowing Rudnicki to paint a very personal portrait of Russell Marshall.

After Roy's direct, Erin began by taking Rudnicki through his own time at the paper and his working relationship with Marshall. Then she turned to the background behind Marshall's suggestion of doing an exposé on a group of New Jersey troopers known as the Lords of Discipline. As she did, she sensed from his responses that he wasn't looking to hurt them.

Sometimes you have to go with your gut, she thought, and in that moment, she decided that unless and until Rudnicki's testimony went sideways, she was going to do a direct examination, and not a cross. She wanted the jury to hear the story directly from him in his words.

"Did Russell tell you why he wanted to do a story on these troopers?" Erin asked.

"Objection. Hearsay," Rivers said, referring to the rule of evidence that prevented a witness from testifying to what someone else had said.

Erin turned to the judge. "Your Honor, Evidence Rule 804," she said, referring to an exception to the hearsay rule that allowed statements of an unavailable witness to be admissible. "I believe this meets the requirements of the rule."

"May I be heard at sidebar?" Rivers responded. "I believe this falls within one of the exceptions to 804," he said, referring to the fact that the proponent of a statement from an unavailable witness cannot be the reason the witness is unavailable.

"I understand your argument, Mr. Rivers, but I'm going to allow it. Overruled," Bader said.

"Yes, he did," Rudnicki replied. "Russell told me that he had reliable information that there was a rogue group of troopers within the New Jersey State Police who targeted minorities both inside and outside the state police. These troopers often stopped motorists based solely on their race or ethnicity. As a Black man, it was important to Russell to try and expose that type of behavior, if it was true."

"As his editor, did you know if he had sources within the state police?"

"He certainly told me he did."

"Do you know who those sources were?"

"He told me they were mostly troopers, but the only name he ever gave me as a source was Jon Mazer."

"But from what Russell told you, he had other sources in the state police, he just never revealed the names to you. Is that accurate?"

"It is," Rudnicki replied. "He did tell me that all his sources were documented and their identity encrypted in the event he was ever ordered to reveal them."

"Do you know why Russell didn't want to provide you with the identity of his other sources?"

"Again, from what he told me, to protect their safety. He was afraid that if they were revealed, they could be exposed to retaliation or worse. So, the fewer people who knew, the less chance of their identities being compromised."

"Did Russell ever tell you why, if he was so concerned for the safety of his sources, he had provided you with Jon Mazer's name?"

"Yes. Mazer had already filed an Internal Affairs complaint with his superiors in the state police complaining about the Lords of Discipline. In other words, his complaints and willingness to speak out against the Lords were already well known, so there was no reason to hide him as a source."

"Did Russell share any drafts of the article he was writing with you?"

"He did. He shared a first draft around the beginning of October 2009, which I reviewed and made suggestions on, and then he shared a revised draft on October 19, 2009, the day he was murdered."

Erin handed several documents to Rivers, who in turn handed them to Roy. "Your Honor, I'd like to show the witness what I've had marked as exhibits D-1 and D-1A. I have previously provided copies to the state, and they're in the exhibit binder we provided to Your Honor."

"Any objections, Mr. Rivers or Ms. Roy?" Bader asked.

Roy looked at Rivers and then slowly stood. "No objection."

"Proceed, Counsel," Bader said.

"Mr. Rudnicki, I'm going to show you exhibits D-1 and D-1A; do you recognize these documents?"

Rudnicki took the documents from Erin, studied them, and then looked up. "Yes, D-1 is an email that Russell sent me, and D-1A is a copy of the article draft that was attached to the email."

"Mr. Rudnicki, what's the time and date of the email D-1?"

"October 19, 2009, at 6:01 p.m."

"And based on the contents of the email, is there anything in the email that would lead you to believe that this was actually sent by Mr. Marshall, as opposed to someone using his computer?"

"Yes, ma'am. The salutation is 'Rud,' a shorthand version of Rudnicki. Rud is what Russell called me."

"Did anyone else at the newspaper call you 'Rud'?" Erin asked.

Rudnicki seemed to hesitate, causing Erin to wonder if she had made a mistake.

He took a deep breath. "At the newspaper, no. Rud is something only my close friends call me." He took a sip of water from a cup on the witness stand. "Russell was the only one at the paper who called me Rud."

Erin walked back to counsel table and shuffled some papers. She wasn't looking for anything, she just wanted to give Rudnicki some time to compose himself, and for the jury to process what had happened.

After several seconds, Erin walked back to where she had been standing and faced Rudnicki. "Please take a look at what's been marked D-1A. Can you identify that document?"

"Yes, this is the draft of the article that Russell sent along with the email."

"How can you be sure, Mr. Rudnicki, that it's the draft that was attached to the email?"

"Because the subject line of Russell's email is *Penultimate Draft—LOD,* and the caption on exhibit D-1A is *Penultimate Draft—the Lords of Discipline.* Plus, I read the draft when I received it, and looking at it now, this is the draft article."

Erin then took Rudnicki through the fact that Marshall had a laptop he worked on at home, but it had disappeared. In fact, exhibit D-1, the email, had been sent from Marshall's laptop. Erin also established that Marshall's desktop computer, which was in his office at the newspaper, had not been touched by anyone at work since his death, and then, on the advice of counsel, turned over to the AG's Office upon its request.

"Mr. Rudnicki, in the article that I've had marked as exhibit D-1A, Russell makes reference in several places to the fact that Mr. Mazer is a gay man. Did you ever speak to him about that?"

"I did," Rudnicki replied.

"Why?"

"Because I was concerned about outing Mr. Mazer, especially

since he's a state trooper, and at least my perception is that law enforcement agencies are not always welcoming to gay men and women."

"Objection, Your Honor, and I'd ask that the answer be stricken as his opinion," Rivers said, only making it halfway out of his chair.

"Overruled, since the witness couched his answer in terms of his perception. However," Bader continued, "I caution the jury that Mr. Rudnicki's perceptions are just that, his perceptions, and are not to be considered by you as evidence concerning any actual bias in law enforcement."

Erin smiled inwardly at the cautionary instruction, which often only highlighted exactly what you didn't want the jury to think about. *Whatever you do, ignore that elephant in the room.*

"How did Russell respond to your concerns about outing Mr. Mazer?"

"He told me that Mr. Mazer had advised him that his IA complaint referenced the fact that he was a gay man, and that was the reason the Lords were coming after him."

"Did Mr. Marshall ever express any concerns about the accuracy of the information Mr. Mazer had provided to him?" Erin asked, knowing that Trooper Britton had said this to the investigators and wanting to get out ahead of him.

"No. Quite to the contrary. Russell believed the information was very accurate, and he had been able to confirm most of it from additional sources."

"After Mr. Marshall's death, did the paper run the story?"

"No," Rudnicki replied.

"Why?" Erin asked.

"Because the AG's Office asked us not to," he replied.

Erin paused for a split second to see if he was going to add the second reason he had told Duane, but when he made no effort, Erin nodded. "Thank you, Mr. Rudnicki."

Roy stood at counsel table, placed her hands on the table, and leaned forward. "Did your paper have any other reasons for not running Marshall's story, besides the fact that you were asked not to run it by my office?"

"Yes," Rudnicki replied. "The main source for the story was under investigation for the murder of the reporter of the story, Mr. Marshall."

"In response to one of counsel's questions, you stated that Mr. Marshall had not expressed any concerns about the accuracy of the information Mr. Mazer had provided."

"That's correct," Rudnicki replied.

"Did you ever verify through other sources the accuracy of the information provided by Mr. Mazer?"

"Me, personally?"

"Yes, you or someone acting at your direction?"

"No, ma'am."

"Nothing further," Roy said, retaking her seat.

Erin stood, and slowly made her way around counsel table. It was always risky to ask a question when you didn't have a good idea of what the response would be. But her calculus was that Rudnicki hadn't been an adverse witness, and based on what he had told Duane, she was confident she'd get the right answer.

"Mr. Rudnicki, generally as an editor, for an investigative story, such as the one Mr. Marshall was working on, would you normally require the author to have multiple sources for the story's factual information?"

"Yes, I would."

"Deputy Attorney General Roy just asked you if you, or others at your behest, had verified the information in Mr. Marshall's story and you indicated you had not. Why not?" she asked, and then literally held her breath.

"Two reasons," Rudnicki said. "First, we were supposed to have an editorial meeting with Russell on Tuesday morning—I'm sorry, Tuesday being the day after he was murdered. At that meeting, we would have gone through the story with Russell line by line and he would have sourced the facts for us. Obviously, that meeting never occurred."

Erin walked to the far end of the jury box, causing the jury to swivel to look at her as she asked the next question. "You said there were two reasons you never verified the information; what was the second?"

The jurors turned to watch Rudnicki.

"We didn't have his computer. As I mentioned, his laptop had disappeared and we were requested to turn over his work desktop computer to the Attorney General's Office, which we did, so we didn't have access to any corroborating information."

"To the best of your knowledge, had anyone at the paper, or on the paper's behalf, accessed Mr. Marshall's computer after you learned he was murdered?"

"No. We were specifically told by our counsel not to access Mr. Marshall's computer. It was disconnected and locked in a closet in my office until the Attorney General's Office took possession of it."

"Would you expect that corroborating information to still be stored on his desktop?"

"I would," Rudnicki replied, exuding confidence.

"Thank you," Erin said, allowing herself to breathe again.

After Rudnicki left the stand, Rivers called Investigator Clayton from the AG's Office, who had led the team that executed the search warrant on Mazer's apartment. He testified that when they arrived at his apartment, Mazer was physically present. After serving Mazer with the search warrant, the team seized Mazer's BlackBerry from his person, two 9mm handguns—one his duty weapon, the other his off-duty weapon, from a lockbox in his bedroom closet—a prepaid cell phone, which was located in his desk drawer, a laptop computer from his bedroom, four pairs of uniform trousers from his bedroom closet, and carpet samples from the living room and bedroom. When he was done on direct, Erin had no cross-examination.

Next Rivers called Detective Sergeant First Class Louis Packel, who was from the state police laboratory's Ballistic Unit. Packel testified that the bullets recovered by the medical examiner from the victim's body, as well as the bullet recovered from the kitchen floor, were too deformed to match to any weapon. However, it was his expert opinion that the casing found in the victim's home was from the 9mm weapon seized from Mazer's apartment, his off-duty weapon, a Glock 26.

"No questions, Your Honor," Erin said, when Packel finished his direct testimony, causing some mumbling among the spectators in the gallery.

The last witness before lunch was Jack Collins, who was a scientist at the state police lab. He testified that fibers from the carpeting in Mazer's apartment matched fibers located in the living room of Marshall's home.

When Collins's direct examination was concluded, Duane stood. "Mr. Collins, am I correct that you have no way of knowing if the fibers from Mr. Mazer's carpeting had been in Marshall's home a day, a week, a month, or a year. Is that correct?"

"It is," he replied.

"Mr. Collins, you also tested four pairs of uniform pants that were seized from Mr. Mazer's apartment looking for bloodstains, correct?"

"Yes, sir. That's correct."

"Did you locate any bloodstains on any of those pants?" Duane asked.

"I did not," Collins replied.

"Nothing further," Duane said, retaking his seat.

Rivers stood up quickly. "Mr. Collins, do you know if any of the trousers that were seized and tested by you had been dry-cleaned between October 19 and when they were seized, approximately two weeks later?"

"I'd have no way of knowing that, sir."

"Thank you," Rivers said with a flourish.

Duane slowly rose from his chair and smiled politely. "I assume, Mr. Collins, that when you tested the pants you used chemicals, infrared photography, and a Polilight laser in an attempt to detect any blood on the pants?"

"Um, well, yes, I did," Collins replied, his manner making it hard to discern if he was surprised or impressed by Duane's question.

"And you've used these techniques in the past with success to detect blood after clothes had been laundered or washed, isn't that true?"

"Yes, you're correct."

"So, when you used these methods, and you didn't detect any blood, you concluded that, even if they had been washed or laundered, there was no blood on any of these pairs of pants, correct?"

"Yes," Collins answered.

"Thank you," Duane said, lowering himself back into his seat.

"I told you I should have drawn more out of Rudnicki on direct," Carol said as she and Rivers sat in the office in the Middlesex County Prosecutor's Office that had been provided to them as a base of operations, Rivers enjoying a sub sandwich, Carol trying to have some tomato soup without spilling it all over her white blouse. "McCabe made him her witness. The jury's sure to pick up on that."

"What the hell are you worried about?" Rivers asked. "We ended the morning with conclusive proof that the weapon seized from Mazer was the murder weapon. This is a cakewalk. Stop being such a nervous Nellie," he said dismissively. "We just put the murder weapon in his hand," he said, picking up his sandwich.

"No, Ward. We've established that the murder weapon was his gun, but we haven't put it in his hand. Never underestimate your adversaries, especially in this case. They know what they're doing. All their little chipping away is part of a plan. Even though they didn't say it in their opening statement, I guarantee you Mazer is going to take the stand, and we need to be prepared."

"Don't worry. I'll take that fag apart on the stand," Rivers said, taking a bite from his sub.

"Ward . . ."

"I know," he said, with his mouth full, causing it to sound like "I mow." When he finished chewing, he said, "Stop being so politically correct. I won't call him a faggot when he's on the stand."

Carol closed her eyes and took a deep breath. *He's hopeless,* she thought.

"Ward, maybe we shouldn't call Trooper Stone. Based on what Collins just testified to concerning the pants, it could make Stone look like he made it up," Carol said.

"Nah, Stone will be fine. Besides, he spent six hours in the car with the guy who just murdered Marshall. It'd look suspicious if we didn't call him. Who's up after lunch?" he asked, peeking at their witness list.

"The cell phone expert," she replied.

"Good. That's your witness. You think we'll get to Lieutenant Maddox?" he asked, referring to the officer in charge of the Somerset barracks.

"Yeah, definitely," Carol replied.

"Shit. Guess I better look at his report," he said. "You have a copy?" he asked after unsuccessfully thumbing through some file folders.

"Here," she said, handing him a file as she pushed her soup away.

CHAPTER 31

After everyone had returned from lunch, Middlesex County Detective Mildred Cannon made her way to the witness stand. She was part of the county prosecutor's Computer Crimes Unit, her specialty being cell phone technology, but her appearance certainly did not fit any nerdy stereotype of a computer expert. Her long blond hair curled gently on her shoulders, and her youthful appearance made it impossible to tell her age. She was dressed in a burgundy business suit consisting of a collarless jacket and a pencil skirt that fell several inches above her knees. Her pink silk blouse and four-inch heels completed her outfit, and as Erin took her in, she had no doubt that the men on the jury would be watching her with rapt attention. Whether they'd hear anything she was saying was a very different question.

Cannon testified that she was brought in early to the investigation to analyze the call and text message history on Russell Marshall's cell phone. Unlike almost all the other MCPO detectives, she remained on the investigation after the AG's Office had taken over the case, mainly because she was such a well-regarded expert. Because she stayed on, she was also asked to analyze Jon Mazer's cell phone records.

Cannon testified that on the day Marshall was murdered, he had received fourteen phone calls and made six. All of the incoming calls, with three exceptions, could be traced to numbers associated with the newspaper, or members of his family. The exceptions were three calls from a prepaid phone. Two of those came from a phone number that matched the number for a prepaid phone seized from Mazer's home. One was a three-minute call at 2:47 p.m. and a twenty-five second call that started at 7:03:36 p.m. After the 7:03 p.m. call, Marshall received a call at 7:05 from an unknown number, there was also an outgoing call to an unknown number at 7:10 p.m., and then, at 8:25 p.m. and 9:45 p.m., he received calls from a number listed to his sister. Neither of the calls from his sister were answered, and she left two voicemail messages.

"Detective," Roy continued, "did you also do a cell tower analysis to determine where the calls on what I'll call the Mazer burner phone were made?"

"Objection, to the characterization of the phone as a 'burner,'" Erin said, as she rose from counsel table. "It's a prepaid phone."

"Reframe the question, Counsel," Bader said.

Roy drew in a breath. "Did you also do a cell tower analysis to determine where the calls from Mazer's prepaid phone were made?"

"I did," Cannon replied. "The call at 2:47 p.m. connected to a cell tower near Franklin, New Jersey. The 7:03 p.m. call connected to a tower near Somerville, New Jersey."

"Did you also analyze what I'll call Mr. Mazer's regular cell phone?"

"I did," Cannon replied.

"What did you find?"

"There was one incoming call from a prepaid number at 2:20 p.m. that afternoon that lasted fifteen minutes, and there were two outgoing calls made to the same prepaid number, at 2:51 p.m. that was for three minutes, and then at 4:52 p.m. that lasted eight minutes."

"Did you analyze the cell tower information for those calls?" Roy asked.

"I did," Cannon replied. "The 2:20 p.m. incoming call and the 2:51 p.m. outgoing call connected to a cell tower near Franklin, New Jersey. The 4:52 p.m. call connected to a tower in Edison, New Jersey."

"Were there any other calls on Mr. Mazer's regular cell phone after 4:52 p.m.?"

"It appears that his cell phone was off from approximately 5:30 p.m. until 9:00 p.m. When the phone was reactivated, there was one outgoing call at 9:59 p.m. to the same prepaid number as the earlier calls, and then the phone was turned off again at 11:30 p.m. and not turned on again until 6:30 a.m.," Cannon said, looking at the jurors.

"How can you tell if a cell phone is turned off, Detective?" Roy asked.

"Because it stops connecting to cell towers. When a phone is on, even if it's not being used, it will connect to different cell towers as it changes locations, making it possible to track the location of a phone, even if it's not in use. However, when it's turned off, we can't track it."

"Meaning that if someone wanted to hide their location, they could simply turn off their phone?" Roy asked.

"Objection, Your Honor. Speculation," Erin said.

Bader seemed to consider the objection for several seconds. "I'll allow it," she ruled.

"Yes," Cannon responded. "Turning off a cell phone is one way to prevent your location from being discovered."

"When Mr. Mazer's phone was turned on at 9:00 p.m., do you have a location as to where his phone was when it connected?"

"Yes. It was near a cell tower in Bridgewater, New Jersey."

"And do you know how far that is from Mr. Marshall's home in Edison?"

"Yes, ma'am. It's about a twenty-minute drive from there to New Durham Road and I-287."

"When Mr. Mazer's phone was on between 9:00 p.m. and 11:30 p.m., were you able to track his location?"

"Well, I should caution, that with cell tower location, we can only get a general vicinity based on where the cell tower is located, but with that caveat, the cell tower data showed that Mr. Mazer was in the vicinity of New Durham Road around 9:45 p.m., and then again at 10:05 p.m. The rest of the data was consistent with driving back and forth on major highways, with the cell pinging off different tower locations every few minutes, until the phone was turned off again around 11:30 p.m.," Cannon offered.

"Thank you, Detective," Roy said, returning to her seat.

Erin stood at counsel table. "Both the 2:51 p.m. and 7:03 p.m. calls from Mr. Mazer's prepaid phone connected to Mr. Marshall's phone, correct?"

"Yes, they did."

"And that means in both cases someone answered Mr. Marshall's phone, correct?"

"Yes," Cannon replied.

"Did you check the cell tower information for Mr. Marshall's phone for those calls?"

"I did," Cannon replied with a hint of pride.

"And where were the cell towers that Mr. Marshall's phone connected to?" Erin asked.

"Both times they connected through a tower in Edison."

"So, since Mr. Marshall lived in Edison, it's at least some indication he was home when he received those calls. Is that fair to say?"

"Yes. That's fair," Cannon agreed.

"You testified that Mr. Marshall also received a call at 7:05 p.m. from another number, correct?"

"Yes."

"How long did that call last?" Erin asked.

"Fifty-eight seconds," Cannon said.

"Were you able to get the cell tower location for the cell phone that made that call?" Erin asked.

"No, we weren't," Cannon replied.

"Why not?"

"Um, because it was a prepaid phone, the carriers, such as Verizon or Sprint, don't maintain the data for that long a period of time, and by the time we asked for it, it was no longer available," Cannon replied.

"And there was also an outgoing call at 7:10 p.m. that lasted five minutes, correct?"

"Yes.

"And I assume you have no cell tower information on the recipient of that call either. Is that correct?"

"Yes, it is," Cannon replied.

"Am I correct that the cell tower information for the 7:05 call Mr. Marshall received and the 7:10 call he made also show that his phone connected in Edison?"

"That's correct."

"You testified that Mr. Mazer's regular cell phone was off from 5:30 p.m. to 9:00 p.m. and you could tell that because it was not connecting to cell towers. What was the status of Mr. Mazer's pre-paid phone after the 7:03 p.m. call?"

"It was turned off after the 7:03 call and it does not appear that it was ever turned on again until it was seized."

"Thank you," Erin said.

Lieutenant George Maddox strode up the center aisle of the courtroom with an air of importance. His hair was cut in an old-fashioned military style crew cut. Standing rigid, he raised his right hand and placed his left on the Bible as the oath was administered, then responded with a booming, "I do."

As the person in charge of the Somerville State Police barracks the night Marshall was murdered, Maddox testified that troopers generally worked twelve-hour shifts. They have three days on and two days off, then two days on and three days off, and a makeup eight-hour shift one day every two weeks. Mazer, who was assigned to the Somerville barracks, had worked from six p.m. on October 19 to six a.m. on October 20. When troopers work the overnight, they are alone in their vehicle from the start of their shift until approximately eleven to eleven thirty p.m., when they return to the barracks and two troopers will double up in one vehicle for safety reasons. On the night in question, Mazer had doubled up around eleven thirty p.m. with Trooper Edward Stone.

When it was time for his cross-examination, Duane rose slowly from counsel table and walked to a point where he was positioned about ten feet away and directly in front of the witness.

"Good afternoon, Lieutenant," Duane began, his voice suddenly commanding the room. "We made a discovery request for all surveillance videos of the parking area at the Somerville barracks and we were told there are none. Is that accurate, Lieutenant?"

"It is," Maddox replied.

"Is that because there's no outside security cameras at the barracks, is that what you're telling me?"

"Yes, sir. That's what I'm telling you," he said, with a hint of impudence.

"We were also told that there are no security cameras inside the barracks, except for the holding area where arrestees are held, is that also true?"

"Yes, sir. It is."

"So, if I wanted to roam around the parking lot of the barracks, I would be unobserved, unless I bumped into a trooper?"

Maddox gave Duane a funny look. "That is correct, sir."

"Is it accurate that most of the time the troopers enter the building through a rear door that leads to the locker room?"

"That's accurate, sir."

"Is it also true that the lock on the rear door is a push-button cipher lock?"

"Yes, sir."

"Meaning, as long as a person knows the lock code—the numbers and order of the numbers—they could punch them into the lock and enter through the rear door. Correct?"

"Only active-duty troopers, assigned to the barracks, know the combination . . . sir."

"That's a nice answer, Lieutenant," Duane said with a small grin, "but how about you answer my question. As long as a person knows the lock code, they could punch it into the lock and enter through the rear door. Correct?"

"As I said, only troopers assigned to the barracks have the code."

"I understand exactly what you said, Lieutenant Maddox, but you apparently are having trouble understanding me."

"Objection," Rivers shouted. "He's badgering the witness."

Bader stared down at Rivers. "Mr. Rivers, the witness hasn't answered the question. Lieutenant, please answer Mr. Swisher's question."

Maddox's eyes narrowed after the question was read. "Correct," he responded.

“Thank you,” Duane said, then continued. “And when you enter through the rear door, you don’t pass the front desk, so unless there is someone in the locker room when you walk in, no one will know you are in the building?”

“That’s possible,” Maddox replied.

“Lieutenant, anything’s possible. Isn’t it likely?”

There was a long silence. “If there was no one in the locker room, a person could enter without anyone knowing,” Maddox finally answered.

“And if I were a trooper assigned to the barracks and realized I needed to come back for something, I could enter through the rear door and then leave through the rear door and no one would ever know I had returned to the building, is that accurate?”

“It’s a possibility.”

Duane tilted his head and eyed Maddox.

“Yes, Counsel. That could happen,” Maddox said through clenched teeth.

“On the night in question, you were on duty that entire shift—six p.m. to six a.m., correct, Lieutenant?”

“Yes.”

“And as you sit here today, you have no way of knowing if anyone who was not on duty between six p.m. and six a.m. entered the building, do you?”

Duane could tell that Maddox wanted to push back on this answer. It sounded absurd that with the right code anyone could walk in and out of a New Jersey State Police barracks, totally unnoticed. It had sounded just as ludicrous to Erin when Mazer had told her this, but Mazer had sworn it was true.

Maddox flashed a scowl. “That’s correct,” he finally conceded.

“Maddox is a pompous piece of shit,” Jon said as soon as they gathered in his holding cell. “He’s one of them. He’s part of the Lords. Fucking asshole. He was always asking me how my boyfriend was, or telling me I didn’t look well, and asking if I had AIDS. You should have gone after him on the Lords. Make him lie under oath.”

"Jon, remember, at the end of the day, your guilt or innocence doesn't depend on whether or not the jury believes the Lords exist or not. What matters is whether they believe you pulled the trigger. We poke holes where we can, but we still need the jury to believe you."

"You're right," Jon said, suddenly deflated. "Shit, all the jury will remember from today is that Marshall was killed with my gun."

Erin hoped her face didn't show what she was thinking, which was *Yeah, that just about sums it up.*

"It's not like the fact that it was your gun is a surprise," Erin said. "Try to keep things in perspective. Hopefully, the points we're making allow the jury to keep an open mind."

"Yeah, until I fuck it up," he said.

"Stop!" Erin admonished. "You're going to be a great witness. Have some faith in yourself," she said, in spite of her own reservations.

Keep the faith, she thought. *That's my mantra—keep the faith.*

CHAPTER 32

ERIN STUMBLED INTO THE KITCHEN AROUND TEN, HER HAIR AN UNholy mess, wearing one of Mark's XL T-shirts as her nightgown. "Why did you let me sleep so late?" she asked Mark with a yawn.

He squinted at her. "Because it's Saturday and you were exhausted. You fell asleep last night ten minutes into the first episode of *Boardwalk Empire*, a show you've been telling me for the last two weeks you were dying to watch because you know the guy who wrote the book."

"I don't know him," she corrected, rubbing her eyes. "He's a judge in Atlantic County—Judge Nelson Johnson. I just think it's pretty cool that before he became a judge, he wrote a book that HBO made into a series." She rubbed the back of her neck, trying to work out a kink. "I'd love to write a book someday."

Mark snorted. "It sure as hell would be a lot safer than your current profession."

"Depends on what I wrote about," she replied with a wink.

"Knowing you, it would probably be about a transgender criminal defense attorney."

She shrugged and gave him an impish grin. "Nah, no one would ever read that."

She sauntered across the kitchen to the cabinet, grabbed a New York City Marathon mug, which also happened to be the largest mug on the shelf, and poured herself some coffee. She threw in some milk and sugar, ran a spoon through the mixture, and took a long sip. She closed her eyes and drew in a deep breath. "Umm, Costa Rican—thanks," she said.

Then she made her way over to the kitchen table, pulled out a chair, folded her legs underneath her, and settled in. "Come, sit," she said, tapping the chair next to her.

Mark added some coffee to his own mug and plopped down next to her. "I presume you're heading into the office today?"

"Yeah. You know me when I'm in trial mode, no such thing as a weekend. Although, I do have to confess it was nice to sleep in."

"Good. You needed it," he said.

"Is everything all right?" she asked, sensing something was off.

He pursed his lips. "Not exactly," he responded.

"Okay," she said, wondering what was coming next.

"I really hoped I wouldn't have to tell you about this. I know how crazy busy you are and how focused you are on the trial."

She put her coffee cup on the table and took his hand. "Talk to me. What's the matter?"

"Molly called me yesterday. Jack and my mom have been interviewed about you and me having a baby, and from what my mom told Molly, it will be part of a segment on one of the Sunday morning shows on WCON."

"Shit, just what we need, more publicity. And coincidently timed perfectly for the argument before Jacobs on Monday on their motion to intervene." She shook her head in disgust. "I'm sure the report will be balanced and honest," she offered sardonically, referencing the station's tagline. "I guess I know whose side they'll be on, but I'm a little surprised they didn't reach out to anyone on our side."

"They did," Mark responded.

"They did? When? Who?" she asked in rapid fire, trying to process what was going on.

"They reached out to Phil on Thursday. He knew you were on trial, so he called me to let me know. Phil said one of the reporters wanted to interview him, but he declined. When Phil spoke to me, he didn't know if they were really going to do a story, but he wanted me to know just in case."

"Why didn't you tell me?" Erin asked.

"E, you're in the middle of a murder trial. I didn't want to distract you with this BS," Mark said.

"I appreciate that, but . . ." She stopped, trying to gauge the look on his face. "There's more, isn't there? More that you're not telling me."

"Yeah, there's more," he said. "Apparently the same producer reached out to the Westfield School Board president and superintendent to inquire about me, what grades I taught and whether they were aware of our situation."

"Oh God, no," Erin said, squeezing Mark's hand.

"No, no, everything's good," he said reassuringly.

She raised her hand to her mouth and inhaled. "Are you sure?"

"Honest, it's all good," he said. "Yesterday, I was asked to go to the principal's office at the end of the day. When I got there, Dr. Neusteen, the superintendent, was there. They told me about the calls from WCON. Apparently, they were asking if they were aware I was married to a transgender woman. From what Neusteen told me, both he and the president of the board told the reporter that I was an excellent teacher, and they were not going to discuss my personal life because it had no impact on my job as a teacher."

Erin slid her kitchen chair as near to his as she could get and threw her arms around his waist, pulling him close. "Mark, I'm so sorry."

"Why are you sorry? You have nothing to do with any of this. We knew my brother was being backed by the ALDA." He took his fingers and gently reached under her chin, lifting her head so she was looking into his eyes. "Don't you dare go blaming yourself for any of this. Remember, I'm all in on us having a child and it was my idea to do it this way. This is what I want. And I'm not going to let my bigoted brother, and the small-minded people who are supporting him, ruin something wonderful."

Erin looked up into Mark's green eyes. "Thank you."

"You're welcome," he said.

"Can I ask you why you didn't tell me last night about your meeting with the superintendent?"

He smiled. "Because you fell asleep."

* * *

When she got to the office around noon, Swish was already hard at work. He looked up from his desk when she rapped on his door. "Hope you're enjoying sleeping late on Saturday mornings while you still can," he joked.

"I am. But we have a problem."

His smile quickly faded and he motioned for her to take a seat. "What's going on?"

When she was done explaining, he asked if she was okay.

"Swish, as furious as I am, especially in light of the motion before Jacobs, it suddenly occurred to me—what happens if jurors see this program tomorrow?"

"Shit. I hadn't thought about that."

"We somehow need to try and get hold of Roy or Rivers, and the judge, and hope the court still has time to get hold of the jurors." Erin said.

It took several hours, and numerous phone calls, but they were ultimately able to get hold of Carol Roy and Judge Bader. At five thirty p.m. Bader convened a conference call where Erin explained that there was likely going to be a segment on WCON about her and her husband having a baby with a gestational carrier and their concern that the jury might see it.

"With all due respect, Ms. McCabe," Roy chimed in, "I'm not sure using a gestational carrier is going to prejudice any of the jurors against anyone."

"I don't disagree with you, Ms. Roy. However, there is one other aspect. The gestational carrier is carrying a baby conceived from my sister-in-law's ovum and my sperm."

"I'm sorry," Roy said. "Did you say, 'your sperm'?"

"I did."

"Oh," Roy mumbled.

"Thank you, Ms. McCabe, for bringing this to our attention. I understand your concern. I will contact the jury manager and have him try to contact each juror by phone to prevent them from watching. Do you know what time the show will be on?"

"I don't, Judge. All I was told was that it will be on one of the Sunday talk show segments."

"Thank you," Bader said. "I might also suggest that we all try and watch it so that we can see if, or how, it may be prejudicial to either side. And let's convene at eight thirty on Monday morning to assess the situation and decide what, if anything, I need to do with the jury. Thank you, Counsel. I'll see you on Monday."

On Monday morning, Bader met with the four attorneys in her chambers, telling them that she had watched the show and found it troubling enough that she was going to interview each of the jurors separately in chambers, without counsel present, to see if any had seen the program. Depending on what she learned, she would let them all know if she felt further action was necessary.

Erin and Duane took advantage of the time to brief Mazer on what was going on. Around nine thirty, Erin excused herself and headed to the ladies' room. When she came out of the stall, Carol Roy was standing near the sinks. Erin nodded, said hi, and proceeded to wash her hands.

"Did you watch it?" Roy asked.

"I'm sorry?" Erin replied.

"The show yesterday, about you and your husband—did you watch it?"

As Erin grabbed a paper towel to dry her hands, she nodded. "Yeah, I did. I didn't want to. I kind of suspected what it would be like."

Roy seemed lost as to what to say. "I . . . I'm sorry. What they said about you was cruel. I know how personal those kinds of decisions are. Having a baby, I mean. We . . . my partner and I . . . we've talked about having a family, kind of doing what you did. Anyway, I can't imagine what it's like to have your private life spread out there for public consumption."

"Thanks," Erin said, wondering if Roy had used "partner" to convey a message.

"Yeah, my partner's another woman," Roy said, grinning, apparently sensing Erin's hesitation.

Erin gave her a weak smile. "Can I ask what your partner does?"

"She's a cop," Roy responded. "Trenton PD—Detective Margot

Turner. She's the reason I left the Mercer Prosecutor's Office. She kept showing up on my homicide cases, which makes sense because that's how we met—on a case. She's in Homicide," Roy added with a shrug. "Look, McCabe—sorry, Erin . . ."

Erin chuckled. "No worries. I'm sure Swish and I are nothing but McCabe and Swisher when you guys talk about us, just like you and Ward are always Roy and Rivers. We work in a last name profession."

"Yeah, we do," Roy said, her face scrunching into a knowing acknowledgment. "Erin . . . well, I just wanted you to know that I respect you for being honest and open about who you are. I'm sure it's not always easy, yesterday's show being exhibit A."

"Thanks," Erin replied.

"I . . . I also learned for the first time that my office is opposing what you're trying to do." Roy took a step forward. "I want you to know, if I ever find out who in my office made the decision to go public on you, I'll tell them exactly what I think of them. You may be my adversary in the courtroom, but outside it, I respect the shit out of you for being you." She paused, giving Erin a sad smile. "Can I give you a hug?"

Erin bit down on her lower lip, trying to keep her emotions in check. "Sure," she said, a catch in her voice.

When they separated, Erin could scarcely believe what had just happened. "Thank you. What you said and did mean a lot to me." Erin hesitated. "And listen, if you and your partner ever decide to go ahead with the family thing, don't hesitate to reach out. I've gotten to know some great docs and lawyers who really know what they're doing. I'd be happy to share the info with you."

Now it was Roy who looked like she was battling with her emotions. "Thanks," she said softly. "That's good to know."

Bader came on the bench at ten fifteen and proceeded to put on the record what had transpired.

"The show in question," Bader continued, "aired yesterday morning at ten a.m., and consisted in large measure of the brother-in-law and mother-in-law of Ms. McCabe demeaning her, misgendering her, and mocking the process Ms. McCabe and her husband are using to create a family. Suffice it to say that neither Ms. McCabe or her husband were portrayed in a positive light. I will also note that neither Ms. McCabe, her husband, their lawyers or doctors were involved in the show or appeared on the show."

Bader looked down at a yellow legal pad in front of her. "The jury manager advised me this morning that, of the fourteen jurors, he had managed to reach ten of them on Saturday night; six he spoke with personally, and four received voice mail messages. Based on my interviews with each of the jurors individually, I am pleased to advise counsel that thirteen of the jurors did not see any of the show. There was one juror, juror number thirteen, Marsha Johnson, who saw the beginning of the show, but as soon as it mentioned Erin McCabe by name, she changed the channel. I asked her if anyone else in her household watched, and she indicated that her granddaughter is the only person who lives with her, and her granddaughter doesn't watch anything on WCON. I also followed up with Ms. Johnson and asked questions concerning her ability to be fair and impartial, and she responded that based on the little that she saw, it wouldn't impact her at all. Finally, I cautioned her that under no circumstances was she to discuss the show with any other jurors."

Bader paused, removed her reading glasses, and rubbed the bridge of her nose. "What I'd like to do is take a ten-minute recess to allow counsel to consider your positions with regard to Ms. Johnson. I will also tell counsel that when we recommence with the jury present, I will once again give them a cautionary instruction not to read any news stories or articles about the case in print or online, not to view any television reports or listen to any radio broadcasts, and remind them not to search for or doing any research on the case." She stood. "Please be back in ten minutes."

Erin stepped out into the hallway and looked at her phone. There was a text message from Song to call. She dialed his number and held her breath.

"Phil Song," he answered.

Erin could tell from the background noise that he was in his car. "Phil, it's Erin. How'd the motion go?" she asked. When seconds went by and he didn't respond, she said, "Phil?"

"Yeah, sorry," he finally said. "I guess it's a terrible turn of a phrase, but she essentially split the baby. She denied their motion to intervene, holding that they had no standing to be parties in the case. Unfortunately, she ruled that when we get to the hearing on our application, she will consider their papers as an amicus brief, supporting the AG's position opposing the application."

"Damn," she mumbled mostly to herself.

"I know that doesn't sound great, but if it's any consolation, my read was that she was furious about the show on WCON yesterday. She didn't say too much about it, but it certainly sounded like she saw it."

Erin inhaled before releasing it. "Okay. Thanks, Phil. I have to get back inside. We're dealing with the fallout from the show here too."

"Good luck," he said before Erin disconnected.

CHAPTER 33

BOTH SIDES AGREED THAT THERE WAS NO REASON TO EITHER QUEStion Juror Johnson any further, or to ask for her to be removed.

"Is the state ready to continue?" Bader asked after repeating the cautionary instruction.

Roy stood up. "Yes, Your Honor. The state calls Investigator Joseph Ash."

This is where things start to get exciting, Erin thought. Ash, unlike Detective Cannon, who was in the MCPO's Computer Crimes Unit, was part of the AG's Computer Crimes Forensics Unit. Because Marshall's office desktop computer was seized after the AG's Office took over the investigation, Ash had done the analysis of his computer.

Using a screen set up so that the judge, jury, and counsel could view what he found, Roy had Ash bring up the working copy of Marshall's computer so he could show the jury what was on it at the time it was seized. Using a computer mouse, Ash opened Marshall's email program, and then his document folder. He testified that when he was requested to do so, he made an exact duplicate of what was on the computer to provide to defense counsel. Ash confirmed that no files or emails were deleted on or after October 19, 2009, the date of Marshall's murder. He recounted that they discovered various drafts of the article Marshall was working on, which concerned whether a group called the Lords of Discipline existed in the state police, and he was able to open the various Word documents to show the jury various drafts.

Roy questioned Ash about the fact that apparently Marshall had deleted emails he received concerning the story, almost all of which were from Mazer, although he also deleted emails that he sent to himself from his personal email address. Based on the IP addresses, it was a different computer, in other words, not his work computer.

"Investigator," Roy began, "you testified that Mr. Marshall deleted emails he received from the defendant, Mr. Mazer, is that correct?"

"It is," he replied.

"When an email is deleted, does that mean it's gone forever?"

"No," Ash responded. "It depends on a lot of variables. Starting with if the company the person works for maintains its own email server, which backs everything up. But even if that isn't the case, most email providers—AOL, Yahoo, Google, Comcast, all of them—will continue to be able to access emails anywhere from sixty to over one hundred and eighty days."

"Were you able to retrieve emails from the defendant to Mr. Marshall that Mr. Marshall deleted?"

"Yes."

"Investigator Ash, I'm showing you what has been marked as S-17; can you tell the jury what that document is?" Roy asked.

"It's my report in which I analyze Mr. Marshall's deleted emails that are relevant to the article he was working on," Ash replied.

Roy then took Ash through twenty-five separate recovered emails that had been sent by Mazer and deleted by Marshall, all of which involved the article on the Lords. Most of them appeared to be Mazer providing information, or about the Internal Affairs complaint he had filed. Many of them were specifically about Troopers Britton and Stone and their roles in the Lords, and their efforts to destroy him.

"Did you discover any deleted emails sent to or from Mr. Marshall regarding the article with any other individuals, other than the defendant?" Roy asked.

"There were other deleted emails such as some spam emails, some work emails about unrelated matters, an email from a guy at a radio station sending him some music, but nothing else that appeared to deal with the article Mr. Marshall was working on," Ash stated.

"Thank you," Roy said. "Nothing further."

Erin stood and made her way around counsel table. "Good morning, Investigator," she said pleasantly, showing a small smile. "Let me clarify one thing: the emails that were deleted, the actual act of deleting them was done by Mr. Marshall, or at least by someone in his office, correct? In other words, Mr. Mazer didn't somehow delete the emails he had sent to Mr. Marshall from Mr. Marshall's work computer. Is that fair to say?"

"Yes, that's fair."

"If I could ask you to go back to Mr. Marshall's desktop, which Ms. Roy had you bring up earlier."

"Yes, I have it," Ash replied, and opened Marshall's computer on the screen.

"Ms. Roy had you bring up various drafts of the article Mr. Marshall was working on. Could you bring up the draft that was saved on October 19."

"Yes. Here it is," Ash said.

"As you read through the article, you see that there are places where Marshall has *according to a source who wished to remain anonymous,* and then he has in parentheses *(source A)*. Do you see that?"

"I do."

"And if you look through the entire draft, in addition to source A, you'll see there are also references to sources B, C, D, and E. Do you agree with me?"

"Yes, I do," Ash replied.

"Investigator, based on your analysis of the information on Mr. Marshall's computer, were you able to determine the names of sources A through E?" Erin asked.

"No, ma'am. I could not locate anything identifying those sources," Ash replied.

"If I understand your testimony, all of these applications here now were on Mr. Marshall's computer on October 19, correct?"

"That's correct. Nothing was added or deleted," Ash volunteered.

"Thank you, Investigator. You anticipated my next question—nothing was added and nothing was deleted to Mr. Marshall's computer after the time of his death, correct?"

"As I just said, that is correct."

"If you look down the list of applications, there's Microsoft Outlook, Word, Excel, and PowerPoint. There are also contacts, photos, QuickTime Player, iTunes, Skype, Adobe Acrobat—correct?"

"I see those, yes."

"If you look down the applications, you'll see about the fifth from the bottom, an application called Steghide. Do you know what that is?"

"Yes, ma'am. It's what's known as steganography software," Ash replied, his face suddenly betraying a concern.

"And for those of us who are not computer experts, what is steganography software?" Erin asked.

"Steganography software allows a person to hide a message or information in something that's visible to everyone."

"I see," Erin said, bobbing her head. "Did you look to see if Mr. Marshall had used the software."

"Ah, no . . . no, I didn't," Ash replied, his eyes darting to counsel table where Roy and Rivers were looking just as puzzled.

In the months leading up to the trial, Erin and Duane had several debates over how to handle what Geiger and Tinsley had discovered. Ash's expert's report made no reference to the steganography software or decoding the picture to reveal Marshall's sources—meaning, the state didn't know Marshall's other sources. This had left them with an agonizing choice to make: serve an expert's report from Geiger, as they were required to do under the reciprocal discovery rules if they were going to call him as an expert witness, or, make Ash try to use the software on the witness stand to reveal the sources. It was a bit of a Hobson's choice. They had settled on an approach they hoped would give them the best of both worlds.

Here goes nothing, Erin thought.

"Investigator Ash, have you ever used or analyzed the steganography software on Mr. Marshall's computer?" Erin asked, dipping her toe in the water.

"Ah, actually, I haven't," he replied, again allowing his gaze to fall on Rivers and Roy, his expression now a bit pleading.

"Could you open the software for me?" Erin asked, trying her best to appear calm.

"Objection," Rivers intoned, jumping to his feet.

"I'll see counsel at sidebar," Bader said, her demeanor indicating she was just as confused as everyone else.

"Where are you going with this, Counsel?" Bader asked, not even requiring Rivers to expand on why he was objecting.

"Judge, this is the state's computer expert. There's software on the victim's computer that, according to the witness, 'allows a person to hide a message or information in something that's visible to everyone.' Certainly, I should be able to explore with the state's witness whether Mr. Marshall took advantage of that software in hiding information relevant to this case."

Bader eyed Erin suspiciously, but turned to look at Rivers. "Mr. Rivers?"

"Judge, this is outrageous. The witness has testified he didn't look at this software, has never used or analyzed this software, and it appears that this line of questioning is designed to do no more than embarrass the witness."

Bader shifted her focus back to Erin. "Oh, I suspect counsel is aiming at more than embarrassing the witness," she said. "Let me ask you this, Ms. McCabe; has the defense provided an expert report involving the steganography software?"

"No, Your Honor. The defense was relying on the expertise of the state's computer expert," Erin replied, hoping her air of sincerity wasn't too transparent. Erin also was banking on Bader putting aside her years as a prosecutor and doing what they needed her to do.

"Despite not providing a report, can I assume the defense has retained the services of an expert?" Bader asked.

"We have, Your Honor, but solely as a consultant, not as a witness. Accordingly, under the court rules, disclosure wasn't required." Erin replied.

Bader's glare was withering. "I'm not happy, Ms. McCabe. My instincts are telling me that there's more involved here, and I don't like either side being blindsided during the trial."

And yet, Bader was hesitating to sustain the objection.

Erin held her breath. True, she and Swish were skirting on the edge, but when the real fireworks came later on, she needed Bader on their side, and she hoped that whatever sympathy she had garnered as a result of the WCON broadcast hadn't totally dissipated.

"Here's what I'm going to do. I'm not going to embarrass Investigator Ash by requiring him to try and analyze something on a program he admittedly has no experience with. Ms. McCabe, if you want to pursue this further with your own expert, I want an expert report served to the state by the close of business tomorrow. If that's not possible for some reason, I want to know first thing tomorrow morning and I will then consider whether I should extend the deadline or bar your witness. Any questions?" Bader asked.

"No, Judge. Thank you," Erin replied.

"Judge," Rivers interjected, "this isn't fair to the state. The rules require that we be served with any expert's reports at least thirty days before trial. If we get it tomorrow, we will be severely prejudiced."

"Mr. Rivers, I'll grant you it's a close call. But I'm going to give Ms. McCabe the benefit of the doubt and accept that she believed whatever testimony she felt was relevant was something she could obtain from Investigator Ash. I will also say that I am less than impressed with an expert witness on computers who admits that he didn't even bother to open software on the victim's computer—software designed specifically to hide information. That, frankly, is baffling to me. Given those circumstances, what I've tried to achieve is the appropriate balance of the needs of both sides. I believe my ruling provides that balance."

Erin was thankful that they had dodged a bullet. It was also becoming clear to Erin that Bader wasn't terribly impressed with Rivers and his histrionics.

Back at counsel table, she looked down at her legal pad. "Investigator, one last question. In any of the emails you saw on Mr. Marshall's computer, saved or deleted, do you see any emails to or from a Deputy Attorney General Albert Holmes?"

Rivers shot from his seat, but said nothing.

"Do you have an objection, Mr. Rivers?" Bader asked.

"Ah, no. No objection," he said, retaking his seat.

"Do you need the question repeated?" Erin asked.

"No, I remember the question. And the answer is yes, there was an email to DAG Holmes from Mr. Marshall, but no reply email from DAG Holmes. However, Mr. Marshall's email had been deleted and when we tried to recover it, it was indecipherable."

"Did you go back and check for that email on DAG Holmes's computer?"

"Um, no. No, we didn't."

"Thank you, sir. Nothing further."

Her reference to Holmes had hit a nerve. She wasn't sure yet what it meant. Maybe just being sensitive and trying to protect a dead colleague, or maybe . . . or maybe something entirely different.

When they broke for lunch, Roy stayed behind to talk to Investigator Ash.

"Look, based on what McCabe asked you, there's something hidden by that software and you need to find it. My guess, based on her earlier questions, is that Marshall's sources are hidden somewhere, but see what you can come up with. Oh, and do me a favor, check Holmes's emails for anything to and from Marshall."

Walking over to the office they used as their base, Roy mulled over what had happened in the morning's session. She hated feeling that McCabe and Swisher knew things that she and Rivers didn't—like she was playing chess in the dark, but they could see the board.

Then there was her trial partner; what the fuck was up with him? Why in God's name had he leapt to his feet at the mention of Holmes's name? It wasn't even close to an objectionable question . . . although to evaluate Rivers's behavior based on his knowledge of the Rules of Evidence was unfair, since he seemed to have so little. Still, even for Rivers, it seemed strange. She really hadn't known Albert that well, beyond getting Mazer's IA from him and bumping into him from time to time in the office. Still, when he took his own life, and then they trashed him by confirming his arrest for solicitation, well, that didn't sit right. Someone had wanted to make sure that Albert's reputation was destroyed. Poor bastard.

Damn, she thought. This was supposed to be an open-and-shut case. Mazer's prints were in the victim's home; he called twice the day of the murder; his gun was the murder weapon; he was clearly in the vicinity of the house. Sure, motive was a little weak, but they didn't have to prove motive.

But why would he murder the guy he had helped for months?

Damn it. If she was starting to wonder, what were the jurors doing?

CHAPTER 34

AS DUANE WATCHED TROOPER EDWARD STONE STRIDE TO THE WITness stand, he couldn't help but think that he looked like the man was selected directly out of central casting. In keeping with his surname, he stood ramrod straight, as if carved from granite, a bearing befitting the former marine that he was. Stone was dressed in a navy-blue sports jacket, gray slacks, a powder blue shirt, and striped tie. He appeared taller than average, with short brown hair, and a glare from his brown eyes that would strike fear into any motorist unlucky enough to be pulled over by him.

Stone testified that on October 19, he had worked the six p.m. to six a.m. shift. He was assigned to patrol I-287, Mazer being the other trooper assigned to I-287. His shift had been uneventful, one speeding ticket, and one disabled vehicle during the early part of his shift. At eleven thirty p.m., he had returned to the Somerville barracks so that, per standard operating procedure, he could double up with Mazer in one vehicle. They had gone back out on the road at midnight.

"If I understand how things work," Rivers said, "from midnight until six a.m., you and Mr. Mazer rode in the same state police vehicle together as a team."

"That's correct," Stone replied.

"Who drove the vehicle?"

"The defendant, Jon Mazer," Stone said, emphasizing "defendant" in a way that made it seem like a personal poke at Mazer.

"Had you ridden with the defendant before October 19?" Rivers asked.

"Yes, sir. Many times," Stone said.

"Did you notice anything unusual about the defendant's behavior during the time you were together that night?" Rivers asked.

"Objection," Duane said, as he rose to his feet.

Bader brought her fingers to her lips, seeming to consider Duane's objection, then turned to the witness. "When you partnered with the defendant in the past, what was his demeanor like?" she asked Stone.

Duane wanted to object to Bader's question, but he was reluctant to do it in front of the jury and risk offending the judge.

Stone pivoted in the witness chair so he was facing the judge. "Quiet," he replied. "We didn't have a lot in common, so other than the business at hand, we didn't talk too much. *Stoic,* I guess would be a good word to describe him," Stone said in a way that made Duane wonder who had given Stone that "good word" to use.

"And was he any different on October 19?" Bader asked in follow-up.

Duane tensed; again his instinct was to object, but it was the judge's question. Instead, he slowly took his seat, his eyes never leaving the witness.

"He was, Your Honor. He appeared nervous. He was very fidgety. He kept checking his phone. He was so out of sorts that I asked him if everything was okay. He gave me kind of a strange look and said there was a lot of stuff—although he may have used a slightly different word—going on in his life, and he proceeded to tell me that he was thinking of leaving the outfit, which is how troopers refer to the state police."

"Thank you. You may continue, Mr. Rivers," Bader said.

"Trooper, did you notice anything else unusual about the defendant that night?" Rivers asked.

From having read the statement that Stone had given as part of the investigation, Duane knew what was coming, and even though Rivers's question was objectionable, it was better to have Rivers asking the questions than Bader. The last thing they wanted was the jury to perceive Bader's questioning as an indication that she was siding with the state.

"Yes, sir. I noticed that on his right pants leg, the leg that I could see from the passenger seat, there was what appeared to be blood about four inches up from the bottom of his pants leg on the front of his pants," Stone replied.

"Did you say anything about this, what appeared to be blood, to him?"

"I did. I sarcastically said, 'What happened to your leg, Jon, cut yourself shaving?' When I said it to him, he appeared startled, then glanced down at his leg, and said, 'Oh, earlier I came across a dead deer in the fast lane, so I stopped and dragged it off to the grass median to avoid an accident. Must've gotten some blood on me.' "

"Did you have any further conversation with him about the blood?"

"No, sir. Nothing further."

"Trooper, what is the protocol if you come across a dead animal in the travel portion of the roadway?"

"In a situation like the one the defendant described, the policy is for the trooper to stop their vehicle behind the carcass, activate their overhead lights, and call in to dispatch for them to get either a Department of Transportation crew out to the scene or an animal control officer from the local municipality. If the trooper feels the situation is extremely hazardous, dragging it off the roadway is permissible, but it must then immediately be reported to dispatch."

"And there would be a record of any calls to dispatch, is that accurate, Trooper?" Rivers asked.

"It is, sir. The state police use a computer-aided dispatch system, CAD for short, and all calls to dispatch are reflected in the CAD records," Stone said with a wisp of a grin as he looked in Mazer's direction.

"Thank you," Rivers said with a faint grin of his own.

Duane rose and walked so he was no more than six or seven

feet from the witness stand. "You and Mr. Mazer didn't like each other, is that fair to say, Trooper?" Duane asked, wasting no time with preliminaries.

"Yes, sir. I think that's fair," Stone conceded.

"In fact, approximately a year before October 19, 2009, Mr. Mazer filed an Internal Affairs complaint against you and others for, among other things, harassing him because he's gay, correct?"

"He did," Stone responded. "Which was unsubstantiated," he added.

Bader gave what looked to be a disapproving frown. "Mr. Stone, just answer the question you're asked. There is no need for you to volunteer information, even if you think it's helpful." Turning her gaze back to Duane, Bader said, "Continue."

"You said Mr. Mazer appeared nervous and kept checking his phone."

"Yes, sir."

"What kind of phone did he have, Trooper?"

"I don't remember, exactly."

"Let's see if we can narrow it down. Was it a smartphone, like a BlackBerry or iPhone, or just a regular old flip phone?"

"My recollection is that it was a BlackBerry, but I don't remember exactly what it was."

"But you do remember he kept checking it, so it was on?"

"Yeah," he said, the "yes, sir" momentarily gone. "It was on," he said, a question hanging in his voice.

"What time was it that you noticed the blood on Mr. Mazer's pants leg?"

"I don't know, sir. I wasn't checking my watch," he replied glibly.

"Well, was it five minutes after you started patrolling together, an hour, four hours—can you give me an estimate?"

"I'm not certain. Maybe an hour or so."

"Was it one big spot, or did it look like it had splattered on him?"

"Um, it was splattered, sir."

"Describe it for us?" Duane said, moving a little closer to the witness stand.

"Again, I really don't remember. I just noticed blood on his pants leg. I wasn't focused on it at the time. Only after the defendant was arrested did I remember about the blood."

"Your Honor, I'd ask that anything after the witness responded, 'I don't remember,' be stricken as unresponsive."

"I agree with you, Mr. Swisher, that it was unresponsive, but the jury has already heard it, and I assume Mr. Rivers would just ask it on redirect, so I'll allow it. But I'm again cautioning the witness to answer the question and trust the state's attorneys to ask any follow-up questions," Bader said.

"You said the blood was on the front of his pants, about four inches up from the bottom of his pants leg." Duane reached down and touched his own suit pants. "Let the record reflect that I'm touching my own pants leg, in the front of my pants, where the crease is, about four inches above the bottom. Trooper Stone, you see where I'm touching my pants—is that approximately where you noticed the blood on Mr. Mazer's pants?"

"Yeah, that looks right," Stone responded.

"The uniform pants that you wear, they're dark navy blue, correct?"

Stone hesitated, seeming to suddenly appreciate the implication of Duane's questions. "Yeah," he said.

"And all troopers wear the same color uniform pants, correct?"

"Yes," Stone responded.

"Thank you," Duane said, ending his cross. Stone looked confused, as if expecting more questions. But Duane hadn't harped on whether it was even possible for Stone to see blood on the front of Mazer's dark navy pants, in a dark car, because when Erin gave her summation to the jury, she could point out how unlikely it was for Stone to have been able to see what he claimed, as well as the fact that the state's expert had found no blood on the pants seized from Mazer. The temptation every lawyer had to resist was asking the one question too many. Save it for the jury and argue that Stone was full of shit.

Besides, Stone had committed an unforced error with his testimony. The state's own expert had testified Mazer's phone was off the whole time Mazer and Stone rode together. *False in one, false in all*, Duane thought, knowing that the judge would charge the jury that if they found that a witness lied about one thing, they were free to disregard any or all other portions of the witness's testimony. Of course, the same charge applied to their witnesses—one that could sink Jon if he lied to protect DeAngelis.

The rest of the afternoon was spent with Roy questioning a witness from the state police on what CAD records were and how they were maintained. He testified that there were no records of any calls by Mazer to dispatch about a deer carcass. He also went through Mazer's dispatch records for October 19, indicating he had made a stop at 7:14 p.m., but there was no indication that he was dispatched on any calls at 7:03 p.m., the time a call was made from his burner to Marshall's number.

When the witness was done with his direct testimony, Erin indicated that she had no cross-examination.

"Who do you have lined up for tomorrow?" Bader asked after she had let the jury go for the day. When Roy went to stand, Bader waved her down with her hand. "We're still on the record, but the jury's gone, so relax a little. No need to stand."

"Thank you, Judge. At this point, we intend on calling Trooper David Britton and, although we'll review things tonight, I believe he'll be our last witness."

"Good," Bader said. "Ms. McCabe, Mr. Swisher, I presume you will have a motion at the end of the state's case?"

"Yes, Your Honor," Erin replied.

"Ms. McCabe, if your motion for judgment of acquittal is denied, do you anticipate that you will be presenting any witness as part of a defense case?"

"I do, Judge," Erin replied. "And anticipating Your Honor's next question, I would expect to have approximately four witnesses. I also anticipate there may be an evidentiary hearing required with regard to certain testimony from one of the witnesses. Finally, Judge, I was able to speak with our computer expert over the lunch break today, and retained him to testify. He advised me that he should have his report by around four o'clock tomorrow. As soon as I can, I will forward it to Mr. Rivers and Ms. Roy."

"Thank you for that, Ms. McCabe," Bader said. "Let's do this: we'll conclude the state's case tomorrow, hear the motion for a judgment of acquittal, and then, again assuming the motion is denied, I'll expect the defense to start first thing Wednesday morning. Anything further?" she asked.

"No, Your Honor," Erin and Roy said simultaneously.

Later, Roy sat in her office. She had just spent two hours preparing Britton for his testimony tomorrow. She didn't need him trying to embellish like Stone had. Jesus Christ, what was Stone thinking, volunteering that Mazer was looking at his phone? He had never told them that before. She knew what McCabe would do with that in summation. The jurors would never believe Stone now. Fortunately, he wasn't critical to prove their case.

Time to go home, she thought. She just needed Britton to hold up tomorrow and she'd be good. There was no way Bader would grant the motion for acquittal—even with Rivers arguing it, she thought, allowing herself a small snort.

The phone on her desk suddenly sprang to life. She glanced at her watch, 6:48 p.m. Who the hell would be calling her now?

"Roy," she answered after the second ring.

"Carol, this is Joe Ash. Do you have a minute?"

"Sure. What's up?"

"I did what you asked me to do, and candidly, I can't make any sense out of this software. I'm sorry."

"No worries, Joe. They're supposed to serve an expert's report on us tomorrow afternoon. As soon as I get it, I'll let you know." She paused. "By the way, did you search for Holmes's email?"

"I did. It's unusual, but shortly after his death, his email was wiped," he said.

"Wiped? What do you mean?"

"I mean, I can't find it on the server. Perhaps it was downloaded, but it's not there."

"Okay, thanks," she said, hanging up. *Weird,* she thought. Why did she have a queasy feeling about Albert? Based on the news after his death, it sounded like he was gay, or at least bi, but he had been on the IA that cleared Stone, Britton, and others. And he had been part of the task force that found that the Lords didn't exist. How was he involved?

McCabe knew something she didn't, and that was the worst place for any trial lawyer to be in. *Shit.*

CHAPTER 35

ERIN HAD BEEN UP SINCE FOUR A.M. SHE WOKE UP TO PEE, THE brain turned on, the adrenaline kicked in, and sleep became impossible. She had tossed and turned for another hour, before finally giving up and getting out of bed. And as she did, some part of her brain laughed at her, whispering, "Get used to it. This is what it'll be like when baby makes three."

As Erin started the coffee, she played back the conversation she had had yesterday with Liz, who was now five and a half months pregnant and feeling great. Liz had laughed when she told Erin that this was definitely Erin's child, because it felt like the baby was already playing soccer, she kicked so much. Her next ultrasound was on Thursday, and Erin was crushed that because of the trial, she couldn't attend, but she took some solace in knowing that Mark was going to be there.

But as excited as she was about the baby, that wasn't the reason she couldn't sleep. Today Trooper David Britton would take the stand, and depending on how her cross went, it could either make or break the case.

Much like Stone, Britton had a commanding demeanor. He knew to look directly at Rivers when being asked a question, and then he would pivot slightly so that his answer was directed to the jury. He was not as tall as Stone, perhaps five nine, but he was solidly built, with short, jet-black hair and ice-blue eyes that were both beautiful and cold at the same time.

"You testified you spoke with Mr. Marshall about the article he was working on; could you estimate how many times you spoke to him about it?" Rivers asked.

"I'd estimate about five times," Britton replied crisply.

"How did you come to talk to him?" Rivers continued.

"He called me and asked if I would talk to him about an article he was doing. I agreed and we met at the Reo Diner in Woodbridge," Britton responded.

"And what did you discuss at that meeting?"

"He told me he was doing an article on the Lords of Discipline, and wanted to speak to me about it. I told him that I had heard all the rumors and there was no such group. He told me that he had information I was involved with a group by that name, and I laughed and said he must be speaking to Jon Mazer, because Mazer kept spreading rumors about me. In fact, he had filed an IA complaint against me that had been dismissed."

"Where did you meet the approximately four other times you met?" Rivers asked.

"I know we met once in the living room of his house. I remember two other times at the same diner, and then one time at a bar in Woodbridge, the Liberty Tavern, I think is the name of the place."

"What did you discuss at those meetings?"

"Mostly he was trying to get me to confirm information he said he had received from other people. He always maintained the confidentiality of his sources, but based on the things he was asking me about, I was fairly certain that his main source was the defendant."

"Why is that?" Rivers asked, now in the flow and seeming to be enjoying himself.

"Because all the things Mr. Marshall was asking about involved allegations Mazer had made up. Mazer was hung up on there being this secret group in the state police and that I was the leader who was out to get him. I told Russell . . . I'm sorry, Mr. Marshall, that I believed Mr. Mazer was paranoid because there were no Lords and nobody was out to get him because he was gay. Honestly, nobody cared who the guy slept with."

"Did you discuss anything else?"

"At one point, after I said something about Mr. Mazer, he asked me why I thought Mr. Mazer would make up these stories. And I told him that I really didn't know. I always felt like I treated him just like I treated all the other troopers, but I warned Mr. Marshall that Mazer had a nasty temper, and I had seen him lose it on a guy we pulled over when we were riding as a team. Not to mention that he had tried to ruin my career with his false IA. After that, most of the guys, I'm sorry, most of the other troopers, didn't want to ride with him because they didn't trust him," Britton said.

"When was the last time you saw Mr. Marshall before he was murdered on October 19?"

Britton blew out a breath and looked up at the ceiling. "I'm not exactly sure when, but I'd say shortly after Labor Day. It was the day we met at the Liberty, and honestly, when I left there, I thought the story was dead because he told me he didn't trust his main source. My last words to him were, 'Watch your back with Mazer. If you publish the story and out him as gay, he'll be pissed. If you don't publish it, he'll be pissed that once again he didn't get me, but this time he'll blame you, instead of the guys in IA.' "

"Thank you," Rivers said, gesturing with his hand to Erin that it was her turn.

"Good morning, Trooper Britton," Erin began with a small grin. "Do you know Drew Smith?"

"Ah, the name sounds familiar. Perhaps you can help me out?" Britton said.

"Sure," Erin replied, her tone soft, her demeanor relaxed. "Drew Smith is a radio talk show host on WTRA, 108.2FM. He has the morning-drive-time show. Does that help refresh your recollection?"

"Oh, yes. Of course. Yes, I know Mr. Smith."

"Did you ever appear on his show, Trooper?" Erin asked.

"No, ma'am. Never," Britton replied confidently.

"Did you ever speak with Mr. Smith?"

"I may have. We might have met once and had a conversation."

"Where did that conversation you had with Smith take place?" Erin asked.

"Oh, I honestly don't recall," Britton responded.

"How about in the studio of WTRA? Does that refresh your recollection?"

Britton's eyes narrowed and his nostrils flared. "I don't recall that."

"Well, you were in Mr. Smith's studio at one point, weren't you?" Erin asked, allowing her tone to shift slightly.

"Like I said, I may have been, but I don't remember being in his studio."

"Regardless of where it was, did Mr. Smith ever record a conversation with you?"

"Not that I'm aware of," Britton said, trying to sound indignant.

"As you've testified on direct, you're aware of allegations that there's a group of troopers within the state police who call themselves the Lords of Discipline, correct?"

By the expression on Britton's face, Erin couldn't tell if he was relieved she had left interrogation about Smith or concerned about the new question about the Lords.

"I've heard that allegation, but I also know that it was fully investigated by a task force set up by the attorney general, which found it didn't exist," he said defiantly.

Erin hadn't really cared that he had gone well beyond her question, but Bader cautioned him nonetheless to answer the question and not volunteer.

"And in fact, you were contacted by the task force requesting information about the allegations, isn't that right?"

"I believe I was," he replied, becoming a little more circumspect.

"And you refused to cooperate with the task force, correct?"

"On the advice of counsel, I did refuse because it was a witch hunt," Britton responded, drawing an icy stare from Bader, but when Erin caught Bader's eye and gave a small shake of her head, Bader said nothing.

"And who was your counsel?" Erin asked.

Erin was a little surprised when it was Roy who stood to object and not Rivers. Nevertheless, the judge quickly asked for counsel to come to sidebar.

"What's the objection, Ms. Roy? Counsel has only asked for the name of the attorney, not what was said."

Roy shifted uneasily from one foot to the other. "Judge, he was represented by Mr. Rivers."

Bader's sardonic grin was priceless. "Well, Ms. Roy, while I understand that may be a bit embarrassing for the state, it's not objectionable."

"Overruled," Bader said when everyone was back in their places. "You may answer the question, Trooper."

"I was represented by Mr. Rivers," Britton responded.

"And just to be clear for the jury, Trooper, you are referring to this Mr. Rivers," Erin said, gesturing in Rivers's direction. "Assistant Attorney General Ward Rivers."

"I am," he replied.

"Have you ever heard any allegations that you are the leader of the Lords of Discipline?" Erin asked, taking a step closer to the witness stand.

"Allegations?" Britton asked.

"Yes, Trooper Britton. Didn't you testify on direct that Jon Mazer had alleged that you, David Britton, were the leader of the Lords of Discipline within the New Jersey State Police?"

"Like I said, I've heard it alleged, but it's not true," Britton responded, smiling.

"In fact, the Internal Affairs complaint filed by my client, Jon Mazer, alleged you were the leader of the Lords of Discipline, correct?"

"I was never shown the IA, Counsel," Britton replied with a self-satisfied smirk. "I was interviewed as part of the IA investigation and I denied under oath being part of any such group, just like I'm denying it now," he answered, his voice growing louder.

"Are you familiar with a book called *The Guardians of Discipline?*"

Britton seemed caught off guard by the sudden shift in subject. "Ah, yes. Yes, I do recall that. And that refreshes my memory to one of your earlier questions that I did speak with Mr. Smith because he told me he was writing a book, and he asked me some questions about 'being a cop,' as he put it."

"Do you recall Mr. Smith publicly thanking you for the help you provided him with his book?"

"No. Unless he mentioned my name on his radio show or something like that. But there's no reason for him to thank me," Britton said.

"Did you ever buy a copy of *The Guardians of Discipline*, Trooper Britton?"

"No," Britton said with a laugh.

"Did Mr. Smith ever give you a copy?"

"I don't remember getting one."

Swish reached into a briefcase sitting next to him and took out copies of *The Guardians of Discipline,* then handed them over to Erin.

"Judge, if I could mark this as exhibit D-3, please," Erin said, handing a copy of the book to the clerk, as Swish handed another copy to Rivers and Roy. Then she handed a copy to Britton. "Did you know that you were specifically referenced in the acknowledgments section?"

"Oh, that was nice of him. If I ever see him again, I'll have to thank him," he responded glibly.

"Do you see the little Post-it Note at the back of the book? Could you please open the book to that page." When he had complied, she said, "Could you please read the portion of the page that I have highlighted in yellow?"

Britton's brow knitted, and his blue eyes seemed to grow even colder. *"I am also extremely grateful to David Britton, who is the inspiration for this book, and who provided me with invaluable insights into what it's like to be on the front lines of law enforcement's current efforts to combat crime."*

"Mr. Smith says you were the inspiration for the book. Do you know what he's referring to, Trooper Britton?" Erin asked, knowing what was coming next.

"No idea," he replied, his anger starting to grow.

Erin walked back and retrieved two documents from a folder, handing one to Rivers and having the clerk mark the second as exhibit D-4.

"Do you recognize this, Trooper Britton?" Erin asked.

Britton looked at the document for several seconds. "It looks like someone played around with an image of a post on my Facebook page," he said.

"Are you saying this really isn't from your Facebook page, Trooper?"

"I'm saying it looks like it was photoshopped," he replied.

"Is your Facebook page the 'Britton Invasion'?" she asked.

"Yeah, but I never posted this."

"So, you never posted on the Britton Invasion Facebook page a recommendation that other troopers read *The Guardians of Discipline*, and implied you were the role model for the main character in the book?"

"No, someone else must have posted that."

"If we went to your Facebook page now," she said as she walked back to counsel table where there was a laptop, "we would be able to see that you never posted that?"

She scooped up the laptop as if ready to bring it over.

"As I'm thinking about it, I remember that someone sent something like this to me as a joke, and I guess I must've just reposted it," he said with a shrug. "I might have added the part about being a role model. It was a joke. I've never even read the book."

"I see," Erin said, placing the laptop back down. "You never read the book *The Guardians of Discipline*, but you joked you were the role model for the main character?"

"Objection. Asked and answered," Rivers said.

"I'll withdraw the question, Your Honor," Erin said, knowing her point had been made.

Erin slowly approached the witness until she was standing about three feet from the witness box. When she stopped, her demeanor seemed to shift.

"Trooper Britton, isn't it true that you referred to Mr. Mazer as a 'cock-sucking faggot'?" she demanded, her voice now that of an avenging angel.

"No! That's not true," Britton fired back.

"How about 'bone smuggler'? Haven't you referred to Mr. Mazer as a 'bone smuggler'?"

"Never," Britton said, his eyes on fire.

"Haven't you referred to gay men as 'fag,' 'faggots' and 'poofs'?" she challenged, her voice angry.

"I object, Judge," Rivers bellowed.

"Ms. McCabe, do you have a good faith basis for these questions?" Bader asked, her skepticism evident.

"Absolutely, Judge," Erin replied, with a certainty that seemed to catch everyone off guard.

"I'll allow it. But I caution you, Ms. McCabe, there had better be proof," she said sternly.

"I fully understand, Your Honor," she said, looking over her shoulder at the jury, who were watching like they were at a boxing match, waiting for the next punch to be thrown. And out of the corner of her eye, Erin caught a glimpse of Roy's mouth agape, in either shock or terror for what was happening.

"How about lesbians, Trooper Britton? Do you recall referring to them as 'dykes'?"

"No," his tone still defiant.

"How about female state troopers, have you referred to them as 'cunts'?"

"I can't remember ever saying that," he said, but this time the uncertainty in his voice was palpable.

"In the last five years, have you referred to Black people using the *N* word?" Erin said, her face now a mask of anger.

Rivers shot to his feet, but before he could even voice an objection, Bader motioned him to sit. Britton, having seen Rivers stand, appeared confused, looking first at Rivers, then at the judge.

"You may answer, Trooper," Bader said.

"No, I would never do that." But there was a hint of doubt.

"How about, in the last five years, have you ever called Hispanic people 'spics,'" Erin asked, her expression seeming to suggest that he knew he had.

"No, not that I recall," he replied.

"After your shift was over at six p.m. on October 19, did you have occasion to return to the barracks that night?"

"No. I went home and went to bed," he replied.

Erin walked back to counsel table. Her adrenaline had her on overdrive and she needed to regain control of her emotions. She took a deep breath and looked at her notes for no other reason than to regain her equilibrium.

"Did you know a deputy attorney general by the name of Albert Holmes?" Erin asked.

"Um, I met a lot of the folks over in the AG's Office. I may have met him."

"Judge, I'd like to reserve the right to recall Trooper Britton on the defense case. There are certain pieces of evidence I need to introduce before I . . ." Erin was going to say confront, but reconsidered her words. "Before I question Trooper Britton concerning that evidence."

"Very good," Bader responded. "Trooper you are free to go, but please stay in touch with Mr. Rivers and Ms. Roy. They will advise you when, or if, you need to return. I also caution you not to speak with anyone concerning your testimony."

Two hours later Erin and Duane sat in the Middlesex County Adult Corrections Center with Jon. After Britton left, Bader had let the jury go. She then made short shrift of Erin's motion for a judgment of acquittal, finding there was more than ample evidence to allow the case to go to the jury.

"Thanks," Jon said to Erin.

"For what?" she replied.

"For taking that asshole down a few pegs. Do you think you'll get in the recording of him and Smith?"

"We'll see. We should know tomorrow."

Jon inhaled and then blew it out slowly.

"How you holding up?" Erin asked.

"Not sure what's worse, solitary or being on trial," he said, followed by a forced laugh. "At least I got some sleep when I was in solitary. Now, I'm up in the middle of the night thinking about my testimony . . . and what's at stake."

"I know this will sound hollow, but try not to worry too much. All you have to do is tell the truth," Erin said, wanting to add "and nothing but the truth," but knew this wasn't the time to revisit what he'd say about Gabe. She was sure they'd have one more fight over that before he testified, but not now.

"Do you think I'll testify tomorrow?" Mazer asked.

"Theoretically, it's possible," Erin said. "But honestly, we'd have to get through both Geiger and Smith, and my bet is there's going to be a lot of fireworks when we call Peter Geiger to the stand tomorrow, and even more with Smith, so I think you're safe until Thursday at the earliest." Erin glanced at her watch. "I'm sure several heads exploded at DCJ when Roy and Rivers received Geiger's report about thirty minutes ago. It should be an interesting day tomorrow."

"How the fuck did you miss this?" Rivers screamed at Joe Ash, shaking a copy of Peter Geiger's expert's report.

"Ward, it was in his iTunes file, under miscellaneous artists, and then as the Britton Invasion, which is right under the British Invasion. Why would I even look there?" Ash said.

"*They* fucking found it!" Rivers yelled. "How the fuck did they find it, and you don't. Explain that fuckup to me, Joe."

"Maybe it's not Britton on the recording?" Ash offered.

"Oh, trust me, that's Dave Britton's voice. We sure as shit heard enough of it this morning as he dug himself a big fucking hole," Rivers said. He suddenly turned to Roy. "And why the hell didn't you know about this? You're supposedly the trial expert."

"Maybe because up until last night, you were the only one to talk to Britton. It was only after good ol' Trooper Stone shit the bed that you even let me speak to him. I told you six months ago to get me access to their social media, but you said you had it covered. You want to know who's to blame, Ward? Take a good look in the goddamn mirror," Roy said.

"You fucking insolent bitch," Rivers spit out. "Who the fuck do you think you are talking to me like that?"

She suddenly stood, placing her hands on the conference room table. "Who do I think I am? I think I'm the only person in this room who knows how to try a fucking case. That's who the fuck I think I am."

CHAPTER 36

As Erin predicted, the shit hit the fan as soon as Bader came on the bench Wednesday morning. The only thing that surprised her was that it was Rivers on his feet arguing; usually he left the legal arguments to Roy. But as Erin watched Rivers bloviate about how the state had been sandbagged by the defense's late service of an expert's report, she couldn't make out what was going on with Roy. Roy had her head down staring at her legal pad, but she didn't appear to be taking any notes. She seemed content to let Rivers run on at the mouth.

"Let me hear from the defense," Bader said, finally interrupting Rivers.

Erin stood. "Good morning, Your Honor."

"Good morning, Ms. McCabe," Bader replied, even though Erin could tell that this was probably not a good morning so far. "It seems the state is upset by the contents and timing of your expert's report. Whom do you plan on calling as your first witness?"

"Peter Geiger, Your Honor, who is our computer expert. However, in response to Mr. Rivers's claims that we sandbagged the state, as Your Honor will recall, I wanted to present the same evidence Mr. Geiger will testify to through the state's expert, Mr. Ash. As Mr. Geiger will testify, he accessed Mr. Marshall's computer and looked at the same computer data, apps, etcetera that the state's expert looked at. The only difference is that Mr. Geiger found things that, apparently, for reasons I don't know, the state's expert did not." Erin stretched out her arms and turned her hands palms up to indicate her lack of an explanation. "As to any prejudice to the state, allow me to take them one at a time." Erin glanced down at the notes on her legal pad before continuing.

"Yesterday, I asked Mr. Ash if he was familiar with steganography software, which he was, and then, whether he had noticed it on Mr. Marshall's computer, which he had—he had just never opened it. Our expert, Mr. Geiger, did. And what he discovered was that the actual names of the individuals listed in the various drafts of Marshall's article as source A, source B, etcetera, were hidden in a picture, and by using the software, Mr. Geiger was able to decode their names. Since all of those individuals, with one exception, have been listed as potential defense witnesses, there is no prejudice to the state, because I assume the state interviewed all of them, or could have, because we had put the state on notice they were potential witnesses."

"You mentioned an exception; who was the exception?" Bader asked.

"Judge, the one exception was Deputy Attorney General Albert Holmes, who unfortunately is deceased."

Bader nodded and Erin took Bader's lack of follow-up as her cue to continue.

"The second thing our expert will testify to is the fact that in Mr. Marshall's iTunes file there is a recording labeled the 'Britton Invasion' that contains a conversation between Drew Smith, the radio host and author, and Trooper David Britton. The recording is approximately forty-five minutes long, and I only plan on having my expert describe where the recording is located on Mr. Marshall's computer. In terms of the authentication of the recording, I plan on doing that through Mr. Smith, who again is listed as a witness on our witness list. And, as I know you will recall, Judge, Mr. Ash testified several times that nothing on Mr. Marshall's computer had been altered since the date of his death. What's there now was there then. The only information our expert included in his report that is technically new is a potential new witness, a gentleman by the name of Scott Lewis, who is a sound engineer for WTRA, and who was the person who sent the recording to Mr. Marshall. Although I believe Mr. Lewis's testimony would, most likely, be duplicative, we have amended our witness list to include him, and given the late notice, if he is needed as a witness, we would make him our last witness to provide the state with ample time to prepare, if they need it."

When Erin paused and looked at Bader, there was the faintest of grins on Bader's face.

"Judge, simply put, all of the individuals who might testify, with the exception of Mr. Lewis, were listed as witnesses, and all of the physical evidence that our expert examined is the exact same evidence the state's had in its possession since it seized Mr. Marshall's computer. If the state is surprised, it's not because we sandbagged them, it's because they failed to find what was right in front of their noses."

Bader laid her reading glasses down in front of her. "The recording, assuming it's admissible . . . will I need to hold a Rule 403 hearing outside the presence of the jury?" she asked, referring to a hearing in which she'd have to decide if the evidence was likely to be so unduly prejudicial that it outweighed any probative value and therefore should be excluded from being considered by the jury.

Rivers was on his feet quickly. "Yes, Your Honor, what is on the recording is highly prejudicial to the state."

Erin gave Rivers the side-eye. "Judge, the only reason the recording is prejudicial to the state is because it proves one of their witnesses perjured himself," Erin said dismissively, turning to face Rivers, who returned her look with a menacing glare.

"I'm going to take a brief recess. I'd like to see counsel in chambers," Bader said.

Once the four of them were assembled in front of Bader's desk, she said, "Listen, we're off the record, so let me ask you, Mr. Rivers, Ms. Roy, is there any doubt as to the authenticity of the recording, and if not, why don't I just do the 403 now? Let me listen to the tape, figure out if I'm going to allow it, and if I am, how much and what parts. Unless you can prove to me that the recording is bogus, don't we have to get to the same spot eventually? Let's just do it now."

"No, Judge. The state doesn't want you listening to the recording," Rivers said.

Bader sighed. "Mr. Rivers, I understand you may want the recording to magically disappear, but unless you can convince me it's a fake, sooner or later, I'll hear it."

Erin watched as Rivers's eyes narrowed and his face grew red, his anger barely contained. But he made no further response.

"What about you, Ms. McCabe, Mr. Swisher, any thoughts?" Bader asked.

Erin looked at Duane, who nodded. "We're fine with going to the 403 now, Judge."

"Judge, the state is adamant in opposing doing the 403 now," Rivers said.

Bader seemed to ponder the situation for a moment. "All right, here's what we'll do. Ms. McCabe, proceed with your expert, but do not have him play the recording, then call Mr. Smith. I want counsel to confer alone with your respective experts and agree on enough of the recording to play to see if Mr. Smith can authenticate it. Then I'll make a determination as to whether I listen to the rest outside the presence of the jury to decide on the admissibility of the recording."

Fifteen minutes later, everyone was assembled back in the courtroom. As Erin had outlined in chambers, Peter Geiger explained to the jury about the steganography software, decoding the photo, and how they had connected the names to the sources. Then, using the large screen displaying Marshall's desktop, he opened the iTunes application and showed where the file called the Britton Invasion was located. He testified that they had found it by opening the "Recently Added" folder and reviewing all iTunes downloads Marshall had received in the last nine months. He then explained that by going to the downloads file, they had been able to locate the original downloading of the Britton Invasion MP3. Next, when they right clicked on it, a drop-down menu appeared with one of the selections being "Get Info." By clicking on that, an information box appeared, which showed that the file was downloaded on June 15, 2009, at 8:03 a.m. and had not been modified since then. The last date it was opened was October 5, 2009, at 4:54 p.m.

Finally, he indicated that the file was received as an attachment from a Yahoo email account belonging to Scott Lewis.

Despite his previous outrage, after consulting briefly with Joseph Ash, Rivers had no cross-examination.

Next up was Drew Smith. When Dylan had served Smith with the trial subpoena eleven days earlier, Smith had threatened not to show up in court. He had screamed at Dylan that he knew nothing about this case, and he wasn't going to tolerate being questioned by some trannie freak. His last words to Dylan were that McCabe would be hearing from the station's attorney, which she had, and who had quickly agreed with Erin that the subpoena was valid and Smith would appear. Yesterday, when Erin called the station's lawyer to confirm Smith's appearance, she had let the lawyer know that he should advise Smith that they had a recording of Smith and Trooper David Britton. Message delivered—Erin had thought when she hung up.

Erin had no idea what would happen when she began questioning Smith. He had refused to speak with Dylan, so it was kind of like walking into a dark, abandoned house at midnight with a penlight flashlight—you knew shit was there, you just didn't know where, and all you could hope was you saw it before you tripped over it.

Smith sauntered up to the witness stand with an air of self-confidence befitting someone accustomed to being treated as a celebrity. He appeared to be in his early fifties, with thick, salt and pepper hair. He wore a sports coat and slacks, his pale blue shirt open at the collar. He answered Erin's preliminary questions easily, boasting about his job as a radio talk show host. Erin quickly realized that Smith was in entertainer mode, not in angry subpoenaed witness mode—it was as if he was trying to charm the jury to gain new listeners for his show.

Smith described being introduced to Britton at a party thrown by a mutual friend who owned a number of bars and restaurants in Princeton, Somerville, and New Brunswick. Smith said he had taken an immediate liking to Britton because they shared a lot of the same political views.

"Mr. Smith, based on this meeting with Trooper Britton, you decided to invite him to appear as a guest on your radio show, is that correct?"

"I did."

"Why did you want to interview Trooper Britton?"

"I thought it would be fascinating for my listeners to hear about what it was like to be a cop in an environment that's very hostile to police officers," he said.

Erin paused, as if contemplating her next question, but she was actually trying to measure the jury's reaction to his last answer. At least based on their body language, not all of them were as enamored with the police as Smith was. "Did that interview ever take place?" Erin asked.

"It did," Smith responded.

"Did that interview ever air on WTRA?"

"It did not," Smith replied, his responses suddenly very clipped and a lot less conversational.

"Was the interview recorded?" she probed.

"It was," he replied.

"Why didn't the interview air?" she asked.

"Let's just say, at some point, I realized both Trooper Britton and I had been talking more as if we were in a locker room, and some of our statements were, how shall I put it, politically incorrect and perhaps offensive to some of my listeners. So, I told my sound engineer to stop the recording."

"Did you tell your sound engineer anything else?" she asked.

"I did. I told him to erase the recording."

"Do you know if he did?" Erin asked.

"I never asked, but I suspect that based on what I've learned about why I'm here today, he didn't," Smith responded, his tone no longer that of a radio host, just someone resigned to their fate.

"Would you be able to recognize the tape, if we played the beginning of it?"

"Probably," he responded in an apparent effort to leave his options open.

"Who was the sound engineer who recorded it?"

"Scott Lewis," he replied.

"And was Mr. Lewis's employment with WTRA terminated last night?" she asked, knowing the answer. Dylan had called her with the news right after speaking with Lewis. Erin felt pretty shitty about costing Lewis his job, but when placed on the scales, Jon's life was far more important. *Sometimes you just have to do shitty things*, she thought.

"He was terminated last night for breaching company policy with regard to providing someone with the recording without authorization." His response apparently aimed at portraying himself as an innocent bystander, not involved in the decision.

Erin suspected it was bullshit, but decided there was nothing to be gained by going there. She had made her point to the jury, and at the end of the day, sending the recording to a reporter probably was a serious breach of company policy.

"Thank you," Erin said, looking up at Bader to indicate that it was now time for the next step.

Erin and Roy had worked out an agreement that they would play the first minute of the recording for Smith, and if he acknowledged this was an accurate recording and represented the interview, the judge would excuse the jury, and then she would hold a confidential, closed hearing—no members of the public or press allowed—to listen to the whole tape with the attorneys and witness present. If the witness confirmed it was accurate, she would then rule on its admissibility.

With both Geiger and Ash gathered around a laptop, they opened the MP3 and hit play. An unknown voice stated, "Recorded February 29, 2008, eleven thirty a.m.—three, two, one." In the next beat, the unmistakable baritone of Drew Smith came out of the speakers set up in the courtroom. He proceeded to provide his standard opening remarks, followed by his introduction of Britton, with Britton then thanking Smith for inviting him to the show and, at Smith's request, Britton doing a brief intro of himself. As soon as Britton concluded his intro, Ash stopped the playback.

"Mr. Smith, was that your voice on the recording?" Erin asked.

"It was."

"And do you recognize the voice of the person who introduced himself as David Britton to in fact be the voice of Trooper David Britton?" Erin asked.

"I do," Smith said.

After that, the jury was told there needed to be a hearing outside their presence and were sent to lunch and told that after lunch they should return to the jury assembly room, not the courtroom. Bader then had the courtroom cleared of all spectators, and directed Ash and Geiger to play the recording.

Forty-five minutes later, Bader took off her glasses, holding them in her left hand, as she dragged her right hand across the bridge of her nose and rubbed her right eye.

She turned to Smith, who was still sitting in the witness box, his shoulders slumped.

"Is that recording an accurate version of your conversation with Trooper Britton?" she asked.

Smith, who was never shy about expressing his views on his show, chewed a bit on his lower lip. "That it is, Judge," he replied, with a touch of gallows humor.

"Mr. Smith, I'm going to excuse you for the rest of the day. I want you back here tomorrow morning at nine to continue your testimony. Counsel, I'm going to break for lunch. Be back at two because I will bring the jury up and release them for the day, and then we are going to have a hearing to determine if I'm going to admit any of this recording, and if I do, what parts. We're adjourned," she said, gathering some papers from her desk and standing. "Oh," she said. "Does anyone have a copy of this on a thumb drive or CD?"

Erin, who had listened to it dozens of times, reached into her briefcase. "I have a copy on CD, Your Honor, which I represent is unaltered."

"Any problems if I use Ms. McCabe's CD?" she said to Rivers and Roy.

Roy glanced at Rivers, waiting for him to respond. When he didn't, Roy said, "No, Your Honor. I accept Ms. McCabe's representation."

"One more thing," Bader said. "I want both Mr. Ash and Mr. Geiger back here at two for the hearing," she commanded, before bounding down the steps and through the door that led to her chambers.

"Whatya think?" Jon asked, when the three of them were sitting in his holding cell.

"I don't know," Swish said. "She's hard to read. There's no question it's prejudicial. Between the two of them, they use the *N* word ten times, 'spics' three times, 'faggot' half a dozen, 'dyke' twice, 'cunts' twice, and then, when they're talking about the IA you filed, Britton calls you every homophobic slur in the books, and honestly, one I had never even heard before."

Erin had listened to Britton and Smith throwing slurs and laughing about it dozens of times. There was no question that the recording was extremely offensive—the venom and hate for people from marginalized communities was front and center. There were no dog whistles there, just pure disdain for people who were different from who they were—white, male, heterosexual. It was painful to listen to, and that worried her. No fair and unbiased juror could listen to that forty-five-minute bonding of bigots and not come away negatively impacted.

"I think I know what Bader's going to do," Erin said. "I don't want either of you to be shocked, so here's my plan and you tell me if you think I'm crazy."

CHAPTER 37

WHEN THEY RETURNED AFTER LUNCH, WHATEVER HAD CAUSED Roy to be benched in the morning had apparently been resolved, because now it was Rivers doodling on his legal pad, as Roy was front and center—and, as Erin knew, Roy was much better on her feet than Rivers. He was all bluster and bombast. Roy spoke in a measured voice, no histrionics. If anyone could convince Bader to keep out the recording, it would be Roy. Methodically she took the judge through the recording, explaining that no fair-minded person could hear the conversation between Britton and Smith and not be offended. That, plus the racial and ethnic composition of the jury, would make the already prejudicial comments even more problematic. Most importantly, she argued, Britton's testimony could be stricken and it would have no bearing on the overwhelming evidence of the defendant's guilt—his cell phone, his fingerprints, his gun—everything pointed to him. And Britton's recording would only distract and confuse the jury as to the real issue in the case—who murdered Russell Marshall.

When Roy was finished, Erin rose to her feet, and from Bader's demeanor, she knew she had her work cut out for her.

"Judge, let me start by saying that I agree with Ms. Roy that the discussion between Trooper Britton and Mr. Smith is highly offensive. But that's not the criteria to be used under the court rule. What the rule provides is that 'relevant evidence *may* be excluded' only 'if its probative value is substantially outweighed by the risk of undue prejudice.' Most respectfully, Judge, and I will admit, somewhat ironically, I believe the outcome of this motion is controlled by the case of *State v. Smith,* a 1968 decision of the Appellate Division, which held that the bias of a witness against a criminal defendant cannot be entirely excluded under Rule 403. Judge, you heard Trooper Britton's comments to Mr. Smith calling Mr. Mazer a 'cock-sucking faggot' and a 'bone smuggler.' That is direct evidence of bias against Mr. Mazer by Trooper Britton," she said, confident that Bader would admit that portion of the recording.

"But that's not all, Judge—how can it be kept from the jury that Trooper Britton perjured himself? When I was asking him questions about how he referred to Black people, Hispanic people, gay men, lesbians, and female state troopers, when Mr. Rivers objected, you specifically asked me whether I had a good-faith basis for asking those questions. Most respectfully, Your Honor put my credibility with the jury on the line. If this recording is excluded, the jury could rightfully think that I had no basis for asking those questions, and was merely trying to play them, when in fact, as we all now know, my questions were beyond reproach. And if my credibility is destroyed, it would have an extremely prejudicial impact on Mr. Mazer's defense.

"Let's also not lose sight of the fact that, in his conversation with Mr. Smith, Trooper Britton came this close"—Erin held her thumb and index finger an inch apart—"to admitting the existence of the Lords of Discipline. The jury needs to hear those comments because they bolster Mr. Mazer's credibility. This is what Mr. Mazer has been saying all along, and what Mr. Marshall's article was all about. With regard to Ms. Roy's comment that you could strike Trooper Britton's testimony and it wouldn't impact the evidence against Mr. Mazer, I respectfully disagree. I didn't decide to put Trooper Britton on the stand, the state did. He's the one who said my client was a liar; he's the one who implied Mr. Marshall didn't believe my client; and he's the one who implied my client posed a physical danger to Mr. Marshall." Her voice grew stronger as she ticked off each reason Britton's testimony was critical. "That testimony cannot go unchallenged," she said, pounding every word with her righteous indignation.

"Your Honor, just as I indicated that the admissibility is controlled by *State v. Smith,* I submit to the court that the resolution of what to admit is also controlled by *Smith.* With regard to the statements that demonstrate the pure homophobic bias Trooper Britton had toward my client, those portions should be admitted in their entirety. With regard to the racial, ethnic, homophobic, and misogynistic comments, under *Smith,* you are permitted to provide a representative sample as opposed to all of them. If Your Honor elected to do that, assuming the comments selected were representative, the defendant would not object. Finally, with regard to the comments hinting at the existence of a group within the state police that sounds remarkably like what Mr. Marshall described in the draft of his article as the Lords of Discipline, I submit those statements should also be admitted in full. Thank you, Judge."

Erin lowered herself back into her seat and stole a glance at Swish, who gave her a tight smile. Then she watched as Bader took several sheets of legal paper, scribbled something on one of the pages, put on her glasses, and looked up.

"Thank you, Ms. Roy and Ms. McCabe, for your excellent arguments. I agree with both of you that this recording is incredibly offensive," Bader began. She then laid out the facts and the procedural history as to how the issue arose. As Erin listened, she knew Bader was doing all of this to make a record for appellate review because the losing side would almost certainly be filing a motion in the Appellate Division asking for leave to file an interlocutory appeal challenging her ruling.

"My initial reaction was that the discussion between Mr. Smith and Trooper Britton was so offensive, and therefore prejudicial to the state, that I had to exclude it. But after listening to the argument of counsel, I am forced to agree with counsel for the defendant that under *State v. Smith,* direct evidence of a witness's bias against the defendant, which in this case we hear directly from the recorded conversation of the witness, must be admitted despite its potential prejudice. I also agree that when the state objected to Ms. McCabe's questions, I made counsel represent that she had a good faith basis to ask them, which, since she had listened to the recording, she clearly had. To prohibit the jury from hearing the recording would make it appear that Ms. McCabe misrepresented her basis for the questions, and I do not believe any cautionary instruction I could give would undo the prejudice to Ms. McCabe and of course, by extension, to the defendant. In light of that, I am going to accept the defense's suggestion that the recording be edited before being played to the jury. I am going to take a recess and listen to it again, and make time notations of the clips I will allow, and then with the help of both experts, we can make an edited version that complies with my ruling, and move on from there."

Roy rose to her feet. "Judge, may we have a temporary stay of your order, to file a motion for leave to file an interlocutory appeal in the Appellate Division?"

"Ms. Roy, here's my thoughts on that. Let me proceed to decide what the jury will hear, and have that composite recording prepared by the experts, and then the appellate court will have the benefit of knowing exactly what I ruled admissible. Make sense?"

"Yes, Judge. Thank you."

It was a little after five p.m. when they all listened to the composite recording one last time to confirm it contained everything Bader had ordered included, and only those things she had ordered included. Her decision allowed the jury to hear Britton's reference to Mazer as a "cock-sucking faggot" and a "bone smuggler"; four of the eight times he used the *N* word; two of the times he used the words "faggot" and "cunt"; and one of the times he used "spic" and "dyke." When it was done, it included about eight minutes of the introductory banter, including a discussion about a group of troopers that sounded like the Lords, and then enough around each of the slurs, to give them context. While the original recording ran forty-five minutes, the composite ran eighteen. Although Erin thought some additional conversation for context should have been included, overall, she and Swish were happy with the final product.

After the recording was finalized, Roy advised the judge that the state would be filing a motion for leave to file an interlocutory appeal. Because this was taking place in the middle of a trial, the appellate court would first have to make a decision on whether they would even allow the state to file an appeal, and if they did allow it, the appellate court would then decide whether to affirm, reverse, or modify Bader's decision. Bader agreed to try and make it easier from a logistical standpoint by providing the original and composite confidential recordings to the Appellate Division under seal. Bader also directed her court reporter to prepare an expedited copy of the transcript of her decision and send it to the appellate clerk's office tomorrow morning. Because of the delay, the jury manager had contacted the jurors and advised them that, unless otherwise notified, to come back on Monday morning.

Standing in the hallway outside Bader's courtroom, Erin and Swish decided that he would be in the office first thing to start working on their response and to receive the state's papers. They both assumed they were going to be on an extremely expedited schedule and, unless the state came up with some novel argument they hadn't made to Bader, Swish would be prepared to file their response quickly utilizing Erin's oral argument as his template.

While Swish was handling that, Erin was going to see Mazer and try once again to convince him to be honest on the witness stand about his relationship with Gabe, and then, based on the change in schedule, she was going to join Liz at her six-month ultrasound.

Rivers was screaming on his cell phone as he barreled down Route 1.

"Listen to me, I need a mistrial. This has turned into a shit show. There's not a doubt in my mind that the Appellate Division is going to uphold Bader's ruling, meaning sometime, probably early next week, the world is going to hear Britton and Smith basically motherfucking every member of the jury except the two white dudes, and I suspect even one of them is a little light in his loafers. I need to hit reset and start over."

Rivers paused, listening impatiently to the response. Finally, when his patience had run out, he said, "Yes. I understand you filed opposition to their application, but I need you to do more. I need you to get hold of Solomon Musto at the ALDA. Tell him to mobilize a protest outside the Middlesex County Courthouse, probably on Monday, but I'll confirm. Make sure he gets McCabe's wacky brother-in-law there . . . Simpson, I forget his first name. I need as many people there as they can muster, carrying signs that McCabe is a pervert and men can't be mothers—basically as offensive as possible, and I need them outside the jurors' entrance to the courthouse at eight a.m. I'm also going to arrange for a leak of the recording to the press. If the recording is going to become public, I want it to happen in a way that compromises this jury so I get a mistrial."

Again, he stopped to listen. "It's not risky at all," he finally said. "Musto's a stand-up guy. He's as committed to the ALDA bullshit as they come. Trust me, he'll be happy to personally take credit for whatever goes down. And the reason I can't call him is because I'm pulling into the parking lot of where I'm meeting with the idiot that caused this mess. Look, I won't forget this. Once Pedersen's nomination to the state supreme court goes through, Anthony Thompson will be named the AG and I'm in line for head of DCJ. Pedersen keeps telling me there's some dumb-ass political reason that it's held up in the Senate Judiciary Committee, but once he goes through, and I get the DCJ job, I won't forget who my friends are." He let out a cruel snicker and added, "Or who my enemies are."

Like Carol Roy, he thought.

"Thanks," he said after several seconds. "I won't forget this. I'll keep you updated on when to tell Musto to have people at the courthouse."

He found Britton in a booth in the back of the dimly lit gin mill.

"Don't start," Britton said, before Rivers had even settled into his seat. "I don't need you to tell me I fucked up with Smith. Trust me, I'm well aware."

"Listen, as bad as it is, the worst they have you on is perjury. I'm working on trying to create a mistrial. If that happens, you'll be good. But even if the recordings come in and you get called back by Ms. Nonuts, you take the Fifth to everything. Talk to the union, have them get a lawyer for you, and take the Fifth."

"Just perjury," Britton said. "Just my fucking job, pension, and everything else. After people hear what I said to Smith, I'll never get a job anywhere."

Rivers laughed. "What, you don't think there's millions of people who think just like you? You just said the quiet part out loud. Just keep your head down and make sure nothing else surfaces and you'll be fine. When I left the outfit and turned the Lords over to you, I gave you my word I'd be there for you. We take care of our own and, no matter what happens, I'll make sure you get taken care of."

Britton picked up the shot glass in front of him, downed it, slammed the glass on the table, and continued to glare at Rivers.

"Just remember, we're in this together, my friend, and you damn well better mean what you say about taking care of me when this is over." He slid out of the booth and stood, looking down at Rivers. "And if I think for one second that you're trying anything to neutralize me, I'll rat you out so fast, you won't know what hit you. Just remember, both of us have a lot to lose."

It was around ten thirty p.m. when Roy finished up the final revisions to the motion for leave to file an appeal. She was both exhausted and despondent. There was no doubt the recording was prejudicial, but she knew in her heart that Bader had made the right call. God, what a pig Britton was, and as much as she knew you shouldn't hold the sins of the client against a lawyer who represented them, she felt in her bones that it was no coincidence

Rivers had represented Britton when he had refused to testify before the AG's task force about the Lords. Those two were cut from the same cloth.

She looked at the two-week pile of mail on her desk. Tanya, her secretary, would have alerted her to any emergencies, but she quickly thumbed through the envelopes. At the very bottom of the stack was a large, white, legal-size, unopened envelope, addressed to her, marked *PERSONAL & CONFIDENTIAL—ATTORNEYS EYES ONLY.*

It also had no postage. What the hell was this? How did it get here, and why the hell hadn't Tanya brought it to her attention? She felt the closed envelope, trying to make sure there were no foreign substances inside, but to the touch, it felt like there was just paper. She picked up her letter opener, sliced open the top, and peeked inside—paper.

It was an affidavit.

I, Deputy Attorney General Albert Holmes, under penalty of perjury, do solemnly swear:

What the fuck, she thought, seeing Holmes's name, which quickly turned to *Oh fuck* as she read what was in the affidavit.

She picked up her cell phone and hit the number 1.

"Go," she said, using the nickname for her partner Margot. "Do you have the private cell phone number for Mercer County Prosecutor Carl Schey?"

"Yeah, everything okay?" Margot asked.

"That would be a negative," she replied. After Margot gave her the number, she said, "Not sure when I'll be home."

"You want an armed escort?" Margot replied.

"No. I'm good for now. But not exactly sure as to what the future holds."

She ran out of her office, made a dozen copies of Holmes's affidavit, then put them in separate envelopes, tucked them in her briefcase, and dialed the number Margot had just given her.

A voice answered with a cautious, "Hello."

"Prosecutor Schey, I'm not sure if you remember me, but this is Carol Roy, I was an AP in Mercer. I left three years ago."

"Of course I remember you, Carol. I was sorry to see you go. Is everything all right?"

"No, sir, it's not. I know it's terribly late, but is there any chance I could see you tonight? It's an emergency."

CHAPTER 38

ERIN SAT IN THE WAITING ROOM NEXT TO LIZ. IT WAS ONLY TWELVE thirty p.m., but it had already been a long day.

She had been at the Middlesex County Adult Corrections Center at eight this morning to see Jon. Because he was on trial, he was allowed extended visiting hours with his attorneys. Things were going well—if the court affirmed and the recording was played for the jury, they would have the moral high ground. But it could be lost if Jon testified and perjured himself over his relationship with Gabe. If he lied and was exposed as a liar, the same false in one, false in all charge that Erin was going to ask the judge to give to the jury about Britton and Stone would be applied to him as well. But, despite everything Erin said, Jon was adamant that he couldn't out Gabe, and Gabe would never out himself. Gabe simply had too much to lose.

"I know you're on trial, but is something bothering you?" Liz asked.

Erin smiled. "I'm sorry. I just have a client who seems intent on snatching defeat from the jaws of victory."

"Sorry," Liz said.

Erin gave Liz a weak smile. "But how are you? You look great."

"Thanks. I feel great. I joked with Sean that maybe we should have a third."

Erin laughed. "What was my brother's reaction to that?"

"He rattled off Dublin, Paris, Rome, Vienna—some of the places we hope to travel to when the boys are a little older."

"They do allow babies in Europe," Erin offered with a grin.

"Sean's right," Liz said. "As much as I know I'll melt when I see your little baby, I won't miss changing diapers or two-o'clock feedings. I think I'm ready to pass the torch," Liz said, giving Erin a hug.

"Thanks," Erin said. "Torch accepted."

Once they had been called in, Erin sat in awe, watching the baby moving around in Liz's uterus as the technician gently moved the wand across Liz's belly.

"Everything looks good," Doctor Grimes said. "The baby seems perfectly normal. So, Liz, whatever you're doing, keep doing it." Grimes faced Erin. "Would you like to know the baby's sex?" she asked.

Erin lowered her eyes, allowing herself a small smile. She was living proof that the baby's sex assigned at birth was sometimes wrong. But she had to admit that, despite her own experience, like most expectant parents, she and Mark had decided that they wanted to know even if they had no plans to share it with anyone else.

"Yes, please. But could I ask you a favor? Would you write it on a piece of paper and put it in an envelope, so Mark and I can find out at the same time?"

Grimes nodded. "Of course," she said graciously.

Erin quickly turned to Liz. "I'm sorry. Would you like to know?"

Liz reached over and took hold of Erin's hand. "No," she said. "I'll wait," she added, with a look that made Erin suspect Liz knew more than she was letting on.

"I know you're on trial right now, but are you still interested in trying to breast-feed?" Grimes asked.

"Yeah, I am," Erin replied.

"Good. When do you think your trial will be over?"

"Probably about a week, two on the outside," she said, trying to factor in the appeal process.

"That's fine. Let's make an appointment today for you to come back at the end of two weeks and we can go over what are called the Newman-Goldfarb Protocols. That's what we use for cisgender women who use a gestational surrogate and want to try and breast-feed. I can use the two weeks to research if I need to modify the protocol in any way because you're already taking estradiol. Assuming we don't, when you come back, we'll start you on birth control pills. Then, after several months, I'll take you off the birth control and start you on an antinausea medication called domperidone, which is known to increase levels of prolactin, which should induce lactation." Grimes paused and gave Erin a look that was both soothing and cautious at the same time. "I know we talked about it before, but I want you to be prepared, because many cisgender women who give birth have difficulty breast-feeding, and, as I'm sure you can appreciate, you have a few more hurdles to overcome. I don't want to sound pessimistic, just realistic. And as wonderful as it is that you are enthusiastic about trying, I don't want you to be discouraged if it doesn't work out."

"I understand," Erin replied. "But I really would like to give it my best shot."

Grimes smiled. "Sounds good. I'll see you in a couple of weeks, and Liz, you're at twenty-four weeks, so I'll see you in four weeks, then I'll start seeing you every two weeks after that."

After leaving Liz, Erin got to the office around three thirty.

"Hey, Momma," Swish greeted her when she walked into his office. "How's everything?"

Erin couldn't help but do a little internal dance of joy with how Swish had welcomed her. Over the years she had constantly tested his boundaries around gender identity and sexual orientation, but Swish was one of those people who had evolved and changed along with her, and his simple act of kindness in recognizing her as a mother had melted her heart.

"All's good," she said. "Baby is healthy and growing and Liz is feeling great. I think if she was my age, instead of forty-one, she'd be convincing Sean to have another baby."

"That's great," Swish said with a warm smile.

"What's happening here?" she asked. "Do you need any help with the appeal?"

"All filed," he replied.

"Already?" she said, unable to contain her incredulity.

"Yep, and not only that, but I think we might hear from the court today."

"Why?" she asked.

"Bader, Roy, and I received an email from the clerk's office around twelve thirty, letting us know that everything, including the transcript of Bader's decision, had been received and sent to the appellate panel of Judges Short, Vantuno, and Byrnes for review."

"Short and Vantuno," Erin repeated.

"I thought you'd remember them," Swish said.

"Only until the day I die," Erin replied. "They kept me from being held in contempt," she said. "Pretty hard to forget them."

"So, my guess is it'll be today, because if they want oral argument, they'll want us in asap to avoid a lengthy trial delay."

"Makes sense," Erin replied.

"How long did the brief take you?" she asked.

"A couple of hours. I basically took your oral argument and turned it into a brief. I have to say, I think *State v. Smith* takes us across the goal line."

"Me too. But we both have been around the block enough not to take anything for granted."

"Excuse me, Duane," Cheryl said, poking her head into his office. "You just got a fax from the Appellate Division."

Erin and Swish exchanged a nervous glance, then he waved Cheryl in and she handed him the fax.

Erin studied his expression, hoping for a clue. It took a few seconds, but then a broad grin stretched across his face. He leaned across his desk and reached out, handing the papers to Erin.

Motion for Leave to File an Interlocutory Appeal

GRANTED	DENIED	OTHER
X		

SUPPLEMENTAL ORDER: Per Curiam. The State's Motion for Leave to Appeal is GRANTED For the reasons set forth on the record by the Honorable Lillian Bader, J.S.C., on September 15, 2010, the admissibility of the recording, as edited pursuant to the trial court's order, is affirmed.

It had taken Erin a moment to understand that the Appellate Division had granted the state leave to appeal, and then affirmed Judge Bader's decision on the merits. It was a win, pure and simple.

She looked up at Swish and smiled. "Looks like there's going to be some fireworks on Monday."

"Yes, indeed," he said. "By the way, I forgot to tell you. Rudnicki called me yesterday, looking for info on what was happening behind closed doors. I need to call him tomorrow and make sure he has a reporter there on Monday."

"Let the games begin," she said with a wicked grin.

Erin cuddled into Mark, the waves of her orgasm slowly receding. "That was wonderful," she said softly.

He kissed the top of her head and then sighed. "Yes, it was. I had forgotten that you become celibate when you're on trial. Glad we had a chance to take advantage of your short break."

"Me too," she moaned. "And I wouldn't call it celibate—it's more that I become asexual."

"Whatever it is, I'm always happier when you're between trials," he said with a small laugh.

She looked at the paper Dr. Grimes had given her lying on the night table and then at Mark. "Are you disappointed we're having a girl?" she asked.

"Why would I be disappointed?"

"I don't know. This is probably our only chance at having a baby, and I guess, well, you know, a father wants a son."

"Don't be silly. I want a healthy and happy baby. I'll love our daughter to pieces. I'm just thrilled we have this opportunity."

"Mark, I wish you could have seen her today. She's so beautiful. Oh my God, she was sucking her thumb."

"I'm just thrilled you got to see her. I know how much it meant to you," he said, giving her a squeeze.

Erin must have dozed off because she was awakened by Mark reaching for his cell phone.

"Hey, Molly, is everything okay?" Erin heard him say. "Okay. Good luck and keep us posted."

"What's going on?" Erin asked, only half awake.

"That was Molly. Robin's starting to have contractions, but they're not really sure if she's in labor. So, they're going to head over to the hospital and see what's what."

"It'll be nice for our daughter to have a cousin to hang out with. Patrick and Brennan are so much older. It'll be good," she said before falling back to sleep.

"Good morning, sunshine," Erin said when Swish walked into her office the following morning.

Then she noticed his face.

"What's with you?" she asked. "It's Friday. We had a big win yesterday. Why do you look like you missed a three-pointer at the buzzer for the win?"

"I just had the strangest call with Rudnicki," he said.

"What do you mean?" she asked.

"He knew everything," Swish replied. "He knew about Bader's decision; he knew about the appeal and the Appellate Division's decision, and . . . and he knew the contents of the recording. And not the redacted content, the content of the entire recording," he said.

"What! How's that possible?" she said, pushing back into her chair. "Who told him?"

Swish closed his eyes and shook his head. "Of course, he wouldn't tell me—confidential source and all. But there are only four of us, well, five if you count the judge, that know, and we know it wasn't us. That leaves only Roy or Rivers."

"Shit. If that hits the press and the jurors see it . . ." She stopped. "Fuck. They're trying to get a mistrial."

Swish's face scrunched. "Mistrial?"

"It's going so badly for them, so what do you do? You hit reset. You heard what Roy said the other day. They didn't need Britton as a witness to prove their case, and they didn't need Stone either. Somebody on that side is trying to get a do-over."

"But even if they did, we'd still get in the recording. We could call Britton and Stone," Swish said. "Plus, we'd have their testimony under oath. Don't they realize that?"

Erin thought through what Swish just said. "It's Rivers. Roy would never do something like this. She's too smart and she plays by the rules."

"You don't know that," Swish said.

"Yeah, I do," Erin replied, and proceeded to tell Swish of her encounter in the ladies' room. "Can we get Rudnicki to hold the story?" she asked.

"I can ask," Swish replied. "But, let's face it, E, chances are if the *Newark Journal* has the story, they aren't the only paper that has the information. Somebody will run the story."

She placed her elbow on her desk and rested her forehead on her hand. "Ah, we're screwed," she said. "Mazer's into us for over a hundred grand. There's no way we can continue like this on a retrial. We're bleeding money." She sighed. "Shit," she said to herself.

CHAPTER 39

DAMN, *HERE WE GO AGAIN*, ERIN THOUGHT AS SHE APPROACHED THE courthouse on Monday. There were about twenty-five to thirty people marching outside the entrance, most carrying signs that read, MEN CAN'T BE MOTHERS or STOP PERVERTS FROM BECOMING PARENTS. There, in the front of the group, in all his glory, was Mark's brother Jack. The ironic part was that, as she weaved her way through the protestors, no one even knew who she was. To them she was a concept, not a real flesh-and-blood person.

When Erin got to the courtroom, Roy was already there. She looked up, and Erin noted that Roy seemed like she was preoccupied.

"Were the protestors here when you got here?" Erin asked.

"Yeah," Roy replied, her mind clearly on something else.

Rivers and Swish arrived about five minutes later. As soon as they were at counsel table, the judge's clerk told them the judge wanted to see counsel in chambers.

When they walked in, Bader, who was holding a copy of the Sunday edition of the *New Brunswick News*, was not a happy camper.

"Does anyone want to take responsibility for this?" she said, flipping the paper so it landed on her desk with the headline facing them. TROOPER AND RADIO SHOW HOST SLAM MEMBERS OF MINORITY COMMUNITIES.

"It had to be the defense, Your Honor. The state has absolutely no interest in spreading this information," Rivers said before anyone else could even speak.

Erin looked at Rivers. Clearly, he had failed Interrogation 101, Erin thought. Rule number one—the person responsible will always try to blame someone else when questioned.

"Your Honor," Erin began, "I will represent to you as an officer of the court that neither I, nor Mr. Swisher, has provided any information to the press. In fact, Mr. Swisher had a conversation on Friday with a person from the *Newark Journal*, who advised Mr. Swisher that he had already received the same information that appears in the *New Brunswick News*, and it was Mr. Swisher who prevailed upon him not to publish it in the *Newark Journal*. Your Honor, why would the defense do anything to jeopardize the trial after we just prevailed in the Appellate Division?"

Bader glanced at Rivers and plopped down in her chair. "I presume you all saw the protesters out front?" Bader asked.

They all nodded.

"You should also know that there will be media in the courtroom today," she said, closing her eyes and exhaling. "Not the way I wanted to start the week." Bader swung her gaze around the room at the four of them. "Does anyone think I need to interview the jurors again?"

"The defense doesn't, Your Honor," Erin said emphatically. "Assuming the jurors even know that the people outside are protesting against me, I have enough confidence in this jury to think they won't be impacted by it. And, as for the article in the *New Brunswick News*, you've already cautioned the jurors repeatedly not to read, listen, or watch anything having to do with this case, and again, I have confidence in the jury's ability to do as instructed by the court."

Out of the corner of her eye, Erin caught Roy looking at her like she had just restored Roy's faith in mankind. Rivers, on the other hand, looked like he was going to explode.

"Your Honor, we definitely think the court must, at a bare minimum, speak to the jurors. The protests outside, the newspaper reports—who knows what they're thinking? A thorough questioning by the court is warranted and required. I hesitate to say this, but the state thinks a mistrial may be required. I can't imagine this jury isn't contaminated beyond the ability of any cautionary instruction."

Bader looked at Rivers. "A mistrial based on what, Mr. Rivers?"

"Judge, the newspaper article was highly prejudicial to the state," he replied.

"Mr. Rivers, at this point we have nothing to suggest any of the jurors have even read the article. They have all been cautioned numerous times not to watch, listen to, or read anything dealing with this trial. In this day and age, with all kinds of media available, we have to have faith that they will follow a judge's instructions, otherwise nothing would get tried to a conclusion. Jurors never cease to amaze me. In my experience, more often than not, they do as their oath requires."

She then turned her attention to Erin, nodding slightly. "You have good instincts, Ms. McCabe." She turned to her clerk. "Bring the jury up. I'll remind the jury of my previous instructions and tell them if any of them have any concerns, they should let my courtroom deputy know at a break. We'll start with Mr. Smith at nine." She looked at the four of them. "See you in a few minutes, Counsel."

"Mr. Smith," Erin began, her manner stern. It was a quality she rarely projected in front of the jury, but for this, she wanted her disdain baked into her questions. "Is it true that you're a published author?"

She was trying to see how Smith was going to play things today. The recording would be red meat to some of his followers, for others definitive proof he was a bigot.

"It is," he replied.

"And the title of the book is *The Guardians of Discipline*; do I have that right?"

"You do," he said in a way that let Erin know he was not in entertainer mode today. He was here to take his lumps and get out. Once he was done, he could spin his testimony whichever way he wanted.

"When you testified last week, we established there was a recording of you speaking with Trooper David Britton. Do you recall that testimony?"

"I do."

"And you stated that, at some point, you told your sound engineer to stop recording, correct?"

"That's correct."

"If I told you that the entire recording was approximately forty-five minutes, would you agree with that?"

"I would," Smith replied.

"And after you told your sound engineer to stop recording, you continued to chat with Trooper Britton for about another forty-five minutes, isn't that true?" Erin hoped that Smith would assume Lewis had spoken to them and would also testify, but even if Smith denied it, this was an appetizer; the main course was about to be served.

"Yeah, probably. I know we spoke for a while after we stopped recording," he conceded.

"And you met with him several times after that, correct?" Erin asked, taking a complete flyer on that one.

"We did," he replied without any hesitation.

"When did you decide to write the book?" she asked.

"Probably after that first session we had," he responded. "I found what he was talking about so fascinating and how the rules and regulations that the troopers, really all cops, have to follow really prevent them from doing their jobs."

"And after coming up with the idea, you spoke to Trooper Britton about writing the book, correct?" Erin asked.

"Yeah, of course. He thought it was a great idea, and offered to help by giving me the inside scoop, and we agreed on what his share of the royalties would be," Smith replied in a tone that implied he believed Erin already knew that.

Erin's mind was doing the Irish jig, but outwardly, she showed no reaction, trying to convey to Smith that he hadn't told her anything that she didn't already know.

"Not that either of us have made a whole lot of money on it," Smith suddenly added.

Never volunteer, Erin thought to herself. And then made a mental note to caution Mazer one more time. Sometimes when you volunteered information nothing happened, and sometimes . . .

"How much have you made so far, Mr. Smith?"

"I'd have to double-check, but we split the seventy-five-hundred advance, and we've probably split another three or four thousand in royalties. Like I said, no one's retiring on the money from the book. It's not exactly a best seller, except maybe in the law enforcement community."

Erin quickly weighed how much Smith would give her on the Lords. She assumed he'd equivocate. Even on the tape, Britton had been smart enough never to admit the Lords existed. She also knew, based on what Bader had allowed, the jury would hear some of Britton's own statements.

"And the title of the book, *The Guardians of Discipline,* that came out of your conversations with Trooper Britton, correct?"

"Well, actually the title was my idea, but when I told him what I wanted to call the book, he laughed and said he thought it was great," Smith responded.

"But your idea was based on what you and Britton talked about, right?" Erin said, trying to draw the final ounce of blood from his response.

"Yeah, and I had no idea about any of this stuff until we started talking."

"And the 'any of this stuff' you just referred to are the allegations concerning the existence of the Lords of Discipline."

"That's right," he replied.

"Judge, I'd like to play the recording at this point, and I'd ask Your Honor to explain to the jury exactly what we are about to play, so that the jury has context for the recording."

Bader nodded and proceeded to explain to the jury that the recording they were about to hear had various segments of the conversations between Mr. Smith and Trooper Britton, and that the entire recording was not going to be played for them. She cautioned them that they should not speculate about what was in the portions they weren't hearing, or blame either side for the fact that they were only hearing portions of the recording, as the decision as to what they could hear was her decision and hers alone.

Erin returned to counsel table and took her seat. She wanted to watch the jury as closely as possible so she could observe their reaction. And she wasn't disappointed. The first time they heard Britton use the *N* word, several of the Black jurors immediately turned their attention to Rivers and Roy. And it only got worse from there. As each racial, ethnic, misogynistic, and homophobic slur echoed throughout the courtroom, the jurors seemed to physically recoil. When it finally ended, they all appeared to be in stunned disbelief.

Erin sat in silence, allowing the vile nature of what they had all just heard to percolate. Then, when she saw Bader look in her direction, she inched out of her seat until she was standing. "No further questions," she said in a voice that was barely audible.

To Erin's surprise, Rivers stood. "Mr. Smith, you just heard pieces of your conversation with Trooper Britton, correct?"

"Correct."

"You mentioned the first day you were here that this was just two guys talking like they were in the men's locker room. What did you mean by that?"

"You know, talking trash and saying things we wouldn't say in polite company. Just being stupid, I guess."

"Thank you, Mr. Smith."

Smith put his hands on the witness box, ready to make his exit, but when he saw Erin stand, he stopped.

"Let me see if I have the definition of locker room talk down, Mr. Smith—talking trash, saying things you wouldn't say in polite company, being stupid," Erin said, repeating his answer. "And brutally honest as well, right?"

Smith inhaled like he had been punched in the stomach. "Ah. Um. I don't know. Maybe. But like I said, it was just stupid talk."

"Mr. Smith, you spoke with Trooper Britton numerous times. Do you, Drew Smith, have any reason to doubt that Trooper Britton believed everything he said to you one hundred percent?"

"Objection," Rivers shouted. "How can he know what Trooper Britton believes?"

"Overruled," Bader said. "The witness was asked if he had any reason to doubt, so the question is focused on the witness's state of mind, not Trooper Britton's. You may answer the question."

"I don't know. I think . . . I mean, just trash talking."

Bader intervened without Erin having to say anything. "The question was do you have any doubt that Trooper Britton meant what he said?"

Smith looked up at the judge, moving his hand to the side of his face. "No," he said in a pained voice. "No doubt."

"Thank you," Bader said.

"Nothing further," Erin said.

They sat in Jon's holding cell, Erin not having the luxury of allowing the adrenaline to subside. Jon was the next witness after the lunch break.

"You were amazing," Jon gushed. "You ripped him a new one."

"Thanks, Jon," she said, not wanting to say too much more, given that he was soon to be on the receiving end. "Just remember what we talked about, tell the truth, and when you're being cross-examined, don't volunteer information. There were a few things that Smith volunteered that were manna from heaven. Just answer the question asked. If there's anything that you're asked that's confusing or paints an incomplete picture, don't worry. I can always come back and tidy things up on redirect. Be patient. Play the long game."

She looked down the table at Swish. They had discussed for hours yesterday afternoon about whether they could avoid putting Jon on the stand. In the end, there was no escaping he needed to testify. If the jury didn't buy Jon's claims that he wasn't the one that had the gun, he was going down no matter how much the jury hated Britton and Smith.

CHAPTER 40

When Roy returned from the lunch recess, she noticed Melanie Thornton, an assistant prosecutor at the Mercer County Prosecutor's Office, in the last row, far away from the gaggle of reporters. When Roy had been an AP in Mercer, Thornton had been an AP in Juvenile, but as Roy had discovered on Friday, Thornton was out of juvie and now in the Professional Responsibility Unit.

Interesting, she thought.

After meeting with Prosecutor Schey Wednesday night, Roy had gotten a message that was relayed through Margot that the prosecutor wanted to meet with her, the cover story being that she was there for an interview because she was thinking of coming back to the office. When she was led into the conference room, Prosecutor Schey; AP Thornton; Director Leonard Smithson, the head of the Professional Responsibility Unit; and to Roy's surprise, Prosecutor Vanessa Talon, the Middlesex County prosecutor; were all sitting around the conference room table.

They had thanked her for contacting Schey, told her they were taking things very seriously, but in light of her sensitive and awkward position, had some questions.

No, she hadn't told anyone in the AG's Office about it. No, she hadn't spoken to Rivers. No, she had no idea how the affidavit got to her desk. No, she had no idea who Diane Fox, the person who had notarized Holmes's signature, was.

Then they told her that given the implications in the affidavit, they didn't want her speaking with anyone about it, and they wanted to make sure that, since she was on trial with Rivers, she could maintain a professional relationship with him. She had laughed and told them that they hadn't had one before, so there was no reason they should have one now.

They asked her if she had copies of the affidavit, and when she admitted she did, they asked for them back.

She had looked around the room, taking the measure of each of them. "No," she had replied firmly. "I don't know what I'm up against here, and that affidavit is my only insurance policy."

She could tell that her response had taken them aback. "Carol," Schey had said. "We need to control who has access to the affidavit. We need your copy back."

"I'm the one who brought it to you. I'm keeping it," she had replied defiantly. "I mean no disrespect, Prosecutor Schey, but you're not my boss and I don't think you're going to report me to my boss or have me arrested for hindering an investigation that I initiated."

Schey and Talon had looked at each other, then after an awkward silence, moved on.

They told her that Diane Fox, the person who had notarized the affidavit, worked at the branch of a bank near where Holmes lived, and she indeed remembered notarizing it, but didn't know him and hadn't read it, since all she was required to do was verify his signature.

Finally, they had asked her if she had any other relevant information to share. She had looked down the table at Talon. "You know the investigation your office had started involving the Edison PD over the incident with Swisher?" she asked. "If you're wondering how it got to the AG's Office, it was Rivers. And if you're wondering what happened to the investigation, the answer is nothing, because Rivers killed it."

They ended by telling her the less she knew what they were doing, the better for her, and if they needed anything, they'd be in touch.

Now here she sat. Wondering how Mazer would hold up, and if he could convince the jury he didn't do it.

As he walked to the witness stand, Roy studied him. He wasn't the buff trooper he had been a year ago. He was thinner, his face drawn, his skin pale; spending a year in protective custody, basically solitary confinement, will do that to you, she thought.

Roy watched as McCabe gently guided her client through his background. Successful athlete and student; disowned by his family when he came out to them; class of 1999 from the State Police Academy; how proud he was to be a trooper and yet the pressure he felt because he was a closeted gay man in an organization that he discovered favored white, straight men; and finally, how he was outed.

Next McCabe had him explain in detail how he was harassed for being a gay man, which ultimately led him to file an Internal Affairs complaint.

"Did you know Deputy Attorney General Albert Holmes?" McCabe asked.

"I did," Mazer replied.

"How?"

"Initially, because he was involved in the task force investigation of whether the Lords of Discipline existed, which came before my IA. But then after my IA was concluded, he called me on my cell phone and asked to meet with me. We met at Carvajal's Mexican Restaurant in Perth Amboy."

"How did he have your cell?"

"I had provided it as part of the task force investigation."

"What was your meeting about?"

"He told me that he knew the Lords existed and that he believed that I was being singled out because I was gay. Holmes suggested that I meet and work with Russell Marshall, who wanted to do an investigative piece on the Lords."

"Did he tell you why, if he knew the Lords existed, the task force report and the IA found to the contrary?"

"All he said was they could ruin him if he didn't do what they wanted."

"Did he say who 'they' were?"

"No. I presume—"

"Objection," Rivers said without even rising from his seat.

"Sustained," Bader said. "The witness is not allowed to speculate."

"Do you know what they had on him?"

"No. I didn't ask and he didn't volunteer."

"As a result of that, did you meet with Mr. Marshall?"

"I did," he replied.

"How often?" McCabe asked.

"In person, probably ten times. Honestly, I don't remember the exact number. But if you include telephone calls, we probably spoke twenty-five to thirty times," Mazer offered.

"Do you know if he had other sources besides you?"

"I believe he did, but honestly, I had no idea. Based on what DAG Holmes told me, I believe that Holmes had spoken to Marshall, but other than that, I don't know."

Roy did a little internal snort. Good answer, and so far, a good witness. Her partner would have his work cut out for him.

Roy listened as McCabe walked him through October 19. Yes, he had called Marshall around 2:45. Any time he called Marshall, Mazer testified he used a prepaid phone, so his calls couldn't be traced back to him. He had called because he knew Marshall was getting close to publication, and he was getting nervous. He had asked Marshall if he could come by and talk. He did go to Marshall's house and got there around 4:15. Marshall had reassured him everything was fine, and let him read a draft of the article. He was there for about thirty minutes and then left. Marshall seemed fine when Mazer left. Because of the time, he didn't head home, but drove to the barracks and changed into his uniform there.

"When you arrived at the barracks, did you have your off-duty weapon and your prepaid phone?" McCabe asked.

"Yes, ma'am," Mazer replied.

"What did you do with them?"

"I have a lockbox in my trunk, and that's where I stowed them."

"At any point in time that evening, after you stored your phone and off-duty weapon in your trunk, did you have possession of either prior to getting off duty at six in the morning of the 20th?"

"No, ma'am," he replied emphatically.

"When you were on patrol that night, where were the keys to your car?"

"In my pants pocket, in my locker at the barracks."

"Where was the key to the lockbox that was in the trunk of your car?"

"It was on the same key ring as my car keys."

"The ones in your pants pocket in your locker?"

"Yes, ma'am."

"At any point in time, after you left Mr. Marshall's home at approximately 4:45, did you return to Mr. Marshall's?"

"I did not."

"Did you call Mr. Marshall on your prepaid phone at 7:03 p.m. that evening?"

"No, ma'am. I did not have that phone with me after I left the barracks to start my patrol that evening."

"Did you ever threaten Mr. Marshall?"

"Oh God, no. I wanted his article to be published as much, if not more, than he did. I wanted the Lords to be exposed for the bigoted, lawless people they are."

"Did you shoot Mr. Marshall?"

"Absolutely not. I had nothing but respect and admiration for the man," Mazer said, causing Roy to look down.

"Did you ever discuss, encourage, or speak to anyone about killing Mr. Marshall?"

"Never!" he said, his baritone booming.

"Do you have an explanation as to how it was that Mr. Marshall was shot with your off-duty weapon?"

"Someone retrieved it from my vehicle using the keys that were in my pants pocket."

When McCabe finished, Rivers rose and walked toward the witness. At this point Roy had lost count of how many times Rivers had boasted about how he was going to "rip this fag apart." She wasn't naïve; she knew there were plenty of people who called queer people all kinds of names. She had been called a "lipstick lesbian" more than a few times, and Margot, being in great physical shape, with short hair, was well aware that some of the cops she worked with called her a dyke behind her back, but damn, Rivers was an assistant attorney general, and New Jersey had a law against discrimination that prohibited discrimination against gay people. And yet, it didn't seem to matter a whit to him.

"You have a lock on your locker on October 19?" he began.

"I did."

"Was it locked?"

"It was."

"Then how do you explain someone getting the keys out of your pants pocket?" he asked with a smirk.

Roy resisted the temptation to bury her head in her hands. Let McCabe ask for an explanation, she wanted to scream.

"Well, sir," Mazer began. "It's a Master combination lock that has a key slot on the back, so it's possible it was opened with a master key. I know I have a couple of master keys, and I know a few others do as well, because sometimes you grab a lock and forget the combination. The other possibility is someone picked the lock. If you know what you're doing, you can pick that kind of lock in about fifteen seconds. Anyone can buy a lock-picking tool set on Amazon for under ten dollars. I know lots of troopers who have a set. You never know when you might need to pick a lock."

"So, what you're asking the jury to believe is that someone knew your keys were in your pants pocket, that they picked the lock on your locker, took the keys, went to your car, removed your gun and phone, drove to Edison, shot Mr. Marshall, drove back to the barracks, replaced your cell phone and gun in the trunk, then picked the lock again on your locker to put the keys back in your pants pocket. Is that it, Mr. Mazer?"

"It is, because I know I didn't shoot him and I have no other explanation," Mazer said.

"I have one, a much simpler one, Mr. Mazer. You spoke with Mr. Marshall around four and tried to get him to pull the article.

When he wouldn't, while you were patrolling I-287, you got off the New Durham Road exit, called him from your burner, met with him a second time, and shot him. Isn't that what happened, Mr. Mazer?"

"Absolutely not, sir. I did not. I repeat, I did not shoot Mr. Marshall."

"You said you went to see him because you were getting nervous. You said you were anxious for the article to come out. What were you nervous about, Mr. Mazer?"

"The article was going to out me as a gay man in a big way. Yeah, I was nervous."

"But you said you were already being harassed because you were gay. So let me ask you again, what were you so nervous about?"

"I told you, it's one thing for some of the people I worked with to know I was gay, it's an entirely different thing for everyone who reads the *Newark Journal* to know."

"Didn't you argue with him over pulling the story?"

"No, sir, we never argued and I never asked him to pull the story."

"Do you know a Father Gabriel DeAngelis?" Rivers asked.

Roy glanced over to where McCabe was sitting, and saw her noticeably stiffen.

"Yes, I do."

"How do you know him?" Rivers asked.

"We're friends," Mazer replied.

"Aren't you lovers?" Rivers asked.

McCabe seemed to be holding her breath.

"No, sir. As I said, we're friends."

Roy didn't know how to feel. The defendant had just lied—that was good for her side. But any satisfaction she felt was short-lived. On one level she knew that if Margot asked her to lie, she probably would. Love made people do funny things. And there were her own doubts about Mazer's guilt.

"Isn't it a fact that your lover, a Catholic priest, was panicked that Marshall's article was going to out him as well, exposing him as a gay man? And in an effort to protect your lover, you went to

Mr. Marshall's house, and when he wouldn't pull the article, you argued with him and shot him?" Rivers demanded.

Mazer seemed stunned, and for the first time he hesitated before answering. "No, sir. That didn't happen," he said, his voice flat, his resolve shredded.

There was no reason for Erin to do redirect. The damage was done. Other than Gabe, Rivers hadn't laid a glove on Jon. But that was kind of like, "Other than that, Mrs. Lincoln, how was the play?" Lying to protect Gabe could put Mazer in jail for the rest of his life.

After the jury left for the day, Bader asked Erin if there were any other defense witnesses.

"Yes, Your Honor. Two more. Trooper Alec Urjinski, whom I don't expect to be long. And per my request at the conclusion of his testimony for the state, I wish to recall Trooper David Britton to confront him with his statements on the composite recording. Honestly, I don't know how long it will take. It depends on his responses."

"Mr. Rivers, any rebuttal witnesses?"

"Yes, Judge. Father Gabriel DeAngelis. I don't believe he will be a lengthy witness."

"Very well, Counsel. Assuming Trooper Britton is a bit of a wild card, let's hope we can finish those witnesses up in the morning. If we do, I'll let the jury go, and we can have our charging conference right after lunch. Anything else?"

"May we have several minutes with our client in the holding cell, Judge?" Erin asked.

"I can give you fifteen minutes, Ms. McCabe, and if you need more than that, I'll have to ask that you head over to the correctional facility."

"Thank you, Judge," Erin replied.

By the time Erin and Swish were let into the cell, Jon already had his face buried in his hands. "Oh shit, oh shit, oh shit," he kept mumbling. He finally looked up. "I'm so sorry. I didn't believe you. I never, never thought he'd testify against me. I'm dead. I should have listened to you."

Despite the urge to say, "Yeah, you should've," Erin didn't.

She and Swish spent the next fifteen minutes trying to convince him that they could recover from this, even though Erin was far from certain they could. The other thing she didn't remind him of was that the last witness the jury was going to hear was the one who would make Jon out to be a liar.

CHAPTER 41

THE NEXT MORNING THE PROTESTORS WERE BACK, BUT NOW THERE was a counterprotest demanding that Britton be fired.

As she ran the gauntlet, Erin wondered how today would go. As she feared, the press had picked up on the salacious details of the alleged relationship between Mazer and DeAngelis, and had barely referenced Mazer's testimony proclaiming his innocence. All she could hope was that she could score enough points with Urjinski and Britton to negate the damage Father DeAngelis was going to do.

As he raised his right hand, Trooper Alec Urjinski's buttoned suit jacket stretched across his chest and looked like it was going to split in two. About five eight, he was built like a tree stump. All Erin could think was he would have been a hell of a football player—no one could ever have tackled him.

Erin ran through his background on the state police and then moved on to the reason he was here.

"Trooper, all troopers work shifts, correct?"

"Correct, ma'am," he responded.

"What's a typical schedule, Trooper?"

"We work three days on and have two days off, and then we have two days on and three days off, each shift being twelve hours, and then every two weeks we have one eight-hour makeup shift," he said.

"Sounds confusing," Erin said.

"You get used to it," he replied with the thinnest of smiles.

"On October 19 were you working?" Erin asked.

"Yes, ma'am. I generally work the overnight, so six in the evening to six in the morning. However, that day, the 19th, was my makeup shift, eight hours, not twelve, so instead of starting at six p.m. like I normally would, I came in to work at around nine thirty that night."

"And did you use the locker room in the barracks that night?"

"I did, ma'am."

"When you arrived that night was there anyone else in the locker room besides yourself?" Erin asked.

"Yes, ma'am. When I arrived, I saw Trooper David Britton in the locker room."

"Where was he?"

"Over by a group of lockers, but I didn't see what he was doing."

"Did he say anything to you?"

"He did. He said, 'What are you looking at, you Ukrainian piece of shit?' "

"Is that how he usually talked to you?"

"We generally don't speak to one another at all, but when he does speak to me, it's not unusual for him to say something crude."

"Did you say anything to him, Trooper?"

"No, ma'am. I have no use for that man."

"Thank you, Trooper."

Rivers stood at counsel table. "How can you be certain, Trooper, that the night you saw Trooper Britton in the locker room was October 19?"

Erin remembered thinking that somewhere along the way Rivers's inexperience would catch up to him. Here it was.

"Two reasons, sir. First, I learned later, after my shift ended, that Mr. Marshall had been murdered and I was devastated because he and I had spoken several times and I had provided him with some information for his article. He was a good man, and as I said, I was crushed. And secondly, when I was contacted by the investigator employed by Ms. McCabe, I double-checked my work records to confirm I started at ten that night."

Rivers looked down at his notes, as if they might somehow save him from the body blow Urjinski had just delivered. "Um . . . ah . . . nothing else," he managed to say.

Erin stood. Rivers had just opened the door for her to produce a record that Urjinski had handed to her this morning and which hadn't been marked as an exhibit prior to the start of the trial. She handed a copy of the document to Rivers and then had it marked as an exhibit. "Trooper, Mr. Rivers just questioned you concerning the hours you worked on October 19 and 20. I've handed you exhibit D-5; can you identify this?"

"Yes, this is my time record for October 19 and 20, which I signed off on."

"Mr. Rivers, will you stipulate this is an official record of the New Jersey State Police?" Erin asked.

Without looking up, Rivers muttered, "Stipulated."

"And, Trooper, what does this document show in terms of your shift for the 19th and 20th?"

"That my shift was from ten p.m. on October 19 to six a.m. on October 20."

"Thank you, Trooper."

"The defense recalls Trooper David Britton to the stand," Erin said, as soon as Urjinski left.

As Britton walked in from the hallway, Erin couldn't help but notice that in a week, David Britton appeared to be a changed man, and not for the better. Gone was the swagger and attitude. Now he appeared resigned to their fate—a dead man walking.

Bader reminded him that he was still under oath and obligated to tell the truth and nothing but the truth.

Erin walked around counsel table and stood near the end of the jury box so he would have to look at the jurors as he answered. "Trooper, since you appeared last, the jury has heard a recording that is a composite of various portions of a conversation between you and Mr. Drew Smith. I'm going to have those played for you now."

After playing the opening introductions where Smith talked and then allowed Britton to introduce himself, Erin indicated to Ash to pause the playback.

"Trooper Britton, is that you on the recording?"

"On the advice of counsel, I take the Fifth," he said in a monotone.

Erin nodded, trying to ignore the murmuring in the courtroom behind her. Unlike a defendant, Britton could selectively invoke the Fifth Amendment. Erin assumed that after Britton learned that the recording existed, any lawyer worth their salt would've advised him to take the Fifth. It didn't protect him against being charged with perjury, but if he testified, he'd talk his way into even more problems.

She took each segment one by one: the *N* word, the *C* word, the *S* word, and then his homophobic slurs, both generally and specifically to Mazer. To each and every one, he said the same thing, "On the advice of counsel, I take the Fifth." At one point, Bader banged her gavel to quiet the spectators in the courtroom.

Then Erin walked past the jury box until she was about five feet away from him. *Here goes*, she thought.

"Trooper Britton, on the evening of October 19, did you break into a locker at the Somerset State Police barracks and remove Trooper Mazer's car keys from his pants pocket?"

Britton looked stunned, and he fidgeted, as if an electric current had suddenly been plugged into the chair. "I . . . um, on the advice of counsel, I take the Fifth," he finally said.

Once again Bader banged her gavel to quiet the courtroom.

Erin took a step closer to the witness box. "Trooper Britton, on the evening of October 19, did you use those keys to remove Trooper Mazer's off-duty weapon and prepaid phone from a lockbox in the trunk of his car?"

Britton inhaled. "On the advice of counsel, I take the Fifth."

Erin moved closer. "Trooper Britton, on the evening of October 19, did you use Trooper Mazer's prepaid phone to call Russell Marshall's number?"

For the first time, Britton hesitated. He was staring straight ahead, and when Erin followed his gaze, it appeared to be locked on Rivers. "On the advice of counsel, I take the Fifth." This time his cadence was slower, giving Erin pause.

She had gotten what she needed and she was no longer certain he'd continue to take the Fifth. If she asked the ultimate question, "Did you shoot Marshall?" and he answered no, it could undo all that she had just done. Based on Urjinski's testimony, there was one more question she was confident he'd refuse to answer, but other than that, it was a crapshoot. *Quit while you're ahead,* she reminded herself.

"Trooper Britton, on the evening of October 19, at approximately nine thirty p.m., did you return Mr. Mazer's off-duty weapon and his cell phone to the lockbox in the trunk of his car and his car keys to his pants pocket in his locker?"

Britton rubbed his hands together and glared at her, his look conveying his unspoken rage. "I take the Fifth," he said.

Erin stood silently, staring at Britton for what seemed like minutes, but was probably only five or six seconds. "I have nothing further," she announced, her voice dripping with disdain.

As she looked over at Rivers and Roy, they appeared to be engaged in a heated conversation.

After several minutes, it was Roy who stood. "No questions, Your Honor," she said, leaving Britton looking stunned.

"The defense rests," Erin announced.

"Does the state have any rebuttal witnesses?" Bader asked.

"Yes, Judge. The state calls Father Gabriel DeAngelis."

DeAngelis was wearing a black business suit, with a black shirt and tie—no Roman collar. He looked calm, far different from the last time Erin saw him when he hastily left her conference room ostensibly to hire a lawyer.

Rivers went through his background, education, and parish assignments before turning to the issues at hand.

"Father, have you been promised anything for your testimony today?" Rivers asked.

"I have," he said.

"And what have you been promised?"

"In return for my truthful testimony today, I will not be prosecuted for providing false information to the law enforcement authorities investigating this case."

"And had you previously provided false information to law enforcement in this case?" Rivers asked.

"I had," DeAngelis replied.

"And what was that false information?"

"I had told you and the investigators from the Attorney General's Office that Jon Mazer and I were only friends."

"And was that a lie, Father?" Rivers said.

DeAngelis lowered his eyes. "Yes, it was."

"And if Mr. Mazer testified under oath to this jury that you were only friends, that would also be a lie, correct?"

"It would."

"And prior to Mr. Mazer's arrest, what was your relationship with him?"

"We were lovers."

"And for how long were you lovers, prior to October 19, 2009?"

"Approximately a year."

"Did you speak with Jon Mazer on October 19, 2009?"

"I did."

"And what did you discuss?"

"He knew Mr. Marshall's article was due to be published in a matter of days, so I asked him to go to see Mr. Marshall because I was terrified that I would be outed in the article along with Jon . . . I'm sorry, Mr. Mazer. If I was outed, I would be defrocked as a priest because the Catholic Church condemns homosexuality. It would also reveal that I had broken my vow of celibacy."

"And do you know if Mr. Mazer saw Mr. Marshall that day?"

"I don't know if he did, but he told me he did."

"Did he tell you anything else?"

"He told me he had met with Mr. Marshall and everything was fine, I had no worries."

"What did you interpret that to mean?"

"I wasn't sure what it meant, quite frankly, so I asked him to go back and speak with Mr. Marshall again and get him to pull the article."

"And what happened?"

"We had an argument and it ended with him saying, 'What part of I told you "you had no worries" don't you understand?' "

"Did you speak to him any further that day or the early morning hours of October 20, 2009?"

"No. He turned his phone off."

"Since then, have you spoken to Mr. Mazer about Mr. Marshall's murder?"

Erin tensed, wondering if DeAngelis was going to be like the jailhouse snitch and rat Jon out in exchange for a "get out of jail free" card.

"I've attempted to."

"What has he said?"

"Just that on the advice of his attorney, he can't talk to me about it."

"Nothing further," Rivers said.

As Erin went to stand, Jon grabbed her arm. Erin leaned over, so he could whisper in her ear.

"He won't hurt me," Jon said.

He already did, Erin thought, but held her tongue.

Erin asked a few follow-up questions about DeAngelis's background, more to dip her toe in the water and test his responses.

"When you first met Mr. Mazer, you hid from him the fact that you were a priest, and it wasn't until months into your relationship that you disclosed that information, correct?"

"That's true," he responded.

"Father, you testified you were concerned that Mr. Marshall's article might out you as a gay man."

"That's correct."

"Is that also why you initially lied to the investigators when they questioned you about your relationship with Jon—you didn't want to be outed?"

"It was."

"Mr. Mazer has been out as a gay man for years, so he has nothing to hide about who he is, correct?"

"That's true," he responded.

"It was only you who was trying to hide the fact that you're also a gay man?"

"That's accurate."

On the fly, Erin tried to work out the right way to frame the question. "So, would you agree with me that Mr. Mazer wasn't protecting his own status when he testified you and he were just friends, he was protecting yours?"

"I would agree with you," DeAngelis answered in a tone that almost seemed to invite Erin to keep going. She wondered if she was walking into a trap.

"As you've testified, for you, being outed carried serious personal and professional consequences. You had made Mr. Mazer aware of those consequences, correct?"

"Yes. I had told him many times that I loved being a priest and I was torn between my love for him and my love for my religious calling, and that if anyone ever found out about our relationship, I'd be removed from the priesthood."

"And that's why you needed Jon to keep your relationship secret—so you could have both?" she said.

"Yes. In retrospect, it doesn't seem like too much to ask to be with the person you love and have a career you love too. But unfortunately, that is not the world I lived in. I needed to live a lie."

There it was, she thought. "And do you have an understanding as to why Mr. Mazer lied about your relationship?"

"I do."

"Why?"

"Because I begged him to lie and I told him if he genuinely loved me, he wouldn't out me."

"When did you beg him?"

"When I asked him to go to Marshall's house on October 19, and then . . . and then again after Jon was arrested. Even after he was charged, I continued to tell him that if he had to testify, he could say we were just friends."

"When were you approached by representatives of the state concerning their belief that you had lied to them about your relationship with Jon?"

"About two weeks before the trial started."

"And what did they tell you?"

"That one way or the other I was going to be outed as Mr. Mazer's lover—either because they were going to prosecute me for providing false information, or I could be given immunity and testify."

"When did you strike the deal with the state that they would not prosecute you in return for truthful testimony?"

"About a week before the trial began."

"When was the last time you saw Jon?"

"Last weekend."

"Did you tell him you were going to testify?"

"No."

"Did you tell him he could tell the truth about your relationship?"

"No."

"Why not?"

"Because Mr. Rivers and the investigators told me not to."

"So let me see if I have this straight. As far as Jon knew, you still wanted him to protect you and show his love for you by lying and not outing you, while at the same time, to save your own skin, you struck a deal with the state to do the very thing you made Jon promise not to do. Do I have that right, Father?"

DeAngelis seemed to stiffen, his face contorting in pain. It took several seconds before he responded in an anguished voice, "You have it right."

"You testified that after Jon met with Marshall and told you that everything was fine, you didn't understand what he meant. Did you think it meant that he had killed Mr. Marshall?"

"Oh God, no. I have no reason to believe Jon Mazer had anything to do with Mr. Marshall's death. Jon was willing to sacrifice everything and anything for that article to be published. . . ." He paused. "Everything, including me," DeAngelis said, letting out a sigh.

"Nothing further," Erin said.

"No redirect," Rivers announced, "and no further rebuttal witnesses."

Bader told the jury that she was releasing them for the rest of the day, and they should return tomorrow morning for summations and then the case would be theirs to decide.

Erin lingered after everyone had left, the courtroom now deserted. She'd join Swish momentarily to grab some lunch, but not yet. Charge conferences could be critical, but not here, not in this case. It was all pretty cut and dry. No, only one more big event for her—summation. The trial had gone almost as well as they could have hoped for, if only Mazer hadn't lied on the stand. And she suspected that if he had lied for a woman he loved, the jurors would have forgiven him. But it was for the love of another man. Would they forgive him for that? Or would some latent bias doom Mazer? The prints, the call, the gun—all his. Had destroying Britton carried the day, or would the jury see that Britton's testimony wasn't necessary to convict Mazer?

Erin was surprised by the sound of the courtroom door being pushed open.

"Sorry, didn't mean to startle you," Carol Roy said, making her way up to counsel table and retrieving something out of her briefcase. "No matter what happens, you tried a good case, Erin," Roy said.

"Thanks." Erin hesitated. "Between you and me, I think my job would have been much harder if you had handled more of the case."

"*Gracias,*" Roy said with a smile. "I don't call the shots, but I appreciate the sentiment nonetheless. Not a hard case from our perspective; Marshall's dead and your guy's gun killed him. We'll see what the jury decides."

"Yeah," Erin mumbled.

"Well, at least I don't have to stress over summations," she said with a chuckle. "Like you're clearly doing."

"True that," Erin replied.

"Catch you later," Roy said, heading back down the main aisle. But she stopped when she got to the door. "Hey, Erin, you play any golf?"

"I've played a few times. Why?" Erin replied.

"Try not to stress too much. I suspect that even if you hit a lousy shot, you're going to get a mulligan on this one." And with that Roy walked out the door.

A mulligan, Erin thought, shaking her head. What the hell was she talking about?

Erin retrieved her phone from her purse. She had six text messages. The first was from Mark. **Congratulations, Aunt Erin. Robin had the baby at 9:47 a.m. Everyone is doing well. Robert Mark Simpson-Hansen—7 lbs, 9 ozs. Talk later.**

The remaining texts were from Molly sending pictures of the baby, who was adorable. Robert Mark, she thought. What a beautiful gesture to use "Mark" as the baby's middle name.

She felt horrible that she had no time to celebrate. She wouldn't even have a chance to visit them in the hospital. Then again, if her mother-in-law, Vivian Simpson, was at the hospital, if Erin went, one of them might wind up getting arrested.

She sighed and quickly texted congratulations to everyone, peeked at her watch, and headed out to join Swish for lunch.

She plopped down in the chair opposite Swish. Her white meat turkey sandwich and diet soda were already sitting on the table.

"Good call not asking Britton if he killed Marshall," Swish said. "My sense is he would have said no."

"That was my gut feeling too. When I asked about using Mazer's phone to call Marshall, he hesitated and looked like he was staring at Rivers," Erin said.

"He was," Swish replied. "From my angle it looked like Rivers shook his head, as if to say no."

"Do you think it means Britton didn't kill him, or just that he was willing to lie about it?" she asked.

Swish shook his head. "Don't know. But if he didn't, who did?" he asked, his tone carrying a whiff of foreboding.

They sat in silence eating. Why it came back to her then, she wasn't sure. It must have been floating around in the dark recesses of her brain and then, for whatever reason, it was suddenly there.

"Shit," she mumbled. *Of course, we'll get a mulligan,* she thought.

"What?" Swish asked.

"It was there all along. We just missed it."

"What was?"

"The name of another one of Marshall's sources."

CHAPTER 42

"WHY? MEMBERS OF THE JURY, ASK YOURSELF WHY."

Erin stood in front of the jury in her lucky outfit. Today the courtroom was packed, including people standing along the side walls of the courtroom. Although the trial had been covered by the *Newark Journal* from the start, the number of reporters had increased when the recording had been revealed, and today they seemed to be everywhere. Bader had advised them that there were a number of media requests to film and photograph the summations, but that pursuant to the supreme court's guidelines, there would be one pool video camera operating today and two photographers. Bader also let them know that some of the video coverage might be broadcast live. But as Erin stood in front of the jury, without any notes, talking from her heart, there were only fifteen people in the courtroom—her and the fourteen people in the box.

No one else mattered.

"The state wants you to believe that Jon Mazer killed Russell Marshall in cold blood to prevent the publication of the article Mr. Marshall was about to have published; an article that Mr. Mazer had collaborated on for months; an article that was going to expose the Lords of Discipline, the very group who had harassed Mr. Mazer and countless others both inside and outside the New Jersey State Police; the article that Jon hoped would change the culture of an organization he was proud to be part of. So, again, I ask you, why? And the answer is very simple. There is no answer to why because Jon Mazer did not kill Russell Marshall."

Erin then dissected the testimony of the various witnesses, poking holes in the state's case as she did. She then pounded on the fact that based on the phone records, Marshall was still alive as of 7:10 p.m.—a time when Jon was on duty. Meaning he would've had to have gone to Marshall's home in his state police vehicle and in full uniform. Something no one in the neighborhood had seen.

"I assume that the state will argue something like 'Trooper Britton and Trooper Stone, yeah, they lied, and yes, Trooper Britton is a bigot who lied about what he called people, but their testimony didn't go to the essential facts. It's still undisputed that Mr. Mazer's fingerprints were in Mr. Marshall's home, and it was Mazer's weapon that killed him. So, throw out their testimony, and the evidence against Mr. Mazer remains.' " Erin paused, walking the length of the jury box. "Really, it doesn't matter. As horrible as Trooper Britton's language and views are, the lie that undoes the state's entire case against my client was Trooper Britton's lie that after his shift on October 19, he went home and went to bed. And we know it's a lie because Trooper Urjinski testified under oath that he saw Trooper David Britton in the locker room of the barracks at nine thirty that night, completely consistent with someone returning car keys to Jon Mazer's locker.

"And ask yourself, if Jon Mazer went to Mr. Marshall's home to murder him, and he left fingerprints in the kitchen, why weren't his fingerprints on the windows that were opened in Mr. Marshall's kitchen, living room, and dining room? The windows that were deliberately opened to make it hard for the medical examiner to determine the cause of death? The answer is obvious. Jon Mazer was in Mr. Marshall's house that afternoon to talk to him, and then he left. He was not the one who came later that evening and murdered Mr. Marshall and then opened the windows.

"If you want further proof that Jon was being set up, ask yourself why an experienced state trooper, one trained in firearms, would pick up two of the three bullet casings, but leave the third, knowing full well that casing could be used to link his weapon to the shooting? The answer is, whoever shot Mr. Marshall wanted to leave a trail that led back to Jon.

"Presumably, the state will argue that the casing was stuck in the grate, and he couldn't find it. Really? You heard Detective Cornish's testimony. He got down on his hands and knees and there it was. But, if you were someone who wanted to make it look like the casing was hard to find, where would you put it? In the grate—leaving the impression that it was left behind because the killer couldn't find it.

"Then there's the phone call at 7:03 from Jon's prepaid phone. Again, if you're trying to set someone up, make a call from their phone to the victim, but when the victim answers, don't say anything. Let the victim think it was an accident—a pocket call, a butt call. Then you call the victim back on a different phone, and set up the meeting. That's why you have the 7:03 call from Jon's phone, and two minutes later, the call from an unknown number to Mr. Marshall from the real murderer. All the pieces fit."

Erin stood about ten feet from the jury box. "Why? You may be asking yourself, why would someone set up Jon? Because Jon was a thorn in their side. Jon had filed an IA against Troopers Britton, Stone, and Lyons. He had pushed back against the Lords. Jon wasn't one of the 'boys.' He was an outsider—the other. He was gay. So they came up with a perfect solution. Remove the nettlesome reporter who is about to expose them to the world, and pin it on the trooper who they saw as a 'fag' and a troublemaker. A perfect solution."

Erin walked over so she was standing directly behind Mazer. "Jon Mazer made one mistake—he was not candid with you about his relationship with Gabriel DeAngelis. The state will argue, and the judge will instruct you, that if you find a witness is untruthful about one thing, you are entitled to discredit their entire testimony. And here I stand telling you that Jon was not truthful with you about one thing. Jon and Gabriel DeAngelis were more than friends, they were lovers."

She walked back so that she was standing directly in front of the jury box, about ten feet away, directly in line with the middle of the box. "Let me ask you, would you lie to protect the person you love? Your husband?" she said, her gaze catching the married women. "Your wife?" she asked, allowing herself to pick out the married men. "Your lover?" she said, her gaze slowly sweeping the jurors. "What if the truth had the power to destroy that person—the person you loved—would you lie then? Would you lie to protect their career, their safety, their secret? Would you lie if they begged you to? Does that justify my client not telling you the truth—no, it doesn't. But does it explain why he did—I submit to you that it does.

"And maybe the state will argue, if Jon was willing to lie to protect his lover, maybe he'd kill to protect him. Remember, the state goes last, so I have no way to respond to the arguments that counsel makes. But remember one thing, when Jon Mazer left Mr. Marshall's home he wasn't worried about the article. You have a draft of the article as an exhibit. I urge you to read it. The article does not out Father DeAngelis, it says nothing about him, and Jon knew that. He knew that when he left Mr. Marshall's house and he knew it when he called Father DeAngelis to tell him not to worry. When Jon wasn't candid, it had nothing to do with protecting himself. He was trying to protect Father DeAngelis from being outed in this courtroom. Jon knows all too well the pain of being outed and he was trying to avoid inflicting that on someone he loved. Unbeknownst to Jon was the fact that Father DeAngelis had already struck a deal with the state to out himself and save himself from prosecution. And then, adding insult to injury, at the request of the prosecution, he hid his deal from Jon and continued to let Jon believe that he needed to protect Father DeAngelis.

"Perhaps some of you look at the relationship between Jon and Father DeAngelis and are offended that a priest, a man who had taken a vow of celibacy, was in a romantic relationship with another man. And maybe some of you don't like the fact that Jon is gay. But does that mean he should be convicted of murder for being gay? If we listen to the words of Trooper Britton, we can conclude that there are people whose criteria for judging folks is the color of their skin, or their ethnicity, or their sex, or their sexual orientation. But all of you took an oath to be fair and impartial and decide this case on the evidence, not on any bias or prejudice. Whatever you think of Jon Mazer, don't convict him of murder simply because he's a gay man.

"And you may wonder, well, if Jon Mazer didn't kill Mr. Marshall, who did? I think we've laid out a pretty good case for who did, but proving who did it is not on Jon. Jon does not have to prove anything to you. Jon Mazer is presumed innocent. The burden is solely on the state to prove Jon's guilt beyond a reasonable doubt. I submit to you members of the jury, the state has not met its burden in this case. There is more than reasonable doubt here. As you promised at the start of the case, all we ask is that you decide the case based on the evidence—not on conjecture or speculation, not on bias or innuendo, but the evidence. And if you do that, I am confident, and Jon is confident, that you will return a verdict of not guilty. Thank you."

Rivers stood, buttoned the suit jacket of his black, pinstriped suit, and positioned himself in front of the jury box.

"Ladies and gentlemen of the jury, let's agree on one thing from the start. Trooper David Britton is a liar and a bigot and his words and attitude are reprehensible, and they will have ramifications. But one of those ramifications shouldn't be to allow the killer of Russell Marshall to get away with murder. What becomes of Trooper Britton for the lies he told you in this courtroom are not for you to decide. Your sworn obligation is to review the evidence, and decide the case based on the facts. Counsel for the defendant and I agree on very few things, but we do agree that bias and prejudice have no place in your deliberations.

"What's ironic is that after telling you bias and prejudice have no place in this courtroom, counsel for the defendant plays the gay card. Her poor client, picked on because he's gay. Her noble client, trying to protect another gay man from being outed. Gay this, gay that—ladies and gentlemen, this isn't a discrimination case. This is a murder case. The defendant doesn't get a free pass because someone was mean to him because he's a homosexual. He's free to engage in a homosexual lifestyle if he so chooses. He's not free to murder someone.

"Counsel for the defendant asked you, 'Why? Why would Jon Mazer kill Russell Marshall in cold blood?' Well, allow me to answer that question—for love. Counsel asked you if you would lie for love. We know the defendant would do that; counsel has admitted he did. But the defendant was willing to do more than lie to protect his lover—he was willing to commit murder. The defendant murdered Russell Marshall to protect his lover—a Catholic priest no less—because his lover was panicked that he would be exposed for the hypocrite he was. A man who had taken a vow of celibacy, a man who made a promise to God to uphold the teachings of the Catholic Church, which condemn homosexuality. A man who begged the defendant to protect him. And when the defendant couldn't convince Mr. Marshall to pull the article, an article we can reasonably infer the defendant felt was as much his as Mr. Marshall's, he argued with Mr. Marshall, lost his temper, and in order to protect his lover, he killed Mr. Marshall.

"Means, motive, and opportunity, ladies and gentlemen, the pillars of any crime, and the defendant had all three. The means—his gun; the opportunity—we know he was in Mr. Marshall's home; and now we have the motive. To silence the man who was going to expose his lover."

Rivers went through witness by witness emphasizing all the connections that led back to Mazer. Then he turned to Mazer, repeating what he had done on cross, trying to show the absurdity of someone breaking into Mazer's locker in a locked police barracks, getting his car keys, taking his weapon and phone, killing Marshall, and then rushing back to return everything to normal before Mazer could discover anything. It was preposterous, Rivers argued.

"Ladies and gentlemen, the defendant, through his counsel, has admitted he perjured himself—end of story. Nothing he told you from the witness stand is worthy of belief, and under the law, you are free to disregard everything he testified to. The evidence in this case is overwhelming. We know that on October 19, 2009, the defendant went to the home of Russell Marshall; we have his admission and his fingerprints. While he was there, he shot Mr. Marshall three times in the chest. Any one of those shots was sufficient to kill Mr. Marshall, but he damn sure wanted to leave no doubt. We know it was him because it's undisputed that it was his weapon that was used to shoot Mr. Marshall.

"Please, ladies and gentlemen, don't leave your common sense outside the jury room. Use your common sense and experience when you examine the evidence. If you do that, and do it fairly and without bias, you will see that the evidence shows the defendant, Jon Mazer, is guilty of murder beyond any reasonable doubt.

"Thank you."

Erin and Swish sat with Jon in his holding cell. It was around two thirty and the jury had just headed off to begin deliberations. The two alternates turned out to be juror number two, a Black female, and juror number four, a South Asian male. The judge then advised the jurors that juror number one, Steven Williams, was to act as the foreperson. Erin and Swish, like all New Jersey lawyers, knew that under the court rules, juror number one was always the foreperson, that's why the person sitting in that seat was especially important. Both Erin and Swish had been comfortable with Williams from the start. Now they'd find out if their gut instincts in terms of how the jurors would react to the blatant racism had been correct.

For Erin, the hard part started now. With the jury out, there was plenty of downtime. Time to run through all the "what ifs" or "should we have done this or that differently?" Lots of time to second-guess. Should she have conceded that Jon lied about only being friends with DeAngelis or should they have stuck with they were only friends? Shit, she thought. DeAngelis was always their Achilles heel.

At four thirty, the jury sent a note asking if they could break for the day. As was customary, Bader repeated her instruction to avoid any news about the trial, specifically noting there had been a much larger contingent of press and media in the courtroom today, and emphasizing they were not to discuss the case with anyone outside the jury room, including family, friends, coworkers, even fellow jurors.

"What do you think?" Erin asked Swish as they walked to their cars, affording them the first chance to talk outside Jon's presence.

"I think I know you well enough to know you are in the midst of playing Whac-a-Mole with your self-doubt—maybe we should have done this, maybe we shouldn't have done that, maybe we shouldn't have admitted Jon wasn't truthful. How am I doing?" he asked.

"Pretty good," she said sheepishly.

"E, it went down just like we knew it would. Marshall was killed with our guy's gun with his prints in the house. It was always going to be a tough case, made harder by the fact that he insisted on lying to protect his boyfriend, who turned around and sold him down the river."

Erin allowed herself a small laugh. "You never did like Father DeAngelis."

"You're right about that. But the bottom line is that we tried a good case. If he goes down, it wasn't because we fucked up. You've got to remember, E, we don't make the facts or the law, we can only play the cards we're dealt."

"Thanks," she said. "See you tomorrow. Fingers crossed," she said, holding up her right hand with her fingers crossed.

When she walked in the door, she was welcomed by delicious scents coming from the kitchen. She dropped her briefcase in the foyer. "Hey," she said as she walked in, stood on her toes, and gave Mark a peck on the cheek. "Whatcha making?"

He gave her a kiss on the forehead. "I figured the adrenaline might still be flowing, so I went with something simple—some breaded chicken cutlets, jasmine rice, and a salad," he said. "And by the way, you were brilliant today."

She gave him a quizzical look. "Was it on the news?"

"I don't know, probably," he said with a grin. "I was there."

"What do you mean you were there?"

"I was in the courtroom. I saw your summation."

"You what?"

"Yeah, I've never seen you in action, so I took a half of a personal day and came to see you."

She looked at him in disbelief. "I didn't see you."

"Of course you didn't. You were so focused on the jurors, you didn't see me . . . or your mom."

"My mom!"

"Yep, your mom. I picked her up this morning and we came together."

"Why didn't you tell me?" she asked.

He laughed. "There are a few things I've learned over the last few years. Telling a woman she looks 'fine' is not a compliment; always make sure I tell you I like your hairstyle, even if I don't. And don't put any more pressure on you when you're on trial, because you're already so amped up, you might explode."

She leaned back and suppressed a laugh. "You don't like my hair," she finally said.

"I love your hair," he replied enthusiastically.

"I'll never be able to trust your compliments about my hair again," she said, throwing her arms around his neck and giving him a deep kiss.

"That was nice," she said when their kiss ended. "What did my mom think?"

"Like me, she thought you were brilliant."

"You're both biased."

"True, but we still thought you rocked it."

"Thanks," she said. "So, if you were on the jury, what would you do?"

"We stayed for the prosecutor guy too, and he made some good points, but as I know from listening to you rehearse things, you don't have to prove your guy didn't do it, they have to prove he did. And for me there's more than a reasonable doubt. So, I think you win."

"Wish you were on the jury," she said. "Speaking of which, were you watching the jurors?"

"Yeah, my read was that you scored some points with almost all of them."

"Almost all?" she said.

"Yeah, there was a woman in the back row, I don't know, she seemed kind of cool to you."

"Juror eight, Karen Cosby," Erin said immediately. "Yeah, we've been worried about her from the start."

"But even if you don't get everyone, it has to be unanimous to convict, right?" he asked.

"And unanimous to find him not guilty," she said in a tone that conveyed her fear.

"But isn't a hung jury a good thing for you?" he asked.

"Sometimes it is, but not in this case," she said. "In this case a mistrial would be a disaster because they'd get to retry Jon and they'd never make the same mistakes on a retrial. No, a hung jury is definitely not a good thing."

CHAPTER 43

AROUND ELEVEN ON THURSDAY MORNING, THE JURY SENT OUT A note asking to have the defendant's testimony read back. When everyone was assembled back in the courtroom, Bader asked the foreman if they wanted Mr. Mazer's entire testimony read, to which he responded they did. Bader's court reporter was both a great writer and reader. Meaning that not only did she get everything down accurately, but unlike some reporters, she had no trouble at all reading back what she had transcribed.

Erin always marveled at court reporters; to her, they were the unsung heroes of the system. Unfortunately, for most proceedings on the civil side, almost all of them had been replaced by a taping system, which Erin knew would sooner or later take over in the criminal courts as well. But for now, Bader's reporter read everything line by line. It took two hours to complete the read back, which meant the lunch break came later than usual, causing Bader to suggest a forty-five-minute lunch break.

When Erin stepped out into the hallway, she noticed she had both a missed call and a voicemail message from Phil Song. She immediately clicked on the message to listen.

"Erin, Phil Song. Give me a call when you can. Judge Jacobs's clerk called. The judge would like to set up the hearing on our application to have you and Mark listed on the baby's birth certificate as the baby's mom and dad. You and Mark, and Liz and Sean will all need to be there to testify, so give me a call back when you can. I know you're on trial because I saw you on the news last night. Good luck."

"Everything okay?" Swish asked.

"Yeah, I think so," she said. "Why don't you go grab lunch? I need to try and get hold of the lawyer who is handling the birth certificate stuff for Mark and me."

"You want me to bring you back something?" Swish asked.

Between worrying about what it meant that the jury wanted Mazer's testimony read back, and now Judge Jacobs wanting to schedule a hearing, her stomach and food wouldn't be a good match right now. "How about a diet soda and a package of M & Ms?" she said, generating a raised eyebrow from Swish. "What?" she said. "The carbonation will fill me up without calories and the candy will boost my sugar and give me energy—breakfast of champions."

After Swish left, she immediately redialed Song. "Hey, Phil, it's Erin," she said when he answered. "I got your message about a hearing. What's going on? I kind of thought everything was going to be on the papers."

"I did too, but apparently the AG's Office was causing a stink, so the judge wants to schedule an in-person hearing. I told her clerk you were on trial, and also that Sean is a doctor with a very busy schedule, so I just need you to get me some dates when the four of you are available."

"Do you know how much time we're going to need—a couple hours, half a day, a day?" Erin asked.

"Honestly, Erin, I don't know. Let's plan on a day for scheduling purposes and see what the clerk says when I get back to her."

"Sure. Thanks, Phil. I probably won't be able to get back to you until next week. Is that okay?"

"Yeah, no problem. Good luck with your trial."

"Thanks, Phil."

After the lunch break the jury requested that Father DeAngelis's testimony be read back.

"This isn't good," Jon said in his holding cell.

"Try not to read too much into it," Swish replied. "You can

drive yourself crazy trying to figure out what the hell the jury is thinking."

"Yeah, but why aren't they asking for Britton's or Smith's testimony?" Jon asked.

"Probably because it's pretty cut and dry," Erin suggested. "I agree with Duane, you'll drive yourself nuts trying to guess," she said, knowing that was exactly what she was doing, and willing to bet that Swish was doing the same thing. It was the nature of the beast. The jury asks a question or wants a readback, and everyone immediately begins playing "what is the jury thinking."

But the readbacks of Mazer and now DeAngelis made her silently agree with Jon—this wasn't good. They were focused on his lie, Erin speculated, why else ask for both?

As they had the day before, at four thirty, the jury once again asked to break for the day.

"Thoughts?" Erin asked Swish as they stood in the parking lot.

"Tomorrow afternoon, we'll have a verdict. My guess is the readbacks were to satisfy one reluctant juror."

"Really?" she said. "And what do you base that on?"

"During readback this morning, it looked to me like nine or ten, maybe even eleven of them were nodding along, like 'See, this is what we told you he said.' "

"Is that good or bad for us?" she asked.

"I'm thinking good, but that's more of a guess. What about you?"

"I look for smiles or body language," she said. "When I catch their eye, how do they react?"

"And?" he asked.

"I feel good about four or five of them. The foreman, I confess, is a bit like you, inscrutable, and our friend, Ms. Cosby, she's a sphinx. I don't know, Swish. I hope we get a verdict tomorrow, because waiting over the weekend will be brutal." She paused. "Unless, of course, if it's a guilty verdict."

"I saw your texts. You know I have a jury out. What's going on?" Rivers asked.

"I thought you'd want to know that the General and the Colonel are going to announce the opening of an IA against Britton, along with his immediate suspension," Sam Walters, the attorney general's chief of staff, said, referring to the AG and the head of the state police, in the way they were known in the law enforcement community—the General and the Colonel. "But they're going to wait until the jury reaches a verdict, to avoid any publicity that could impact the verdict."

"I kind of figured that was going to happen. He really shot himself in the foot with that interview he did with Smith. Does he know it's coming?"

"Yeah, there was a reach-out to the head of the union last night to alert him. Obviously, Britton's not happy about it." Walters paused. "Just an FYI, you had better keep your head down too. Let's just say folks from the governor on down are none too happy with that tape."

Shit, Rivers thought. "So they're pissed at me, even though I had nothing to do with it," he finally said.

"The General just felt you should have given him more of a warning as to what was coming. He felt like he was blindsided."

"Jesus, Sam, it's not like we didn't try everything we could to keep it out."

"I hear you, Ward. But like I said, he's pissed off at the world right now."

"All right, thanks," Rivers replied. "I appreciate the heads-up."

Fuck, Rivers thought after he hung up. Why in God's name had Britton spoken with Smith and then allowed it to be recorded? Even the edited recording was a fucking disaster. There was no question that Britton was fucked. But it wasn't just the recording. He took the Fifth on whether he took Mazer's phone and gun. That opened up a whole can of shit. Fucking McCabe had walked them right into a trap and now he had to figure out how to play this. And if it was only Britton's fate in play, he wouldn't give a shit. But Britton was definitely trapped in a corner and trapped animals were dangerous. Britton knew a lot—too much actually. Rivers snorted to himself. Who the fuck was he kidding? Britton wasn't the only cornered animal. Based on what Walters had just told him, he was fucking cornered too.

He needed to find a way out, and he needed it quickly.

"I am so fucked," Britton said as he looked across the table in Horgan's, a local cop bar, at troopers Ed Stone and Kiernan Lyons.

"What did Nash tell you?" Stone asked, referring to Kyle Nash, head of the troopers' union.

"The Colonel told him they're ready to start the IA, and as soon as there's a verdict, they'll publicly announce it and suspend me, initially with pay, and then once the IA complaint is sustained, unpaid. Then they'll file Major Disciplinary Charges against me, looking to terminate me."

"Nash think you have a shot at beating it?"

Britton's laugh was bitter. "Nash's words were something like, 'As long as you didn't kill Marshall, maybe you can cut a deal to resign and plead to perjury, so they don't charge you with second-degree Official Misconduct. Hopefully that'll keep you out of jail.' "

"Jesus," Lyons said. "Sorry, bro."

"Rivers have any thoughts?" Stone asked.

"Don't even get me started on that son of a bitch. When I was on the stand, he could've asked me if I killed Marshall, so I could've denied doing it, but he wouldn't even throw me a fucking lifeline," Britton said through gritted teeth. "But I can't fuck with him, because I need him if they try to come after me. That said, between us, even though he ran the Lords when he was in the outfit, I don't trust the motherfucker," he said, signaling to their waitress for another drink.

"And then there's Smith," Britton continued, shaking his head. "Told me not to worry. The recording had been destroyed." He stopped and drained what was left of his beer. "Shit," he said. "I'm a fucking pariah, which is pretty fucking ironic since all I did was get caught saying out loud exactly what we all say in private."

"You talk to a lawyer yet?" Stone asked.

"Yeah. The union got me one. He's the one who told me to

take the Fifth. I'm supposed to see him again next week as soon as they get a verdict in the Mazer case. Need to get a divorce lawyer too. Fucking bitch threatened me with a DV complaint if I didn't leave. Just what I need, a domestic violence beef. The papers would have a field day with that."

"Shit, dude," Lyons said. "Whatya gonna do?"

Britton flexed his jaw, looked up at the ceiling, and exhaled. "Not sure yet, but I suspect it won't be pretty."

CHAPTER 44

IT WAS ELEVEN THIRTY ON FRIDAY WHEN BADER CALLED COUNSEL INTO her chambers. "I have a note from the foreman indicating that the jury is deadlocked," she said. "From my perspective, with readbacks and everything else, they've been at it for less than two days, so my initial reaction is to give the instruction on further deliberations, but wanted to make sure we were all on the same page."

"Judge," Rivers began, "as I've indicated earlier, this jury has clearly been tainted, and the state once again renews its request for a mistrial."

Bader turned her head to look at Erin.

"Judge, we're fine with your suggestion. The jury hasn't been out that long and I don't think any of us are anxious to try this case again."

Bader nodded and directed her attention back to Rivers. "Mr. Rivers, I'll note the state's position, as well as the defendant's when we go back on the record, but my position remains unchanged. If the jury is hopelessly deadlocked, we'll find out in due course, but we need to let them work at it a bit longer."

Ten minutes later, Bader turned her chair to the twelve jurors sitting in the box. "I've received a note from the foreman indicating you have not been able to reach a unanimous verdict. Despite that, I'm going to ask you to keep trying. I want you to remember that each of you took the oath as a juror. It is your duty, as jurors, to consult with one another and to deliberate with a view to reaching an agreement. Each of you must decide the case for yourself, but only after an impartial consideration of the evidence with your fellow jurors. Do not hesitate to reexamine your own views and change your opinion if you're convinced it's wrong, but do not change it solely because of the opinion of your fellow jurors, or for the mere purpose of returning a verdict. You are not partisans. You are judges—judges of the facts. With those instructions in mind, please return to your deliberations. Thank you."

Erin had studied the jurors as Bader gave her instructions. Despite her best efforts, she couldn't figure out who was on which side of the guilty/not guilty line.

Mark had once asked Erin what it was like waiting for a jury verdict, and she had told him it was one of the most helpless feelings in the world. Twelve strangers, who days or weeks earlier had known absolutely nothing about the case, were deciding the fate of her client and there was absolutely nothing else she could do.

"You still thinking today?" Erin asked Swish when they took a break from sitting with Jon.

"Yeah, I am. If they're as astute as I think they are, they probably read between the lines of Bader's demeanor. She'll bring them back on Monday if necessary. Meaning, if they want to be done with this and enjoy their weekend, they'll find a way to do this today."

"I'm never sure whether that kind of pressure is good or bad for us," she replied.

"Having spent some time with prosecutors, they think it's more of a push to a not guilty verdict. After all, who wants to spend the weekend thinking they just voted to convict an innocent man so they could enjoy a round of golf?"

Bader's clerk stuck her head out of the courtroom door. "The jury would like part of the judge's instructions reread. Please come inside."

When the jury was back in the box, Bader said, "I understand you'd like me to instruct you again on reasonable doubt. Under New Jersey law, a reasonable doubt is an honest and reasonable uncertainty in your minds about the guilt of the defendant after you have given full and impartial consideration to all of the evidence. A reasonable doubt may arise from the evidence itself or from a lack of evidence. Proof beyond a reasonable doubt is proof, for example, that leaves you firmly convinced of the defendant's guilt. In this world, we know very few things with absolute certainty. In criminal cases the law does not require proof that overcomes every possible doubt. If, based on your consideration of the evidence, you are firmly convinced that the defendant is guilty of the crime charged, you must find him guilty. If, on the other hand, you are not firmly convinced of the defendant's guilt, you must give the defendant the benefit of the doubt and find him not guilty.

"You may now resume your deliberations," Bader said with a tight smile.

Steve Williams leaned back in his chair. His fellow jurors were starting to get antsy. None of them wanted to come back on Monday, but that was beginning to look more and more likely. If he had known he was going to wind up as foreman, he probably would have tried to come up with an excuse to get off. It would've been fairly easy. He truly was sick and tired of white cops killing Black people. Folks in his neighborhood had tried and convicted Mazer the day he was arrested, and when they found out he had been picked for the jury, they smiled knowingly whenever they saw him in the store or walking in the neighborhood.

And initially it had looked easy—Mazer's fingerprints in the house, Mazer's gun, Mazer's phone used to call—but he had promised to keep an open mind.

When they had started deliberations, the preliminary vote had been six guilty, four not guilty, and two undecided. One thing they all agreed on was that Trooper Britton was a racist, lying sack of shit. But, as Williams saw it, even after they threw out everything he testified to, there was still enough to convict Mazer.

Todd Harris, juror number seven, had argued that Mazer had no reason to kill Marshall, but Todd was white, and liked cops.

Williams had tended to agree more with Mildred Jackson, juror number ten, who thought Mazer had done it to protect his homosexual boyfriend, although Mildred still had trouble believing that any man as handsome as Mazer could be gay.

He had to admit that he had been stuck on the fence until Karen Cosby, juror eight, started analyzing the evidence and the testimony bit by bit, witness by witness. She was a paralegal, and even though she worked in the bond department, the woman knew how to break things down and wasn't afraid to tell you why she thought you were wrong—and damn if she wasn't convincing. Now they were down to one holdout. Hopefully, Karen could work her magic one more time.

Erin, Swish, and Jon sat in his holding cell, each lost in their own thoughts. With Jon's future hanging in the balance, small talk seemed painful. So, silence was the order of the day—awkward silence. Erin's stomach was in knots. She guessed they were down to one, but were they holding out for guilty or not guilty?

Erin glanced at her watch, four o'clock. Suddenly there was a stirring outside the cell.

"Judge wants everyone in the courtroom," a sheriff's officer announced.

When they entered the courtroom, Erin knew immediately there was a verdict. Members of the press were taking up positions in the back of the courtroom so they could leave as soon as the verdict was announced and call their respective outlets. There were extra sheriff's officers stationed strategically around the courtroom to provide additional security if needed. In the second row, behind the railing that separated the spectators from the lawyers, she saw Rich Rudolph and Doug Rudnicki. Sitting directly in front of them were Marshall's family members, who had been present throughout the entire trial.

Here we go, Erin thought, suddenly glad that she hadn't eaten lunch.

Bader walked up the three steps to her bench. "I've received a note from the jury that they have reached a verdict. I want to caution everyone in the courtroom that when the verdict is read, I will not tolerate any outbursts, and if there are, I will have anyone involved removed from the courtroom." She then turned to her clerk. "Bring the jury in, please."

Erin leaned over and whispered to Jon, "The judge will ask you to stand before the verdict is read. Duane and I will stand with you."

Jon looked at her, his face drawn and ashen. "Okay," he mumbled.

"Mr. Foreman," Bader said once they were all settled in, "has the jury reached a verdict?"

Steven Williams rose from his seat in the jury box. "We have, Your Honor."

"Is your verdict unanimous?" she asked.

"It is, Your Honor."

"Will the defendant, Jon Mazer, please rise."

With Erin and Duane on either side of him, Jon stood and turned to face the jury. Erin felt her heart pounding as she looked at Williams standing in the jury box. He was staring at the judge and not at them.

"Mr. Foreman, what is the jury's verdict in the matter of the State of New Jersey versus Jon Mazer?"

Erin held her breath.

"Your Honor, we the members of the jury, find Jon Mazer not guilty of the murder of Russell Marshall."

When the words "not guilty" left Steven Williams's mouth, Erin closed her eyes and inhaled for what seemed like the first time in minutes. Mazer seemed to go momentarily weak in the knees, and she heard him whisper to himself, "Thank God."

Despite Bader's admonition, Erin heard some muffled noises behind them, causing Bader to rap her gavel gently. "Quiet, please."

"Mr. Rivers, Ms. Roy, do you want the jury to be polled?"

Rivers stood. "Please, Judge," he said softly.

Bader then asked each of the jurors individually if they agreed with the verdict announced by the foreman.

After each answered that they agreed, Bader said, "Ladies and gentlemen, I want to thank you for your service. Jury duty is one of the most important civic duties you can provide as a citizen and I commend you all for your diligence, patience, and service to the state of New Jersey. I tell you so you are aware; you are under no obligation to speak to anyone about this case or the jury deliberations. I suspect each of you may be contacted by members of the media. In the event you are, you are free to discuss or not discuss the case, as you choose. With that, you are discharged with my personal thanks for all your hard work."

After the jury had made their way out of the courtroom, Bader turned to Jon, Erin, and Duane. "The jury having found you not guilty of the charges against you, the matter is concluded and you are free to go, Mr. Mazer. Good luck, sir."

The three of them joined in a group hug, with Jon repeating, "Thank you. Thank you. Thank you."

After several minutes, Erin broke away and headed over to Rivers and Roy. Extending a hand toward Rivers, she said, "Nice job."

Rivers looked at her outstretched hand and grabbed his briefcase. "Fuck you. You sandbagged us. We both have long careers ahead of us, McCabe, and I won't forget what you did."

He then turned and headed for the door, ignoring the questions from reporters, and made his way out.

Erin was still looking in his direction when she heard Roy's voice. "Sorry, Erin."

Erin turned to see Roy with her hand outstretched. Erin gave a sad smile, reached out and took Roy's hand. "Thank you, Carol. You are a worthy adversary, and between me and you, I'm thankful Rivers didn't utilize your skills more fully. Who knows how this would have turned out?"

Roy laughed. "It still would have been not guilty. And if it's any consolation, I don't feel sandbagged. Your expert found the recording, ours didn't. Shame on us."

"Thanks," Erin said.

"And one more thing," Roy said, reaching down into her briefcase and removing a legal-size envelope. "You never got this from me. And my recommendation is that you keep it confidential. It's pretty fucking sad, actually. But I think you need to see it," Roy said, her tone having shifted from congratulatory to foreboding. "Here's your mulligan."

Erin took the envelope, totally mystified. "Thanks."

Britton sat on the love seat in his family room, his hand shaking, the barrel of his gun deep into his mouth. *Fuck them all,* he thought. They pushed him to this. And now . . . now he had truly ruined his life. He didn't want to be here for the announcement of the charges against him. He didn't need the headlines or the perp walk. No, he'd go out on his own terms.

Suddenly, his phone vibrated. He looked down to see there was a text message from a Middlesex County sheriff's officer he knew who worked in the courthouse. He took the gun out of his mouth, and picked up his phone.

Not guilty.

He laid his weapon down and looked at his watch—4:10 p.m. He walked into the kitchen, trying to avoid the blood that had spread across the floor from his wife's body. Rigor mortis was already starting to set in. He stood by the refrigerator staring at her.

You got what you deserved, bitch. I told you not to push my buttons. Maybe next time you'll listen to me. He let out a mocking laugh. *Oh yeah, guess there won't be a next time.* He grabbed a beer from the fridge, twisted off the cap, and took a healthy swig. *Not fucking guilty, the final insult,* he thought. He sat at the counter, finishing his beer. Then the plan hit him.

He went into the bedroom and took his off-duty weapon out of the closet, checked the magazine and grabbed an extra magazine, just in case. With his duty weapon and this he was set. One way or the other, this was his last day on the planet. May as well go out in a blaze of glory.

From Erin's perspective the news conference outside the courthouse went great. She had let Swish do most of the talking, and Jon was effusive in his praise for them. When each of them was asked about Britton and Smith, they all said variations on the same theme. "What they said was reprehensible and should be dealt with." At this point, exhausted from the trial, none of them were in the mood to pour more gas on the fire.

When they finished the news conference, Rudnicki pulled Swish aside and told him that Jennifer Savage, the reporter for the *Journal,* had spoken to one of the jurors. Apparently, since early this morning, they were eleven to one for acquittal. The lone holdout was juror number twelve, Jason Washburn, the young literary agent. He believed Mazer had killed Marshall in order to protect his lover's secret. He finally agreed with the others, apparently not wanting to come back on Monday. Savage had also been told that Karen Cosby, who didn't like Erin because she was transgender, had put aside her personal feelings, and had argued convincingly for Mazer's innocence.

Since Jon had no car, and there was no one at the courthouse to give him a ride, they agreed Swish would take him over to the correction facility so he could pick up his wallet and personal property, and Erin would meet them there. Afterward, Swish would give him a ride home and they'd plan a celebratory dinner for next week.

It was around six thirty by the time they had gotten Jon processed out of the correctional facility. As they walked down the sidewalk three abreast with Jon between her and Swish, a car pulled up and parked in the semicircular driveway in front of the building. Erin wasn't paying much attention, having too much fun laughing with Swish and Jon.

"Well, if it isn't the three little bears. Fucking pretend mamma bear, a fucking Black pappa bear, and the gay fucking baby bear."

They stopped and Erin looked up to see David Britton standing about ten feet away.

"My lucky day," he said with a sneer. "But not yours," he added, pulling his weapon from his hip holster.

The next thing Erin knew, Jon shoved her so hard she was flying through the air sideways, Swish's scream of "GUN!" reverberating in her ears, followed by the deafening roar of gunshots.

CHAPTER 45

ERIN WASN'T SURE HOW MANY SHOTS WERE FIRED. SHE HEARD CORrections officers running out of the building screaming, followed by another shot.

When the shooting stopped, she looked up to see Jon and Swish both on the ground, blood pooling by their unmoving bodies. Britton was also down, part of the top of his head missing. Sirens wailed and there was pandemonium as nurses and EMTs who worked in the facility came running out and began working furiously on Swish and Jon. She scrambled to her feet.

"Swish!" she screamed. "Oh my God, Swish!"

She attempted to run to him, but a burly corrections officer grabbed her around the waist. "Stay here," he said, his voice commanding, yet soothing. "Let the medical people work on them. There's nothing you can do but get in the way."

She fell to her knees, screaming in agony.

Suddenly there was a nurse at her side. "Honey, you're bleeding. Are you hurt?"

She quickly took stock of herself. She had some superficial cuts on her arms and legs from where she had landed on the concrete sidewalk, but as best she could tell, nothing else. "I'm okay," she said. "Please take care of them," she pleaded, pointing at Swish and Jon.

The wail of the sirens filled the air as ambulances came flying into the same area that Britton had parked, and gurneys were wheeled over to where Swish and Jon were lying.

"I need to go with him," Erin screamed, pointing to the gurney they had placed Swish on.

"We'll get you there," said a lieutenant she recognized from visiting Mazer. "They need to work on him in the ambulance."

"Is he going to make it?" she asked, terror in her voice.

"I honestly don't know, ma'am. They're doing everything they can."

As the ambulances sped off, one with Swish, the other with Jon, she saw the EMTs moving away from Britton's body. He was clearly gone and this was a crime scene. He'd lay there until the medical examiner ordered his removal.

"Come with me, ma'am," the lieutenant said, ushering her to a waiting sheriff's vehicle.

"What hospital?" she asked. "Robert Wood Johnson?"

"Yes, ma'am."

Somehow in the chaos, she had managed to find her purse and she dragged out her cell phone, hitting Mark's number.

"Hey, congratulations," he answered. "Where are you?"

"Mark, there's been a shooting. Swish and Jon have been shot. I need you to get hold of Cori, and JJ, and whoever else you can think of, and get to Robert Wood Johnson as soon as possible." And then she completely lost it, crying into the phone. "Oh my God, Mark, please hurry."

Erin was sitting in the surgery waiting room when Mark arrived. He hurried over and sat next to her, allowing her to throw herself into his chest and sob. She tried to explain, but every time she tried to talk, she was overcome with emotion.

"I'm sorry. I'm sorry. Hopefully Swish will be okay. I heard it on the news on the way here. They said it was Britton."

All she could do was nod.

"I called Sean to let him know what was going on, and I'm hoping with his connections maybe he could get us some information on Swish," Mark said.

"Thanks," she said, grateful that Mark had thought of Sean.

About ten minutes later, JJ, his husband Gary, and Corrine

came running in. As soon as Erin saw Corrine, she jumped up, rushed over, and hugged her.

"Oh God, Cori," she said, both of them crying as they rocked each other. When they broke their embrace, Erin said, "I don't know," without being asked. "They took him to surgery as soon as we arrived. I don't know anything."

Erin tried to fill them in as best she could, but after Mazer's shove had sent her flying, she didn't know what had happened.

At one point a resident came out to let them know Swish was still in surgery. When they pressed her as to how he was, all she said was she had no other information.

About an hour later, Erin looked up to see Sean. He immediately walked over and knelt in front of Corrine, taking her hand in his and giving it a reassuring pat.

"Corrine, I just spoke to the doctor who operated on Duane, who is probably the best trauma surgeon in the state, and I asked him if I could speak with you first. He's going to come in and talk to you, but what he told me is that Duane made it through surgery, but it's still touch and go." Corrine covered her mouth with her hand and muttered, "Oh please, God." Sean squeezed her hand. "He lost a lot of blood. He was hit twice, once in the left shoulder, the second on the left side of his chest, puncturing his lung. But miraculously, it doesn't look like it struck any major arteries or deflected and hit any other major organs. The next forty-eight hours are going to be critical." He gave her a hug. "He's getting the best care possible."

"Thank you," Corrine said as she folded into JJ, who was sitting next to her.

Sean then knelt in front of Erin.

"Sis," he said, his face turning very somber. "I'm afraid I have some awful news. Jon Mazer didn't make it. He died of his gunshot wounds about an hour ago. They tried everything they could to save him, but one of his wounds severed his lateral descending artery, and another destroyed his lung. They tried. I'm so sorry."

Erin was riding a roller coaster of emotions. Swish was alive—Jon was dead. Dead? How could Jon be dead? How could Swish be critically wounded? They'd just walked out of the courtroom together, laughing, crying—Jon was free. They'd won. And now he was gone, and Swish was fighting for his life. She bent forward and began to weep. Her brother caught her in his arms and held her tight.

"I know, E. I know."

Mark gently pulled her from Sean's arms and embraced her with his. "I'm sorry, babe. I'm so sorry."

"Excuse me, is there an Erin McCabe here?" an imposing gentleman standing in the doorway asked.

Mark looked up. "She's here. What do you need?"

He displayed a badge. "I'm Captain Jenkins, Mercer County Prosecutor's Office. A few folks would like to speak to her for a moment." He paused, looking at the emotions on full display around the room. "I'm sorry, I realize this is a very difficult time, but it's important."

Erin looked up, blew her nose in the tissue she was holding, and stood up.

"I'm coming with you," Mark said.

Erin gave a weak nod, and they followed Jenkins down the hallway, where he opened a door and motioned with his arm for them to enter.

As Erin entered the room, she noticed Carol Roy, Middlesex County Prosecutor Vanessa Talon, and several other individuals she didn't recognize.

Talon stood and came over and hugged Erin. "We're all praying that Duane is going to make it," she said.

Erin pursed her lips and nodded. "Thanks," she managed to squeak out. "Jon's dead," she sobbed.

"We know. I'm sorry."

Talon then introduced the other people in the room, starting with Mercer County Prosecutor Carl Schey and several detectives and assistant prosecutors from Middlesex and Mercer. "And of course, DAG Carol Roy."

Carol got up from her chair and gave Erin a hug. "I'm sorry," she said, a catch in her voice.

'Thanks," Erin said. "Oh, this is my husband, Mark."

"Erin, Mark, have a seat," Talon said. "We know this is an incredibly difficult time, but we wanted to give you some information, and were hoping that after that, you'd be willing to provide a statement to the detectives."

Erin chewed on her lower lip and nodded.

"I'm going to let Carol start," Talon said.

"Erin, I'm sure you haven't had a chance to look at what I gave you after the verdict today, but it's an affidavit of Deputy Attorney General Albert Holmes that was left on my desk during the trial."

Holmes, Erin thought. *How could he do an affidavit? He's been dead for months.*

As if reading Erin's thoughts, Roy continued. "He signed the affidavit the day he died. Turns out he had left a copy in a sealed envelope on his desk with a note on the outside that it was for me. Apparently, when his supervisor and paralegal were cleaning out his desk several months after he died, they found it, and his secretary left it on my desk. In the affidavit, Holmes described what hadn't come to light yet, but was widely reported after he died, about being caught in the undercover sting operation in Branch Brook Park, and how when Rivers found out about it, he used it to blackmail Holmes, first when Rivers was in private practice in connection with the task force investigation, and then later, when he became an assistant attorney general and Holmes was handling Mazer's IA. Holmes admitted to being the initial source for Marshall about the Lords and recruiting Mazer to assist. He stated he was in frequent contact with Marshall, and Marshall would call him on a prepaid phone. Most importantly, Holmes stated in his affidavit that on the evening of October 19, 2009, at 7:10 p.m. he received a call from Marshall telling him that another confidential source in the AG's Office had just reached out to him and Marshall wanted to know if Holmes knew any reason why someone from the AG's Office would want to see him that night. Holmes told Marshall he had no idea why. Holmes speculated, although he had no proof, that the individual who had called Marshall was Assistant Attorney General Rivers."

Erin looked up, her eyes wide, the final piece of the puzzle falling into place. Rivers called Marshall to meet. Erin looked down the table at Carol. "The mulligan," Erin said. "You knew that at the very least, even if Jon was convicted, you'd have to disclose the information in Holmes's affidavit and he'd get a new trial."

"Erin, I'm very sorry," Schey said. "But letting the trial continue was my decision."

"Which I supported," Talon added.

"Obviously, we didn't know how things were going to turn out at the trial," Schey said. "And at that point, all we had was the affidavit of a dead man filled with speculation. Certainly hard to make a case based solely on that. Further complicating things were Rivers's connections to the attorney general, and rumors that Rivers was next in line for head of DCJ. Let's just say in terms of the normal chain of command, Vanessa and I had to go way outside the lines. We believed that letting the trial continue was the safest course. Never for a moment did we anticipate what would happen today.

"To complete the picture for you," Schey continued, "we're trying to put together enough information for probable cause to get search warrants on all of Rivers's cell phones and computers. While we suspect Rivers and Britton were working together, other than Holmes's speculation, which won't be enough, we don't have anything connecting Rivers and Marshall."

"I know the connection," Erin said, knowing all the pieces now made sense.

"What connection?" Schey asked.

"Between Marshall and Rivers," she replied. "Rivers was one of Marshall's sources."

Erin's statement was met by a collective, "What?"

"Carol," Erin continued, looking down the table at Roy. "The steganography software that hid the sources—there was a random letter in the middle of the picture. None of us could figure out what the letter meant. The letter was *W* and it was located in what we mistakenly called a stream. It's not a stream—it's a river—'W

River.' Ward Rivers was one of Marshall's confidential sources. I figured that part out right before summations, but there was nothing I could do at that point, and obviously, I didn't have this piece—that he was the one who had called Marshall the night of the murder. I'm sure Rivers was smart enough to use burner phones and probably has burned any he used, but his burner number will be on Marshall's cell, especially the call at 7:05, the one that came in two minutes after the call from Jon's cell. That number may be on Britton's phone as well. And unless Rivers was smart enough to turn off his AG-issued cell phone, you should be able to triangulate his location on October 19 from the cell tower data. That's the connection."

"Rivers was a source for Marshall?" Schey asked.

"Sure," Erin replied. "Rivers had been a trooper and then represented a lot of the troopers who were asked to provide statements as part of the task force investigation. He'd have an insider's knowledge on the Lords, and could have fed Marshall misinformation, or by talking with Marshall, Rivers would've known if Marshall had uncovered the truth—a truth he never wanted to see the light of day." Erin looked across the table at Schey. "Marshall had only two confidential sources in the AG's Office—Holmes and Rivers. Marshall called Holmes, leaving only Rivers as the one on his way to Marshall's house. There's your probable cause."

"That makes sense," Talon said, jotting something on a yellow legal pad.

Schey looked over his shoulder. "Jenk," he said to Captain Jenkins. "Get to work on an affidavit. We have our PC and I want to hit Rivers asap, before he has a chance to destroy things."

"Will do," Jenkins replied.

There was a knock on the door, and a man peered inside. "Prosecutor Talon, can I see you for a moment."

"Excuse me," she said as she left the room.

"Erin, we want you to know that we will do everything in our power to see that justice is done," Schey said.

"Thank you," Erin said. "I appreciate that." Her mind drifted, replaying the events of the afternoon, and as she did, she realized she didn't know how it had ended. "I'm sorry, I know this is a strange question, but who shot Britton?"

One of the assistant prosecutors from Middlesex spoke up. "We believe Britton was initially wounded when he and Duane struggled for the gun, but when he managed to scramble to his feet, he was shot by Trooper Alec Urjinski."

Urjinski, she thought. *That makes no sense.* "I'm sorry, Trooper Urjinski? What are you talking about?"

"Apparently, Trooper Urjinski heard the news that Jon had been found not guilty and drove to the courthouse to congratulate him. When he got there, he was told that all of you had headed over to the jail to get Mazer's stuff, so he drove over to the jail. He pulled up just as Britton started firing. I'll say this for Urjinski, he's a good shot. He hit Britton in the skull with one shot from thirty feet. He saved Duane's life."

Erin leaned up against Mark, feeling exhausted and heartbroken.

The door suddenly opened and a very ashen Talon came back into the room. "More bad news, I'm afraid," she said. "Detectives from my office went over to Britton's home to execute search warrants. When they finally forced their way into the home, they found the body of Michelle Britton, David's wife, dead in her kitchen, shot three times in the chest. Based on the condition of the body, it appears she was shot around noon today."

"Shit," Prosecutor Schey said to no one in particular.

"Amen," Talon replied.

CHAPTER 46

OVER THE THIRTY-SIX HOURS SINCE SWISH HAD BEEN SHOT, EITHER Corrine, Erin, Mark, or JJ was at Swish's bedside in the ICU. Erin had just relieved Corrine so she could go home, shower, and be with the kids for Sunday morning breakfast. Swish remained in critical condition, but other than a scare yesterday afternoon when his fever spiked, he was holding his own.

Erin reached over the bed rail and rubbed his biceps, the only part of his arm and hand that wasn't punctured by some tube or line. She studied the tubes, the lines, the electrodes all running from Swish's body to various machines and monitors, trying to trace their origin and end point. Almost involuntarily, she mumbled a silent prayer.

The alarm from the monitor keeping track of his heart rate, respiratory rate, blood oxygen, temperature, and blood pressure suddenly screamed, jolting her back to reality. *The nurse,* she thought. *I need to get the nurse.*

Before she could even get to the door, Swish's nurse was in the room and yelling into the phone, "Code blue, ICU room ten. I repeat, code blue, ICU room ten."

When the alarm had gone off yesterday because of a spike in Swish's temperature, the nurse had turned it off, left the room for a few minutes, and hung one more IV bag on the pole next to Swish's bed. But this was different. There was a different look in the nurse's eyes, not panic, but one that conveyed a message—this wasn't good.

The nurse turned quickly toward her. "Go to the ICU waiting room. Someone will come and speak to you there."

"Should I call his wife?" Erin asked.

The nurse seemed to quickly weigh her response. "Yes. I'll be down to see you in a few minutes. Go!"

"Please save him—please!" Erin said, before fleeing the room.

Erin ran to the waiting room. An emergency team had rushed past her and had disappeared into Swish's room. She called Mark and explained the situation, and they decided he would call Cori and head to her house to drive her. Even though it was Sunday morning, it would still take a good forty minutes to get back to the hospital.

Her watch said it was only fifteen minutes, but it seemed like hours, before someone came into the waiting area.

"Ms. McCabe?" the person asked, looking down at the clipboard in his hand that would have contained the authorization from Corrine to allow Erin to receive information on Swish's medical condition.

"Yes," she said nervously.

"I'm Doctor Matthews," he said. "Mr. Swisher's blood pressure had dropped to eighty over forty, which is what triggered the alarm. We've dramatically increased his IV fluids and we're monitoring for any internal bleeding, but for now, we've stabilized him and we're confident that any immediate danger has passed. Of course, we're continuing to watch him closely."

"Thank you," Erin replied. "Has his wife been notified?" she asked.

"The nursing staff is on the phone with her now," he replied.

"Thank you," she repeated.

Later, after she had talked to Cori, she sat next to him, her hand resting on his biceps. "Damn it, big guy," she said gently. "Cori is not raising those kids alone, and I'm not practicing law without you. Now get your ass in gear, and get better."

She would never be certain if she had imagined it or not, but, in that moment, she swore she felt his biceps flex.

* * *

Four days later, Erin and Mark had just gotten into bed when her cell phone buzzed. She grabbed it off the night table and saw it was Cori. *Oh no*, she thought.

"Hi, Cori. Is everything okay?" she answered.

"Hope I didn't wake you," a very raspy voice said.

It took her several seconds. "Swish?" she said. "Swish, is that you?"

"Who else would be calling you at this time of night?"

"Oh my God, Swish." She tried not to cry. "It is so wonderful to hear you."

"It's wonderful to be heard," he replied. "But it hurts. I'll let you talk to Cori."

When Cori got on, she let Erin know that Swish had opened his eyes around four in the afternoon, and then around nine had started to say a few words. He was still tired and not totally with it, but the doctors were now confident he was going to make a complete recovery.

Jon's funeral, which took place ten days after the shooting, had left Erin bereft. For her, it had been both somber and infuriating. As befitting a fallen trooper, the funeral was attended by representatives from police departments from around the state and even some from other states and countries. What particularly irked Erin was the hypocrisy of people. Some of the same officials and members of the state police brass who had condemned Jon publicly when he was arrested, now joined the chorus heaping praise on him as a hero. Even his family, who had ostracized him in life, were in the front pews grieving his loss.

Erin and Mark had lingered long after the various entourages had left the cemetery. The grave workers lingered in the distance waiting to lower Jon's casket into the ground, but she needed to say her own goodbye to the man who had saved her life. Unlike some of her clients, she had never grown personally close to Jon. She liked him, he seemed like a good man, and he certainly was loyal to a fault—willing to risk spending his life in jail to protect his lover. But now his actions had carved a place in her heart that was unlike any other.

Standing there, she leaned into Mark, wrapping her arm around his waist. She was still here and Jon wasn't. How serendipitous this thing called life. Here today, gone tomorrow with no apparent rhyme or reason. The tears rolled down her cheeks. Jon might not have been the client she was closest to, but he was the client she'd remember for the rest of her life—a life she owed to him.

She saw him when she and Mark finally turned to leave. He was standing among the gravestones about thirty yards away. She told Mark to wait, then walked over. His eyes were red and puffy. His face bore the look of someone in torment.

"I really did love him," Gabe said.

"I'm sure you did. I'm sorry for your loss, Gabe, and sorry that you'll never have a chance to make amends. I know how badly that can hurt."

"This is my fault," he babbled between sobs.

"Gabe, you're not responsible for Jon's death. What happened would've happened even if you had testified you and Jon were just friends. Don't blame yourself for this," Erin said.

He stood there shaking his head. "He died hating me, thinking I betrayed him . . . because I did . . . I betrayed him."

"I don't think he hated you, Gabe. He loved you. I suspect he did feel betrayed, but my guess is he would have gotten over it and forgiven you. It's time you forgave yourself."

He stared at her, his look conveying his desire to believe her. "I left the priesthood," he said. "I . . . I just couldn't stay after everything that happened." He gave an ironic snort. "I'm sure I would've been thrown out if I didn't leave. All I did was save them the aggravation of a Church trial under Canon Law. Not that I had a defense, having admitted under oath I was gay and had a lover."

Erin took several steps forward and hugged him. "Jon would have wanted you to be happy. Live a good life, Gabe, and find happiness in who you are and whatever you do."

When she and Mark got to their car, she turned and looked back to the grave site and saw Gabe standing there, his head bowed, his shoulders heaving.

* * *

By the time of Jon's funeral, Swish's condition had been upgraded to stable, and he was moved to a critical care unit, which allowed Erin to have longer visits and talk to him. He remembered most of what had happened, and one of his first questions was to ask how Jon was. When Erin told him that Jon was gone, Swish had put his head back on the pillow and closed his eyes.

"I guess I knew," he said. "I saw him shove you out of the line of fire, which ironically not only saved your life, but probably mine as well."

"Why yours?" Erin had asked.

"Britton squeezed off two or three rounds at you, but Jon's shove caused Britton to miss you. As soon as I saw the gun, I started running at Britton. Because he had pushed you, Jon was a split second behind me in trying to get to Britton. But after missing you, Britton took aim at Jon, who was directly in the line of fire. By the time Britton had time to move his arm to try and take me out, I was on him. If it hadn't been for those missed shots at you, I think he would have had time to take me out too. I wasn't hit until we wrestled for control of the gun." Swish paused, appearing to let the memory move on. "I think Britton was also hit as we wrestled on the ground."

Erin filled in the gaps. The medical examiner's report showed Britton had two bullet wounds caused by his own weapon, one in the abdomen, and one in the left bicep. Like everyone, Swish was stunned when he learned that the shot that killed Britton had come from Urjinski.

By the third week in the hospital, Swish started to take some tentative walks around the ward and, after a month, was released to Hope Rehabilitation Center.

Schey kept Erin updated on the ongoing criminal investigation of Ward Rivers for the murder of Russell Marshall, and the death of DAG Albert Holmes. Ward had resigned from the AG's Office. Search warrants had been executed on all his electronic devices and a grand jury had been convened in Middlesex County. In addition to the criminal allegations, Schey had also let Erin know that the investigation had turned up evidence that Rivers had encouraged a deputy attorney general in his office to oppose Erin's and Mark's application to be listed as the mom and dad on the baby's birth certificate. His emails also showed that Rivers had reached out to attorneys for the ALDA coordinating with them to represent Jack and Vivian Simpson in opposing the application. In a bizarre way, Erin had actually been somewhat relieved to learn that her mother-in-law and brother-in-law had been co-opted into opposing their application. It didn't necessarily take all of the sting out, but she could at least take solace in the fact it wasn't their idea.

CHAPTER 47

FIVE WEEKS AFTER THE SHOOTING, ERIN, MARK, SEAN, AND LIZ SAT AT counsel table with Phil Song waiting for Judge Jacobs to take the bench. It was the first time Erin had been in court since the verdict in the Mazer trial.

"All rise," the clerk intoned.

"Be seated," Jacobs said before she even reached her chair.

Jacobs then laid out in detail the nature of the application that Song had made on behalf of Erin and Mark to be listed as parents on the baby's birth certificate.

"For the record," Jacobs continued, "I have previously denied the application of Jack Simpson, Mark's brother, and Vivian Simpson, Mark's mother, to intervene in this matter for purposes of objecting to Mark and Erin being listed as the baby's parents, having found that they lacked standing to object. I did permit them through their counsel, the American Liberty Defense Alliance, to submit papers as amicus joining in the attorney general's opposition.

"As I just indicated, the Office of the Attorney General has filed opposition to the application. Based on that, and in the interest of court efficiency, what I'd like to do, Mr. Song, is, with your permission, have all of your clients sworn in for their testimony."

Jacobs then swore the four of them as witnesses and Song proceeded to go through the surrogacy agreements that he had prepared, confirm the marriage license between Erin and Mark, the consent of all of them to the arrangement they had reached, including a waiver of conflicts, which allowed Song to represent both couples and Erin's birth certificate, which had been reissued after she transitioned with the correct gender marker—female. Song then rested.

"Deputy Attorney General DeLeo, do you have any questions?"

"Judge, may I initially question Ms. Erin McCabe?"

"Of course, Counsel," Jacobs responded.

"Ms. McCabe, it's my understanding that the baby that will be born from this arrangement was conceived using your sperm. Is that correct?"

"It is."

"So shouldn't you be listed as the father and not the mother?"

"Mr. DeLeo, as in many parenting situations, for example adoption, a woman or man who has no genetic connection whatsoever to the child is listed as the child's mother or father. In this case, although I have a genetic connection to the child, from a societal standpoint, because I am a woman married to a man, I will be the baby's mother and Mark will be the baby's father. I suppose technically we could be listed as parents, but it just makes more sense for our baby's sake for me to be listed as the child's mother."

"But you're not a woman, Ms. McCabe," DeLeo said.

"Objection," Song said.

Jacobs looked down at DeLeo. "Sustained. Please ask a question."

"Are you a woman, Ms. McCabe?" DeLeo asked.

"I have a birth certificate that says I'm female," Erin replied. "It's been marked into evidence."

"But you produced the sperm that created this child, didn't you?" DeLeo said.

"I did," Erin replied.

"But women don't produce sperm, do they?" DeLeo said.

"Mr. DeLeo," Jacobs interrupted. "We all understand that the child was conceived using the sperm that Ms. McCabe banked prior to her transition. That's not in dispute. What you're doing is arguing with the witness. Leaving aside your argument, do you have any questions for the witnesses?"

"No, Your Honor," DeLeo responded, his frustration evident.

"Let me ask Elizabeth McCabe and her husband, Sean McCabe, a question," Jacobs said. "Do both of you consent to Erin McCabe and Mark Simpson being listed on the baby's birth certificate as the baby's parents?"

Liz looked at Sean, and he nodded for her to go first. "Most definitely, Judge. It was our idea for me to act as the surrogate for Erin and Mark because we think they will be amazing parents."

"I agree, Your Honor," Sean added. "Both Liz and I, and our sons, are in full support of this application."

"Thank you," Jacobs said. "And Ms. McCabe, sorry, Elizabeth McCabe, are you aware that you have seventy-two hours after the birth of the baby before you're allowed to surrender your parental rights? In other words, all these legal agreements that you entered into can be voided by you anytime within seventy-two hours of birth. Do you understand that?"

"I do, Your Honor. Mr. Song fully explained my rights to me, but I can assure you I won't change my mind. There has been no greater honor for me, short of being the mother of my own children, than acting as a surrogate for Erin and Mark."

"Thank you all very much. Anything further, Mr. Song?" Jacobs asked.

"No, Your Honor."

"Deputy Attorney General DeLeo, I've read your papers, and understand the state's position that Ms. McCabe should not be listed on the birth certificate as the baby's mother, but as the father. Anything further?"

"No, Judge."

"For the record," Jacobs continued, "I note that the ALDA in its amicus brief, in addition to joining the attorney general's arguments, has taken the position that Erin McCabe and Mark Simpson should be treated as a same-sex couple, and therefore not married, but in a civil union. ALDA also argues that Ms. McCabe is unfit, but at the very least should be required to go through a full adoption procedure, including a home study and psychological evaluation, prior to being listed on the child's birth certificate as a parent. I have considered these arguments as well as those of the Attorney General's Office," Jacobs said.

Erin lowered her head and took a deep breath. She reached out under the table, found Mark's hand, and squeezed it. He squeezed back.

Jacobs looked down at the legal pad in front of her. "Under New Jersey law, a birth certificate must be issued within five days of birth. The law also provides Elizabeth McCabe with seventy-two hours to change her mind, and request her name to be placed on the birth certificate. Accordingly, I'm going to deny plaintiffs' request for a prebirth order, which would effectively cut off Elizabeth McCabe's legal right to change her mind. I don't believe I'm allowed to do that."

Erin winced. The thought of having to file an appeal and the publicity that would result caused her to recoil.

"However," Jacobs continued, "pursuant to the case of *A.H.W. v. G.H.B.*, I will issue an order that allows the names of plaintiffs Erin McCabe and Mark Simpson to be placed on the birth certificate *after* the seventy-two-hour statutory waiting period has expired, but before the birth certificate must be filed, which is five days after birth, assuming Elizabeth McCabe doesn't change her mind within the seventy-two hours. It is clear to me that under the law Erin McCabe is a woman; she will be listed on the baby's birth certificate as the mother. In addition, based on the case of *In Re: The Parentage of the Child of Kimberly Robinson*, I find that as the lawful husband of Erin McCabe, Mark Simpson shall be listed on the birth certificate as the father. With regard to the argument of the ALDA that Erin McCabe should be required to adopt the child, I find no basis in law or fact for that argument, and it is denied.

"Finally, I note that in 1976, in the case of *M.T. v J.T.*, the Appellate Division held in a published decision written by then Judge Handler, later to be Justice Handler, that the marriage between a transsexual woman, the terminology used in 1976, and a man was a lawful marriage of a man and a woman. Accordingly, since this has been the law in New Jersey for over thirty years, I find the conduct and arguments of the ALDA to be frivolous and they appear to have been made in an attempt to embarrass and harass the parties. As such, if a fee application is made on behalf of Erin McCabe and Mark Simpson for reimbursement of their fees in opposing the original application of the ALDA to intervene and in responding to their amicus brief, I will consider it." Jacobs laid her reading glasses on the bench in front of her and peered at counsel for the ALDA. "Both against the ALDA and their attorney," Jacobs added. "Thank you, and good luck to all of you."

When they left the courthouse, the four of them headed to the Hope Rehab Center to celebrate. Cori had checked with the facility, and Duane's doctors all agreed a little party might brighten his spirits. So, unbeknownst to Swish, they had agreed that after the court hearing they'd head to the center to celebrate.

But what had started out as just the six of them celebrating quickly morphed into a much grander affair as word of the party spread. First, JJ and Gary asked to come, then Cori's parents, then Peg, and Molly, Robin, and baby Robert, then all the guys on the basketball team, and finally Rachel and Logan. By the time they totaled up the final RSVPs, over fifty people had decided to attend.

"Hey, big guy," Erin said when Swish hobbled in with Cori.

"What the hell's going on?" he said, looking around the room.

"We're celebrating!" Erin announced.

"Celebrating what?" he asked.

"The judge granted our application, so Mark and I will be on the baby's birth certificate. And . . ." She walked to the chair he had parked himself in and hugged him. "And the fact that you're here to celebrate with all of us who love you," she said, sweeping her hand around the room, as everyone gathered broke into spontaneous applause.

CHAPTER 48

ERIN HELD HER GLASS OF WATER OUT IN FRONT OF HER AS HER MOM made her second Thanksgiving Day toast. As she had last year, Peg toasted Pat and how much they missed him, but this year she added the joy of having Molly, Robin, and their baby join them for Thanksgiving, and how excited she was that, hopefully by Christmas, there'd be another baby for her to spoil. When Peg finished, Sean held out his glass and said, "Here's to the second annual last Thanksgiving dinner at Mom's. May there be many, many more."

As everyone clinked their glasses, Erin looked around the room, reminding herself of how incredibly blessed she was. Looking across the table at Liz and Sean, she knew she would never be able to repay them for the gift they had given her.

There was also a poignancy to this year's celebration that was hard for Erin to ignore. In addition to it being the second Thanksgiving without her dad, the fact that she was even here to celebrate while Jon and Albert Holmes would never celebrate another Thanksgiving wasn't lost on her. Life was so fickle. She and Jon had been mere inches apart. But she was alive and he wasn't. And the chain of events she had set in motion when she called Holmes continued to haunt her.

"Everything all right?" Mark asked, rousing her from her thoughts.

"Yeah," she said, giving him a rueful smile. "Just giving thanks for all I've been given. Most of all for you," she said, leaning over and kissing him on the cheek.

In the beginning of December, Swish returned to the office for a few hours, and seeing him back had a healing effect on Erin. His presence seemed to anchor her in ways she hadn't realized. He was the yang to her yin, and for the first time since the shooting, she enjoyed being in the office.

"Good to have you back," she said, plopping down on the opposite side of his desk.

"Good to be anywhere," he replied, bringing a smile to her face.

"How you feeling?" she asked.

"Honestly, not too bad. The ribs and shoulder are still painful, and I'm still not sleeping very well, but I know I'm pretty damn lucky to have taken two bullets and be here. So, no complaints."

"How you doing mentally?" she asked. "You talking to someone?"

"Still having nightmares and some flashbacks, and yes, I started talking to a therapist when I was in rehab. I'm trying to stay on top of it. What about you? Just because you weren't shot doesn't mean you can't have PTSD."

"I know," she said. "Between the shooting and the baby coming, I've been seeing my therapist regularly."

"Good," he said. "What's new here?"

"I've sent a letter to the state for reimbursement of our fees in the Mazer case, which, since he was found not guilty, I think we should get without too much of a fight," she said, folding her hands as if in prayer.

"Anything new with the Marshall case?" he asked.

Erin nodded. "Talon and Roy check in periodically, and it sounds like they're trying to put together a case against Rivers. Kind of ironic, but it turns out that the cell phone he had through the AG's Office was on all day on October 19, and, according to cell tower data, he was in Edison between seven thirty and eight p.m. the night Marshall was murdered. They think he and Britton were in on it together. Britton took Mazer's cell phone and gun out of his trunk, met Rivers, and handed it off to him. Rivers called Marshall, went over to the house, shot him, and then he got the gun and phone back to Britton to put back in the trunk of the car. That's why Britton wanted to deny on the stand making the call to Marshall and why Urjinski caught him in Mazer's locker—putting the car keys back."

"Yeah, but with both Holmes and Britton gone, sounds like it could be tough to prove Rivers did it," Swish offered.

"I don't disagree," Erin said. "With no direct proof, a good defense lawyer would have a good chance of creating a reasonable doubt."

"They have a motive?" Swish asked.

"From what Talon told me, they've squeezed Trooper Stone really hard with potential perjury, obstruction and official misconduct charges, and in order to avoid prosecution, he talked. He told them that, when he was a trooper, Rivers ran the Lords, and he continued to protect them once he was in the AG's Office. From what Britton had told Stone, Marshall was already planning a second article, exposing the AG connection, and when Rivers found out he went ballistic. Talon also thinks that's why Marshall's laptop disappeared—it had the only draft of the second article."

Swish nodded. "Takes a ballsy son of a bitch to murder someone and then prosecute someone else for the crime."

"Yeah," she said. "Ballsy and evil."

"What about the Lords—they going after them?" he asked.

She shook her head. "Neither county has jurisdiction to investigate the state police—sole province of the AG's Office."

"Guess we know how that'll go," he said, unable to hide his disappointment.

She knew Swish was right. Even with Britton gone, and Rivers no longer in a position to run interference, she had little faith things would change. The problems within the state police were so systemic and deeply rooted she couldn't help but believe that racial profiling would continue even if the Lords didn't. And given that culture, anyone speaking out against it might suffer the same fate as Russell, Albert, and Jon. She looked at Swish and remembered an earlier conversation, and it pained her to know how right he was—driving while Black was still going to get you pulled over on the highways of New Jersey.

"And how are you and Mark doing? All ready for the baby?" he asked, trying to lighten the mood.

"Is anyone ever ready for a baby?" she replied.

Swish let out a knowing laugh. "You got that right; you're never ready."

"Which leads to something I guess we need to revisit," Erin said.

"What's that?" he asked.

"Well, when we planned for this, we figured I'd be off for about three months or so, and you'd hold down the fort until we had the baby in day care and I could get back to work, but . . . I don't know that it's fair for me to expect you to do that at this point."

Swish gave her a gentle smile. "Let's see what happens. Liz isn't due for another two weeks. Hopefully, I'll be recovered enough to handle most of the things here, and I'll know where to find you if I need you. Besides, assuming you're right and we get the Mazer fee, we should be able to coast for a few months. Try not to worry about me. I want you to enjoy your baby. They grow up fast, E. Savor every moment you can."

"Thanks, Swish," she said, getting up and giving him a gentle hug on his good left side. "I appreciate you more than you'll ever know."

She took a step back and looked at him. "I'm not sure I even thanked you."

"For what?" he asked.

"For saving my life. If you and Jon had hesitated even a split second, I wouldn't be here. Instead, both of you ran right at Britton. I know Jon paid the ultimate price, but what you did almost cost you your life too."

She reached her arm around his neck, and gently pulled his head down toward her, and as she did, she leaned over and kissed his cheek.

"I know we're not keeping score, but I haven't forgotten how differently my encounter with the Edison cops might have turned out if you hadn't done what you did," he said, kissing her on the top of her head.

Two weeks later, Erin and Mark were cleaning up after dinner when her cell phone rang.

"Hey, Sean," she answered.

"Hey, E, just wanted to let you know that I just called Mom and asked if she could come down to be with the boys. Liz is having some contractions. They're still pretty far apart, but based on what happened with Patrick and Brennan, she can go into hard labor pretty quickly. You and Mark may want to head this way just in case. For now, I'd say head to our house, but if things change, I'll call you on your cell."

"On our way," she responded.

They were about halfway to Sean and Liz's house in Princeton when Sean called back.

"We're on our way to Princeton Medical Center. This looks like it, E."

"See you there," Erin replied.

She turned and looked at Mark, who was silhouetted by the lights from the dashboard.

"You still good with the baby's name?" Erin asked.

"Yeah. Molly doesn't want us to use her name as the baby's middle name. Apparently, my family doesn't know about her involvement, and she'd like to try and keep it that way."

"Okay," Erin said, feeling bad that they couldn't acknowledge Molly in the same way Molly and Robin had acknowledged Mark.

"You excited?" she asked.

"Scared shitless," he responded.

"Oh, good. I thought it was only me," she replied.

When they arrived at the hospital, Doctor Grimes's staff had done a good job of preparing the folks at the hospital on how to handle things, and Mark and Erin were immediately sent up to the delivery room. When they got there, Liz was already eight centimeters dilated and fully effaced. When Liz saw Erin, she immediately asked her to come hold her hand. Sean was on the other side, wiping her forehead and encouraging her.

"Won't be long now," Liz said.

Doctor Grimes came in and examined Liz. "Are you getting the urge to push?" Grimes asked Liz.

"Yeah," Liz replied, arching her shoulders in reaction to a contraction.

"You're doing great, Liz. You're almost there. Try not to push yet. I'll tell you when. Just a little longer.

Liz squeezed Erin's hand and moaned.

Grimes looked up at Erin, and then turned to one of the nurses. "Get a gown for Erin. She and Mark are the intended parents. Liz, as we discussed, when the baby is born, I'm going to give her to Erin. Is that okay?"

Liz managed a tight smile. "Of course. This is her baby, not mine." Then Liz squeezed Erin's hand.

Erin quickly got her top and bra off, and put on a hospital gown, and then returned to Liz's side.

"The baby's head is right there," Grimes reported, crouched in front of Liz.

Erin could see the top of the baby's head protruding slightly, the hair matted, but visible. Her baby's head, she thought. *Her baby!*

"Okay, Liz. Bear down and give me a really hard push."

Erin watched as Liz gritted her teeth and groaned, her face contorted. Erin had never seen a baby being born and she was trying to process how messy and beautiful and awe-inspiring it was all at the same time. When Erin looked down, the baby's head was out, and Grimes was maneuvering the baby's shoulders to gently free them from Liz. And then the baby was fully out and in

Doctor Grimes's capable hands. Grimes laid the baby on Liz's belly, waiting a minute before clamping off the umbilical cord.

"Erin, have a seat over there," Grimes said, motioning to a reclining chair.

Erin hopped in the chair, and reclined it so she was almost prone, and pulled the front of her gown down to expose the top of her chest.

Grimes cut the umbilical cord and brought the baby over to the nurse, who cleaned her up, placed a little cap on her head, and performed the Apgar test. Then Grimes walked over and gently laid the baby on Erin's chest, and a nurse came over and laid a blanket over both of them.

Erin looked at her daughter. Her eyes were closed, her tiny hands clenched into fists. She had streaks of dark hair peeking out from beneath the cap on her head. She was so tiny and helpless and the most beautiful little person Erin had ever laid eyes on. Tears of joy slalomed down Erin's cheek.

Mark came around and stood by the side of the chair staring at Erin and the baby.

"Come say hello to our daughter," Erin said.

Mark crouched down so he was on eye level with both of them, leaned over and kissed Erin on the cheek.

"Bridget Alice McCabe-Simpson, say hello to your dad."

"She's beautiful," he said.

"Yes, she is," Erin replied.

Erin then got Mark and Sean to push the chair over so it was parallel to Liz's bed.

Erin reached out and took hold of Liz's hand, giving it a gentle squeeze. "I don't know how to even begin to thank you for what you did. Would you like to hold your niece?" Erin asked.

"Thank you," Liz said. "I'd love to."

Erin gently handed the baby to Mark, who then laid her on Liz's chest.

"Well, look at you, my beautiful niece. You are the luckiest baby in the world, because you have the best parents in the world."

"And the best aunt and uncle," Erin added.

After a few minutes, Liz said to Mark, "I think it's time for Bridget to spend some time with her mom."

Mark picked up his daughter and laid her back on Erin's chest, and covered them with the blanket, his face beaming.

"Oh, my little Bridget. I love you, sweet baby," Erin said, feeling the warmth of her daughter on her chest.

CHAPTER 49

December 25, 2010
2:00 a.m.

BRIDGET WAS NESTLED IN ERIN'S ARMS, GENTLY FEEDING FROM ERIN'S breast. Much to Erin's delight, a week before Bridget was born, she had begun lactating. On Doctor Grimes's recommendation, Erin and Mark had found an accepting and understanding pediatrician in town, Doctor Virginia Bradley, who, aware of Erin's situation and the protocol Grimes had put her on, had encouraged her to breast-feed. Erin was a little unsure of herself and had struggled initially, but now, nine days after Bridget was born, despite Erin's nervousness, Bridget had gained back most of the weight she lost after birth and seemed to be having no trouble breast-feeding.

Erin gazed down at her daughter. There were still times she had trouble fathoming the reality of her journey and that somehow this beautiful child was her flesh and blood. Had anyone told her when she was going through the gender affirmation process that some six years later, she'd be married and holding her newborn daughter, she would have thought they had gone insane—and yet, here she was, married and with her child suckling on her breast.

Her mind drifted, as if wandering through a labyrinth, bouncing between the twists and turns of her life that had led her to this point. Her internal struggle to deal with a body that didn't match who she knew she was; her futile efforts to fit into the male world she had been to; the painful collapse of her marriage when she finally acknowledged her truth; the joy of living as the person she always knew she was; the resulting strain that tore at her relationship with her father; the love of her mother, which never wavered; Sean, Liz, and the boys who had given her a gift that was beyond measure; and the love of two men who had saved her from her own despair—Swish and Mark. Mark, who had single-handedly navigated through the minefield she had erected around her heart and, in the process, allowed her not only to love him, but to love herself as well. Mark, a man without ego, who willingly gave up his place as a birth parent to allow her the experience of having a child who was truly her descendent.

Mark, who loved her for who she was.

Erin gently moved Bridget from her left breast to her right and looked into her bright blue eyes. Bridget's tiny fingers splayed as she nestled contently into Erin. *Oh Bridget,* she thought. *I hope I'm as good a mom to you as my mom is to me.*

When Bridget had finished nursing, Erin cradled her in her arms and rocked her gently. Bridget's wide eyes were still locked onto Erin. *Oh, my sweet child. I hope you never suffer because of who I am. I hope you're confident and fearless in who you are. And I hope that you always know that you are loved beyond measure.*

After several minutes, Bridget's eyes fluttered several times and then closed as she fell back to sleep. Erin softly kissed the top of Bridget's head, soaking in her sweet smell and laid her back in her cradle. *I don't know where life is going to take you, my little one, but as long as I'm here, I'll always be there for you. Mommy loves you.*

As she stared down at her sleeping child, she recalled something her mom had once told her about the reason why her father struggled to come to terms with her being transgender—it was fear—fear of how it reflected on him as a father, and the fear of a loving parent who wanted nothing more than to protect their child from a world that could be cruel and hateful. Erin hoped that her own fears would never stand in the way of allowing Bridget to follow whatever road in life she decided to travel. But, as she hovered over her darling daughter, perhaps for the first time, she understood her father's desire to protect her, to keep her safe and to shelter her from the storm. She knew deep in her heart that's what she'd always want to do for Bridget—protect her from the world—even as she knew it was an impossible dream.

After she crawled back under the covers, Mark rolled over and draped his arm over her. "Everything okay?" he asked in a sleepy whisper.

She kissed his cheek. "Yeah. Everything's good," she said softly. "Merry Christmas."

She put her head back on the pillow, thankful for the life she'd been given. Despite its ups and downs, she knew she had been blessed. To her left was her sleeping daughter; to her right, her sleeping husband. She closed her eyes and in the moments before sleep washed over her, she found contentment in knowing that wherever their journey took them, as long as they were together, she would always find the courage to face whatever came her way.

ACKNOWLEDGMENTS

Writing wouldn't be as much fun if there was no one to read (or hear) what I wrote. So, to those of you who have read or listened to my book, thank you. I hope you've enjoyed it as much as I enjoyed creating it.

I want to thank my agent, Carrie Pestritto, at the Laura Dail Literary Agency, and my editor at Kensington Books, John Scognamiglio, both of whom have helped guide me through four novels—thank you to both of you for all your help and guidance.

I also want to thank all the people at Kensington Books who have worked so hard to make this novel the best book it could be, and to all the folks who work behind the scenes to help promote me and my books, in particular Michelle Addo and Vida Engstrand. I am so grateful to have such a great team working with me.

I am indebted to Andrea Robinson, an independent editor, who has worked with me on all of my novels. She has been incredibly helpful with her thoughts, suggestions, and edits. Andrea's input has made this a much better book. Trust me, if you saw the first draft I sent to her, you'd thank her too.

Special thanks to my good friend Captain John Hayes from the New Jersey State Police, whose advice, technical assistance, and friendship were all invaluable. As the first openly gay male New Jersey State trooper, John helped inspire this novel. Bravery takes many forms and John checks all the boxes.

I'm also grateful to Bill Singer, Esq., a friend and colleague who is a national expert in helping people, in particular LGBTQ+ folks, in finding alternative methods of creating families. Bill literally saved me hours of legal research by generously sharing his knowledge and expertise. All of the cases referenced in the book are real New Jersey cases, and one of them, *In Re: The Parentage of the Child of Kimberly Robinson,* is a case that Bill litigated. If I made any technical mistakes, they're my fault, not Bill's.

I also wish to acknowledge that because this novel is a legal thriller, I did not have the luxury of doing a deeper dive into all the medical and personal issues surrounding alternative reproductive techniques. I know for many people it is a physically, emotionally, and financially exhausting process, which is often not successful. To anyone who has been through the process, or for various reasons could not utilize the process, and is offended or triggered in any way by my description of the process, I sincerely apologize. That was not my intent.

To the people who have read various drafts of this along the way—Gerry Carbine, Lori Becker, Janet Bayer, Celeste Fiore, Lynn Centonze, Lori Linskey, and Jan Gigl—thank you for your help and suggestions. And to my son, and fellow author, Colin Gigl, thank you for our Wednesday night chats. You kept me going when I struggled with this story. Thank you for your encouragement.

I owe so much to my family—Jan, our children, Tim, Colin, and Kate, their significant others, and grandkids—I love all of you more than you'll ever know. To my sister Virginia and cousin Lynn, who have shown up at so many of my events they know my story better than I do—thank you for your support. To my brother Tom, who never fails to find my typos. To my sister Doreen, whom I admire for all she has accomplished. And to my mom, who passed away in December 2020. It is no secret that Peg McCabe is an homage to my mom. As long as Peg lives on in my books, I feel like a part of my mom is still with me.

I want to thank all the authors in the crime/mystery/thriller community. What a wonderful and supportive group of people. In particular, I'd like to thank the members of Queer Crime Writers for their friendship and support.

Thanks also go to Wanda Akin, Esq., and Brian Neary, Esq., who have graciously appeared on several CLE panels with me to discuss the real-life lessons offered by my novels. None of those panels would have been possible without the help and support of Lisa Spiegel at the NJ State Bar Association.

Although this book is critical of some in the law enforcement community, I am sensitive to the fact that there are many dedicated people working in law enforcement—I've had the pleasure of working with any number of them. It can be a difficult and dangerous profession. However, those dangers should never blind us to the fact that there is room for improvement in the way the public, and in particular, marginalized communities are treated by members of law enforcement.

It is no secret that these are especially difficult times for the transgender and nonbinary communities. Trans and nonbinary folks, especially young people, are under attack by people who deny our very existence and seek to take away our basic human rights. Some have vowed to eradicate us. I am an out, proud, and open transgender woman, and if Erin McCabe as a character offers any lessons, it's that none of us choose to be trans or nonbinary—it's not a lifestyle choice or a fad—it's just who we are. Like everyone else, we are human beings trying to live our best lives possible. So, to everyone in the LGBTQ+ community, and especially those in the trans and nonbinary communities, thank you for your strength and inspiration. Finally, thank you to our allies who stand with us, you are invaluable.